dancing in the palm of his hand

A novel
of the witchcraft
persecutions in
17th century Germany

Annamarie beckel

dancing in the palm of his hand

*A novel
of the witchcraft
persecutions in
17th century Germany*

Annamarie beckel

Breakwater Books Ltd.
100 Water Street P.O. Box 2188
St. John's NL A1C 6E6
www.breakwaterbooks.com

Library and Archives Canada Cataloguing in Publication

Beckel, Annamarie L.
    Dancing in the palm of his hand / Annamarie Beckel.

ISBN 1-55081-217-3

1. Trials (Witchcraft)--Germany--Fiction. I. Title.

PS8553.E29552D35 2005   813'.54   C2005-902612-X
Copyright © 2005 Annamarie Beckel

Design: Rhonda Molloy
Editor: Tamara Reynish

The Canada Council | Le Conseil des Arts
for the Arts | du Canada

We acknowledge the financial support of
The Canada Council for the Arts for our publishing activities.

We acknowledge the financial support of the Government of Canada through the Book Publishing Industry Development Program (BPIDP) for our publishing activities.

Printed in Canada.

Historians estimate
that between 80,000 and 200,000 people,
75 percent of them women,
were executed for witchcraft
in Europe between 1500 and 1750.

ॐ

This novel
is dedicated to the
memory of the innocents who suffered.

ᘓ

"A belief that there are such things as witches
is so essential a part of the Catholic faith that obstinately
to maintain the opposite opinion savors of heresy."

–Heinrich Kramer and Jakob Sprenger, 1486,
Malleus Maleficarum, known in the Holy Roman Empire
as *Der Hexenhammer, The Hammer of Witches.*

foreword

ᘒ

Dancing in the Palm of His Hand is a work of fiction. Prince-Bishop Philipp Adolf von Ehrenberg and his chancellor, Johann Brandt, lived and ruled in early 17th century Würzburg, and historians estimate that von Ehrenberg burned 900 witches between 1623 and 1631. Throughout the novel, characters quote from theologians' and jurists' treatises on witches. These treatises are real historical documents: *Tractatus de Confessionibus Maleficorum et Sagarum* (Peter Binsfeld, 1589), *De la Demonomanie des sorciers* (Jean Bodin, 1580), *Discours des sorciers* (Henri Boquet, 1602), *Disquisitionum Magicarum* (Martin Delrio, 1599), *Malleus Maleficarum* (Heinrich Kramer and Jakob Sprenger, 1486), *Demonolatreiae* (Nicolas Remy, 1595), and *De Praestigiis Daemonum* (Johann Weyer, 1563). With the exception of *De Praestigiis Daemonum*, which was written by Johann Weyer, an opponent of the witch persecutions, these documents were the guides for the witch hunters. Moreover, the universities in the Holy Roman Empire, Italy, and France regularly issued "opinions" on legal procedures in witch trials, which in the Holy Roman Empire were guided by the *Constitutio Criminalis Carolina*, popularly known as the "Carolina Code," the basic criminal law code formalized under Emperor Charles V in 1532.

Witch trials existed during one of the most creative and dynamic periods in the history of Europe. The theological and legal aspects of "demonology" were considered serious intellectual pursuits, and these horrific and misogynistic treatises on witchcraft existed side by side with brilliant Renaissance art and literature, with the works of Michelangelo, Shakespeare, Galileo, Montaigne, and Descartes.

1

They conjured me into being. Floods of pious words were my birth waters. The Dominicans served as midwives, the Jesuits wet-nurses. The black ink flowing from their quills was the bitter milk I suckled. The dark stream sustains me even now, giving me life and strength.

They call me Lucifer, Prince of Devils. The Antichrist. I am as real to them as the Virgin's Son. And nearly as powerful. I bring fire and hail, death and pestilence, impotence and barrenness. I take the shape of a handsome man, an alluring woman. I seduce the unrighteous. So they say.

I am awed by the number of souls they claim I have won. Yet, I care not for a single one of them. So they say.

The end-time is near, and I am at war with God. In the dark of night, deep in the forest, my army gathers around me. We desecrate the host, trample with cloven hoof all that is sacred. We make an ointment from the flesh of unbaptized babies, use it to fly through the air, to kill and to maim. So they say.

They have granted me extraordinary powers, almost unlimited. I am nearly an equal to God, they say. Yet, because no Dominican or Jesuit can find a pathway around his belief that God is omnipotent, they say I can act only with God's permission.

I should think such a notion offensive to God.

2

14 April 1626

People began gathering at dawn, just as the cathedral bells rang out. Eva watched from the window as men and women streamed past the bakery on their way to the town hall. Everyone came: craftsmen and journeymen, merchants, priests and monks, peddlers and beggars, town councilmen, peasants from outside the Würzburg city walls. Some brought children: little boys astride their fathers' shoulders, babies squirming in their mothers' arms, younger sisters and brothers clinging to the hands of older siblings.

Eva did not join them. She tried not to hear the trial, but the town hall was only a few buildings away from the bakery on *Domstrasse*, and the voice that read out the *shrift* was loud and resonant. The reading of the women's crimes lasted nearly two hours: they had turned away from God and signed a pact with the Devil, attended the sabbath where they fornicated with the Devil and his demons, caused illness and death among their neighbours, curdled milk and caused grain to spoil, raised up fierce storms with lightning and hail to ruin the crops, caused men's members to go limp and women's wombs to close or their babies to die within, dug up the graves of unbaptized infants to make a flying ointment from their flesh.

The voice and the crimes chilled Eva and made her heart quicken. She tied and retied the lacing of her bodice, trying to relieve the tightness she felt within. She kept herself busy and distracted by standing behind the counter, taking people's *kreuzers* and *pfennigs* in exchange for the heavy dark loaves the journeymen had baked before first light. She tried to distract her daughter as well, to keep her from hearing and from seeing. Katharina was too young, only eleven. She would have nightmares, and the child was already plagued with disturbing dreams and visions.

No matter what she did, however, Eva's thoughts returned again and again to the three accused women. She had no need to hear the voice. Leaflets listing the women and their crimes, shown in etchings for those who could not read, had appeared in the marketplace the day before. She'd not been surprised to see an old woman, a beggar, among the accused, but she'd been shocked to see Frau Basser's name – and her crimes. She was the wife of a prosperous tavern-keeper just down the street, a plump jovial woman who'd known everyone in Würzburg. She'd come to the Rosen Bakery for her family's bread, and Eva had thought her a good woman, a pious woman, a woman she'd never have suspected of witchcraft. Never. But Eva had read the litany of crimes Frau Basser had confessed to. She'd even admitted to poisoning one of the tavern's patrons.

And there was a girl, too, just sixteen, only five years older than Katharina.

The bakery was vacant now; everyone was outside, watching. Eva heard loud cheers and knew that old Judge Steinbach, in his tremulous voice, had rendered a verdict. The accused had been condemned. Eva leaned against the counter and tried to breathe, but there was not enough air. The roar of the crowd grew louder, and Eva found herself drawn yet again to the window. The enraged mob, waving fists and shouting curses, followed the slow-moving cart as it lurched through the street. The monks, in sombre black robes, chanted, warning that all that had been predicted was coming to pass; the end of the world was near.

The crowd surrounding the tumbrel parted slightly, and Eva saw the three wretched women behind the wooden bars: the girl, barely old enough to be considered a woman, Frau Basser, and the old beggar. A priest sat with them, a small black book clutched in his hands. Frau Basser leaned close to him and shouted, but her words were lost in the boisterous din. Eva's throat closed, and she had to look away. The women had been stripped to the waist, their heads shaved, their arms bound behind their backs. Their pale skin was mottled blue with cold. Blood streaked their bare mutilated breasts.

Katharina had crept up beside Eva and now stood on tiptoe trying to gain a better view, her white-gold braid swinging as she bobbed her head. Then, she stood still. Eva put an arm around her and tried to pull her close, to turn her away from the window, but the slight girl stood as solid and resistant as a pillar of stone. Eva placed her hand over her daughter's eyes. "Don't watch," she said.

Katharina pulled the hand away. "But Mama, I saw an angel come out of the flames. She had big white wings." The girl held out her thin arms as if she were cradling an infant. "She carried a white dog."

Eva grabbed the girl's shoulders. "You must not say such things!" There were no flames. Not yet. And certainly there were no angels. "You saw nothing of the kind." She released her daughter, giving her a small shove. "Go back by the ovens."

"But Mama, can't we go, too?"

"*Nein*! Go fetch yeast and flour for the men."

Her face in a pout, Katharina walked toward the back of the bakery, her left foot dragging like the whisper of brittle leaves across the wooden floor.

Eva turned from the window. She never went to the burnings, and she would not allow her daughter to go. There'd been no burnings when she was a child, and when they started, about sixteen or seventeen years ago, she'd gone only once, when she was twenty and still working as a maidservant. Even now Eva sometimes woke in the middle of the night hearing echoes of the old woman's screams and smelling the nauseating stench of scorched flesh. Ten or twelve years ago there'd been so many burnings, hundreds, that the stink had hung over Würzburg for three solid years. Then the burnings stopped, and Eva hoped it was finished, that all the witches were dead, but now there seemed to be more of them than ever.

The door creaked open. Eva stepped behind the counter as three women came in, each wearing the small embroidered cap of a matron. Eva's fingers went to her own black cap, a widow's cap, and smoothed her brown hair beneath it.

One of the matrons held fast to a little boy's hand. She brushed her fingertips over the youngest woman's belly. "Perhaps there will be more babies now," she said, "and the harvests will improve. There'll be more grain, cheaper bread." She glanced sharply at Eva, then pointed to a dark loaf. She opened her hand and held out eight *pfennigs*.

Eva shook her head.

"It's all I have," the woman pleaded.

Eva thought of the tattered ledger in the bedchamber upstairs. She kept the accounts, adding and subtracting the numbers each night. The bakery would fail if she didn't keep raising her prices to match the rising costs of wheat, barley, and rye.

The boy gripped the edge of the counter and stared at the loaf. His fingers were grimy, his cheekbones sharp under sallow skin. His huge eyes glinted like a stray dog's. He swallowed.

Eva wiped her hands on her apron. Were he still alive, Jacob would beat her for what she was about to do. She took the loaf from the shelf and handed it to the woman, taking only four *pfennigs* from the callused palm.

The woman clutched the bread to her chest. "*Danke*," she whispered.

The three women left quickly, and two younger women came in, one tall and angular, the other small and too thin, but comely nonetheless. Both wore plain dark gowns, much like Eva's own, laced over muslin chemises, and each carried a woven basket. Their long hair was tied back, but neither wore a cap. Unmarried maidservants. The smaller one leaned toward the other. "The harvests will be better now," she said, her face bright. "And Karl will be able to save money."

"Enough to think of marrying?" said the other girl.

The first young woman blushed prettily, then reached into her basket and held out three *kreuzers*. "*Bitte*, two loaves of rye."

Eva placed the loaves on the counter and picked up the *kreuzers*.

"But there are undoubtedly more of them," warned the tall girl. "Because the end-time is near. That's what the priest says. Ruining crops and killing babies." She shuddered. "I hate them all."

Eva counted out six *pfennigs* in change.

"I wish them all dead," said the other girl, "then the emperor's generals would win the war, and everyone would return to the true faith." She gave Eva a sidelong glance, as if seeking her agreement.

Eva gave it, nodding, sure that the girl was only repeating what she'd heard from her employer, or priest. Eva could feel the unspoken fear hovering just below the young maidservants' fierce words. They might hate witches, but, like her, they'd chosen not to attend the burnings.

The girl placed the loaves in her basket, then she and her companion left.

Eva went to stand before a small painting of the Virgin and Son she'd hung in the alcove under the stairway. Her fingers trembled as she made the sign of the cross. "Mary, Mother of God, have mercy upon me for I have sinned," she prayed. When she'd seen Frau Basser, she had not felt what she was supposed to feel: fury at the witch and satisfaction at the rightful punishment meted out by the court. She had felt only pity. And pounding fear.

She considered Mary's calm and kindly face, the golden light surrounding her and the child, and felt reassured. The Holy Mother would feel pity, even for a witch. And perhaps those three women were the last in the city. The harvests *would* improve now. Würzburg would be spared from plague. There *would* be more babies. And there would be no more burnings. The tall girl's words entwined themselves around her hopes. *There are undoubtedly more of them. Because the end-time is near.* Eva knew the words to be true. And now even women she knew and thought to be good and righteous were being revealed as witches.

Eva crossed herself again. When there were so many witches, and they appeared in such guises, how could anyone know who was a witch and who was not?

3

14 April 1626

Herr Doktor Franz Lutz tugged his fingers through his tangled white beard and stared into the distance where row after row of grapevines striped the sunlit hillside. In a small patch of untrammelled meadow, yellow and white flowers bloomed amidst the tall grasses. A few bony cows grazed, apparently unalarmed by the noisy crowd that had gathered so near to them.

Father Herzeim stepped down from the tumbrel. One witch, Frau Basser, tried to follow the priest, and the executioner had to shove her back into the cart. Lutz kept his gaze locked on the priest. He felt a vague sense of shame when his eyes strayed to the witches and their nakedness, particularly the young one. She must have been a great beauty, he thought, a young woman of generous and comely proportions.

Father Herzeim's face was haggard, and Lutz wondered for the hundredth time how his friend managed it, visiting witches in their stinking cells, hearing their final confessions, going with them to their deaths. It was a dangerous ministry, coming face to face with witches and the Devil. The priest, a professor of civil and ecclesiastical law at the university, was entirely unsuited for such crude work, and Lutz wished the Prince-Bishop had never appointed him. Father Herzeim, a Jesuit, rarely spoke of it, except to say "it is our way of proceeding," but Lutz could see the terrible toll this onerous duty was taking. His friend had been the final confessor for witches for less than a year, and in that brief span, premature streaks of silver had crept into his dark hair and beard, the lines on his handsome face had deepened, though he was not yet forty.

Lutz raised an arm, and Father Herzeim made his way toward him, his broad-brimmed hat bobbing above the crowd. People warily stepped away from the final confessor for witches, and the priest took his place beside Lutz. Drops of blood, witches' blood, spotted the pale yellow cincture around the waist of his black cassock. He made the sign of the cross, his long fingers sweeping from his forehead to his chest, left shoulder to right. "*In nomine patris, et filii, et spiritus sancti.*" He clasped his hands over his breviary and bowed his head.

The executioner, masked and gloved, led the witches from the tumbrel, one by one. Frau Basser was first. Shrieking, she tried to pull away from his grasp. He cuffed her across the face, then untied her wrists only long enough to bind her to one of the three tall stakes

Lutz resisted the urge to plug his forefingers into his ears, to shut out Frau Basser's screams, the mob's curses and jeers, and, especially, the monks' chanting, which unnerved him even more than the screams. He feared that the monks might be right. The end of the world was near; everything predicted in The Apocalypse was coming to pass. He tallied the evidence, keeping count by tapping his fingers against his wool breeches. One: hunger. Last autumn's grain harvests had been the worst in years and people were starving. Beggars were thick on the streets, not just in Würzburg, but throughout the southwest. Two: plague. It was breaking out everywhere around them, Ansbach, Rothenburg, Nuremberg. At yesterday's Lower City Council meeting, the councilmen had voted to direct the city gatekeepers to allow no strangers to enter Würzburg nor any citizen to re-enter who was returning from a city with plague. Three: war. The Holy Roman Empire now had a new and powerful enemy. The Netherlands had just joined England and Denmark on the side of the Protestant Union. Four: witches. The Devil was actively recruiting more witches. Scores had been executed, not only in Würzburg, but in Bamberg, Eichstatt, and Ellwangen as well, and still there were more of them. Only two days earlier, at Easter mass, the priest had read from The Apocalypse: *Woe to the earth, and to the sea, because the devil is come down unto you, having great wrath, knowing that he hath but a short time.* The priest had followed that verse with words from the Dominicans' *Der Hexenhammer, The Hammer of Witches.* No matter how hard he tried, Lutz could not erase the words from his mind: *And so in this twilight and evening of the world…the evil of witches and their iniquities superabound.*

Lutz pulled a linen handkerchief from under his starched cuff and pressed it against his sweating forehead. He could admit, at least to himself, that he was not a brave man. Thoughts of the end-time scared him. Witches and their depraved deeds scared him. Even now he feared that if he met their eyes they would put a curse on him. He wanted to be nowhere near this place. Now, or later. The ghosts of those who died violently lingered in the place of their death, and if witches had done such vile things in life, what might they do in death? Were Lutz not a member of the Lower City Council and his attendance required, he'd never have come. Yet here he was, standing near the front of the raucous crowd so that Father Herzeim would have one welcoming face to walk toward.

The executioner placed a thick wire around Frau Basser's neck. She screamed. Once. He quickly twisted the iron rod to tighten the wire. Her face purpled, her eyes bulged. Her tongue protruded and her body convulsed.

Lutz felt his head floating away. The bright sky closed in, then receded. The noise of the crowd faded away in echoes, and he could hear his own blood pulsing. He blinked hard, then lowered his head and took a deep breath. His wife Maria had fussed at him that morning to bring his pomander filled with hartshorn to keep himself from fainting, but Lutz, wanting to forget where he was going, managed to forget that as well. He regretted the oversight. It would be unseemly for a member of the Lower City Council to be seen swooning at an execution. He tried to calm himself. Over the bulge of his belly, he studied a small blue flower near the toe of his boot, wondering how it had escaped trampling. He counted the petals. Five, and a bright yellow centre. The strangling was a mercy really. The witches would not have to endure the horrendous pain of the fires, and he would not have to endure their screaming. He hated it when witches retracted their confessions and had to be burned alive, with green wood to prolong the suffering. The shrieks were unbearable.

Lutz heard cheers, then smelled the smoke. His stomach roiled. His breakfast had worked its way up, lodging in his gullet. He could taste bitterness at the back of his throat. Maria had warned him not to eat.

Lutz's ears rang in the silence. His back and legs ached. He'd been standing for hours, but he knew Father Herzeim would not leave until the witches had been burned to ash, as prescribed by law. Even their bones were dangerous. The executioner would gather the ashes and throw them into the river to be carried far away from Würzburg.

Lutz could risk looking up now. The flames had burned down and nearly everyone had left. Only a few ragged beggars patrolled the grounds for scraps of food. With a long pole, the executioner stirred the ash. A glowing ember flickered, then died, releasing a final smoky breath.

Father Herzeim turned his face to the sky. Dark clouds had gathered overhead. "Why must they bring the children?" he said.

"To instruct them," said Lutz. "To show them the wages of sin."

A small muscle at the corner of the priest's mouth twitched. "The wages of sin," he said softly. He turned abruptly and strode toward the city gate, his black cassock flapping around his ankles. Lutz, his short legs pumping, hurried to keep pace. His close-fitting doublet squeezed his chest and belly so tightly he could hardly draw breath. "Father," he panted.

"I must speak to the Prince-Bishop. At once."

"Not now, surely. It's nearly time for evening prayers."

Father Herzeim slowed, waiting for Lutz to catch up. "There's been a new opinion from the theologians at the University of Ingolstadt," said the priest. "You've read it?"

"I'm a contract lawyer, not a theologian," Lutz huffed.

"It's important, Lutz. They argue that people should not be arrested for witchcraft on the basis of accusations made by condemned witches. There must be other evidence. I must inform the Prince-Bishop."

"Isn't tomorrow soon enough?"

Father Herzeim shook his head. "I must talk with His Grace before he sends out the bailiff to arrest the people who've been newly accused."

"The opinion directly concerns capital crimes, so the head of the *Malefizamt* will have read it. Herr Hampelmann will inform the Prince-Bishop."

"Of that, I am not so sure." Father Herzeim laid a hand on Lutz's arm. "*Bitte*, will you come with me? The Prince-Bishop is weary of my complaints, but if you, a member of the city council, are with me, he will be more likely to grant me an audience."

Lutz cleared his throat. "Lower City Council, Father, only newly appointed."

"No matter. You're still a member."

Lutz considered his friend's earnest face. What the priest had told him did seem important: to arrest, or not to arrest, on the basis of witches' accusations when there was no other evidence. If Lutz were to go to the Prince-Bishop with new and valuable legal clarifications in a matter as pressing as witchcraft, it would be a stroke in his favour. It could just win him an appointment to the Upper City Council. "All right," he said.

"Bless you."

Lutz shrugged his shoulders as if trying to throw off a burden. There were risks to this errand. He'd like to serve on the prestigious Upper City Council, but he was reluctant to come under the close scrutiny of the Prince-Bishop, or to annoy him. And there was the added danger that His Grace might assume Lutz was interested in prosecuting witches and appoint him to the *Malefizamt*, the office in charge of investigating capital crimes. Lutz knew almost nothing about capital crimes and didn't particularly want to. He'd go with his friend, but speak as little as possible.

Lutz and Father Herzeim stopped in front of the Sander Tower, the south gate into Würzburg, and waited for the watchman at the high narrow window to acknowledge them. Father Herzeim looked toward the Prisoners' Tower in the distance. The circular tower was built into the inner city wall and stood at least five stories high, its conical roof pointing into the slate sky. Dark green ivy crept over the grey stone walls. The priest closed his eyes.

He's spent too much time within those walls, thought Lutz, far too much time.

At the watchman's nod, the men passed through the gate and into the city. They continued in silence, walking at a slower pace, much to Lutz's relief. His feet hurt from standing all day, his stiff breeches had begun to chafe his thighs, and the lacings that held his breeches to his doublet were beginning to come loose.

The Angelus bells rang out from Saint Kilian's Cathedral just as they reached *Domstrasse*. Father Herzeim turned toward the cathedral, paused a moment to make the sign of the cross, then he and Lutz headed the opposite direction toward the bridge. Beggars hunched against the walls of the closed shops. Now and

again, one called out, "A *pfennig. Bitte*, just a *pfennig* for bread."
When the petitioner was a child, Lutz reached into the pouch in
the lining of his breeches and tossed a coin, then he and the priest
hurried away before other beggars could pursue them.

As they passed the Rosen Bakery, Father Herzeim gave a slight
nod, then smiled, the first smile Lutz had seen from him in weeks.
Lutz followed his friend's gaze and caught a glimpse of a girl at
the window. Then she was gone. The image behind the thick
circles of glass was so fleeting, so pale, that Lutz would have
thought the child, with her white-gold hair, a ghost, or an
angel, but he'd often seen the odd little girl before, standing at the
bakery window, watching.

In front of the town hall, the priest stopped and made the
sign of the cross on the very spot where the public trial had been
conducted, just below the Green Tree of Justice painted on the
outside wall of the imposing stone building. While listening to the
lengthy *shrift* that morning, Lutz had committed to memory
every line and shading of the painting, as if holding the image in
his thoughts could protect him from witches and their crimes and
the terrors of the end-time. A respected citizen and a beautiful
young girl in league with the Devil? He'd been so shocked, his
heart beating so fast, that he'd had to find a place to sit down. Lutz
still found it hard to believe, even now, and would have liked to
sit down again, but Father Herzeim continued on.

The two men climbed the slight incline to the stone bridge
spanning the River Main. Halfway across the river, the priest
stopped and adjusted the broad brim of his hat to shield his face
from the mist that had begun to fall. "I am in need of courage,"
he said, "before I face the Prince-Bishop." He bowed his head and
began to pray, too softly for Lutz to hear. The light wind off the
river ruffled the cassock's billowing sleeves. Blue-backed swallows
twittered and dipped over the dark water.

Lutz dutifully recited his own evening prayers. Finishing long before the priest, he leaned against the thick stone wall and studied his friend's sharp profile. He'd known Father Herzeim since the Jesuit first came to Würzburg eight years ago, but they'd become intimately acquainted only recently. Last fall, Lutz had gone to the university to seek advice on a complex contract between two merchants, one in Augsburg and one in Würzburg. At the university, he was directed to Father Herzeim, who impressed Lutz with his quickness of mind and breadth of knowledge. The consultation ranged far beyond mere contract law, and at the end of two hours, the priest invited Lutz to return.

Father Herzeim's lips continued to move. Shivering, Lutz pulled his hat lower to keep the drizzle off the back of his neck. Just a few months ago, their friendship deepened when they discovered that they shared a secret dislike for the work of the poet Martin Opitz, who'd just been crowned poet laureate by Emperor Ferdinand. *Too stilted and cold. No passion, no feeling,* they'd agreed, then quoted to each other lines written by Walter von der Vogelweide. Father Herzeim even recited a poem he'd composed himself. Emboldened, Lutz had asked the priest his Christian name. Lutz never used it, of course, even in private, but he knew it: Friedrich.

Lutz scanned the grey clouds, so low they seemed to merge with the dark river. A barge loaded with wine casks approached, then passed through a granite archway under the bridge. The Prince-Bishop's castle, Marienberg, as stern and forbidding as His Grace's perpetual scowl, stood across the river, high on the mountain overlooking the city. Lutz lifted his hat and ran a hand through his shaggy hair, then jammed the hat back on his head. He should tidy himself before he met with the Prince-Bishop. He examined his white cuffs. Smudged. Nothing he could do about that now. He reached down to pull up his sagging hose, then retied some of the loose lacings between his breeches and doublet.

"*Dei glorium*, amen," said Father Herzeim. His dark eyes searched the misty twilight to one side, the other, then behind him. No one, not even a beggar was near to them on the bridge. "There is more to this errand, Lutz, than just the new opinion from Ingolstadt," he said quietly. "On the way to the fires, Frau Basser pleaded with me to speak to the Prince-Bishop. She was terrified of having innocent blood on her immortal soul."

"Innocent blood?"

"She claims that none of the five she accused is guilty, that she accused them only to end the torture."

"Did the other two witches accuse the same five people?"

The priest nodded.

"Then it's simple," said Lutz. "The witch was lying to save her accomplices, so they could continue their evil work."

"I am not so sure."

"Why, then, did all three witches give the commissioners the very same names? If they wanted only to end the torture, they'd give the first names that came into their heads."

"Frau Basser said those names were suggested to her."

Lutz took a step back. "Suggested to her! By whom?"

"I cannot tell you that."

"It can't possibly be true. She's lying."

"And her final confession," the priest whispered. "I can say nothing of it, except that it leads me to believe that Frau Basser was innocent."

"Innocent!" Lutz crossed his arms over his chest. "The men who serve on the commission are learned jurists. They'd never commit such a grievous error. Nor would God allow it."

He leaned closer and peered into Father Herzeim's pallid face. "I'm concerned about you, Father. *Bitte*, ask His Grace to relieve you of this appointment."

4

14 April 1626

Herr Doktor Wilhelm Hampelmann raised the silver goblet to his lips and sipped clear white wine. He stared out the open window, at the wisps of grey smoke curling and twisting over the tile roofs. The heavy clouds held the smoke low, close to the earth. It was only right and good that the smoke should not ascend to the heavens. It vexed him, though, that he could still smell the stink of burning flesh. The odour clung to his nostrils. *Hexen gestank.* Witches' stench. How had the smoke crept all the way up to Marienberg? He brought his pomander to his nose. Inhaling the pungent fragrance of lavender, he turned to the Prince-Bishop, who sat behind a broad oak desk studying an open ledger.

The Prince-Bishop plucked a grey quill from its stand and dipped the nib into black ink. The pen's scritching filled the room, a counterpoint to the insistent piping of the canaries flitting about in the silver cage that hung beside the desk. He blotted the ink, then heaved himself up. He held out the ledger. "These filthy vermin infest all of Würzburg. Read this and verify that Chancellor Brandt has recorded them all."

Hampelmann reached for the ledger, then brought the pages close to his face, squinting to bring the writing into focus.

First execution, 14 January 1625, two persons: Frau Bayer, a widow and beggar. A woman, a stranger.

Second execution, 3 March 1625, four persons: Frau Immler, a midwife. Fraulein Bayer, a prostitute, daughter of Frau Bayer. Old Hof-Schmidt, a beggar. Her daughter, also a beggar.

dancing in the palm of his hand
༜

*Third execution, 11 April 1625, five persons: Fraulein
Ritter, a maidservant. Three women, strangers. An old
peddler named Schwan.*

Hampelmann ran a hand through his pale hair. It was
exhausting, these never-ending trials. Over the past three years,
he'd participated in at least a score of inquisitions – a repugnant
dangerous undertaking. The depravity of witches knew no
bounds, and they were especially intent on harming those
who dared to prosecute them. Yet, as head of the *Malefizamt* and
a member of both the Upper and Lower City Councils, he felt
it was his duty, not only to the people of Würzburg and the
Prince-Bishop, but to God himself, to investigate every case of
suspected witchcraft. There could be no greater offence to God
than to renounce him and make a pact with the Devil.

The Prince-Bishop turned to the noisy birds, thrust a thick
finger between the silver wires, and cooed. A bright yellow canary
flew to the fleshy perch, but at the clanging of the Angelus bells,
the Prince-Bishop withdrew his finger and reached for the gold
and crystal reliquary on his desk. Clutching it awkwardly to his
chest with one hand and dangling a bejewelled rosary in the other,
he knelt before the wooden crucifix mounted on the stone wall
and began murmuring his evening prayers.

Hampelmann remained respectfully silent, preferring the
Jesuit practice of meditation to the Dominicans' recitation of set
prayers. As the Jesuits recommended, he went to confession
weekly and examined his conscience daily. In that meticulous
soul-searching, he'd discovered that his own personal defect was
pride, Saint Thomas Aquinas' first deadly sin.

He twisted the gold ring on his right hand, the Hampelmann
family crest. How could he not be proud of his noble lineage, his
quickness of mind, his achievements by the age of forty-one: head
of the *Malefizamt*, first burgomaster of the Lower City Council,

second burgomaster of the Upper City Council, favoured advisor to the Prince-Bishop? It was a bitter struggle to humble himself, and every morning he went to mass at Saint Kilian's Cathedral, then to meditation in the Lusam Garden at Neumunster. There, beside the grave of the poet Walter von der Vogelweide, he laboured to compose his own verses about his Lord's suffering. Hampelmann knew he was not a skilled poet; his poetry served to provoke him to humility.

At the moment, Hampelmann was also struggling with covetousness, Saint Thomas' second deadly sin. He realised, with chagrin, that he coveted the Prince-Bishop's relic. The precious reliquary His Grace held close to his heart contained a thorn from the true crown. The Prince-Bishop had paid dearly for the thorn, but in these dangerous times it was worth every *pfennig*. It protected him. Hampelmann touched the ball of wax fastened to the narrow cord at his throat, wax from the cathedral candles that contained consecrated salt and herbs. That was what the Jesuits had prescribed for his protection. Would it truly protect him from the Devil's wrath?

He bowed his head, ashamed of his fear and the weakness of his faith. He was doing God's work. Of course, God would protect him. He crossed himself and thought of the great French lawyer, Jean Bodin, whose words so reassured him that Hampelmann had committed them to memory: *It is a wonderful secret of God's and one which judges ought to ponder well, that God keeps them under his protection both against earthly powers and against the power of evil spirits. This is why we read in the law of God "when ye judge fear no one, for judgement is God's."* Bodin's words, however, always brought to mind those of the Jesuit scholar, Martin Delrio, who claimed that avarice, ambition, cruelty, or thirst for revenge could render a judge vulnerable to spells; only those who put God before their eyes and carried out their duties piously would be inviolate. During his morning meditations,

Hampelmann regularly examined his motives, determined to keep
God before his eyes.

He returned to Chancellor Brandt's report.

*Ninth execution, 16 December 1625, five persons:
An old woman who sold pigeons. Frau Niebur, a midwife.
Fraulein Schwarz, a laundress. Two women, strangers.*

Always, it seemed, the investigation began with charges raised
against some tongue-ripe hag, charges of *maleficium*, dark curses
and potions she'd employed to work ill upon her neighbours.
Hampelmann felt a prickling cross the back of his neck. With
her snaggled yellow teeth, floating eye, and humped back, one
had only to look upon the loathsome old crone - and to hear her
sharp tongue - to know that she was a witch. If the Devil gave
her strength, it ended with her, but if he abandoned the wretch,
as so often he did, she weakened and named her accomplices.

*First execution, 16 January 1626, four persons: Old Frau
Stolzberger, a widow and beggar. Another woman, a
stranger. A young man named Niebur, son of Frau Niebur,
a thief and sodomite. Executed at the same time was a
guard who had helped a prisoner escape.*

*Second execution, 23 February 1626, two persons: Frau
Stolzberger, widowed daughter of Old Frau Stolzberger. A
butcher's widow, Frau Dietrich, was burned alive.*

*Third execution, 14 April 1626, three persons: Frau
Imhof, a widow and beggar. Fraulein Stolzberger, a beggar, daughter of Frau Stolzberger. Frau Basser, wife of a
tavern-keeper.*

Hampelmann picked up the quill and signed the report in
his elegant hand: *Herr Doktor Wilhelm Hampelmann.* He
rubbed his aching eyes. His duties weighed heavily upon him.
He was especially troubled by what he'd recently learned about a

young man, a law student at the university who was rumoured to be openly questioning how the Würzburg *Malefizamt* investigated charges of witchcraft. During the most recent hearings, Hampelmann had even asked the witches about those rumours. To his surprise and horror, all three confirmed them and then named Herr Christoph Silberhans as an accomplice. It disturbed Hampelmann that denunciations of men contradicted the Dominicans' witch-hunting manual *Der Hexenhammer*. He closed his eyes to bring the words clearly to mind: *All this comes to pass because of the carnal appetite that is insatiable in women…and this is why they have dealings with demons, so that their lust may be satisfied…Hence it is but logical to speak of witchcraft as a matter of female witches, and not of men…And may the Lord be praised, who hath seen fit unto this day to preserve the male sex from this depravity.*

Then again, thought Hampelmann, perhaps there was no contradiction. Lust. That was the key. The Dominicans had known well enough that the Devil worked his evil through lust. *From the moment of his fall, the Devil has been seeking to destroy the unity of the Church, to injure love, to mar the sweetness of the saints' holy works with the gall of his envy, and to extirpate and destroy mankind in every way. His strength is in the loins and in the navel, because they hold sway over man through the lusts of the flesh. For the sea of lust in men is in the loins, for it is here that the semen is secreted, as lust is in the navel in the case of women.*

Hampelmann closed the window against the chilly air. Like women, he reasoned, male witches were excessively lustful men who had succumbed to, rather than controlled, their lust. He thought of his own lovely wife Helena and considered, with some satisfaction, how rarely he allowed himself to touch her. He strove to make his love for her pure and chaste, like the love he felt for his daughter. Yet, when he thought of Helena, it was with some regret. If he'd never loved her, never desired her, he'd have been ordained. Hampelmann was quite sure of that. And then he'd have become a member of the Cathedral Chapter, who were, to a man, clerical nobles. It was from the Cathedral Chapter that the next Prince-Bishop would be chosen. Because of Helena, that prize was now forever beyond his grasp. He did not blame her, though. He knew that the fault lay with his own weakness, for which his Jesuit confessor had referred him to First Corinthians, chapter 7: *It is good for a man not to touch a woman. But for fear of fornication, let every man have his own wife, and let every woman have her own husband.*

There was a soft knock on the door. The Prince-Bishop's florid face contorted with annoyance as he struggled up from his knees. He carefully set down the reliquary, then dropped into his chair. "And what will be his complaint this time?" he groaned.

A serving man stepped into the room. Father Herzeim swept in behind him. Herr Lutz followed, his steps hesitant. Water dripped from their broad-brimmed hats, which they held clutched in front of them.

"Your Grace," said the servant, "I informed Father Herzeim and Herr Lutz that you were far too tired to see them now." He flicked a hand toward the priest. "He, however, insisted."

With a smile that quickly turned to a grimace, the Prince-Bishop addressed the servant. "Leadership carries with it grave responsibilities. Unlike the peasants, who can take their rest whenever they choose, those of us in authority go to our eternal rest only when we pass from this earthly existence. On earth, we must endure–" his gaze slid to Father Herzeim "–continual tribulations."

The priest leaned forward. "Your Grace-"

The Prince-Bishop raised a hand, his gold rings flashing. "*Bitte*, a moment. Wine, Father? Herr Lutz?" Without waiting for a reply, the servant scurried from the room.

Hampelmann lifted his goblet and, over its silver rim, studied the priest – head bowed, breviary and hat clutched before him, a supplicant. By no means a stupid man, but weak. He'd been a thorn in their sides ever since his appointment as final confessor. There were times when Hampelmann wondered if he'd been sent by God to test their resolve. He was so different from the other Jesuits. Was it a lack of courage? Or a lack of faith?

Father Herzeim raised his head. "*Bitte*, Your Grace–"

"Patience, Father. *To every thing there is a season.*"

The serving man returned with two goblets. Lutz bobbed his head gratefully and reached for the wine. Father Herzeim waved it aside.

The Prince-Bishop thrust out his lower lip. "An excellent vintage, Father, from the Stein vineyards. What matter presses upon you so heavily that you would eschew such a wine…and risk offence to your superior?"

The priest held out his breviary, as if making an offering. "I must speak with you about the recent opinion from the University of Ingolstadt." He spoke quickly. "It rejects the use of accusations made by condemned witches to arrest anyone when there is no other evidence of witchcraft."

Hampelmann stepped forward. "With all due respect, Your Grace, I have studied the document, and it bears the mark of sceptics…and heretics. Nevertheless, if read carefully, the opinion states that in a crime as heinous as witchcraft we must proceed with utmost caution." He looked at Father Herzeim. "But indeed we must proceed."

"I, too, have studied the Ingolstadt opinion," said Father Herzeim, "and believe that it concurs with the opinion of the theologians at the University of Dillingen: *The protection of the innocent must be as close to the heart of the judge and the prince as the care of the public good against sorcerers.*"

Hampelmann tasted sour wine at the back of his throat. *Protection of the innocent.*

The Prince-Bishop's eyes narrowed. "The Commission of Inquisition carefully protects the innocent, Father. God protects the innocent." He turned to Lutz. "And what is your opinion in this matter, Herr Lutz?"

Lutz shifted his considerable weight from one foot to the other. "It…it does seem that this opinion raises an important question." He spread his hands, hat in one, goblet in the other. "When there is no other evidence…" His voice trailed off, and his bulk seemed to shrink beneath the Prince-Bishop's scowl.

Father Herzeim persisted. "How can we know that the Devil has not deluded these women into naming innocent people? That's why the theologians at Ingolstadt rejected the use of denunciations. They questioned how, when we believe deluded old women in no other matter, we can take their accusations as truth." He touched the wooden cross on his chest. "Moreover, if a witch is truly guilty, can't we assume that she wishes to harm others and that her accusations are false? And if she is innocent, then her denunciations must be false."

"Innocent!" shouted Hampelmann.

The Prince-Bishop laid a hand on the reliquary, his thumb caressing the crystal that enclosed the thorn. "It is the duty of the commissioners to sort out truth from falsehood, to separate the guilty from the innocent. If any of the accused are innocent, the commissioners will discover that truth during the hearings."

The flutter of wings was loud in the silence. The Prince-Bishop stood and opened a drawer from which he pulled a silver ladle. He scooped black thistle seed from a stoneware jar and moved toward the cage. "I trust, Father, that you will be attending the banquet tomorrow evening?"

Father Herzeim nodded, his face grim.

The Prince-Bishop fumbled with the tiny latch on the cage door. "Herr Lutz," he said, "you appear to be a man who enjoys good food and wine. You must serve on the commission soon.

Then you, too, may attend the banquet." Black seeds rained from the ladle into a porcelain dish. "You are both dismissed now."

Lutz set down the goblet and hurried toward the door. Father Herzeim did not move. "There is yet another matter," the priest said quietly.

The Prince-Bishop's eyebrows came together in a thick dark line. "Oh?"

"On the way to the fires, Frau Basser withdrew her accusations against the others. She said they are innocent, that she named them as accomplices only to end the torture. They must not be arrested."

The Prince-Bishop set down the ladle, then folded his arms over the gold cross nestled against his velvet robes. "This witch signed her confession to the commission. And her accusations. It does not matter that she withdrew them later. These people—" he looked toward Hampelmann.

"Herr Silberhans, Fraulein Spatz, Frau Bettler, Frau Lamm, and Frau Rosen, Your Grace."

"*Danke*, Herr Hampelmann. These people can – and will – be arrested."

"But Frau Basser insisted that they are innocent," said the priest. "And I believe her. Where is the evidence that any crime has been committed? Herr Silberhans is a student of mine. A fine young man. There are no *indicia* of witchcraft for him."

"I beg to differ," said Hampelmann. "It is widely rumoured that Christoph Silberhans has expressed open scepticism about the way we conduct the hearings. Some of his fellow students even came to the *Malefizamt* to report that Silberhans is a defender of witches."

"I teach my students to examine the law," said Father Herzeim. "It is not enough merely to learn it. Naturally there are questions. Neither questions, nor hearsay, constitute evidence."

The Prince-Bishop pointed a finger at the priest. "Some laws are too important to be questioned. Do not forget the rule of obedience."

Father Herzeim took a deep breath. "What then of Frau Rosen? She is known as an honest and pious woman, of no ill repute."

"No ill repute?" laughed Hampelmann. "As I recall, and do correct me if I am mistaken, Herr Lutz, she and her husband were nearly fined for having a child too soon after their wedding. They would have been fined had the midwife not testified before the Lower City Council that the child was born early. A claim I do not believe. The girl was born crippled, I might add. Moreover, it is widely known that Frau Rosen's husband had to discipline her often, and severely."

Hands clasped behind his back, Hampelmann walked toward the window. He'd known Eva Rosen years ago, known her quite well in fact, when she was still Eva Hirsch and worked as a maidservant in his father's household. The woman was beautiful and so seductive that it was a real possibility she was a witch. Certainly worth investigating. It made the hair stand up on the back of his neck to think that there might have been a witch working in the Hampelmann household and that he'd nearly been fooled by her charms.

He pivoted slowly. "About three years ago, Herr Rosen died suddenly, mysteriously, leaving a trade corporation membership for his widow to offer to a new husband. Yet Frau Rosen has chosen not to remarry, though I understand she's quite a handsome woman."

"It's hardly a sin, or an indication of witchcraft, to remain unmarried," said Father Herzeim. "The Church commends it, in fact. First Corinthians, chapter 7: *But I say to the unmarried, and to the widows: It is good for them if they so continue.*"

"Have you forgotten, Father, how the verse ends?" Hampelmann did not wait for an answer. "*But if they do not contain themselves, let them marry. For it is better to marry than to be burnt.* Frau Rosen is an experienced woman. I seriously doubt that she has *contained herself.*"

Hampelmann smoothed his beard. "God has placed woman under man's authority, and yet there's Frau Rosen, on her own, subject to the authority of no man, running the bakery with only journeymen. No master. The bakery is losing money and she's not even chosen a legal guardian to manage her financial affairs. Though the Lower City Council has recommended it. Three times. Is it not true, Herr Lutz, that the master bakers have complained to the council about Frau Rosen?"

Lutz hovered near the door, hand on the latch. Even with his blurred eyesight, Hampelmann could see that the councilman's white hair and beard needed trimming, his soiled hose drooped at the knees, his white collar was rumpled, and there were copper buttons missing from his doublet where it stretched over his protruding belly. Lutz's slovenliness and corpulence disgusted Hampelmann. The man was at least fifty, a lawyer and a Würzburg councilman. One would think he could muster a greater dignity, especially in an audience with the Prince-Bishop.

Lutz chuckled uneasily. "Ach, they're always complaining about something."

"But you cannot deny that Herr Kaiser became seriously ill after he registered his complaint. So ill that he nearly died."

Father Herzeim stepped toward Hampelmann. "There is nothing in what you say to indicate witchcraft."

Clenching his fists, Hampelmann willed himself to be patient with the priest. He would not yield to Saint Thomas' sixth deadly sin: anger.

"Your Grace," said Father Herzeim, turning away from Hampelmann, "Frau Basser pleaded with me that those whom she'd accused not be arrested. I pray that you will show mercy."

"Do I not order that witches who confess and repent be

strangled or beheaded before they're burned? But just as the surgeon is cruel in cauterizing a wound, so must we be cruel in burning away bad flesh from good. If it became known that condemned witches could retract their accusations of others, all of them would do so. Why would they not want their accomplices to go free?" The Prince-Bishop's face hardened. "Frau Rosen – along with all the others – shall be brought in for investigation. As the law requires."

The Prince-Bishop considered the broad tapestry covering one wall. Hampelmann could not see the scene clearly, but he knew it depicted the martyrdom of Saint Kilian, who'd brought Christianity to Würzburg more than 600 years ago, then been murdered by Turkish infidels right there in Marienberg.

"We must be as dedicated to the true faith as Saint Kilian," said the Prince-Bishop. "And just as courageous."

Father Herzeim reached out to touch the gold cross on the reliquary. "Saint Kilian converted by words, not the sword. These women need religious instruction, not death."

"Saint Kilian died by the sword," said Hampelmann, "murdered by those who would not be converted by words. Witches will do the same to us if we allow them to live."

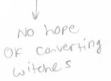

No hope
of converting
witches

5

15 April 1626

Eva had roused the journeymen hours before dawn. Talking quietly to each other, the two men worked at long wooden tables worn smooth and shiny by years of kneaded dough. With floured hands, Eva shaped sweet buns, the only bread the bakers' trade corporation allowed her to mix and bake.

There had been four journeymen before Jacob died, but two had left, taunted into quitting "a workshop run by a woman." Eva was glad they were gone. Barley and rye had become so dear she could not have paid wages to four men.

She suspected the other two stayed only because each yet hoped to marry her, Herr Rosen's widow, and thereby gain the position of master baker. Both were hard steady workers, and Herr Stolz, with his sandy hair and strong teeth, could even be considered handsome. Watching his muscled arms and shoulders lifting heavy trays from the ovens, she'd been tempted, more than once, to invite him to her bed. She had little doubt he'd accept the invitation. But Eva knew how men changed when they got what they wanted. Before their marriage, Jacob, a childless widower, had been kind and attentive whenever she came in his bakery to buy bread. After they wed, he was gentle at first, and appreciative that she knew her numbers and could keep the accounts. He was delighted when Eva conceived so soon, but when she gave him only Katharina, his disposition hardened. He cared little that his daughter was born early, so small and scrawny the midwife predicted she would not survive. Jacob cared only that Katharina was not a son, and that her foot was misshapen. Later, Katharina's limp would sometimes provoke him to rage.

In the succeeding years, Jacob worked as diligently as an old man could to achieve an heir, and when he could not manage a husband's duties, he blamed Eva, wondering aloud about midwives' potions and witches' spells. It had been nearly three years since Jacob's death, but Eva could still recall the blows of the birch rod on her back and, even more painfully, the thud it made striking Katharina.

Eva slapped a sweet bun onto the greased tray. Her reluctance to remarry had cost her a few customers, *hausfrauen* who now went to other bakeries. The women who remained sometimes studied Eva from the corners of their eyes. They might as well speak their suspicions aloud, Eva thought, and simply ask whose husband warmed her bed. A flush rose from her neck to her cheeks, and she again felt the anger, and the shame, she'd known the day she dared to wear a blue gown instead of her widow's weeds. She'd felt the women's sharp measuring looks, and less than an hour after the bakery opened, she went upstairs to change back to her black gown, though it reeked of stale sweat and wood smoke.

Eva dusted her hands on her apron and set the sweet buns to rise. She walked to the window that looked out on *Domstrasse*. The sky was beginning to grow light. She cracked open the window and heard the clang of hammering from a nearby smithy, then the distant bellowing of cattle being driven through the streets and out the gates to graze in the meadows beyond the city walls. A skeletal bright-eyed mongrel circled a heap of refuse, snarling at a scrawny pig rooting through the garbage. When the dog dashed in to snatch a bone, the pig squealed and trotted away.

Eva smelled it then. Again. She'd closed the window and door tightly the day before, but the greasy stench of burning flesh had crept in. She was sure she'd seen grey wisps seeping in around the windowsill. Eva hated the stink. It made her skin prickle, and she'd tried to wipe it from her face and neck with a damp cloth. When the Angelus bells rang out and the Rosen Bakery closed for the day, she'd hauled out the rags and pail, hiked up her black skirts, and gone down on her knees to scrub the floors with lye soap. Then, she'd washed the counter and walls. Even so, the odour lingered. It always did, underlying the fragrance of baking bread.

She heard a soft uneven tread on the stairs behind her. Eva turned and saw Katharina, still in her sleeping shift. In the candlelight, her long braid, twining over one shoulder looked white. Her eyes glittered like emeralds. Eva's throat tightened even as she tried to smile. Just the day before, those beautiful eyes had seen visions of orange flames and white-winged angels.

The girl's strangeness made Eva afraid for her, and she forbade her to speak to anyone of her dreams and visions. There was little danger of that, however, as Katharina avoided other children and rarely even spoke to anyone but her mother. She spent her days at the window, watching the street, or walking the riverbank, collecting coloured stones, plants and flowers, and white feathers. Angel wings, she called them. Once she'd returned home after dark, telling Eva that the *feurige mannlein*, the little glowing men, had helped her to find her way. Eva had put her trembling fingers to her daughter's lips and told her not to speak of such things. Ever.

Katharina looked like a wraith, her milky skin never darkening in the sun. Her limping gait only added to her oddness. Jacob had claimed the girl's misshapen foot was a sign that Eva had sinned.

Eva knew which of her sins had crippled her daughter. Her limp was a daily reproach.

Katharina yawned. "Some bread, Mama?"

"Of course, *Liebchen*." Eva walked back to the ovens and picked up a fresh loaf of barley bread. Herr Stolz jerked his chin at the shelf, at the day-old loaves. Ignoring his sidelong glance, Eva cut off a thick slice from the still-warm loaf.

The journeyman wiped a forearm across his sweating brow. "You spoil the child."

Eva spread the coarse bread with a thin layer of cherry jam. No, he would not make a good husband. She filled a mug with beer. As she brought the food to Katharina, the morning bells began. A faint far-off tinkling at first, then a growing cacophony of pealing, clanging, booming, and jangling as other bells chimed in. She tried to identify each of the city's cathedrals and chapels by the distinctive pitch of its bells: Saint Kilian's, Neumunster, Saint Burkard's, Mary's Chapel, Saint Augustine's, Neubau. Eva loved this time of day, the soft light of dawn, the bells ringing, the fragrant golden loaves ready to sell.

While Katharina ate, Eva roamed the workshop, extinguishing as many of the tallow candles as she could. She paused by the painting of the Holy Mother and Child. The candlelight made the faces glow as if lit from within. The oil paint had begun to crack and peel, but Eva thought the web of lines only made Mary's face more lovely, wrinkled softly, like a kindly grandmother's. She crossed herself, then ran her fingers over the leather-bound Bible she kept on a small table beneath the painting. It had cost so much that Jacob had refused to buy it at first. Why have a Bible, he reasoned, when neither of them could read? Eva begged, then persuaded him that a Bible would bring good fortune upon the bakery, that it would protect them from loss and harm. He finally relented. She was careful then not to let him discover that the nuns at the Unterzell Convent, where she'd lived for six years after her parents died, had taught her not only numbers but letters as well.

Eva flipped open the pages and read a favourite passage from Psalms. *Give glory to the Lord, for he is good: for his mercy endureth forever.*

She hardly heard, above the bells, the clip-clop of horses on the stone street. There was the squeaking complaint of leather, then a loud pounding on the door. Eva smoothed her apron and straightened her widow's cap, but before she could step to the door, it was pushed open from the other side. A man in a broad-brimmed hat with long grey and white plumes ducked through the narrow doorway. He carried a lance. An ornate red scabbard hung from his broad leather belt, and a chain of iron links spanned his chest. The Prince-Bishop's bailiff.

Eva gasped and put her shaking hands to her mouth.

Slowly, deliberately, the man unrolled a scroll. "On the authority of Prince-Bishop Philipp Adolf von Ehrenberg," he read, "Frau Eva Rosen is placed under arrest until such time as an inquiry can be made into the charges of witchcraft against her. She has been accused of turning from God and the Holy Roman Church and making a pact with the Devil."

Her heart in her throat, Eva was nearly unable to speak. "Who has accused me? Never have I turned from God."

The bailiff called over his shoulder, to the men pushing through the door behind him. "We are to bring the girl as well. Attend to them both while I search the premises. Herr Baunach, you question the journeymen."

6

15 April 1626

The canaries flitted to the porcelain cup filled with bread crumbs. Hampelmann, who sat to the right of the Prince-Bishop, was disgusted by their insipid chittering and the bits of dark excrement that fell from amidst their glossy yellow feathers.

The Prince-Bishop pushed back his chair and folded his hands over his velvet robes. His eyelids drooped, blinked open at the canaries' piping, then drooped again.

Hampelmann's stomach was full, but not excessively so, and he congratulated himself on his restraint. He'd eaten only sparingly of the lavish banquet for the Commission of Inquisition for the Würzburg Court, taking only small portions of the roast pork, partridge and swan, the poached trout in cream sauce, the baked goose stuffed with chestnuts, the white and yellow cheeses and dark rye bread, the dried African figs, currants and hazelnuts. He was vastly pleased that the meal had ended with apricot pastries flavoured with ginger and cinnamon from the Levant, costly spices kept under lock and key. Hampelmann hadn't particularly enjoyed the sweets, a cloying indulgence to his abstemious palate. But serving pastries containing expensive spices was a sign that the Prince-Bishop approved of the commission's work – despite Father Herzeim's complaints.

Sitting to the right of Hampelmann, the Jesuit had eaten almost nothing, though he'd emptied his wine goblet again and again. His face was downcast, and he'd hardly contributed a word to the jovial banter during the meal. It was clear the priest's thoughts were far away from Marienberg Castle, and

Hampelmann wondered if they were still in the Prisoners' Tower with those whom the Prince-Bishop's bailiff had arrested early that morning. The final confessor for witches seemed far too concerned for the earthly welfare of the accused, too little concerned for the fate of their eternal souls.

The Prince-Bishop stood and bent toward the silver cage behind his ornately carved chair. Cooing to the birds, he slipped a brocade cloth over the cage. Herr Doktor Johann Brandt, the Prince-Bishop's chancellor, rolled his eyes, then carefully recomposed his face when his hooded gaze met Hampelmann's across the table. Hampelmann looked long at the chancellor, to be sure that Brandt understood that he had seen his indiscretion.

The Prince-Bishop sat down and picked at his front teeth with a long thumbnail. "Good news, gentlemen. I've heard that General Wallenstein has gathered an enormous army for the emperor. He'll put the Protestants to rout."

"I've heard, though, that he's ruthless in requisitioning men and supplies," said Herr Doktor Lindner, the ruddy-faced physician who'd served on the commission. His bulbous nose glowed red from too much wine. "Wallenstein simply takes what he wants. Let's hope he keeps the war in the north."

"There's little enough in Würzburg to take," sniffed Chancellor Brandt. "Plenty of extra men. He could requisition all the beggars. But there's no supplies to be had."

Judge Steinbach, who sat beside Chancellor Brandt, raised a frail palsied hand. "Even so, there are the taxes the emperor is demanding. How can Würzburg possibly pay them? The council has been debating the question for days."

Hampelmann dabbed his mouth with a linen napkin, then held it in place to hide his clenched jaw. Steinbach was Judge of the Würzburg Court and first burgomaster of the Upper City Council only because of his wealth and reputation in the city, not because the old man was competent – at anything. The Upper

City Council ended up debating nearly everything for days because the timid judge could not maintain order at the meetings. As second burgomaster, Hampelmann always had to intervene.

The Prince-Bishop waved a hand dismissively. "Increase the wine tax."

"We've considered that," said Judge Steinbach. "But the harvests in the vineyards have been nearly as poor as those in the fields."

"Mark my words," said Lindner. The physician's voice was overly loud, his words slurred. "With soldiers travelling about, there'll be outbreaks of plague everywhere."

Hampelmann studied the dark freckles sprinkled across Lindner's face and wondered if the drunken boor had been listening to anyone but himself. How could anyone take seriously the opinions of a man who had freckles, as if he worked in the fields like a common peasant?

"War. Famine. Plague. It's all punishment from God." Father Streng's high-pitched lilt was ill-suited to the harshness of his pronouncement. The young Jesuit, who sat to the left of the Prince-Bishop and across from Hampelmann, was so slight, his fair skin so smooth, that he looked and sounded like a boy, though he was at least twenty-five. "To quote my fellow Jesuit, Martin Delrio," continued the priest: *The wrath of God grows ever fiercer and more dreadful. If this evil of witchcraft is not suppressed, the whole country can expect nothing more certain than the punishment and curse of God. Witches are at the root of it all, gentlemen.*"

Hampelmann nodded stiffly. He found Father Streng's habit of quoting authorities verbatim exceedingly tedious, but he rarely disagreed with the priest. He did, however, recognize his own sin of pride in the young man, pride in his nobility and his membership in the Upper City Council. And the Cathedral Chapter. Hampelmann suspected that Father Streng coveted the

Prince-Bishop's power and authority. With precious little subtlety, the Jesuit vied with Hampelmann to be His Grace's favoured advisor.

Father Herzeim absently rolled a silver goblet between his hands. "When I was a boy growing up in Nuremberg, bad weather and poor harvests, plagues and other misfortunes were blamed on nature or thought to be acts of God." He gazed into the emptiness of the goblet, then set it upright. "Now it seems that everything is blamed on witches, or God's wrath at witches, or his wrath that we are not prosecuting witches. Why is that?"

Chancellor Brandt's lip curled. "You speak like a Lutheran, Father, not a Jesuit."

Father Streng's grey eyes were huge behind his spectacles. "*Nein*, even that Devil's spawn Luther knew the evil of witches. *I would have no compassion on these witches*, he wrote, *I would burn them all.*" He plucked up an embroidered napkin and twisted it, as if wringing the neck of a goose. Hampelmann groaned inwardly and wished that Chancellor Brandt had not mentioned Lutherans. He sat back in his chair and readied himself for one of Father Streng's long-winded lectures.

The young Jesuit cleaned his spectacles with the napkin, then placed them back on his nose. "So you would question the wisdom of the authorities, Father Herzeim?" Without waiting for the older priest to answer, Father Streng drew back his narrow shoulders and launched his verbal salvo. "Ephesians, chapter 6: *Put you on the armour of God, that you may be able to stand against the deceits of the devil. For our wrestling is not against flesh and blood; but against principalities and powers, against the rulers of the world of this darkness, against the spirits of wickedness in high places.*"

His left eyelid twitched, making the small mole above his pale eyebrow jump. "And to quote the great French lawyer, Jean Bodin: *If there is any means to appease the wrath of God, to gain his blessing, and to punish the most detestable crimes of which the human mind can conceive, it is to punish with the utmost rigor the witches."*

Father Herzeim considered the young man's flushed face. "I do not dispute the authorities, Father Streng, but I am persuaded that Jean Bodin and the others have given insufficient attention to the parable of the cockle in Saint Matthew."

"How so?" Father Streng panted, as if he'd just run all the way up Marienberg Mountain to the Prince-Bishop's castle.

"Chapter 13: *The kingdom of heaven is likened to a man that sowed good seed in his field. But while men were asleep, his enemy came and oversowed cockle among the wheat and went his way. And when the blade was sprung up and had brought forth fruit, then appeared also the cockle. And the servants of the goodman of the house coming said to him: Sir, didst thou not sow good seed in thy field? Whence then hath it cockle? And he said to them: An enemy hath done this. And the servants said to him: Wilt thou that we go and gather it up?"*

One of the beeswax candles flickered, then burned out. A servant stepped forward to replace it. Hampelmann glanced from one Jesuit to the other. Father Streng's spectacles reflected the yellow candlelight, hiding his eyes, but his mouth was a tight pucker. Father Herzeim was not nearly so drunk as he ought to be.

Father Herzeim stared at his own reflection in the silver goblet. *"And he said: No, lest perhaps gathering up the cockle, you root up the wheat also together with it. Suffer both to grow until the harvest, and in the time of the harvest I will say to the reapers: Gather up first the cockle and bind it into bundles to burn, but the wheat gather ye into my barn."*

"And just what is it you think the authorities have missed?" said Father Streng.

"We are the servants, not the reapers. Who are we to judge who is cockle and who is wheat? Might we not be uprooting the wheat with the cockle in this zealous hunt for witches?"

The Prince-Bishop placed both hands flat on the table. "So you would allow witches to destroy the Holy Church for fear of hurting an innocent?"

"The protection of the innocent must be utmost in our minds, and in our hearts," said Father Herzeim.

"*Nein*," shouted Father Streng. "It is the prosecution of witches that must be utmost in our minds."

"We are doing God's work," said Hampelmann. "He would never allow us to condemn an innocent." He pulled at the scratchy white ruff encircling his neck and caught a whiff of *hexen gestank* on his sleeve. His fingers went to the ball of wax at his throat. *God's work*

Father Herzeim turned to Hampelmann. "Surely you have not forgotten that not long ago Duke Maximilian himself ordered the execution of a witch judge in Bavaria for precisely that – condemning innocents."

Judge Steinbach suddenly sat straight up, his lashless eyes blinking rapidly. He tugged at the little tuft of white beard on his bony chin. "What did he do?" His voice quavered.

Spineless, thought Hampelmann. The Judge of the Würzburg Court twitched all through the commission's hearings, and now the fool was fretting that he might be executed himself.

"Judge Sattler's legal errors were egregious," said Hampelmann. "We are far more careful in our procedures."

Judge Steinbach ran his tongue over his teeth, then spoke haltingly. "With all due respect, Your Grace, some of these recent accusations do trouble me. Frau Rosen and Herr Silberhans – they're not beggars. Frau Rosen is a baker's widow, Herr Silberhans a law student at the university."

"The end-time is near, Judge Steinbach," said the Prince-Bishop. "Witches are becoming ever more numerous. And more and more clever at disguising themselves in the world."

"In these dangerous times it is quite proper to take the

strongest measures to root out evil," said Father Streng. "Let the trials hit who they may."

"Even the nobles?" said Father Herzeim.

Father Streng pounded a small fist on the table. "Even the nobles! Because if we are negligent, God will punish us all."

"All right," said Father Herzeim, "investigate. But must they die?"

"That is what God demands of us," said Father Streng. "It is God's will that they die. And as Jesuits, we are but instruments in the hands of God." He dabbed the sweat on his forehead with a napkin. "You would remind us that a judge was executed for condemning innocents. I would remind you of the words of Martin Delrio: *Judges are bound under pain of mortal sin to condemn witches to death; anyone who pronounces against the death sentence is reasonably suspected of secret complicity; nay, it is an* indicium *of witchcraft to defend witches.* Would you be a defender of witches, Father Herzeim?"

"I am a defender of the faith. Remember our way of proceeding, Father Streng, *noster modus procedenti.* We are here to console, not to condemn."

The Prince-Bishop crossed his arms over his velvet robes. "It is a mercy to kill them."

Father Streng nodded vigorously. "Indeed, Cardinal Bellarmine has written: *It benefits obstinate heretics that they be cut off from this life; for the longer they live, thinking their various errors, the more people they pervert, and the greater the damnation they lay up for themselves.* We are saving their eternal souls by ending their earthly lives."

Father Herzeim fixed his dark eyes on the ceiling. "Might I raise a small point of practicality? If the commission requires, under pain of torture, that condemned witches name others, then proceeds to arrest those so named on the basis of those accusations, simple mathematics predicts that the trials shall become more and more numerous. Is it not inevitable that eventually the accusations will encompass all of us? That we, too, will be burned?"

He smiled crookedly into the Prince-Bishop's scowl. "But then, who will be left to light the fires?"

1

⌘

16 April 1626

Eva huddled on the thin layer of straw. She'd been awake all night, her thoughts wild and confused, and now she waited for the dawn, hoping that in the light of day she could begin to tease apart the dense and terrifying tangle, find one thread she could follow to a reason.

Why was she here? Who had accused her?

She watched the grey stone wall emerge from the murky dark. A shaft of pale light crept in through the high narrow window and caressed her face, but it brought with it no warmth, no understanding, no reasons.

She heard a thump, then scraping on the low wood ceiling. Someone was imprisoned above her.

The cathedral bells rang out. Eva made the sign of the cross. "*In nomine patris, et filii, et spiritus sancti.*" Placing her palms together, she saw the dried blood crusted on her sleeves. Her eyes followed the heavy iron links from the cuffs encircling her wrists to the metal plate where the chains were bolted to the wall.

She bowed her head and tried to pray, but all that came to mind was the look of revulsion – and fear – on the bailiff's face when his gloved hands grasped her arms and bound them in front of her. Her protests and screams had echoed as if they came from a place far away, from some other woman. She heard again Katharina's whimpers, "Mama, Mama." Eva had not been able to protect her daughter. And no one would help them; no one would even answer her questions. The men only crossed themselves and muttered "*hexe, hexe*" as they pulled her behind their horses, so that she had to run to keep from falling forward and being dragged. Her heart had beat fiercely from exertion and terror. And humiliation. At the Prisoners' Tower, the men used a birch rod to prod her up a narrow spiral staircase and into this dimly lit cell hardly more than two body lengths across. Gloved hands clamped her wrists into the metal cuffs, as if she were dangerous. And there she'd sat, until the cell grew dark, then light again. A day and a night. Already, it felt like forever.

Eva groped for the rosary that hung from a loop inside the waist of her gown. She fingered the wooden beads and prayed, "Dear Mother of God, help me in my hour of need, and please protect my child." She felt tears gathering. She did not know where they'd taken Katharina or what they'd done to her. She blinked back the tears. She would be strong. She would not weep. Her throat ached with the effort. A single tear escaped and made a cold trail down her cheek to her chin.

A key rasped in the lock, metal scraping metal. Eva turned, but could see nothing but grey stone through the door's small barred window. The heavy door creaked open, and an old woman shuffled in, her scrawny back bowed, as if she carried a heavy load of hay or kindling. A large ring of keys hung from the belt at her waist. She held a wooden bowl in her left hand. With her right, she made the sign of the cross.

Eva shifted on the straw, away from the place where she'd relieved herself during the night. There was a wooden pail in the cell, but her shackles had not allowed her to reach it.

Keeping a wary eye on Eva, the woman held out the bowl. Eva put out her hands, but when she smelled the rancid broth, she gagged, and the bowl slipped from her grasp. The stinking grey broth splashed on the woman's apron, then soaked into the straw.

"A few days, and you'll be wanting it bad enough," the woman lisped through missing teeth.

"Who are you?"

"The one who brings your food and cleans up your messes."

"Where is my daughter? Where is Katharina?"

"If you mean the little girl, the one with the golden hair, she's here."

"Can you bring her to me? Please."

The woman shook her kerchiefed head. "*Nein*. The commissioners want the witches kept apart, so's they can't conspire."

"But I'm not a witch. And neither is Katharina."

"You've been arrested, haven't you?"

"Please. She must be terrified."

The woman fingered the dark mole on her cheek. "It could be done. For a price."

"Price?"

The woman licked her chapped lips. "Two *gulden*."

"Two *gulden*! Where can I get two *gulden* in here?" Eva touched the small silver cross at her throat. "I can give you this. It's worth far more than two *gulden*."

The woman recoiled. "I'm taking nothing worn by a witch." She looked down at Eva. "If you want to see your daughter bad enough, you'll find two *gulden*. I was told you owned your own shop, a bakery right on *Domstrasse*."

Eva rubbed the rosary through the thin wool of her gown. Herr Stolz. He must have seen everything. He had to know where she and Katharina had been taken. Surely he would help them. "Go to my shop and ask for Herr Stolz," she said. "He's one of my journeymen. Tell him I sent you. Tell him the money is for Katharina. He'll give you two *gulden*." Mother of God, please let Herr Stolz believe this woman.

"How do I know he'll give me the *gulden*?"

"I know he will. He...he cares for me."

The woman winked. "A widow with a young journeyman, eh?"

Eva felt her face grow hot.

"She is a pretty little thing," the woman muttered to herself, her face softening. "I always feel sorry for the children. And no matter what the high and mighty commissioners say, I can't see much harm in having a mother and daughter together. Seems like you've already done as much conspiring as you're going to do." She moved the wooden pail closer to Eva. "And it would mean one less cell to clean."

"Bless you."

The woman laughed. "You may be blessing me now, but before this is over, you – and all the others – will be cursing me." She made the sign of the cross, then put a gnarled hand to her throat. "I have this bit of wax the Jesuits gave me. With herbs they blessed. It protects me so I don't have to be scared of you – or the others."

"There are others?"

"A big lot of you this time. Six. And I have to cook for all of you, and clean up. Climbing up and down those stairs all day." She wrinkled her nose. "And I'm seeing – and smelling – that you're needing new straw already."

"Six?"

"*Ja*, six."

"Who are the others? Who has accused us?"

The woman frowned. "As if you don't know already."

"*Nein*, I don't."

The woman's eyes narrowed. "You mean with all your powers, you don't know who else is in here with you or who accused you?"

"I have no powers."

"Humph! No powers? Judge Steinbach and Chancellor Brandt will see about that." She raised one finger. "There's a maidservant. Her baby, a bastard, was born dead. Or so she claims." She lifted a second crooked finger. "Then there's the midwife who delivered the baby." Leaning forward, she cupped a hand to her mouth. "I'd be willing to bet those two *gulden* the midwife offered the child to the Devil while it yet breathed, before it could be baptized." She backed away, as if she'd just remembered what Eva was. "But then you'd be knowing all about that."

"I know nothing. You must believe me."

"It's true, you don't look much like a witch." The woman poked around under her kerchief, scratching her head. "But then neither did Fraulein Stolzberger. She was a beauty, just like you. But then, it don't matter much what a jailer's wife thinks. What matters is what the commissioners believe."

"And…and the others?"

The woman raised a third finger. "An old beggar. Now there's a wicked old hag if ever I saw one, threatening people with her ugly face, trying to scare respectable citizens into giving her more *pfennigs*. She's a witch for sure."

The jailer's wife held up a fourth finger, her dull grey eyes suddenly bright, like polished silver coins. "And this time there's a young man, a high born. And handsome, too. They say he's a defender of witches."

Eva saw the sheen of excitement on the woman's face, as if she relished possessing so much information. It was probably the only valuable thing she owned, thought Eva, and yet she gave it away freely, or so it seemed. How much did she carry outside these stone walls? And to whom?

"The commissioners will have to work hard to get the truth out of all of you."

"I'll tell them the truth at once. Katharina and I are innocent."

The woman cackled, revealing a scattering of broken and missing teeth in her lower jaw. "That's what they all say."

The jailer's wife returned a short while later, Katharina's small hand enclosed in hers. Still in her muslin sleeping gown, now soiled and torn, the girl stood in the doorway, her eyes straight ahead, as if she did not see her mother.

Eva called out. "*Liebchen*."

Stiffly, Katharina limped toward Eva and sat down beside her.

"If I don't get those *gulden*," the woman said, jerking her thumb over her shoulder, "back she goes." She turned, and the door slammed shut behind her.

Eva lifted Katharina's arms and kissed the purple bruises on her wrists. "Are you all right?"

Katharina trembled, but did not answer.

Eva, her arms still shackled, cradled her daughter as best she could. "Tell me, *Liebchen*, are you all right?" Her fingers worked to smooth the girl's mussed braid.

Katharina lifted her head from her mother's chest. "I saw him last night, Mama. He watched me with his red eyes."

"Who?"

"Him. The Devil."

"You must not say such things!" Eva felt the blood drain from her face. "You saw a rat. Only a rat."

"*Nein*, it was him. But it's all right. Angels came, angels in golden gowns. There were orange flames at their feet, but their gowns did not burn up. I was scared at first. I screamed. I screamed at them, and at him. But the angels came close and stood between me and him, so that I couldn't see his red eyes anymore. They touched my face with their soft fingers. When they left, he was gone."

"*Nein*, Katharina. This cannot be so." Eva held Katharina's head tight to her chest.

"You don't believe me?"

"Did you say anything of this to the old woman who brought you here?"

"*Nein*."

"Katharina, you must not speak of these things, to anyone!"

The key scraped in the lock. The door opened, and a tall priest in a broad-brimmed hat stepped into the cell. The jailer's wife followed. Folding her hands at her waist, she dipped her head toward the priest. "Father Herzeim has come."

Eva leaned forward. Thanks be to God! A priest. He would see that a terrible mistake had been made. He would order that she and Katharina be released.

After the jailer's wife had closed the door behind her, Father Herzeim picked up a small stool and set it beside Eva and Katharina. He sat down, smoothed his black cassock over his knees, and laid his breviary in his lap.

Embarrassed at the foul odours rising from the straw, Eva wished that he'd not come so near. She studied his face for a look of disgust, but he gave no sign that he'd noticed the rank smell. He took off his hat and set it aside. There were two broad streaks of silver through his dark hair.

Katharina pointed at the streaks. "Look, Mama. Angel wings."

The priest almost smiled, then folded his hands over the wooden cross on his chest. "I am here to offer you spiritual consolation. Is there anything you wish to tell me?"

"Why have we been arrested?"

"Your daughter has not been arrested. She is here because you are." The corner of his mouth twitched. "You have been accused of witchcraft."

"Who has accused me?"

"The women who were executed two days ago."

"But they do not even know me."

"You knew none of them?"

Shamed by her small lie, Eva looked away. "Frau Basser bought bread from the bakery now and again, but she did not know me well. Why would she accuse me of witchcraft? Why would any of them?"

Father Herzeim rubbed his forehead, as if to smooth out the lines. "Have you done anything, Frau Rosen, that might be construed as witchcraft? Sold tainted or mouldy bread that might make someone ill? Said anything that might be taken as a curse?"

"*Nein*, nothing."

The priest peered at her, his dark eyes searching. "I've been told that your husband died suddenly, and with no explanation."

"That's true, Father, but surely no one thinks–"

"Apparently, they do."

Her heart beat faster. It was true that she'd feared Jacob, that she'd never really loved him. But how could anyone think she'd killed him?

"I did not kill my husband."

Father Herzeim bit the inside of his cheek. "You've been a long time without a husband. Nearly three years, I'm told. Have you been chaste?"

Eva thought of Herr Stolz and felt a flush rise from her throat to her cheeks. She could not look at the priest when she answered. "*Ja*, Father."

"Have you gone to a sorcerer or a midwife for a love potion? Or tried to concoct one yourself? Many desperate women do."

"I have done none of those things, Father. I…I did not wish to marry again."

"I've heard that as well. The master bakers and the city councilmen do not approve, Frau Rosen."

"But doesn't the Holy Church?"

"As long as you live chastely."

Eva clasped her hands together, making the chains clank. "And never…never have I – or my daughter – had anything to do with the Devil."

"But Mama," said Katharina.

Eva pinched the girl's thigh, hard. Katharina let out a yelp. Father Herzeim raised a dark eyebrow.

"She's frightened by all these questions." Eva could hear the tremor in her own voice. "There's been a terrible mistake. My daughter and I are innocent. You must order them to release us."

"Only the Prince-Bishop can order your release."

"Then please, Father, you must speak with the Prince-Bishop."

The priest ran a hand through his hair, mussing the silver streaks. "I have spoken with His Grace. He will recommend that the Commission of Inquisition release you only after the hearings, after he's read the commission's report on your crimes."

"Crimes? There are no crimes." Eva grabbed his arm. "You said that Katharina has not been accused. Take her out of here. Take her to the Unterzell Convent. The nuns will care for her until I am released."

Father Herzeim looked at Katharina, his eyes surprisingly kind, and sorrowful. "Would that I had the power to do that."

"What power do you have?"

"I will help you and your daughter as best I can."

"What good is your help if you cannot get us released?"

"I can offer consolation and strength."

"Consolation and strength?" Eva closed her eyes. No, the silver streaks were not the wings of an angel. "You'd best bring me an image of the Holy Mother," she said bitterly. "She is the only one who can help us now."

"Let me confess you."

"Confess!" she hissed. "I have nothing to confess."

"Nothing?"

Chastised, Eva bowed her head. She'd confessed to her parish priest less than a week ago, just before Easter. What had she done since then? Turned away a beggar because she had no more bread, scolded Katharina too harshly, had impure thoughts about Herr Stolz. As she whispered her sins to the priest, they all seemed so distant now, so unimportant, so very far away.

"That is all? There is nothing else?" asked Father Herzeim.

"I have spoken angry words to a priest. Please forgive me, Father." Eva looked up and saw Father Herzeim's small smile.

She bowed her head again when he raised his hand in the sign of absolution.

"*Ego te absolvo, in nomine patris, et filii, et spiritus sancti.*"

She was startled when he touched her. He put a hand under her chin and lifted her face. His fingers were soft on her skin. She could smell the clean scent of his soap.

"Frau Rosen, listen to me. You must insist on your innocence. No matter what the commissioners say, no matter what they do to you, you – and Katharina – must insist on your innocence."

8

17 April 1626

Dropping a *pfennig* into the grubby hand that clawed at his breeches, Lutz hurried away from the gaping mouth filled with brown stubs and red swollen gums. He dashed into the town hall, to the small room where the councilmen kept their black robes. His were the only ones still hanging there. Pulling them quickly over his doublet, Lutz strode to the small chapel on the ground floor. There, he knelt, made the sign of the cross, and murmured a brief prayer for guidance in the decisions he would make that morning. He climbed the stairs to the Wenceslaus Hall, cracked open the double doors, and slid into his place on the long bench, inconspicuously, he hoped.

Hampelmann cast Lutz a chastising frown. As first burgomaster of the Lower City Council, Hampelmann sat at the table in the centre of the room with Herr Bayer, the second burgomaster, who picked up a quill to record Lutz's name in the ledger.

Lutz was surprised to see Judge Steinbach sitting between Hampelmann and Bayer. What concern could have brought the first burgomaster of the Upper City Council to a meeting of the Lower City Council? Perhaps they would be debating the new war taxes imposed by Emperor Ferdinand. Lutz groaned. With Judge Steinbach presiding, that debate could go on all day.

Hampelmann passed the gavel to Judge Steinbach. It shook in his hand. "We must come to order now," he said, looking sourly at a small gold watch. "We are already late." Grimacing, he pushed himself up, straightened his rheumatic knees, and crossed himself, as did the councilmen, who then muttered the Latin invocation with which they began their morning meetings.

"*Ad majorem Dei gloriam.* Amen," wheezed the judge, crossing himself again. He passed the gavel back to Hampelmann.

Bayer pushed the ledger toward Hampelmann, who squinted at the open pages. "Councilman Rausch," said Hampelmann, "have the gatekeepers been informed of the council's decision not to allow strangers into the city nor any citizens who are returning from cities with plague?"

Rausch rose from his seat beside Lutz. "They have been so directed."

Hampelmann nodded, then continued. "At the meeting on Monday last, Councilman Rausch, you were assigned the task of investigating the recent increase in requests for begging licenses. Do you have a report for the council?"

Rausch dipped his head toward the three burgomasters and then at the assembled councilmen, who sat on two long benches facing each other, eleven to a bench. Rausch held up his open ledger. "My enquiries reveal that the unprecedented increase in requests for licenses is, not surprisingly, related to the poor harvests of last fall, which left Würzburg with exceedingly low grain stores." He turned to the Würzburg Grain Steward, who nodded his agreement.

"Finding no work in the countryside," Rausch said, "a large number of day labourers and their families have come into the city. Finding no work here, they resort to begging. The question before the council is whether to increase the number of licenses given out. Those who argue in the affirmative claim that people are starving and if additional licenses are not issued, people will die."

A few councilmen watched Rausch intently. Others, their faces blank, gazed at the smouldering fire in the hearth. Still others studied their hands. Judge Steinbach's chin, with its tuft of white beard, rested on his chest. His eyes were closed, and his long white hair had fallen forward. Obviously, thought Lutz, it wasn't the question of begging licenses that had brought the burgomaster to the meeting.

"Those who argue in the negative," said Rausch, "claim that people of a certain station will beg, with or without a license. This point seems well taken, as we have all witnessed the increase in beggars in Würzburg, licensed or not."

Staring at the large arched window behind the row of black-robed councilmen, Lutz imagined the hordes of ragged children just outside. They loitered near the town hall, on the cathedral steps, all along *Domstrasse*, and everywhere in the marketplace, begging and picking through piles of refuse. What Rausch said was true: their numbers were increasing daily. No matter where Lutz went, they followed, their voices trailing after him, high and plaintive. Maria scolded him for the number of *pfennigs* he gave out – never mind that she was guilty of distributing far more. She could not bring herself to turn away from the small open palm of a child, especially a little girl's.

Rausch raised a thick forefinger, poking it forward for emphasis. "Secondly, the primary advantage to withholding licenses is that, lacking a license, beggars can be expelled from Würzburg should their continued presence threaten the well-being of the citizens." He paused expectantly.

"Comments?" said Hampelmann.

Lutz stood, smoothing his robes over his belly. "Last year's cold spring hit the whole of the Rhine valley. Harvests were poor everywhere. No town has any grain to spare."

"*Ja?*" said Hampelmann.

"If we expel people from Würzburg," said Lutz, "we are almost certainly condemning them to starvation."

Rausch sighed loudly. "But they would not be Würzburg's responsibility. They would be outside the city walls." He waved his closed ledger. "And away from the city, they could search the meadows and woods for roots, wild birds and hares, new spring growth, that sort of thing. They might even be better off if we forced them to leave."

Herr Meier, a master carpenter, stood. "But haven't you just told us, Councilman Rausch, that people have fled the countryside because they can find nothing to eat?"

Rausch gave Meier a patronizing smile. "*Nein*, Councilman Meier, I did not say that. I *said* they had come into the city because there is no work for them in the countryside."

"But there are so many children," said Lutz.

Hampelmann held up both hands, palms out. "*Danke*, Councilman Rausch, your report and the comments of Councilman Lutz and Councilman Meier are all well taken. But first and foremost, we must remember the teachings of our Lord, and be generous to those less fortunate than ourselves. We must take pity on those who suffer. And look, instead, to punish those agents of the Devil responsible for their suffering." He banged the gavel. "Are we prepared to vote on the question of increasing the number of begging licenses issued by…one quarter?"

"One quarter?" grumbled Rausch.

Hampelmann banged the gavel again. "Those in favour?" He raised his own hand.

"*Ja*!" said Lutz and Meier. Under Hampelmann's stern gaze, Bayer and at least a dozen other councilmen voiced a staccato chorus of *ja*s.

"Those opposed?"

A few disgruntled *nein*s from Rausch and the remaining councilmen rumbled through the council room.

Bayer dipped his quill and recorded the vote.

Hampelmann glanced at Bayer's ledger. "It is decided then. Eighteen *ja*s to six *nein*s. I shall direct the city office to increase the number of begging licenses issued by one quarter." He picked up the ledger. "Burgomaster Bayer," he said, "do you have a report on the allegations of rape made by..." he brought the pages closer to his face "Frau Greta Himmel against Herr Karl Seiler?"

Bayer stood. "I do, and the allegations have proved to be groundless. Herr Seiler, a respected goldsmith and a trade corporation master known to nearly all of us, does not deny that he has *known* Frau Himmel." He surveyed the councilmen, his pale eyebrows arched. "But he denies the woman's charges."

Bayer leaned forward. His words floated like a conspiratorial whisper on the hazy smoke from the hearth. "After all, gentlemen, Frau Himmel was married for thirteen years. She's been a widow for five. It stretches credibility to imagine that such a woman, so long without a man, would spurn the attentions of Herr Seiler, or those of any other man for that matter."

There was soft knowing laughter throughout the room. Lutz found himself chuckling as well.

Hampelmann banged the gavel. "Gentlemen, lust and fornication are hardly to be laughed at. Lust is the Devil's tool. And it's no secret that Herr Seiler is much given to lustful indulgences. Burgomaster Bayer, are you certain there's no merit to Frau Himmel's charges? She's reputed to be a pious and honourable woman."

Bayer waved his hand dismissively. "*Nein*. Herr Seiler's journeyman, Herr Konrad Lambrecht, is willing to testify that he saw Frau Himmel encourage Herr Seiler's attentions. Albeit, as a matter of record, it should be noted that, because Herr Seiler has damaged the honour of his trade corporation, the other masters have agreed to discipline him for his indiscretions. They have levied a fine of five *gulden*."

The trade masters among the councilmen nodded their approval.

"Are there any objections to dismissing Frau Himmel's charges against Herr Seiler?" said Hampelmann.

The room was silent but for the shuffling of feet and the clearing of throats.

"Done then," said Hampelmann. He nudged the sleeping judge.

Jerking to attention, Judge Steinbach sat up. He took the gavel from Hampelmann. "The next order of business," he said, "is the impending inquisition into the accusations made by the three witches who were executed Tuesday last."

Lutz's stomach lurched. So that was why Judge Steinbach had come to the meeting: witches, not taxes.

"I have been informed by the Prince-Bishop's bailiff that all five of the accused–" the judge read from his own ledger "–Frau Eva Rosen, Frau Lilie Lamm, Frau Gertrude Bettler, Fraulein Ursula Spatz, and Herr Christoph Silberhans – are now in custody. The first question before us is: Do we wish to retain the services of Herr Georg Freude?"

Bayer sneered. "The man is vulgar and offensive, but he seems an able executioner, quite skilled at eliciting confessions."

"I agree," said Meier. "Herr Freude knows his business. And his fees are not unreasonable. I recommend he be retained."

"Do you all agree?" said Judge Steinbach. There were nods from both benches.

Bayer recorded the decision, then picked up a small ivory-handled knife and sharpened the quill with a few quick strokes.

"The second question," said Judge Steinbach, "concerns the Commission of Inquisition for the Würzburg Court. As judge of the court, I will, of course, preside at the preliminary inquisition. Prince-Bishop Philipp Adolf has appointed his chancellor, Herr Doktor Johann Brandt, to represent the central government. Herr Doktor Wilhelm Hampelmann is to represent the *Malefizamt*. His Grace has also appointed Father Streng from the Cathedral Chapter and Upper City Council. The physician, Herr Doktor Hans Lindner, has also been reappointed. That leaves only the representative from the Lower City Council."

The councilmen looked at the floor, the windows, their hands, the hearth. Through his robes, Lutz toyed nervously with a loose button on his doublet.

Judge Steinbach blinked his watery eyes. "His Grace has honoured Herr Doktor Franz Lutz with the appointment."

Lutz's hand jerked. The copper button hit the slate floor with a ping that echoed off the walls.

Hampelmann regarded him with undisguised contempt. "You agree then to serve, Councilman Lutz?"

Lutz pulled out his handkerchief to wipe his wet palms, then mopped the sweat from his brow. "*Ja,*" he squeaked, his throat tight.

Walking from the town hall to his home on Augustinerstrasse, Lutz looked up toward the Prince-Bishop's castle high atop Marienberg Mountain, its pale towers gleaming in the sunlight. He tried to convince himself that the appointment was a good thing. If he served well on the commission, His Grace might reward him with an appointment to the Upper City Council, perhaps even as second burgomaster when old Judge Steinbach finally died and Hampelmann took his place.

Maria, the wife of a burgomaster. She would be so pleased and proud.

The sun was almost directly overhead. Lutz felt its warmth on his face. Pink blossoms covered the cherry trees, the fallen petals forming a carpet beneath his feet. Hadn't both the Dominicans and the Jesuits written that God protects those who do his work? Hampelmann himself was evidence of that. He'd served on the commission time and time again, and he and his family prospered.

As soon as Lutz stepped through the doorway, Maria began fussing. He feigned mild irritation while she tut-tutted over his rumpled doublet and the missing button, straightened his wide white collar, and made him pull up his sagging hose. She sat him down in the dining room, then bustled about, setting the table with silver and porcelain. They retained two maidservants, but Maria preferred to prepare and serve meals herself.

Breathing in the heady fragrance of simmering carp and onions, Lutz felt his stomach begin to settle, then rumble with hunger. He watched his wife open the damask drapes to let in the midday sun. Twenty-four years of predictable fussing, predictable ritual. Some men found it constricting. Lutz found it comforting. He'd never tell her so, but he'd miss it if Maria didn't fuss. And he enjoyed the good food and drink prepared by his wife's capable hands. He laced his fingers over his protruding belly. He knew what the parish priest said, but was it really such a grievous sin to enjoy God's gifts? Did it make him any less holy to be portly, to savour what he ate and drank?

Maria lifted silver spoons from a drawer, her back to Lutz. He considered the ample curves under her plain dark gown, the long silver-streaked hair, plaited and coiled under her embroidered matron's cap. He recalled then, with some discomfort, Frau Himmel's charges against Herr Seiler, his own laughter at her presumed lustfulness, the lustfulness of all women. Except Maria, of course. Maria was different. She was affectionate, but he would hardly call her lustful.

He watched his wife's graceful hands as she set a spoon and knife before him. He smiled into her smile, so familiar. Lutz sighed then, with gratitude and with mild longing. He was grateful that Maria was more virtuous than other women were. But he couldn't help thinking that a little show of lust now and again might well be a very pleasant thing. Lately, since her courses had stopped, Maria had shown hardly any inclination at all, and he'd begun to wonder if her only real source of desire had been her desperate longing for a child.

Maria set a covered tureen on the table, left the dining room, and returned with a plate of dark bread.

There had been a child, years ago. They'd waited eight long years, through half a dozen miscarriages and stillbirths, for a living child. But the tiny girl took only one short breath, let out one weak whimper. She had not been baptized, and now her soul dwelt in limbo. Every morning, without fail, Maria went to Saint Kilian's Cathedral, lit a candle for the child's soul, and prayed. Her prayers saddened Lutz, and he recalled with deep sorrow and anger the words the parish priest offered as comfort to his wife.

He stared at the dust motes floating in the small square of sunlight. If only he'd recognized the book the priest had pulled from the shelf, he would have stopped him from reading to her the words of the Jesuit, Martin Delrio, cruel words Lutz had regretted so many times they were etched into his memory: *If, as is not uncommon, God permits children to be killed before they have been baptized, it is to prevent their committing in later life those sins which would make their damnation more severe. In this, God is neither cruel nor unjust, since, by the mere fact of original sin, the children have already merited death.* At hearing those words, Maria had wept even harder, begging the priest to tell her how she could pray the child into heaven. He could not. He had no more words to give her.

There had been several conceptions since, but no living children. Lutz felt almost relieved that Maria's courses had stopped, that there would be no new grief for his wife to bear. She had a surfeit of old ones.

Only a few months ago, the same dull-witted priest had pulled Lutz aside, his breath reeking of wine. He congratulated Lutz on his recent appointment to the Lower City Council. "Such a pity," he'd said then, "that you have no son to carry on your tradition of service to Würzburg. Yet a woman's barrenness is a judgement from God." Lutz had spun away, his fists clenched, ready to strike the priest's doughy face. No, his wife was not to blame for their childlessness. How could the priest, or God, for that matter, find fault with the gentle and generous Maria?

She set a bowl of soup in front of him, filled a bowl for herself, and sat down.

If she was not to blame, who was? Lutz knew what *Der Hexenhammer* suggested: *It is witchcraft…when a woman is prevented from conceiving, or is made to miscarry after she has conceived.* Was it possible his wife's barrenness was the result of a curse?

Maria lifted a spoon to her full lips and blew on the steaming broth. "What happened at this morning's meeting?"

"The council decided to increase the number of begging licenses issued."

"Good. Now if the Grain Steward would just release more rye and barley from the stores."

Lutz reached for a thick slice of bread. "There is little enough to release, Maria."

"I think there is more than he claims." She bent her head over the bowl. "What else did the council decide?"

Lutz pursed his lips. "They voted to dismiss Frau Himmel's allegations against Herr Seiler."

"Fra-a-anz!"

He held up a hand to ward off her rebuke. "Herr Meier's investigation found no grounds," he said.

"No grounds? Everyone knows Herr Seiler is a pig."

"A pig? He's a respectable goldsmith, a trade master."

"Respectable to men perhaps. To women, he's a *schwein*. No woman wants to go into his shop alone."

"Is this just women's gossip? Or is there something you haven't told me?"

She bowed her head. "It is shameful to speak of such things."

Lutz studied her down-turned face. "Maria?"

"We must not speak of it. The poor woman will be humiliated by the council's decision." She toyed with her spoon and knife. "What else?"

Lutz swallowed. "I've been appointed to the Commission of Inquisition."

Her hands flew to her mouth. "Oh my God."

"It is my duty as a city councilman."

"But it's so dangerous." She blinked back tears.

"Where is your faith, Maria? God protects those who do his work." Lutz laid a hand over hers. To comfort her? Or himself? "We will be safe."

9

17 April 1626

Lutz walked slowly along the narrow street, his fingers combing absently through his beard. He stopped and leaned against the stone wall of a courtyard. The unopened buds held the promise of colour amidst the drab greys and browns of mud and stone and wood, a promise that would normally gladden Lutz's winter-weary heart. But on this sunny afternoon, he felt faint-hearted, not light-hearted. Despite his brave words to Maria, and to himself, he was afraid, and ashamed of his fear.

He breathed deeply of the soft spring air, taking in the sweet fragrance of the white blooms of a horse chestnut, then proceeded on. He could think of no better man to seek out for advice than the final confessor for condemned witches. Father Herzeim knew their wicked ways better than anyone. Certainly he could tell Lutz how to protect himself and Maria from their vindictiveness.

As Lutz approached *Dommerschulstrasse*, an old beggar hobbled toward him. He snatched at Lutz's breeches. "*Bitte*, a *pfennig*, just a *pfennig* for bread," he rasped. Quickly, Lutz reached into the lining of his breeches, grabbed a coin, and tossed it at the man's hand so he would have to release the breeches to catch it. As the beggar did so, Lutz noticed his eyeless socket, the clean lines of the scars indicating that the eye had been deliberately plucked out. Lutz drew back, wondering what crime the man had committed to warrant such a punishment.

Lutz hurried away from the beggar and maintained his quick pace past the Jesuit House. He'd gone there only once, just after his first consultation with Father Herzeim. The cool glances from the rector and the other Jesuits had made Lutz feel so unwelcome he'd never gone back. Which was what they wanted, he supposed. Now he always met the priest at his office at the university, and though it was late in the day, Lutz knew Father Herzeim would still be there. It wasn't hard to understand why. On his single visit to the Jesuit House, Lutz had seen Father Herzeim's stark room: a narrow wooden bed, a plain desk and chair, a single tallow candle, a small shelf for books, a crucifix on a wall the colour of mud, and little else, not even a window.

When Lutz reached the university, he proceeded through the arched gates into the inner courtyard, entered a tan stone building, and made his way through the empty corridors. His footsteps echoed off dark walls. Knocking softly on the door to Father Herzeim's office, he heard a muffled, "*Bitte*, a moment," then the stacking of books, quick footsteps, and the scrape of a chair or table. When Father Herzeim finally opened the door, he was breathing rapidly and his cheeks were pink. If Lutz hadn't known him better, he would have suspected that there was a woman hidden somewhere in the office.

"It's always good to see you, Lutz," said the priest, "but what brings you here at this hour?"

Lutz surveyed the room, trying to discern what Father Herzeim had been doing. The tall shelves of leather-bound volumes were unusually neat. Tidying up? Remembering his mission then, Lutz laid his hat to the side. "The Prince-Bishop has appointed me to the Commission of Inquisition."

Father Herzeim inhaled sharply. "I am sorry to hear that." He sat down behind the desk, which was piled high with books and ledgers, all neatly stacked. "But it was bound to happen." He gestured toward the wooden chair across from the desk.

As always, Lutz lowered himself gingerly, wondering if the rickety chair would support his bulk. "Maria is concerned, and fearful. We've never had any dealings with witches." He thought briefly of their dead daughter and all the babies who'd never been born. "None that we know of anyway. What can we do to protect ourselves?"

Father Herzeim's long fingers smoothed the edges of a leather binding that had begun to split. "Prayer. Faith. Confession. Daily meditation and examination of your conscience."

"That's it? What about consecrated wax and herbs? Relics?"

"None of that would hurt, but…" the priest shrugged.

"Aren't you afraid when you go into their cells?"

"I believe it's not so easy for witches to work their mischief as many men seem to think."

"You believe, but don't know? There must be something else you can advise us to do."

"What could be more powerful than prayer?"

"I don't know, but…" Lutz teetered on the chair.

"When is the first meeting of the commission?"

"Monday morning."

His fingers still worrying the damaged binding, Father Herzeim scanned the corner of the room as if searching for something. "Three days. Not much time."

"For what?"

"For you to familiarize yourself with the laws concerning witchcraft."

"I already know more than I want to about witchcraft."

Father Herzeim turned to Lutz, his dark eyes piercing, as if he could see into Lutz's chest and examine his cowardly heart. "Would you allow innocent people to be condemned because you are afraid?"

Lutz picked up his hat and ran his fingers around its broad brim. The priest was right. Somehow he must summon his courage. "All right, Father. But my gut feeling is that people accused by known witches are almost certainly witches themselves."

Father Herzeim's lips curved into the crooked smile that had become so familiar to Lutz. "Your considerable gut may say they are guilty," said the priest, "but my heart says that at least some of them are not."

"And the commission will recommend release for those who are innocent."

The smile faded. "There are some on the commission who are overly zealous to execute."

"So you still believe that Frau Basser was innocent?" said Lutz.

"I do."

"But the Church teaches that God protects the innocent."

"*Ja*, it teaches that." Father Herzeim put a hand to his chin and pinched his bottom lip between a thumb and forefinger. "But could it be that God protects the innocent by moving the truly faithful to search out the truth? It is your duty to the accused, and to God, to pursue truth. Despite whatever fears you have." He stood and went to the window. "I do not fear witches, Lutz, because I am doing God's work: offering these lost souls comfort and consolation, bringing them back to God."

"The commissioners are doing God's work as well."

Father Herzeim turned to Lutz. "You will be doing God's work if you are as zealous to protect the innocent as to prosecute the guilty."

"I will try, Father." Lutz studied the hard angles of the priest's face and hoped that his friend's strength and fearlessness would help him find whatever fragments of courage lay hidden within his own heart.

"We say God is love," said Father Herzeim, his hand over the cedar cross that hung near his heart. "Yet the world is consumed by hate." He looked as if he were in pain. "Catholics and Protestants hate each other, both hate witches, and both imagine that God hates with them."

"Surely God hates evil."

"The sin, but not the sinner. I believe God wants the sinner brought back to him, not killed."

In the silence, Lutz could hear the soft coos of wood-pigeons outside the window. "What is it I need to learn?" he said.

"More than you can imagine." Father Herzeim started pulling books from the shelves. "Let's start with the recent opinion from the theologians at the University of Ingolstadt."

"I have given that some thought," said Lutz, "and despite what Hampelmann says, I do see some problems with accusations made by condemned witches. It is quite reasonable to assume that they'd want to do additional harm by denouncing innocent people. It also brings up the legal difficulty of allowing testimony from a *testes infamis*, a disreputable witness."

"There's more than that. Much more." The priest's face was animated as he flipped through a leather-bound volume. "You must raise those questions, and also the question of evidence, *corpus delicti*. Where is the evidence that a crime has been committed? Particularly for Frau Rosen and Herr Silberhans. There is absolutely no evidence but hearsay. By law, that should not be admissible at the hearings."

Father Herzeim glanced up from the book. "You must get them both released, Lutz. I am convinced they are innocent." As if it were a mask, the excitement dropped from his face, replaced by a look of profound melancholy. "The cases of the beggar, the maidservant, and Frau Lamm are... more complicated."

10

~

19 April 1626

Holding her breath, Eva sipped the rancid broth. The jailer's wife was right. Eva and Katharina had begun to eat the food, even though the smell of it made them gag. Twice a day the woman brought them thin greasy soup and hunks of stale bread. Katharina whined for the loaves from their own bakery. Warm barley bread and cherry jam. Just thinking of it made Eva's mouth water.

She set down the empty bowl and allowed herself to take a deep breath, then put a hand over her nose. There were times when she believed she could bear the stench not one moment longer. Everything reeked: the spoiled food, the dank stone walls, the foul slop bucket filled with their own wastes, the soiled straw, her own body. Even Katharina smelled of piss. When it rained, the dampness made the stench even worse; it hung so heavy Eva could almost see it, a grey-brown fetid haze.

Eva tried to conjure pleasant smells: baking bread, freshly laundered linens, lye soap, hay that had just been scythed, beeswax candles, wild pink roses. And for just a moment she could catch the fragrance, just a whiff, before the stench intruded. She had asked the jailer's wife to open the window, but they'd grown so cold during the night, Katharina shivering uncontrollably, that Eva had had to ask her to close it again.

During those long nights, Eva held her daughter, and while the girl slept, tried to think of why Frau Basser had accused her. Always she came to the same conclusion: the witch had denounced her out of sheer malice and evil. The commissioners would realize that as soon as they questioned Eva. They had to. The priest believed in her innocence. Eva had seen that in his eyes, heard it in his words. *You must insist on your innocence. No matter what they say, no matter what they do, you must insist on your innocence.* But what if Katharina told them of her strange visions?

The girl wrinkled her nose, then set down the bowl, most of the broth uneaten. She wrapped her thin arms around her knees and bowed her head, her eyes open and staring.

A prickling chill crept across the back of Eva's neck. The night before, Katharina had seen them again: angels in golden gowns, orange flames at their feet, the Devil, with his red eyes and leering grin, crouched against the wall. Eva had seen nothing, and as she listened to her daughter's whispers in the darkness before dawn, Eva's heart beat against her chest like a wild bird, trapped. "Don't listen to him," she'd said. "No matter what he offers, accept nothing…from him or the angels."

"But they're beautiful, Mama. Why don't you like them?"

"You are not to speak of them," she'd said. "To anyone. Ever." Then Eva had hugged Katharina to her chest to quiet her own heart.

Now, in the morning light, Eva studied the huddled girl, so pale and listless. The Devil was tempting her daughter. It was just as their parish priest had warned: the Devil took advantage of misery. And if witches could appear in the guise of the righteous, surely the Devil could conjure images of angels. He'd been one himself.

The cathedral bells rang out. Eva's eyes filled. She longed for the comfort of the morning mass, with Katharina sitting safely by her side. She and her daughter had not missed a Sunday in more than a year, and now their seats would be empty. Hushed whispers would fill Saint Kilian's, passing from mouth to ear, mouth to ear. Everyone would know, even those who'd not seen them dragged through the streets.

Eva heard the familiar scrape of the key. Katharina crawled into Eva's lap as the door swung open and the jailer's wife stepped in. The bony jailer or one of the guards came every day to check that Eva's shackles were secure, but it was always the jailer's wife who brought their food, emptied the slop bucket, and changed the straw.

The woman crossed herself, looked long at Katharina, then rubbed her thumb and middle finger together. A sign she'd been paid the two *gulden*? She reached for the bucket. The keys at her waist jangled as she lugged it across the floor. When she'd locked the door behind her, Eva relaxed her grip on Katharina. The jailer's wife had not taken her away.

Eva picked up Katharina's hand and traced a long line in her palm with her forefinger. "We'll work on your letters today."

"But it's Sunday, Mama. We can't."

Eva had not forgotten the day, but time had no meaning in this place. "We'll recite Psalms then," she said. "The first verses of Psalm 5."

Katharina rattled off a sentence. "*O Lord, rebuke me not in thy indignation, nor chastise me in thy wrath. Have mercy on me, O Lord, for—*"

"*Nein,*" interrupted Eva, "that's Psalm 6."

The girl tipped her head to the side, finger to her chin. "*When I called upon him, the God of my justice heard me.*"

"*Nein,* that's Psalm 4."

Katharina's pale brow furrowed. "A hint?"

"*Give ear, O Lord, to my words—*"

"I know it, Mama. *Give ear, O Lord, to my words, understand my cry. Hearken to the voice of my prayer, O my King and my God. For to thee will I pray. O Lord, in the morning thou shalt hear my voice. In the morning...*" Katharina chewed her lip.

Eva finished the verses. "*In the morning, I will stand before thee, and will see: because thou art not a God that willest iniquity.*"

Neither shall the wicked dwell near thee. Nor shall the unjust abide before thy eyes. Thou hatest all the workers of iniquity. Thou wilt destroy all that speak a lie."

Eva had purposely asked for Psalm 5. It comforted. *Thou art not a God that willest iniquity.* God would protect them. Eva clasped her shackled hand around her rosary. "Mother of God," she prayed, then stopped. Could the Mother of God hear her in such a place?

11

One man lights the pine torches on the wall. One by one, the other men step down into the chamber. Their fingertips move from forehead to chest, left shoulder to right. They slide silently onto wooden chairs set round the curved table. The young Jesuit records their names, all seven. The men believe there must be seven at this meeting, just as they believe there must be thirteen when my disciples gather.

They are soldiers of God. They have come here to do battle with evil.

They wear masks of calm, but flinch at the sound of skittering mice. I wave a hand just to see them cower when the flames flicker, crack my knuckles just to hear their sharp gasps. Under the table, where their bouncing knees are hidden, their jittery feet dance a tarantella.

The men dare not look at the shadows cast upon the stone walls, shadows broken and dismembered by shelves filled with ropes and birch rods, gouges, pincers, and thumbscrews. The grey walls bear silent witness, storing up, like sacred confessions, the screams they have heard. The porous floor hoards the rain of tears and blood.

The men mutter prayers and touch the balls of wax and herbs at their throats. As if mere wax can protect them from my charms.

Their fear smells of sour sweat and fevered breath.

It is their fear that brings me here, their fear that sustains me. Alone, I can do nothing. In their belief, all things are possible.

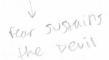
fear sustains
the Devil

12

~

20 April 1626

The men sat around the rough pine table set opposite the door leading to the narrow spiral staircase and the prisoners above. They waited patiently as Father Streng recorded Chancellor Brandt's answer to Herr Doktor Lutz's most recent question. Hampelmann shifted on the wooden chair, careful not to let his elbow nudge Judge Steinbach, who sat to his left. Hampelmann could hear the judge's wheezing breaths in the stillness of the cramped chamber.

The wooden floor of the cell above them creaked. Judge Steinbach swallowed, the noise from his throat audible. A furtive mouse, its bright eyes reflecting the yellow flames of the torches, scrabbled over the thumbscrews, its nails clicking on grey iron.

Holding his spectacles on his nose, Father Streng frowned in concentration as he wrote. Clarity of vision. Hampelmann wondered if he should consider getting spectacles. Then again, that might be thwarting God's will. Perhaps God had blurred his vision so that he might see more clearly what lay beneath the obvious.

The obvious and what lay beneath. Hampelmann surveyed the men at the table. Judge Lorenz Steinbach: old and faint-hearted. The burgomaster slept through every city council meeting, but here, in the Prisoners' Tower, he was alert and watchful. He sat hunched at the centre of the curved table, twitching like a nervous hare every time the torches flickered. He might wear the judge's black robes and hold the gavel in his gnarled hands, but, as always, it would be Hampelmann,

◡◠

Father Streng, and Chancellor Brandt who would actually conduct the hearings.

Chancellor Johann Brandt: forceful and crafty. He sat across from Hampelmann and the judge, calmly studying the report prepared by the *Malefizamt*, his eyebrows a thick dark line. Hampelmann didn't particularly like the man, or trust him, but he respected his authority. A gold medallion bearing His Grace's coat of arms hung from his neck. He'd been the Prince-Bishop's chancellor for nine years, and he knew how to prosecute witches.

To the right of the chancellor, Father Streng: irritatingly brilliant and zealously devoted to the cause. The diminutive Jesuit was a true soldier of God, *militare Deo*. The young priest scribbled furiously while the quaking judge looked on from across the table, sliding the gavel from hand to hand.

Herr Georg Freude: disgusting in his vulgarity, but skilled at his profession. He sat at the end of the table nearest the tools of his trade: hemp ropes and birch rods, eye gougers, pincers and thumbscrews, leg vises, a large wooden wheel attached by a rope to a pulley on the ceiling. The executioner combed his fingers through his scraggly dark beard, searching out lice, which he pinched between his thumb and middle finger. His forefinger was missing. Hampelmann surmised that Freude had been a thief before he came to his current profession. Or, thought Hampelmann, he could have lost the finger in a botched execution rather than as punishment for petty theft. Hampelmann found the man's scarred pockmarked face revolting and wished that he wore his black mask during the hearings as well as the executions. Hampelmann tried to keep his distance from the executioner, who always stank, carrying about his person the sour miasma of a beggar. There were also his lice to consider. And the way the man scratched at his crotch, he no doubt had crabs as well.

To the right of the executioner and the left of the judge,

Herr Doktor Hans Lindner: thick-headed, boorish, and ridiculous looking with a fringe of sandy hair ringing his bald head and a face dotted with freckles. He was here only because, by law, a physician must be present at the preliminary inquisition. He had the authority to stop the torture from going too far, but Lindner, a pompous buffoon, overestimated his importance, and his knowledge of witches. Thick arms crossed over his broad chest, fat lower lip thrust out, the physician appeared relaxed, but Hampelmann could feel the vibrations from his bouncing knee coming through the table.

Hampelmann glanced at the man sitting to his right. Herr Doktor Franz Lutz: slovenly, of middling intelligence, and almost as twitchy as the judge. Constantly touching the ball of wax at his throat, Lutz sat nearest to the outside door, as if he hoped to be the first to flee should one of the witches or the Devil attack. His pale moon face was framed by shaggy white hair, shadowed by dark circles under his eyes. The man was obviously losing sleep. A simple contract lawyer, Lutz was, no doubt, spending hours poring through law books, terrified of making an error in such a weighty matter. Which was, of course, as it should be. And yet his simple-minded questions had led Hampelmann to wonder if it had been a mistake to recommend the councilman for the commission, if the man were too dense to grasp the enormity of the crimes they were there to investigate.

Lutz raised a beefy hand. The long shadows cast by his outstretched fingers on the circular walls appeared to be reaching to enclose the men. "Another question, gentlemen. I have some concerns about *corpus delicti*. According to the Carolina Code, article 44, there must be evidence that a crime has been committed before a person can be arrested. What is the evidence, the *corpus delicti*, if you will, against the accused?"

Judge Steinbach pointed his gavel at the ledger in Chancellor Brandt's hands. "There, in the confessions of the witches who were just executed," said the judge. "All three of them named the accused as accomplices."

"But those are only accusations, not evidence," said Lutz. "Moreover, those accusations came from disreputable witnesses. What about *that* question, gentlemen, the admissibility of testimony from a disreputable witness? According to the Carolina Code, the testimony of a *testes infamis* is not admissible in court."

Hampelmann ran a thumbnail along a deep scar in the table. Despite Lutz's obvious intellectual limitations and his irksome questions, Hampelmann found himself developing a grudging respect for the man. Where had the bumbling lawyer mustered the temerity to question the procedures of his betters: nobles and clerics who'd served on the commission a dozen times?

Chancellor Brandt tipped back his head so that he looked down his narrow nose at Lutz. "I would remind you, Herr Lutz, of two very basic points, the first being that this is a preliminary inquisition, not a trial. We are here to gather and evaluate the evidence, to discover the truth, not to render a verdict. The strict legal requirements of a trial do not apply to these initial hearings. Secondly, witchcraft is a *crimen exceptum*, an exceptional crime. Strict rules of evidence do not apply. Therefore, the testimony of disreputable witnesses can be accepted."

"Witchcraft is the most secret of crimes," added Father Streng, pointing the brown plume of his pen at Lutz. "How could we possibly know of its existence except through the testimony of the witches themselves? How could a God-fearing person know who has attended the sabbath?" He smirked at Lutz. "Or do you imagine that people who associate with witches are of good reputation?"

"Because you are new to the commission, Herr Lutz, your errors in thinking are understandable," said Chancellor Brandt. "It would be best if you merely observed for a while. Your questions will then be answered to your satisfaction...without delaying our deliberations this morning."

Lutz scanned the wall behind Freude, his gaze settling on the thumbscrews. "It is true that all of this is new to me, but ever since I was honoured by being appointed to the Commission of Inquisition, I have been thinking hard about such questions as these. I beg your indulgence, gentlemen. *Bitte*, just a few more questions."

Judge Steinbach gave a small reluctant nod.

"While it may be true that for investigations of witchcraft we must accept the testimony of persons of bad reputation, it has struck me that there is a problem inherent in accusations made by condemned witches." Lutz's eyes were drawn back to the thumbscrews. "If these women are truly guilty of witchcraft, aren't their accusations questionable precisely because they are witches? Obviously, they wish to harm innocent people. On the other hand, if they are not witches," he raised his palms, "then, as Father Streng has pointed out, they cannot possibly name accomplices."

The priest laid a hand on his breviary. "Are you suggesting that the commission has condemned innocent people?"

"Not at all. I'm just trying to sort out the problem of accepting as truth the testimony of witches."

"It's a moot point, Herr Lutz," said Hampelmann, reaching across the table for the ledger held by Chancellor Brandt. "In searching their homes, the bailiff found plenty of evidence." He brought the open ledger close to his face. "The most alarming was found in Frau Lamm's quarters. There were more than two score plants and roots, most of unknown origin. Many were bundled together and hung to dry. There were both dried and fresh toadstools, three small pots of greasy ointments, one of which the bailiff recorded as having the colour and odour of human flesh. There were at least two dozen small leather or cloth bags marked with cryptic characters and filled with powders of various colours, as well as pots containing odd mixtures – most definitely not food. Hanging above the doorway was a large stone shaped like a human heart with a hole in the centre."

"But aren't the plants and powders, the odd concoctions, just part of a midwife's trade?" said Lutz.

Lindner cleared his throat. "Precisely," said the physician, "and those who use herbs for cures do so only through a pact with the Devil, either explicit or implicit."

"Surely, Herr Lutz," snapped Father Streng, "you are familiar with what *Der Hexenhammer* has to say about midwives: *No one does more harm to the Catholic faith than midwives. For when they do not kill children, they take them out of the room and, raising them up in the air, offer them to devils.* And this particular midwife delivered Fraulein Spatz's stillborn child."

The priest stroked the plume of the pen against his smooth chin. "I should correct myself. While both Frau Lamm and Fraulein Spatz claim the bastard child was stillborn, others claim they heard a child's cries in the night."

"Fraulein Spatz has been in custody for several weeks now, awaiting trial on charges of infanticide," said Hampelmann. "She was discovered trying to bury the unbaptized infant in consecrated ground."

Judge Steinbach sucked in his breath.

"Indeed, gentlemen," said Hampelmann, "though the bailiff found few suspicious items in Fraulein Spatz's quarters – just several odd pebbles – I think we can agree that there is quite enough evidence against both Frau Lamm and Fraulein Spatz to proceed with the initial inquiry into the charges of witchcraft."

He leafed through the pages. "Now, with regard to Frau Bettler. As a beggar, she had no quarters to search, but when the bailiff questioned townspeople who live near to where she was known to ply her trade – Saint Kilian's Cathedral and the town hall – four men and two women, of *good* reputation, Herr Lutz, testified that they'd heard the old woman muttering curses.

Two of them claim that they became violently ill after refusing to give Frau Bettler more than a *pfennig*, and one woman reported that a child the beggar had touched on the shoulder became ill and died within three days. It's possible that these reports are groundless – merely malicious gossip. But again, gentlemen, I believe there is sufficient evidence to proceed. Any objections?"

"*Nein*," squeaked Judge Steinbach, his voice barely audible.

The men waited silently while Father Streng sharpened his quill. Hampelmann pulled his fur-lined cape more tightly around him. The pine torches gave off little heat, and he wished that Freude or the jailer had built a fire in the wire mesh basket used to heat the chamber for the guards who were there when the commissioners weren't meeting.

"The evidence against Herr Silberhans is more problematic," said Hampelmann when Father Streng had finished. "He is accused of being a sceptic, even a defender of witches. Yet the bailiff found nothing suspicious in his quarters. They were, in fact, remarkably ascetic. A point in his favour, I think. And given the nature of the accusations against him, it is somewhat surprising that Herr Silberhans possessed neither books nor pamphlets of a questionable nature. Nothing, for example, on the *Index of Prohibited Books*."

Hampelmann pulled at his starched white ruff. "Albeit, I believe we would be remiss to release the young man. I propose that we bring him in and question him gently. He's a law student at the university. His crime may be one of a dangerous foolishness in repeating aloud some nonsense he's heard from one of his professors."

Freude paused mid-pinch, a wriggling louse trapped between his horny fingernails. "The boy must be shaved and examined for *stigma diaboli*. If he has a Devil's mark –"

"Of course," said Father Streng. "That must be done."

"We are agreed then in how to proceed with Herr Silberhans?"

said Hampelmann. He waited a moment, ignoring Lutz's raised hand, then continued. "And now, finally, we come to Frau Rosen."

Freude pounded a fist on the table. "She and her daughter are together in one cell. A violation of procedures."

Hampelmann avoided looking at the man's stained and broken teeth. "*Nein*," he said slowly, "it is not a violation. The daughter has been detained only for questioning. She, herself, has not been accused. It would be a violation of the law to hold a mere witness, and a child at that, in solitary confinement."

"I don't like it," said the executioner. "Mother and daughter should not be held together."

"What can it hurt?" said Lutz. "The girl is young, only ten or eleven."

"Humph! I've seen witches as young as five," said Freude. "What say you, Judge Steinbach?"

The judge's eyes slid to Chancellor Brandt, then to Hampelmann. "We'll leave things as they are," he said softly.

Hampelmann nodded, then referred back to the report. "In searching Frau Rosen's premises – her bakery and living quarters – the bailiff found more than a dozen white feathers and nearly ten oddly shaped stones, as well as carvings, one of which had been made into the likeness of a woman."

Lutz raised his hands so quickly a torch flared, making Judge Steinbach jump. "Items any child might collect," he said.

"My daughter collects nothing of the sort," said Hampelmann. "She would be admonished severely for doing so. Items such as these are an invitation to the Devil."

"Surely," Lutz protested, "you can't take these few items as evidence of witchcraft."

"*These few items*, as you choose to call them, are not the only evidence. Have you forgotten that Frau Rosen's husband died suddenly, with no warning or explanation? And Herr Kaiser became ill and nearly died after registering his complaint against her with the Lower City Council."

"Moreover," added Father Streng, "her daughter was born crippled – almost surely a sign of the sinfulness of the mother."

Lindner uncrossed his arms and leaned forward. "And then there is the bad weather for two years running. *Hexenwetter*, witches' weather. The poor harvests have left many people starving."

"The mere occurrence of *hexenwetter*," said Lutz, "hardly indicates that Frau Rosen is responsible. That could have been the work of the witches just executed."

Chancellor Brandt flicked a finger against Hampelmann's ledger. "Since Herr Lutz seems so eager to explain away the evidence and to defend the accused, I propose, Judge Steinbach, that he be appointed their lawyer."

Lutz's mouth dropped open. "But...but I was only raising questions."

Hampelmann twisted his gold ring. Dare he contravene Chancellor Brandt? The words of Jean Bodin came immediately to mind: *avarice, ambition, cruelty, or thirst for revenge could render a judge vulnerable to spells.* The chancellor's motive was revenge, a desire to punish Lutz. Hampelmann had to speak up. Duty demanded it.

"With all due respect to Chancellor Brandt," he said carefully, "I'm not sure that such an appointment would be fair to either Herr Lutz or the accused. The man has little experience with witches. Perhaps he should be permitted to observe and learn from these initial hearings before he is assigned such a demanding and dangerous responsibility."

Judge Steinbach folded his gnarled hands and laid them gingerly on the table. "It is a difficult question."

Chancellor Brandt's hooded gaze went around the table, meeting the eyes of each man in turn, Hampelmann's last. "Are we all agreed then?"

A trio of *ja*s sounded: Father Streng, Freude, and Lindner. The chancellor gave Hampelmann a tight smile. "*Ja*," he said.

Looking as if he might faint, Lutz gripped the table.

Judge Steinbach picked up the gavel and tapped it once. "It is done then."

13

✧

20 April 1626

Standing outside the Prisoners' Tower, Lutz looked up at the narrow windows. He would have to talk directly to witches now and visit them in their cells. Alone. His stomach clenched like a fist, his throat burned.

He turned away from the tower, toward the warmth and light of the sun. It hung low in the sky above Marienberg, giving the Prince-Bishop's castle a rosy celestial glow. From his castle on the mountain, the Prince-Bishop watched over Würzburg the way God on high watched over Würzburg. God would protect Lutz because he was doing God's work. Hampelmann had assured him of that. Those encouraging words had done little to hearten him, though. Did he lack faith as well as courage?

Lutz pulled his handkerchief from under his cuff and dabbed his forehead, then tucked it away and set out for the university, only a few minutes' walk from the tower. His long shadow trailed him, just off to the right. He wished that he really were that tall. Instead, he felt small, a timid mouse wanting nothing more than to hide in some protected crevice.

He entered the inner court of the university and proceeded to Father Herzeim's office. Lutz knocked, then waited for the soft *ja* before opening the door. He blinked at the evening light pouring in through the window. It fell like a golden mantle across the narrow desk where Father Herzeim sat. The priest looked up from the books and ledgers that lay scattered before him. "It's good –"

"The Commission of Inquisition has appointed me to defend the accused witches."

"*Nein*," the priest breathed.

"It was Chancellor Brandt's doing." Lutz shook his head, disgusted with himself. "I was stupid, a *dummkopf.* Asked too many questions and did not see how annoyed they were getting until it was too late."

Father Herzeim's hand closed over his cedar cross. "I never should have encouraged you to ask those questions."

"That hardly matters now. It's done, and I need your help. I'm a practical man, Father, not a mystic. I need something more than just prayer and faith and a bit of wax to protect me." Lutz touched the ball of wax Maria had tied around his neck that morning. It seemed small and inconsequential, hardly the shield he needed.

"There is nothing greater than prayer and faith," the priest said quietly.

"That may well be, but I need something more." Hands clasped behind his back, Lutz started to pace. "I want you to come with me when I go into their cells. With you there, they'll be reluctant to speak falsely to me, and I'll know whether they're guilty or not."

Lutz stopped in front of the desk. "I am not a brave man, Father. I'll admit that I'm scared to death of meeting witches face to face." He looked down at the floor, at the pattern of scuff marks on the dark wood, ashamed that he'd had to make such a cowardly admission to his friend. "With a Jesuit there, I would be less afraid. Of them and the Devil. Please, will you come with me?"

Father Herzeim's mouth twisted oddly, almost a smile, but not. "I've visited the accused," he said. "I am convinced that most of them are innocent. But if my presence brings comfort and courage, I will go with you."

"*Danke.*" Lutz picked up a poker and stabbed at the small fire in the hearth. "I also need your help in preparing their defence."

"That I will not do."

Lutz whirled to face the priest. "What! It's your damned questions that got me into this mess." He saw the priest flinch and immediately regretted the accusation. He set the poker back in its stand, then sat down in the rickety chair opposite the desk. "Ach, I'm not blaming you. But, Father, you're the one who knows these laws, the one who's always telling me how concerned you are that innocent people might be condemned. You must help me."

Father Herzeim quietly closed the book that lay open on his desk: *Essais* by Michel Montaigne. Lutz recognized it as a work his friend often quoted in their debates. "*Nein,*" the priest whispered. "I have my students to attend to."

"Your students!"

"If I become any more involved in these inquisitions, I'll be neglecting my duties at the university."

Lutz jumped up and leaned across the desk. "One of the accused, Herr Silberhans, is a student of yours. What about your responsibility to him?" He jabbed his finger at the book. "Wasn't it just last week that you quoted to me from your precious book? Tell me again what Montaigne has to say about witch trials."

Father Herzeim took a deep breath. "*It is putting a very high price on one's conjectures to have a man roasted alive for them,*" he quoted mechanically.

"I'm just asking for a little help," pleaded Lutz. "I'm a contract lawyer, not an expert on witchcraft." He laid his hand on the book so that it lay beside Father Herzeim's. The priest's hand was trembling.

"Remember your own question to me just a few days ago?" said Lutz. "*You would allow innocent people to be condemned because you are afraid?*"

Father Herzeim's dark eyes searched Lutz's face. "It is not for my life that I fear, but for yours. I never should have advised you to raise those questions. I have placed you in terrible danger. I fear that if I help you now, I will be helping you directly into your grave."

"Into my grave?" Lutz snorted. "Father, I'm far more likely to find myself in a grave if you *don't* help me."

The priest stared into the corner, at a small table, as if hoping to find an answer there. "I will agree to help you," he said finally, his voice weary, "but only to protect you. And not from the dangers you imagine. You *must* understand that there is little you can do to affect the outcome of this inquisition."

"But that's precisely what a lawyer does — try to affect the outcome. And the evidence in these cases is remarkably flimsy, mostly hearsay and circumstantial."

"Evidence will matter little."

"Of course evidence matters," said Lutz, stepping back from the desk. "Evidence always matters."

Father Herzeim clenched his jaw. "Listen to me, Lutz. You must be very, very careful. You are legally obligated to defend the accused, but do not give them grounds to accuse you of being a defender of witches."

"Give who grounds?"

"The commissioners."

Lutz laughed uneasily. "But they have assigned me this task. Why would they accuse me of anything…except incompetence?"

"Because they are men who take the writings of the Jesuit, Martin Delrio, as seriously as scripture. Delrio says that it is an *indicium* of witchcraft to defend witches."

"But Herr Hampelmann and Judge Steinbach know me," Lutz protested. "Never could they imagine that I would choose to defend the accused because I am one of them."

Father Herzeim tapped a slender forefinger on Montaigne's *Essais*. "I am coming to believe that the commissioners can imagine nearly anything. You run a terrible risk in defending the accused."

"Seems to me the risk lies in prosecuting them. I've been studying *Der Hexenhammer*. According to the Dominicans, the evils perpetrated by modern witches exceed all other sin that God has ever permitted."

"Of that I am not so sure. I believe the Devil deludes witches into believing they have powers. Their real powers are limited."

The logs in the hearth shifted. Red sparks flew upward. Father Herzeim's face was sallow in the fading light. "The commissioners' powers are not," he said.

14

21 April 1626

Cradling Katharina in her lap, Eva felt a deep weariness of heart and soul. When the Angelus bells rang out for evening prayers, she laid a hand over her rosary and fingered the beads, but could not find within her the words, or even the will, to pray.

Everything around her was grey stone or brown wood, except the sliver of sky in the narrow window, which was pale blue tinged with pink. She concentrated on that sliver of sky and tried to bring to mind the flowers that would be blooming in the bakery courtyard: glossy yellow buttercups, sweetly perfumed lily-of-the-valley, dainty blue forget-me-nots with bright yellow centres, soft pink cherry blossoms.

The metal scrape of the key. So familiar now that Katharina didn't even lift her head from Eva's chest. Eva could see Father Herzeim's dark eyes peering through the small barred window.

The door opened and the priest stepped into the cell, his half smile both sorrowful and hopeful. A stout man stood behind him. He craned his neck to look over Father Herzeim's shoulder. Eva hugged Katharina to her chest, jangling the chains attached to her wrists. The stout man winced and made the sign of the cross, his eyes darting around the cell, to the window, the wooden stool, the pail, but not to Eva. He wrinkled his nose and reached for a small silver pomander hanging by a looped chain from a button on his doublet. Eva watched him bring the pomander to his nose and inhale deeply. She no longer had the energy to be embarrassed by the stench.

"This is Herr Doktor Franz Lutz," said Father Herzeim. "He is to be your lawyer."

The man tipped his broad-brimmed hat toward her. "I will be your defence lawyer for the preliminary hearings, Frau Rosen."

"I don't need a lawyer. The judge will see at once that a mistake has been made, and he will release us."

"It may not be that simple," said Father Herzeim. "It would be best if you allow a lawyer to help you."

Eva had never sought help from a lawyer, not even for the bakery, and the man before her did not inspire confidence. His round face was kindly but somewhat befuddled, his smile too tight, as if he were in pain. He swayed from one black boot to the other, and his fingers flitted from tugging on his white beard, to tapping the silver pomander, to touching the cord at his throat, to toying with the buttons on his dark doublet.

Father Herzeim pulled up the stool and sat down close to Eva. Lutz began to pace, all the while rolling the pomander in his palms. "There are, as yet, no formal charges against you," the lawyer said. "There are only the accusations made by other witches and a few rumours. And, of course, the evidence found by the bailiff."

"Evidence?" said Eva.

"Some feathers, a few odd rocks and pebbles, some carvings."

Katharina raised her head. "Did you bring my doll? Or the angel wings?"

Lutz turned abruptly, his blue eyes meeting Eva's for the first time. "Angel wings?"

Eva looked at Father Herzeim, who nodded encouragement. "The white feathers," she said softly.

Lutz coughed into his hand. "*Nein*, child, I did not."

Katharina slumped against her mother.

"Am I to understand, Frau Rosen," said the lawyer, "that these...this so-called evidence belongs to your daughter?"

Eva inhaled sharply. Was it more dangerous to say those things were Katharina's? Or hers? She touched her rosary. She'd sworn to herself and to God that she would speak nothing but truth. That was the only way she could be sure the Holy Mother would help her in her hour of need. She would speak the truth. But no more truth than necessary.

Lutz looked at her expectantly.

She gave a small nod. "*Ja.*"

To her enormous relief, his hunched shoulders relaxed. "That's what I thought," he said. "What the bailiff calls evidence is merely a child's playthings." He studied the floor. With the toe of a scuffed boot, he pushed straw into a small pile. "Now, Frau Rosen, I must ask you a few more questions, and it is absolutely imperative that you tell me the truth."

Lutz took another deep breath through the pomander. "The accusations made by the condemned witches are far more serious than the evidence. All three claimed to have seen you at the sabbath."

"Lies. Never have I gone to a gathering of witches."

Lutz's gaze shifted to the priest. "Do not forget that your confessor sits at your side. You must tell us the truth."

Father Herzeim laid his fingers on Eva's shoulder, so lightly they seemed barely there, and yet, through the thin wool of her gown, they created a small circle of warmth. Eva breathed in the clean fragrance of his soap.

"For the sake of your eternal soul," said the priest, "you must tell Herr Lutz the truth."

"That is the truth. I swear it – upon my eternal soul. I know nothing of witchcraft."

Lutz scratched his chin through his thick beard. "What is most puzzling, and damning, is that all three of the condemned witches, independently, named you as an accomplice. If you are not a witch, why would all three name you as such?"

"I don't know," said Eva. "Never have I – or my daughter – had anything to do with the Devil or with witches."

Katharina started to lift her head. Eva pulled it back to her chest. "Please, you must believe me."

"Did you know any of the condemned witches?" the lawyer asked.

Eva glanced at the priest. He gave her his sad half smile. "I knew Frau Basser, but only to sell her bread," she said quickly. "I have thought and thought about it, Herr Lutz, and I cannot think why any of them would accuse me except out of sheer malice and evil."

"Do you know any of the others who were named with you?"

"The jailer's wife told me a few names – a midwife and a law student, I think. But I know none of them. I swear."

"The jailer's wife told you?" said Lutz. "Damn that old crone and her wagging tongue! She'll be locked up herself if the other commissioners hear of this."

The truth. Eva hesitated before she spoke. "I do know *of* Frau Lamm, but only by her reputation as a skilled midwife. I have never consulted her." The truth. But no more truth than necessary. There was no need to tell them that Frau Lamm was rumoured to provide remedies to *frauleins* who found themselves in trouble. That was malicious gossip, not truth.

"Have you done anything that someone might misinterpret as witchcraft?" said Lutz.

"Nothing."

"Sold someone bread that made them ill? Said something that might be thought of as a curse?"

"*Nein.*"

"What about your husband? Didn't he discipline you rather severely?"

Eva bowed her head. "*Ja.*"

"Did you ever curse him for that, wish him ill, or even dead?"

Eva studied the pattern of cracks in the wood floor. She knew them by heart, could see them even when she closed her eyes.

It was true, she'd feared and hated Jacob, but she hadn't wished him dead. Or had she?

"I never wished him ill, or dead." She felt Katharina shiver. Had her daughter?

The lawyer stood with his back to her now, his face tilted up toward the window. "Never?"

"Never." Surely that was the truth. She might have wished to be free of him, but she never could have wished for his death. Nor could Katharina. That would be evil. She and her daughter were sinful, but they were not evil.

Lutz spun to face her. "Herr Rosen died quite suddenly. Of what?"

"I-I don't know. He was all right in the morning when we rose from our bed. The journeymen said that when Jacob was unloading sacks of flour he gasped and fell to his knees. And died. Just like that. I wasn't there, and no one could tell me why he'd died, not even the physician who examined him. Jacob was old, Herr Lutz, and cruel, but I did not wish him dead."

"But you haven't remarried, though I understand there have been suitors."

"None has been suitable," Eva mumbled. Did everyone think it a sin that she hadn't remarried?

"Have you consulted a sorcerer or diviner to find a suitable match? Or used a love charm?"

"*Nein.*"

Lutz flicked his blunt fingers against the pomander. "We know that the Devil comes to those who are desperate. Has he ever come to you or approached you in any way?"

Eva held Katharina tightly. "Never. I put my faith in God and pray to the Holy Mother."

Lutz leaned closer. The brim of his hat nearly touched her forehead. Close up, his clear blue eyes looked younger than the web of lines around them. She caught the sharp scent of sweet marjoram from his pomander.

"You must tell me the truth," he said. "I cannot help you unless you speak the truth."

She held his gaze. "I speak the truth. I swear it." Katharina's dreams and visions were a child's fantasies. Nothing more.

He stepped back. "Then you must insist on that to the commissioners. The first hearing is tomorrow morning."

Finally, after six days and six nights in this horrid place, she would talk to the men in charge, the commissioners. They would see the error at once, and free her and Katharina. She and her daughter would go home. Home to the scent of baking bread, freshly laundered linens, and the flowers in her courtyard.

Eva reached out a shackled hand. "*Bitte*, might I have your pomander for just one moment?"

Lutz jumped back. "*Nein*! I cannot give you anything, or accept anything from you. Until it is proven that you are not a witch."

The key in the lock. Eva jerked awake, limbs stiff, eyes gritty. The jailer's wife shuffled in. She carried a large stoneware bowl and a mound of coarse cloths slung over one shoulder. A candle enclosed in a square glass lantern swung from her wrist. She set the bowl beside Eva. A cake of yellow soap floated in the steaming water. Eva nudged Katharina awake, then leaned forward and inhaled the fragrance of the soap. Thanks be to God. A bath.

A burly man strode into the cell. His face was scarred and pockmarked. In one black-gloved hand, he carried both scissors and a razor, in the other, a lantern. He set down the lantern and crossed himself, his fingers lingering at the cord around his throat. He handed the razor to the jailer's wife and stepped close to Eva. Katharina shrank away.

The man yanked the widow's cap from Eva's head.

ɔɔ

"What are you doing?" she shrieked.

Without a word, he grabbed her hair and began cutting. Eva kicked at his legs. He laid down the scissors, drew back his arm, and slapped her across the face so hard her head hit the stone wall.

"No use to fight it," said the jailer's wife. "Has to be done. It's the law."

The man pulled Eva upright, picked up the scissors, and resumed cutting. Stunned, Eva watched thick chestnut clumps fall in a ring around her. Katharina crouched against the opposite wall, fist to her mouth.

"This is a mistake," Eva whimpered. "We are to be released tomorrow."

The rasp of the scissors stopped. The man laughed harshly. "Where did you get that foolish notion? You're to be questioned tomorrow. Not released."

He finished cutting her hair and stepped to the side. While the jailer's wife lathered the wet soap over what was left of Eva's hair, the man scratched at his crotch, then took the glove off his right hand and combed his fingers through his greasy beard. Finding a louse, he pinched it between his fingernails, thumb and middle finger. His forefinger was missing. He pulled the glove back on, then stepped toward Eva, waving the razor. "Move, and it might slip to your throat. Or take off an ear." He braced her head against his thigh. The razor scraped against her scalp, making her skin burn.

Katharina screamed when the man came toward her, his shadow huge on the wall. He grabbed her hair. The muscles of his hand and forearm worked, but the scissors could not sever the thick braid. He cursed, snatched the razor from the woman's hand, and sawed, then tossed the white-gold braid to the floor.

Eva's hands explored her smooth bare scalp and the tenderness at the back of her head. "Why are you doing this?"

"To look for Devil's marks," said the jailer's wife, "and so's you can't hide no charms."

"Shut up, old woman, or I'll soon be doing the same to you." The man grinned a mouthful of stained and broken teeth. "With that ugly face of yours, and that gossiping tongue, I've often thought you might be a witch yourself."

The woman covered the dark mole on her cheek with a soapy hand.

"Unlock the shackles," he ordered.

The jailer's wife moved quickly to do his bidding. Eva rubbed her raw and swollen wrists, free for the first time in six days.

"Take off your clothes," he growled.

"*Nein!*"

"You heard him," said the woman. "Take off your clothes."

"*Nein!*"

The man jerked his chin toward the jailer's wife. "Do it for her."

Without bothering to undo laces or ties, the woman ripped the gown and chemise from Eva's body, pulled the shoes and stockings from her feet, and tossed the clothes aside. Frantic, Eva tried to cover herself with her hands and arms. She huddled against the wall and watched the man shave Katharina's head, each pull of the razor revealing the delicate outlines of her daughter's skull. Katharina stared, her eyes the flat green of a stagnant pool.

He turned to the jailer's wife. "Go get different shifts. Those are stained."

"I can't leave now. The commissioners say—"

"Go get the shifts, Frau Brugler! And find ones that are clean. And one that'll fit the girl. Take your time."

"There…there's none that'll fit the girl." The woman stood, her thin lips clamped tight.

"Go on, you old hag, or I'll have you locked up and shaved before sunrise."

Frau Brugler picked up a lantern and scurried from the cell, locking the door behind her. The man turned to Eva. "Lay down," he said.

She swallowed hard, her throat dry. Mother of God, this couldn't be happening.

"Lay down." He pointed toward the door. "Over there."

Eva edged toward the door, then slumped down. She pulled her legs to her breasts and wrapped her arms around them. He came closer and stood above her, holding the razor loosely in his hand. He knelt down and leaned over her. His breath stank of sour red wine. He slid a gloved hand between her legs and tried to force them apart. Eva resisted. The razor sliced across her thigh, the lightest of touches. A thin line of blood welled.

Eva closed her eyes and hoped desperately that Katharina had turned her face to the wall.

"Spread your legs," he said hoarsely, his voice low. He dipped his hand in the water, then rubbed the yellow soap over the hair between her thighs, sliding it front to back, front to back. He dropped the soap into the bowl and put his hand where he'd soaped her. Leaning closer, he pressed her against the door, caressing her. Moaning, he poked his thick fingers into her. His mouth over hers muffled her scream.

He rubbed his own crotch. Then, with one hand still holding the razor, he started untying his breeches, his gloved fingers fumbling with the laces. Eva turned away, but could hear the rasp of buckram. She saw the pale glow of candlelight at the barred window above her.

"Herr Freude?" Frau Brugler's voice was high and plaintive. "Herr Freude, where are you?"

The man scrambled to retie his breeches, and by the time Frau Brugler cracked open the door and peeked in, her lantern held before her, he'd pulled Eva away from the door and was kneeling beside her, shaving her. "I couldn't see you," said the jailer's wife. "Gave me a bit of a start."

Freude didn't answer. His eyes held the metallic glint of rage. He scraped Eva roughly, as if to inflict as much hurt and shame as he could. Leaning close, he whispered into her ear, "You nearly had me, you bitch, with your witch's charms."

Finally, when he'd finished and Eva was allowed to stand, the jailer's wife handed her a pale linen shift. Frau Brugler pointed at her thigh. "There's blood on her leg," she said.

"A slip of the razor," said Freude.

The woman's thin eyebrows came together, but she said nothing. She went to Katharina and undressed her, much more gently than she had Eva. The girl did not resist, but only stared straight ahead, unseeing. She looked small and fragile, easily crushed.

Eva gagged and nearly vomited when Freude ordered Katharina to lie down. Mother of God, she begged, please help us in our hour of need.

Katharina did not move. Frau Brugler took her small hand and coaxed her to the floor. "I always feel bad for the young ones," she said.

Freude rolled his eyes, then stooped to examine Katharina. The woman stood near and watched him closely. "Nothing to shave," he muttered.

The jailer's wife lifted Katharina to her feet, pulled a shift over her head, and smoothed it over her thin body. It dragged on the floor. She locked Eva's wrists in the shackles, then she and Freude searched the small cell, lifting the pail and the stool, kicking at the straw and the cut hair, and poking into every crevice. Frau Brugler gathered the discarded clothes.

"Wait," said Eva. "My rosary. Please let me have my rosary."

"Not allowed," said Freude.

After they'd left, Katharina came to sit in her mother's lap, her frail body rigid beneath the thin shift. "That was him, Mama. The Devil. Did you see his red eyes? Why didn't the angels protect us?"

"I don't know, *Liebchen*. I don't know."

꙳

Eva wrapped her arms around her daughter and rocked. She felt the chill air on her scalp and a burning between her thighs where the man had scraped her skin raw. She tried to draw breath, but choked. The smell of lye soap was foul and hateful.

15

22 April 1626

Holding up a glass lantern, Chancellor Brandt pushed open the heavy door. The men had to duck to follow him through the doorway into the lowest chamber of the Prisoners' Tower. As they filed in, each made the sign of the cross and whispered a prayer, *in nomine patris, et filii, et spiritus sancti.*

Chancellor Brandt set the lantern on the curved table, and the men took their places along one side, sitting nearly shoulder to shoulder, thigh to thigh, hat brim to hat brim. Judge Steinbach sat at the centre, Chancellor Brandt to his left, Father Streng to his right. The windowless chamber was less than eight paces across, and the table opposite the door where the accused would enter was hardly large enough to accommodate all seven men. All but the judge took off their hats and hung them on pegs behind them.

Freude lifted the pine torches from their iron holders on the wall, lit each in the sputtering fire in the wire basket set off to the side, then carefully placed the burning torches back in the holders. A black rat scrabbled away from the light, its pointed teeth clamped on a pale scrap of food. It slipped into a crevice between the grey stones.

Father Streng carried his breviary, a large wooden cross, a ledger, several quills, and a pot of black ink. He set the cross and breviary to the side, opened the ledger, dipped a quill into the ink, and recorded their names: Judge Lorenz Steinbach, Chancellor Johann Brandt, Herr Doktor Wilhelm Hampelmann, Herr Doktor Hans Lindner, Herr Georg Freude, and Father Rudolf Streng.

dancing in the palm of his hand

The priest, who sat on Hampelmann's left, glanced pointedly at the vacancy to Hampelmann's right. Hampelmann hunched his shoulders. He had no idea where Lutz was. Perhaps his courage had failed him. It had happened before. Many men lacked the strength of character and the faith needed to serve on the commission. The Prince-Bishop would have to appoint another man, a braver man, to take Lutz's place.

Judge Steinbach laid out a gold watch in a wavering pool of candlelight. "Another few minutes," he said, his face sour, "and then we'll begin without him."

Hampelmann coughed, the acrid wood smoke an irritant in his throat, and thought wistfully of the sweetness of cherry blossoms in the Lusam Garden. He'd gone there for meditation early that morning, the sun warming his back, the blackbirds warbling while he prayed, then laboured to compose verses. Concern about the morning's hearing intruded, however, and he'd managed only one passable line.

The tallow candle burned high in the lantern, dripping pale yellow globs into the grease pan beneath. It stank of burning fat. Hampelmann almost wished that another man would take his place at the table, at least for a while. It was an onerous duty to study the evidence, question the accused, and then tease from them the truth. It was sordid, and frightening, to hear about the depraved and filthy things they'd done. And the commissioners had to be so attentive to detail, so terribly careful. There could, after all, be an innocent among the accused. And if God gave a sign, Hampelmann didn't want to miss it for lack of paying attention. He rubbed his eyes. Tired, he was so tired. But God had called him to this work. It was his cross to bear.

The outside door creaked open. Lutz stepped in, a sheepish smile on his face. He clutched a ledger to his chest. He crossed himself, then took his place at the end of the table near Hampelmann. He removed his hat and hung it behind him.

Chancellor Brandt picked up the judge's watch and made a conspicuous show of examining it while Father Streng recorded the last name: Herr Doktor Franz Lutz.

Judge Steinbach tapped the gavel. "We may now begin. We must first decide who should be questioned first." He nodded stiffly at Lutz and then at Freude, who sat at the end of the table opposite Lutz. "Can you tell us which one you believe to be the most timid and feeble?" asked the judge.

"I don't know about timid and feeble," said Lutz, "but all of them claim, quite sincerely, to be innocent of the charges against them."

Freude laughed. "I've yet to meet a witch who didn't claim to be innocent. At first, that is." He clapped his grimy hands. "But then, that's my job. To make them reveal the truth. Bring in the child first. She'll confess right away."

"The child has not been accused," said Lutz. "She cannot be questioned except as a witness."

"A formality," muttered the executioner.

The torchlight cast Freude's repugnant face in shadow. The man might be skilled at his profession, thought Hampelmann, but he failed, again and again, to comprehend the importance of following the letter of the law. God would protect them only if they carried out their duties meticulously and piously.

"In Würzburg," Hampelmann said loudly, "we do not depart from the law, Herr Freude. The girl has not been accused. Moreover, we must always be mindful that there may be an innocent among the defendants. And that person must be protected. As Jean Bodin has written: *It cannot be denied that witches occasionally conspire maliciously to accuse a totally innocent person of complicity in their crimes.*"

"An excellent point, Herr Hampelmann," said Lutz. "All of the accused spoke to me in the presence of their confessor. Certainly they'd have been reluctant to lie while Father Herzeim was there."

Hampelmann stared at Lutz's bland amiable face. The man's ignorance and naiveté were nothing short of astounding. Surely he didn't believe that the accused were innocent simply because they'd said so in the presence of their Jesuit confessor.

Willing himself to be patient, he took a deep breath. "Herr Lutz, witches are very, very clever in feigning innocence. It may take time, but as this inquiry proceeds, you will come to see that. And since you seem somewhat…" Hampelmann searched for a word less offensive than ignorant "…unfamiliar with the ways of witches, I suggest that you take the utmost precautions. They are far more dangerous than they appear."

"And the more innocent they seem, the more dangerous they are," said Judge Steinbach, touching the ball of wax at his throat.

Freude pulled on his black gloves. "If we can't bring in the child, then I say either the maidservant or the beggar. They're both scared out of their wits, especially the old hag. She's feeble, easy to break."

"What say you, Herr Lutz?" said Judge Steinbach.

"I could make no sense of anything Frau Bettler said. I believe the old woman is demented."

"Or possessed?" said Lindner, who sat to the right of the executioner. The fringe of hair around the physician's bald head looked like a bristling copper halo that had slipped.

"I don't think so," said Lutz, opening his ledger. "She exhibited no strange contortions. When I visited her cell, she knelt before Father Herzeim and wept. When I tried to question her, her answers were incoherent, but she did not speak in voices or threaten us in any way."

"Bring her in," said Judge Steinbach. Freude left the chamber through the low doorway that led to the cells above them.

Father Streng stood, and the other men rose and bowed their heads. "Almighty God," said the priest, "guide us, your humble servants, in the execution of our duties. Help us to be discerning, yet merciful, as you, yourself, are the font of all mercy. And in the carrying out of your work, Lord, protect us, your dutiful servants, from Satan's evil. *In nomine patris, et filii, et spiritus sancti,* amen."

The men sat down and waited. Father Streng sharpened his quills. Judge Steinbach slid the gavel from one trembling hand to the other, the white plume on his hat quivering. Lutz flipped through his ledger. Chancellor Brandt straightened the lace on his broad white cuffs. Lindner clicked a thumbnail on his front teeth, a noise irritating to Hampelmann, who brought his pomander to his nose and inhaled deeply of the pungent and faintly repellent mixture of lavender and hellebore: lavender for his recurrent headaches and fatigue, hellebore to reduce the excess of black bile that caused his ever more frequent bouts of melancholy.

The door swung open and an old woman entered, shuffling backwards on bare feet. A web of blue veins criss-crossed her shaved scalp. Freude prodded her with a birch rod and turned her to face the commissioners. She wore only a coarse linen shift laced loosely at the neck. Her gaunt face looked like a skull. Parts of her nose were missing and her mouth gaped; her lips had sunk back over her toothless gums. She swayed and nearly toppled over, but Freude grabbed the rope binding her wrists and held her upright. He pulled a heavy wooden chair into the centre of the chamber, then placed her hands on the back of the chair.

Father Streng came forward and held up the large wooden crucifix. "By the belief that you have in God and in the expectation of paradise, and being aware of the peril of your soul's eternal damnation, do you swear that the testimony you are about to give is true, such that you are willing to exchange heaven for hell should you tell a lie?"

The woman's milky eyes stared straight ahead.

The priest spoke sharply. "Do you swear?"

Lutz stepped toward her. "Truth," he said slowly. "Frau Bettler, the commissioners want you to swear to speak the truth."

dancing in the palm of his hand

Her whole body shook. "*Ja*," she mouthed.

Returning to his seat between the judge and Hampelmann, Father Streng recorded her answer. "State your name and age," he demanded.

The woman's mouth moved. She licked her cracked lips.

"State your name and age," Chancellor Brandt repeated.

"I don't think she understands," said Lutz. "Her name is Old Frau Bettler. I've asked around, but no one can tell me her age. Most likely about sixty or so. It's hard to tell. She lives as a beggar."

Hampelmann checked his own ledger, the report prepared by the *Malefizamt*. "Let the record show that she has no license. She's been begging illegally."

Judge Steinbach waited for the priest to finish writing, then said, "Frau Bettler, do you know why you've been brought here?" His thin voice cracked.

Again, the woman's mouth moved, but she said nothing. Her claw-like hands clutched the chair.

"I've tried to explain," said Lutz, "but she doesn't seem to understand the accusations made against her."

"How do you know Frau Imhof, Fraulein Stolzberger, and Frau Basser?" asked Chancellor Brandt.

Lutz lifted his hands imploringly. "Chancellor Brandt, she does not understand."

"Then she will be made to understand."

Freude loosened the leather lacing of the shift, untied the hemp rope binding the woman's wrists, then pulled at the shift, so that it fell down around her ankles. The old woman howled. Though Hampelmann had seen it many times before, the sight never failed to startle. The woman tried to cover her sudden nakedness with an arm over her flaccid breasts and a hand over her bald crotch. She was exceedingly thin, all knobs and bones, and her skin was covered with dark crusty patches and boils. Lutz stepped away.

"Hardly a need to examine her closely," said the executioner, pulling a long pin from a leather case. He thrust it into the back of her thigh. The woman did not react. Freude turned her so that her back was to the commissioners. Pus dripped from the boil he'd pricked. "Note that she did not cry out in pain," he said. "And there is almost no blood. These are Devil's marks, gentlemen, not ordinary sores."

Lindner came forward and peered closely at her skin, but was careful not to touch her. "I concur with that assessment," said the physician. "And from all these sores and pustules, I would venture that the woman made her living as a prostitute when she was younger." He smiled darkly. "Pity the man desperate enough to go to her."

While Father Streng recorded the finding, Freude pulled the shift up and over the woman, tightened the laces, and bound her wrists. He again placed her hands on the back of the chair.

"When did you first meet with the Devil, Frau Bettler?" said Chancellor Brandt.

The woman's toothless gums opened and closed.

"Have you ever met with the Devil?" Lutz said quietly.

Father Streng raised his quill. "That is not the question, Herr Lutz. The marks upon her confirm that she has met with the Devil. The question is when and where. When did you first meet with the Devil, Frau Bettler?"

The woman's head lolled from side to side.

Chancellor Brandt cracked his knuckles, one by one, making Judge Steinbach cringe with each pop. "If she does not speak to us, Herr Lutz," said the chancellor, "she will be recorded as taciturn." He glanced at the executioner. "And then tortured until she does speak."

"Please, Frau Bettler," pleaded Lutz, "answer the question. When did you first meet with the Devil?" He touched her arm, then pulled back as if burned.

Hampelmann heard the gasps, his own among them. How could Lutz forget the terrible danger in touching them? The degrading memory of his own carelessness came, unbidden, to his mind. Like Lutz, he'd been a novice on the commission. There'd been a young woman with clear sapphire eyes, unclouded by a trace of guilt, and flawless skin, even when shaved. Hampelmann persuaded himself that she must be innocent. When he visited her in her cell, her graceful hand reached out. He could have stepped back. Instead, he let her soft fingers rest lightly on his cheek, her thumb wiping away a tear he didn't even know he'd shed. That night, lying beside Helena, he dreamed of her. The young woman came to him, her full breasts showing through her gown of sheer red silk. Her dark hair fell loose to her narrow waist. She danced like Salome, just out of reach, then coyly came closer, onto the bed, and sat astride. He could feel the inviting wetness between her thighs. He saw then that her eyes were not blue, but orange and glowing, like hot coals. Her teeth were black points in a red grinning mouth. He awoke, terrified, and choking on *hexen gestank*. He knew then that the woman was a witch, a succubus. If God's hand had not shaken him awake, his soul would have been lost to the Devil. His arousal shamed him, but also taught him how easy it was to be deceived. He should warn Lutz.

The old woman rocked back and forth. "*Gott. Gott. Gott.*"

Father Streng leaped up. "The woman dares to blaspheme? A violation of Article 106 of the Carolina Code."

"She is praying," said Lutz. "She cannot speak coherently."

"I've seen this woman begging on the steps of the cathedral," said Hampelmann. "Heard her cursing. She was coherent enough then. I suspect that she just needs a bit of convincing."

"Show her the first instrument of torture, Herr Freude," said Chancellor Brandt. Judge Steinbach folded his arms over his stomach and shrank into his chair.

The executioner reached for the set of thumbscrews on the shelf. He'd polished the metal plates and the large centre screw so that the iron gleamed. He held the instrument in front of the woman. She stared blankly.

"She cannot see," said Lutz. "Frau Bettler is almost totally blind."

Freude draped her hands over the thumbscrews so that her fingers could explore the instrument, but her hands lay still, except for their continuous tremor.

"When did you first meet with the Devil?" said Chancellor Brandt.

"She does not understand," said Lutz.

Chancellor Brandt nudged Judge Steinbach, who then sat up. "Record the woman as taciturn," he said. "Take her back to her cell, Herr Freude, and bring us…"

"The maidservant," said Hampelmann. "Fraulein Spatz."

Freude prodded Frau Bettler from the chamber. Lutz sat down at the table and flicked through his ledger. Hampelmann saw that the pages were wrinkled and smudged. Notes were scrawled in corners and margins. Hampelmann squinted to read them: *Carolina Code, article 58. Evidence? Ask F. Herzeim.* What a dangerous foolishness to consult that man, a suspected sceptic. He should warn Lutz about that, too.

While they waited, Chancellor Brandt replaced the nub of tallow in the lantern with a new candle. Lindner added a few pieces of wood to the fire in the mesh basket. Lutz drummed his blunt fingers in an irregular rhythm that Hampelmann found unsettling, a sound like soft chuckling. Hampelmann's hand went to the ball of wax at his throat. Then he smelled it: *hexen gestank.* He glanced into the shadows. Red eyes. A rat, surely, but he could not see its outline, only the glowing eyes. He crossed himself. *In nomine patris, et filii, et spiritus sancti.* God protects those who do his will. He had nothing to fear from the Devil.

Freude returned with the young woman, who, when she turned around, had the appearance of being simple-minded. Her eyes were dull, her mouth slack, her face pasty and pockmarked.

Father Streng came forward, held up the crucifix, and commanded her to swear.

"*Ja*," she said eagerly, bobbing her head.

"State your name and age," said Judge Steinbach.

"Fraulein Ursula Spatz, age 18, sir."

"Date of birth," said Chancellor Brandt.

"March 22. Or maybe 23 or 24. I-I'm not sure."

Father Streng, having returned to his seat and his ledger, waved the quill. "Year?"

The girl stood, her face blank.

"Never mind," he said. "I'll do the subtraction. You say you are 18?"

"I-I think so."

Father Streng made no effort to hide his contempt. "Apparently then you were born in 1608. Does that make sense to you, Fraulein Spatz?"

The girl gave a small shrug.

"Parents?" said Chancellor Brandt.

"My mother died when I was born. I never knew my father."

"An orphan then, probably a bastard," said Father Streng. "Do you know your real name?"

"I was named by the director of the Julius Hospital. I lived there with the other orphans until I was hired out by Herr Zwingen." She spat the name.

"Do you know why you've been brought here?" asked Judge Steinbach.

"*N-nein.*"

"You do not know, Fraulein Spatz, of the accusations made against you?" said Chancellor Brandt.

Her face crumpled. "I-I know about them, but they're all lies."

"How did you know Frau Imhof, Fraulein Stolzberger, and Frau Basser?" asked Hampelmann.

"I didn't."

Hampelmann cocked his head. "You claim not to have known them and that their accusations are lies. Yet all three witches testified that you attended the sabbath with them."

"*Nein*," she shouted. "I've never been to a witches' meeting."

Chancellor Brandt nodded toward the executioner. Freude loosened the shift's laces, untied the girl's wrists, then quickly pulled the shift from her shoulders so that it fell to the floor. Though her shocked face was plain and doughy, her large body lumpy and ungainly, her heavy legs widely bowed, Hampelmann felt himself respond to the nakedness she tried so desperately to hide. Chiding himself for his body's weakness, he concentrated on the pulley on the ceiling. This was exactly what witches wanted, for men like him to be made weak and stupid by lust – so stupid they might actually believe them to be innocent.

The executioner drew out his pin and poked it into a large pockmark on the girl's shoulder. "O-o-ow!" she wailed. With a hand now free from restraint, she tried to cover the place he'd pricked. He slapped her hand away.

"What am I to record, Herr Freude?" said Father Streng, his quill poised.

"She feels the pain, but there is little blood. She could be feigning. Most of her marks would appear to be from smallpox."

"Then search her more thoroughly," the priest said impatiently. "It is repugnant, I know, but *Der Hexenhammer* requires it. Accused witches must be searched: *even in the most secret parts of their bodies, which must not be named.*"

The girl's neck and face flushed scarlet when Freude forced her to bend forward so he could examine her buttocks and crotch. The commissioners watched closely. Whimpering, she covered her face with her hands. Hampelmann looked away and saw that Lutz had bowed his head. Torchlight played across the lawyer's blanched face.

"I see nothing unusual," said Freude. "Herr Doktor Lindner, would you have a look?" The physician came forward and directed Freude where to poke and prod with the birch rod. They stepped back and consulted, then Lindner pointed, and Freude poked her again in the crotch, carefully separating the folds. The girl bit down on her lip, but did not cry out.

Lindner returned to his seat. "She bears the *stigma diaboli* in the most secret of places," he announced. "It could have been given to her in only one way. The girl has copulated with a demon."

"*Nein*," she screamed. "Never."

Freude smacked the back of her bald head. "You are not to speak except to answer questions." He held out the shift to the girl, who pulled it over her body as quickly as she could. He bound her wrists.

"Where and when did you first meet with the Devil?" said Hampelmann.

"Never. I go to mass every Sunday, and confession. Just like I'm told. I'm a good girl."

Chancellor Brandt laid a hand over the gold medallion on his chest. "You claim to be a good girl, but didn't you bear a child out of wedlock?"

"I-I was forced."

"Forced?"

"By my employer, Herr Zwingen."

Snorting incredulously, Lindner leaned forward. "Fraulein Spatz, you conceived a child. Medical evidence proves that conception cannot occur unless there is pleasure. How can you possibly insist you were forced? Have you forgotten that you have sworn to tell the truth?"

"*Nein*. I mean *ja*, Herr Zwingen forced me. I did not do it willingly."

Chancellor Brandt whispered into Judge Steinbach's ear. "Let the record show," said the judge, "that the initial testimony of the accused has proved to be false."

Lutz lowered his head into his hands.

"There are people who claim they heard a baby crying the night your son was born," said Hampelmann, "but you made a statement to the Prince-Bishop's bailiff that the child was born dead."

"That's the truth," she said. "They heard some other baby."

"You are absolutely certain the child was born dead?" said Chancellor Brandt.

"*Ja.*"

"During the birth, could you see the midwife at all times?" said Father Streng.

"*Ja.*"

"Was there ever a time when you fainted from pain or fell asleep, or even closed your eyes to rest," said Hampelmann, "a time during which the midwife might have murdered the child without your knowing?"

Lutz stood. "Wait! What evidence is there that the baby was murdered? Did anyone examine the body? Were there marks of strangulation or smothering? A crushed skull?"

"The body was examined by a qualified physician," said Lindner, "a respected colleague of mine. According to his report, there were no bruises or abrasions. In fact, the infant was perfect, and of such size and weight that he should have lived. That and the secrecy of the birth are what make this death so suspicious. Smothering leaves no marks."

"But did anyone check the lungs?" said Lutz. "Were they still filled with birth waters or had the child drawn breath?"

Lindner thrust out his fat lower lip. "Doesn't matter. A midwife could easily smother a baby before it ever draws breath."

Lutz sat down, his shoulders slumped.

 ✧

"Herr Lutz," said Chancellor Brandt, "*bitte*, let us continue without further interruption. We have much to do today. Fraulein Spatz, could the midwife have murdered the baby?"

"*Nein.* My son never breathed."

"Are you sure?" said Hampelmann.

"*Ja.* I felt no movement during the final month. Frau Lamm told me, before he was born, that the baby was dead."

Chancellor Brandt's nose twitched like a rodent's. "The midwife told you the child was dead? Even before it was born?"

Father Streng smoothed the brown quill. "Tell us, Fraulein Spatz, did the midwife show a special interest in the infant's body?"

"*Nein.*" She sniffed, her face angry. "Frau Lamm wanted nothing to do with it. She made me bury it myself."

"Why were the birth and the burial so secret?" said Father Streng. "You were discovered all alone, in the middle of the night, trying to bury the infant near Saint Stephan's Cathedral."

The girl's head hung low. "I hid my…my condition, cause I didn't want anyone to know." She looked up at the priest. "But I wanted my son to be buried in consecrated ground."

Judge Steinbach wagged a bony finger at her. "An unbaptized baby in consecrated ground? The Church does not allow it. Moreover, Fraulein Spatz, you violated the lantern ordinance. You were out that night without a lighted lantern."

Father Streng's eye twitched, making the mole above his eyebrow jump. Lindner's oafish face contorted in puzzlement. Hampelmann rubbed his temples. Leave it to Judge Steinbach to worry about the lantern ordinance when they were investigating charges of witchcraft and infanticide.

"Show her the first instrument of torture," said Chancellor Brandt.

Freude held out the thumbscrews. The girl turned to Lutz, her eyes round and dark in a face completely drained of colour. "Sir?"

"The truth," Lutz said. "Just tell them the truth."

"Do you still insist you were forced?" said Chancellor Brandt.
"*Ja.*"

"Do you still insist that the bastard son resulting from this illicit union was born dead?" said Hampelmann.

"I-I think so."

"So now you're not sure? said Chancellor Brandt. "Did the midwife have any opportunity to kill the baby without your knowing?"

Freude held the thumbscrews only inches from the girl's nose. Tears trickled down her cheeks. "Sh-she might have."

"Have you changed your mind about anything else?" The chancellor's words were clipped and harsh. "How did you know Frau Basser, Fraulein Stolzberger, and Frau Imhof?"

"I didn't. I swear I didn't."

Chancellor Brandt persisted. "When and where did you attend the sabbath?"

"I've never been to a sabbath."

"When did you receive your mark?" said Lindner.

She shook her head, her eyes locked on the thumbscrews.

"You must answer, Fraulein Spatz," said Father Streng.

"I got no mark," she wailed.

"Take her back to her cell," Chancellor Brandt said with disgust. "Very often meditation and the misery of imprisonment dispose the accused to discover the truth." He pointed at the judge's gold watch.

Judge Steinbach tapped the gavel. "We'll adjourn for dinner and reconvene in two hours."

Chancellor Brandt glowered at Lutz. "*Bitte*, do not be late."

16

I laugh and the shadows dance. The men cross themselves then touch the balls of wax at their throats. They believe I always attend the interrogations of my followers. Of course I am here. Their fear has brought me here. Yet they refuse to hear me, or to see me. I can shout as loud as I please, and still, they pretend not to hear.

The men are waiting for the one who has not yet come, and while they wait, they drum their fingers on the table, pick the wax from their ears, smooth the lace on their collars and cuffs, cross and uncross their legs. And pretend they are not thinking of me. Nearly all are wishing they were at home, lounging in a sunlit courtyard, sipping wine with a friend, or reading, contemplating God, or embracing a wife - or lover.

The boyish priest beholds their flagging zeal. His iron eyes narrow behind the glass disks. He jumps up, startling the old man, who blinks and cowers. Infusing his words with fiery passion, the priest reminds the men of the great importance of their work, reminds them that the end-time is near and God will punish them all if they do not seek out and punish witches.

He reminds them of their most terrifying fears.

To bolster the men's fervour, and their courage, he quotes the labyrinthine arguments of Dominicans and Jesuits, arguments that circle and double back like deer paths through a thicket of willow and alder. He speaks with such a potent and slippery tongue that his words straighten the sharpest switchback, make clear the faintest trail. Only now and again does he talk himself into a dead end. His eye twitches then, and I chuckle at the little priest's conundrum.

He paces before them, waving his small black book as if his wrist were attached to strings pulled from above. I listen with interest to his strident logic. He lectures about what the Dominicans have written in their manual, what the Pope has declared to be true. They claim I have three types of followers: those who can injure but cannot cure, those who can both injure and cure, and those who can cure but cannot injure. I raise my hand, making the torches gutter, and shout out my question. The boy stands alert, peering from side to side. If he would just allow himself to hear me, I am quite certain he could explain why women who cure but do not injure should still be burned.

The priest points the book at the men. The most powerful witches, he says, are found among those who can injure. They can perform every sort of spell. The list is long and impressive. To invigorate the men's fear, he names each crime: witches can raise hailstorms, hurtful tempests and lightning, make the generative desires ineffective and even destroy the power of copulation. They can kill infants in the mother's womb by a touch to the belly. They devour unbaptized children.

And all of them practice carnal copulation with me. I sigh morosely. Would that it were so.

The priest has not yet come to the end of his list. Not by any means. I must admit to some pride that the Dominicans and Jesuits believe my followers and me to be so powerful. The Dominicans have written that witches can make horses go mad under their riders; they can transport themselves from place to place through the air; they can affect judges and commissioners so that they cannot hurt them. That is why witches must walk backwards when they enter the chamber. The men have been told - and they always believe what the Church tells them - that witches cannot lay a curse upon them if they see the witches before the witches see them.

My followers can cause themselves and others to keep silent under torture, he says, and can bring about a great trembling to the hands and horrors to the minds of those who arrest them. They can show to others future events, can see absent things as if they were present and turn the minds of men to inordinate love, or hatred. They can bewitch men and animals with a mere look, without touching them, and cause their deaths.

They dedicate their own children to me. I am perplexed. Why would the Dominicans and Jesuits imagine I have any interest in the weak and helpless? I scratch my head in puzzlement, the sound like the scrape of a boot on stone.

The young priest begins to speak quietly, in a whisper, as if he were telling a secret. Or a lie. This last crime is my favourite.

The Dominicans, he says, report that witches sometimes collect male organs in great numbers, as many as twenty or thirty together. They put them in a bird's nest or shut them up in a box, where they move like living members and eat oats and wheat. There is a story of a certain man who lost his member. The young priest blushes, and I laugh out loud at his unease. The man approached a known witch, he says, to ask her to restore his member to him. She told the afflicted man to climb a certain tree, told him he could take whichever one he liked out of a nest in which there were several. But when he tried to take a big one, the witch said, You must not take that one…it belongs to the parish priest.

Only the stout man with the shaggy white hair dares to smile. When he sees that no one else is amused, he hides his grin behind his hand. Then his face takes on furrows of bewilderment as he struggles to follow the tangled twists and turns of the priest's logic. He will learn. Or he will learn to keep silent.

The chancellor arrives, and the men are ready now. The priest has restored their zeal. They bring in the midwife and search her naked body for the mark they believe I have made upon her. Her limbs are sturdy, her breasts large and pendulous. The members the men are so afraid of losing stiffen within their loose breeches.

The Dominicans say I can enter only the heart that is bereft of all holiness. In this, as in most things, they are quite mistaken. I can enter only the heart that contemplates God.

We dwell in the same heart, God and I.

11

The midwife stood, chin thrust forward, shoulders back, arms at her sides. Unashamed of her bald nakedness. A hot flush rose from Lutz's neck to his cheeks, and he found himself unable to meet Frau Lamm's bold gaze. He'd never even looked at Maria's body that closely. An unsettling mix of shame, fear, and carnal prurience made his heart – and his member – throb.

Freude jabbed the woman with the birch rod and turned her around so that her back was to the commissioners. He pointed to a wine-coloured stain, a small *fleur-de-lis* blooming on her shoulder. "There, gentlemen, is the *stigma diaboli*."

Father Streng's quill scratched across the paper.

"Shouldn't you test it?" said Judge Steinbach.

"No need. The evidence is clear." Freude handed the linen shift to Frau Lamm, who slipped it over her shaved head and tugged it down to cover her sturdy body. Tying her wrists, Freude gave the hemp rope an extra twist. The midwife bared her teeth at him, teeth that were straight and strong, and looked sharp enough to bite into a man's throat and hang on like a wolfhound.

Lutz shuddered, and felt himself shrink. Of all the accused, Frau Lamm was the one he most suspected of being a witch. She'd been a widow for twenty-three years, a midwife for thirty-two, since she was nineteen. She was as old as Maria, but that was where the similarity to his wife ended. Frau Lamm was brash and outspoken, her face hard and angular, especially without her bushy silver hair. She was not a large woman, but her arms and legs were heavily muscled. When he visited her cell, she'd treated him with derision, and told Father Herzeim that he'd do better to confess his own sins than to ask to hear hers. When Lutz tried to question the midwife, her unflinching stare and dark laughter had stopped his breath in his throat, making him choke and stammer. He'd have fled the cell if the priest hadn't been there with him.

"When and where did you first have dealings with the Devil?" said Chancellor Brandt.

"I know nothing of the Devil."

Father Streng pointed the quill. "Your mark says otherwise."

"I've had that mark since the day I was born. It's why my mother named me Lilie."

"Which is even more damning," said Freude, pointing at her shoulder with the birch rod. "A child marked in the womb, who carries the name of her mark, as if her mother were proud."

"It is the sign of peace," said Frau Lamm, "the symbol of Saint Katharina."

Freude struck her across the face with the rod. "You'll not foul the names of the saints with your filthy mouth."

"If you've had no dealings with the Devil," said Hampelmann, "how do you explain the evidence?"

"What evidence?" The midwife licked the blood from her split lip.

Hampelmann flipped through his ledger, then ran a finger down the page. "The Prince-Bishop's bailiff found more than two score plants and roots," he said, squinting at the page, "as well as pots of ointments. And there were bags filled with powders of various colours." He looked up. "If these are not potions for poisoning and hexing, what are they?"

"Medicines for healing."

"Those who use herbs for cures do so only through a pact with the Devil," said Lindner, "either explicit or implicit." The physician's oily face glowed in the torchlight.

dancing in the palm of his hand

"I have no pact with the Devil," she said firmly.

Hampelmann stabbed a finger at the page. "What about the ointment the bailiff found, the one with the colour and odour of human flesh?"

The woman's face crinkled in puzzlement, then cleared. "Oh, that's just a salve made from lard and goat's milk. It smells like goats, not men." She smiled grimly. "Well, I suppose some men smell like that."

Chancellor Brandt was clearly not amused. "What about the stone shaped like a heart?" he said. "The stone that hung above your doorway?"

"I found that stone when I was a girl, while I was walking by the river. My mother had just been taken away by the Prince-Bishop's bailiff."

"The charges against her?" said Father Streng.

"Witchcraft."

The commissioners nodded knowingly to each other. Lutz rubbed his thumb over a smudge on his ledger. He'd warned Frau Lamm not to speak of that, told her that being the daughter of a suspected witch was damning evidence. She'd grinned into his face, bubbles of spit at the corners of her mouth, and said she was as good as dead anyway.

"I found that stone while I was praying," she continued, "and my mother was released a few days later. So you see, the stone was a gift from the Holy Mother. It hangs above the door so that no evil can enter my household."

"And what about the evil that comes from your household?" said Judge Steinbach, rubbing the swollen knuckles on his right hand.

"There is no evil in my household. I use herbs and potions to heal, not harm. And, sir, if you would have your maidservant prepare for you a tea made from the root of Solomon's Seal, the pain in your hands would ease."

"Or he'd die," said Lindner.

The judge shrank away from the table and pulled his gnarled hands into his lap.

"Have you ever heard of *Der Hexenhammer*, Frau Lamm?" said Father Streng. "It was written long ago, before you, or even your mother, were born, by men of God who knew the evil of witches." He smoothed the quill with his fingertips. "It says that no one does more harm to the Catholic Faith than midwives. And Fraulein Spatz has intimated that you do harm others."

"The bitch lies."

Lutz raised a warning hand to silence Frau Lamm, then turned to the priest. "*Bitte*, Father Streng, that is not quite correct. Fraulein Spatz maintained that both she and Frau Lamm are innocent."

"As you *ought* to recall, Herr Lutz," said Chancellor Brandt, "by the end of the questioning, Fraulein Spatz had begun to cast doubt upon her own innocence as well as Frau Lamm's. And now, please allow us to continue the questioning. Without interruption."

Lutz placed an elbow on the table and rested his chin in his hand. As a student, he'd been taught that a defence lawyer was supposed to interrupt, to correct and clarify, to challenge. Never before had he attended a hearing where the defence lawyer was told to remain silent. It was exasperating. Frau Lamm might be guilty, but he strongly suspected Fraulein Spatz was not. How could they ever discover that if they allowed no contrary evidence to be presented? Now he understood why Father Herzeim had said that evidence wouldn't matter.

"Fraulein Spatz said that you told her the baby would be born dead," said Father Streng. "How did you know that?"

"She'd felt no movement for weeks, and her skin was sallow. It showed in her eyes. I did nothing to harm that child."

"But it was born dead."

"Some babies are stillborn. Sometimes it is no one's fault."

Father Streng's eyes widened behind his spectacles. "That is heresy, Frau Lamm. A child's death is always someone's fault. The sin of the mother, or the father, visited upon the child. Or the work of witches."

Lutz thought uneasily of Maria and his own dead child. He was certain his gentle wife had done nothing to bring harm to a baby. Had he? What sin could he have committed that was worth the life of a child? Or was it witchcraft? Maria had gone to midwives for help in conceiving. She'd worn bundles of herbs tied in muslin, suspended between her breasts for months at a time. Could she have been bewitched rather than helped?

"I did not harm that child." Frau Lamm stood, unmoving, not a sway or even a tremble.

"There are witnesses who say they heard a child crying that night," said Chancellor Brandt.

"It must have been some other child. Ursula Spatz's baby was born dead."

"Why was everything so secret?" Judge Steinbach's voice rose in a petulant whine.

"The girl is quite large. No one knew she was carrying a child, not even the father." Frau Lamm ran her tongue over her sharp teeth. "May he live to receive the reward he so richly deserves."

Father Streng's quill came to an abrupt halt. "You would threaten Herr Zwingen? Now, in this chamber?"

"*Nein*," said the midwife. "There is no need. The Holy Mother will see to his punishment, since the earthly authorities will not. I think she is not so sweet as many would claim."

"Punishment?" said Father Streng.

"Fraulein Spatz's employer forced her."

"The evidence indicates otherwise," said Lindner. "A child was conceived."

"*Ja*, a child was conceived." Frau Lamm stared at the

physician until he blinked and looked away. "And the child was a bastard," she said. "Fraulein Spatz was planning to take it to the Julius Hospital to be cared for as an orphan."

"Or perhaps she was planning to use it in your foul rituals," said Judge Steinbach.

"We have no rituals."

Lindner ran a palm over his shiny pate, his fingers stopping at the fringe of sandy hair. "The Lower City Council has ordered that midwives report the births of all illegitimate children to the proper authorities. Why did you not do so?"

"The child was born dead."

"Even more reason," huffed the physician, "why the birth – and death – should have been reported. It makes the death all the more suspicious."

"I did not harm that child." Frau Lamm studied the pulley on the ceiling. "It is possible, I suppose, that Fraulein Spatz sought out some other midwife to give her a potion to kill the child in her womb. But not me. I do not do that."

"But you know of these potions?" said Lindner.

"I know of them. But I do not use them."

Lutz suspected otherwise. When he visited her cell, the midwife had spoken bitterly about Fraulein Spatz and her plight. Lutz doubted that Frau Lamm would have any qualms whatsoever about helping unwed girls who'd sinned. She'd even intimated that many in that predicament had been forced, or lied to. All that talk of wombs and private things had made Lutz even more uneasy. Despite the chill in the cell, his forehead and palms had run with sweat. The back of his linen shirt was soaked by the time he and Father Herzeim left.

"Could Fraulein Spatz have smothered the infant when your back was turned?" said Chancellor Brandt.

"*Nein*," the midwife said wearily. "The boy was dead when it came from her womb."

"And that is the truth?" said Hampelmann.

"That is the truth. I swear it."

Chancellor Brandt nodded at Freude. "Show her the first instrument of torture."

The executioner reached for the thumbscrews. Frau Lamm drew back, then stepped forward, her face close to Freude's. "Show me anything you like, you bastard, but you'll not frighten me, or torture me, into saying anything but the truth."

"Watch your tongue," snapped Chancellor Brandt. "And show proper respect for your betters."

"He's a better?" Frau Lamm laughed out loud.

Freude cuffed her on the back of the head so that she stumbled forward into the curve of the table where Judge Steinbach sat. He pushed back his chair so quickly he nearly fell backwards. The executioner grabbed her wrists and pulled her back to the centre of the chamber. The plume on the judge's hat bobbed with each laboured breath.

"Did you harm that child?" said Hampelmann.

"*Nein.*"

"Or any child?"

"*Nein.*"

"Have you harmed anyone with your herbs and potions?" said Lindner.

Freude held the thumbscrews close to her face.

"*Nein,*" she snarled.

"When did you first meet with the Devil?" said Father Streng.

"Never."

"When and where did you attend the sabbath?"

"Never."

Hampelmann held up his open ledger in both hands. "How did you know Frau Basser, Fraulein Stolzberger, and Frau Imhof?"

"I did not know them."

He slammed the ledger on the table. Judge Steinbach jumped

and put a hand to his heart. "Then why did all three name you as an accomplice?" said Hampelmann.

"I do not know."

"You do not know?" said Chancellor Brandt. "Three condemned witches name you as an accomplice, and you don't know why?" He slowly crossed his arms over the medallion on his chest. "I believe that you do know. Herr Freude, take her back to her cell and let her contemplate truth. Before you leave, Frau Lamm, take a good look at the tools in this chamber. I believe you shall come to know them all quite intimately."

Ignoring Chancellor Brandt's instructions, the midwife stared into the face of each commissioner. Every man, even the chancellor and the executioner, looked away before she did. Chancellor Brandt's face reddened. "Take her away," he shouted, "and bring in the young man."

Straining to draw breath, Lutz tugged at the tight starched collar Maria had tied around his neck that morning. He felt as if a hand were clamped over his mouth and nose. The midwife had sucked up all the air. Lutz cracked open the door behind him and gulped fresh air like a man drowning. When his breathing and heartbeat had slowed, he pushed the door closed and turned back to the table.

Chancellor Brandt was scowling. "That door must remain closed during the hearings, Herr Lutz. For everyone's protection, these proceedings must be kept secret."

"I desperately needed fresh air."

"Witches do have a way of poisoning the air around them," Father Streng said sympathetically.

Witches. Poisoning the air. Everything pointed to Frau Lamm's guilt: the Devil's mark, her suspicious name and lineage, her sharp tongue, her knowledge of herbs and potions, the death of the baby. There was nothing Lutz could do to help her. And he shouldn't. If she was in league with the Devil, she deserved to die – despite whatever Father Herzeim might say about bringing a sinner back to God. The midwife was a menace to them all.

Lutz brought his pomander to his nose and breathed in the spicy fragrance of sweet marjoram. And if Frau Lamm was guilty, there was no reason he had to go back to her cell. Ever.

Freude returned with Herr Silberhans. Lutz pretended to study his ledger. He'd learned the routine by now: the accused walking backwards, the oath, the same questions asked over and over again, the bald nakedness, the searching for Devil's marks in the most private of places. It was no longer quite so shocking, although Chancellor Brandt and Freude did seem startled to hear what Lutz had already learned from questioning the young man in his cell. Silberhans was from a wealthy family in Augsburg.

The slender youth stood before them. His penis hung pale and limp, shrunk with fear. Freude searched every inch of his body. "A few scrapes, ordinary moles, and boyhood scars," he finally announced. "Nothing suspicious." He did not call upon the physician's expertise nor pull out his consecrated needle to prick any marks. Freude handed the linen shift back to Silberhans and allowed the young man to cover himself before he gently bound his wrists.

Hampelmann began the second round of questioning. "Herr Silberhans, you have been accused by known witches of being an accomplice. Moreover, there have been reports to the *Malefizamt* that you have publicly questioned the procedures of the Commission of Inquisition for the Würzburg Court. What do you say to these charges?"

"I deny them. And whatever coward has made them, let him accuse me to my face."

"Not possible," said Hampelmann. "The three witches are burning in hell. And as for the others, it would be too dangerous to bring them here."

"Too dangerous?" Lutz blurted.

"Of course," said Hampelmann. "If the accused sees them, or even knows their names, he could lay a curse upon them. For that reason, the *Malefizamt* never releases the names of those who make reports."

"Never?" Lutz said. "Even to me?"

"Especially to you…and Herr Silberhans."

"Are you telling me that Herr Silberhans cannot confront those who've made such serious charges against him?" Lutz could hear the rising pitch and volume of his own voice. "And that I can't have their names to question them, even though these people may have base motives for speaking ill of Herr Silberhans?"

"Too dangerous, Herr Lutz," said Father Streng.

Lutz threw up his hands. "What kind of trial is this?"

Father Streng laid down his quill. "This is a preliminary inquisition, Herr Lutz, not a trial. The strict rules of a trial do not apply. And do not forget Jean Bodin's admonition: *The proof of such crimes is so obscure and so difficult that not one witch in a million would be accused or punished if the procedure were governed by ordinary rules.*"

Lutz pressed the heels of his hands into his eyes. This was like no legal proceeding he'd ever known. No rules of evidence, testimony from disreputable witnesses was considered legally acceptable, and now this: the accused could not confront his accusers. As a defence lawyer his efforts were futile. He could not possibly protect this young man, who, Lutz was almost certain, was innocent of any crime.

"As a student of the law, Herr Silberhans," said Father Streng, "you must be aware of the writings of the Jesuit, Martin Delrio."

"Certainly," Silberhans said quietly.

"Ah, but you seem to have forgotten Delrio's specific words." Father Streng picked up a small knife and sharpened his quill. "*No one is to urge judges to desist from prosecution. It is an* indicium *of witchcraft to defend witches, or to affirm that witch stories which are told as certain are mere deceptions or illusions…Anyone who pronounces against the death sentence is reasonably suspected of secret complicity.*"

"I have never defended witches. Nor opposed the death sentence for witches."

"You're a student of Father Herzeim's," said Hampelmann. "Is that correct?"

"*Ja.*"

"Could it be that you merely repeated, without thinking, what one of your professors said about witchcraft, or about the commission's procedures?"

Lutz jerked to attention. Now it made sense, what Hampelmann had said to him when they returned from dinner, warning Lutz to be careful about seeking advice from a sceptic and heretic. He'd meant Father Herzeim. Hampelmann was using Silberhans to get at a man he considered to be a dangerous sceptic.

Lutz willed the young man to use his wits. Silberhans had to know that if he said no, he was condemning himself. Yet, if he said yes and blamed Father Herzeim, he would be accusing the priest of heresy, and, by extension, condemning himself as well, by admitting he'd repeated the heresy.

"My accusers are quite mistaken when they claim I have spoken in defence of witches," said Silberhans. "I condemn them with all of my body, heart, and soul. And with my spoken words. I do not know what man my accusers heard defending witches or criticizing the commission, for it was not I. Perhaps they were deceived and prompted by the Devil to accuse an innocent man. As to Father Herzeim, I have never heard him speak of witches or witchcraft. Nor have I ever heard him instruct any man to question the authority or teachings of the Church."

Lutz breathed out. Smart boy.

"Father Herzeim never mentions Johann Weyer or Adam

Tanner?" Hampelmann spat the names as if they were bitter fruit on his tongue.

Silberhans pressed his lips together. "Who?"

Lutz rubbed his forehead. Silberhans was feigning ignorance, and not very well. The commissioners, especially Father Streng and Hampelmann, would never believe that a law student at the University of Würzburg did not know the names of the two most infamous sceptics.

"How did you know Frau Basser, Fraulein Stolzberger, and Frau Imhof?" said Hampelmann.

"I did not know them," said Silberhans. "I believe it is as the great French lawyer, Jean Bodin, has written: *It cannot be denied that witches occasionally conspire maliciously to accuse a totally innocent person of complicity in their crimes.*"

"Have you forgotten Bodin's next sentence?" Father Streng shot back. "*But in such cases, Almighty God has invariably revealed the innocence of such persons in a miraculous manner.*" He smirked at the youth. "By what miraculous manner will Almighty God reveal your innocence?"

"I cannot know the mind of God, but I believe he will find a way to reveal my innocence, precisely because I am innocent."

Father Streng took off his spectacles and polished them on his cassock. "You have indicated, Herr Silberhans, that you are familiar with *Disquisitionum Magicarum*, in which Delrio proved that to doubt witchcraft was not only wrong but heretical."

"I have never doubted the existence of witches."

"So you are familiar with Martin Delrio and Jean Bodin," said the priest, "but have never heard of Johann Weyer or Adam Tanner?"

Silberhans' face paled. "I-I may have heard of them, but I've never read them. I believe they are heretical sceptics."

Father Streng placed his spectacles back on his nose. "You indicated before that you did not even know who they are."

"I-I have so rarely heard their names…and never read their work. I had forgotten them."

"Forgotten?" said Hampelmann.

There was a long silence. The logs settled in the wire basket. Lutz wanted desperately to intervene, but what could he say?

Finally, Judge Steinbach spoke. "Have you obeyed the Prince-Bishop's decrees regarding attending mass and confession?"

"*Ja.*"

"I've spoken with his parish priest," Lutz said quickly, before he could be cut off, "and what Herr Silberhans says is true. He attends mass and goes to confession, more often than His Grace's decrees would require."

Freude stepped within the curve of the table opposite Judge Steinbach. The other commissioners leaned forward. "I can find nothing about the young man to indicate that he is a witch, or even a defender of witches," said the executioner, his voice hushed. "*Der Hexenhammer* does say that witchcraft is primarily a woman's crime." His voice dropped even lower. "And Herr Silberhans is from a respected, and well-connected, family in Augsburg. If he's executed, there will be hell to pay in Würzburg."

"*Nein,*" said Father Streng. "It doesn't matter what family he's from. If he's guilty and he's not executed, there will be a real hell to pay, for all of us." He tapped the nib of the quill on the ledger. "Herr Silberhans should be brought back and tortured. If he is innocent, torture will reveal that."

"Tortured on the basis of what evidence?" said Lutz. "We cannot ignore the principle of *constare de delicto* in the Carolina Code." He thumbed through his ledger. "Here it is: *No person may be examined under torture unless sufficient evidence has first been found of the criminal act being investigated.*" He slammed the ledger closed. "For Herr Silberhans, there are only the accusations made by condemned witches. And unnamed persons who assert that he questioned the commission's procedures."

"Very serious charges," said Hampelmann. "Those students were so alarmed they reported Herr Silberhans directly to the *Malefizamt*. And although he denies it, I think he has been reading Weyer and Tanner. I, for one, do not believe that he merely *forgot* the names of those heretics."

"Nor do I," said Father Streng.

"There is no evidence," Lutz insisted. He began counting on his fingers. "No Devil's mark. No mysterious deaths. No claims that he's made anyone or their livestock ill. No charges that he's conjured bad weather. No herbs or potions found in his quarters. Not even any questionable literature there. There are absolutely no grounds for torturing this young man."

"Even so," said Hampelmann, "there is still the question of why all three witches denounced Herr Silberhans as an accomplice."

"Ach, a clear case of malicious conspiracy," Freude said authoritatively. "If witches can foretell the future, surely they can conspire…even when they can't talk to each other."

Judge Steinbach chewed his lip. "Herr Freude has had more experience with witches than any of us. And the boy is from a respected family in Augsburg. What say the rest of you?"

"We must recommend release," Lutz shouted.

"Release," said Freude. Lindner raised a hand to indicate agreement, and Chancellor Brandt gave a small reluctant nod. Father Streng and Hampelmann shook their heads.

Judge Steinbach tapped the gavel. "The decision is made then. Father Streng, draft a report to the Prince-Bishop recommending release for Herr Silberhans."

The young man looked as if he might faint with relief.

"The report should also recommend that Herr Silberhans be expelled from Würzburg," Father Streng said acidly.

"Agreed," said Chancellor Brandt.

"Nonetheless," said Father Streng, "the young man should not be released without a strong admonition." He picked up his breviary and walked toward Silberhans, who shrank away from the small priest.

"You have indicated that you are familiar with the writing of Jean Bodin," said Father Streng. "Do you recall what he wrote about craving knowledge?"

"He wrote that the c-craving for knowledge can lead to bl-blasphemy," Silberhans said, his voice small and shaking, "since any man who could explain the reason for all things would be the equal to God, who alone has knowledge of all things."

Father Streng's thin lips curved into a smile. "Very good, Herr Silberhans. Bodin also wrote that those who call into question things that cannot be explained according to the laws of physics are blinded by arrogance." He began pacing, his breviary clasped behind his back. "The best proof against witches is that the infallible law of God expressly condemns them. And only those, as Bodin himself would say: *who balance everything on the point of a needle and doubt whether the sun is bright, or ice cold, or fire hot, could doubt the existence of witches.*"

The priest pointed the breviary at Silberhans. "It is no less a form of atheism to doubt the existence of witches than to doubt the existence of God."

Hampelmann stood. "*And those who seek deliberately, by means of printed books, to excuse and to redeem witches…are themselves led by Satan's halter.* That's also from Jean Bodin, and—"

Father Streng spoke quickly, interrupting Hampelmann. "Do not forget the names Johann Weyer and Adam Tanner. They are the Devil's own specially appointed men, who write and teach that all that is said of witches is but fairytales and fancy. Do not be so foolish as to follow those who are led by the Devil."

"*N-nein*, Father, I will not."

"And do not forget," said Hampelmann, "that we are recommending release only because there is a lack of evidence,

Herr Silberhans. Not because you have been found innocent."

"Herr Freude," Chancellor Brandt said wearily, "return Herr Silberhans to his cell and bring us Frau Rosen."

Freude scratched at his crotch. "And the girl?"

"Not yet."

18

>

22 April 1626

Eva leaned against the wall, her neck and shoulders taut, her head aching where it had been slammed against stone. Katharina lay listless in her lap, her fingers trailing over her scalp again and again, as if she could not believe her white-blond hair was gone.

Earlier, Eva had heard footsteps passing on the stairs outside the door, at least two sets going up, as many or more coming down. She'd heard no voices, though. Whoever had passed by, had passed in silence.

The sound of footsteps had paralysed Eva, so that even her heart stopped beating. Her greatest hope was that Herr Lutz would come to take her before the commission so she could prove her innocence and be set free. But even as she hoped, she was terrified that Freude would return. She was ugly now, but to a man like him, her ugliness and her revolting stink would offer no protection.

Eva heard footsteps approaching, at least two sets, one light and quick, the other slow and shuffling, and perhaps a third. She crouched closer to the wall, but the footsteps did not stop. They climbed past her door.

She longed for the comfort of her Bible, to cradle the soft leather in her hands, to smell it, to turn the fragile pages, and read again the story of Job, the story of how God allowed the Devil to test Job, and of how he suffered. Job was a good and righteous man, a prosperous man, yet he lost everything: his sons and daughters, his cattle and land, his health. Everything. Except his faith. Perhaps, like Job, she was being tested. And like God's faithful servant, she would be steadfast. In the end, her life would be restored. Like Job's. But would she have to lose Katharina?

The rasp of the key. She shuddered with hope. And terror. And tried to see who was behind the door before it swung open. Freude filled the doorway. He held ropes and a birch rod. Frau Brugler stood behind him.

Eva tried to pull Katharina closer, but the girl scooted across the floor like a spider, then pressed herself against the wall. Without a word, the jailer's wife unlocked Eva's shackles. The man came toward her. The smell of him, and her own fear, made her gasp for air. He grabbed her arm with his gloved hand and pulled her to her feet. Her legs were so weak she could hardly stand. He bound her wrists and shoved her through the door, using the rod to prod her down the dark winding staircase, the steps so narrow and smooth she nearly slipped. They descended past two wooden doors before they finally reached the bottom of the stairs. He poked her in the back. "Turn around."

Confused, Eva hesitated.

"Turn around, you bitch. You can't see them 'til after they see you."

The man pushed the door open and prodded Eva in the stomach. She stepped backwards into the dimly lit chamber. Light and shadow flickered on grey stone walls. The bright bulbous eyes of a rat shone from a crevice between two stones. The man prodded Eva again. She turned and faced the men sitting at the table: Judge Steinbach; Chancellor Brandt; a boyish looking priest with a brown quill poised above a ledger; a plump freckle-faced man wearing a physician's loose robes; Herr Lutz, smiling as if his round belly ached. And Wilhelm Hampelmann. Eva nearly collapsed with relief. Wilhelm knew her. He had to know she wasn't a witch. Under his cool gaze, however, Eva's relief turned to shame. Her scalp was as smooth as an egg, her feet bare, the shift dirty, her breasts visible through the thin linen, and she carried the same rank odour as the man who had brought her there.

"Father Streng," said the judge.

Holding a large wooden crucifix before him, the priest stepped forward. "By the belief that you have in God," he said, "and in the expectation of paradise, and being aware of the peril of your soul's eternal damnation, do you swear that the testimony you are about to give is true, such that you are willing to exchange heaven for hell should you tell a lie?"

"I swear, by all that is holy, to tell the truth."

Father Streng took his seat at the table and picked up the brown quill. "State your name and age."

"Frau Eva Rosen, age 37."

"Date of birth," said the priest, still writing.

"March 2, 1589." In the wavering torchlight, Eva could see iron pincers hanging on the wall. Ropes and birch rods were piled on wooden shelves, which also held thumbscrews and other instruments she didn't recognize. Stone weights were lined up beneath the shelves. A huge wooden wheel stood off to one side. Her throat went dry; her tongue felt thick.

"Parents," said Chancellor Brandt.

"Joseph and Anna Hirsch."

"From Würzburg?" said the judge.

"*Ja.*"

"And are they still in Würzburg?" The judge's voice shook as much as the gavel in his hands.

"They passed away when I was a child."

"How did they die?" asked Chancellor Brandt. Father Streng looked up from his ledger, his face curious.

"Plague. I was eight."

"Who raised you then?" said Chancellor Brandt.

"I was taken to the Julius Hospital. I lived there for two years until the Prioress of the Unterzell Convent chose me from among the other girls to be a maidservant for the nuns. Her intention was that I should become a nun myself."

"Quite obviously, you didn't," said Father Streng.

"I lived and worked at the convent for six years, until–"

Hampelmann interrupted. "Frau Rosen, do you know why you've been brought here?"

The chancellor and the priest exchanged puzzled glances. Eva, too, was bewildered. Why had Wilhelm stopped her from telling them she'd worked in his father's household?

"False accusations have been made against me," she said.

Hampelmann persisted. "How did you know Fraulein Stolzberger, Frau Imhof, and Frau Basser?" His voice was cold, as if he were angry, or didn't know who she was.

Eva tried to imagine her Bible in her hands, the image of the Holy Mother before her. She must be like Job, always faithful, always truthful. "I did not know them," she said. "Frau Basser came to my bakery now and again. But that is all. I hardly even spoke to her."

"You did not know them, yet all of them made accusations against you?" said Chancellor Brandt. "Do not forget, Frau Rosen, that you have sworn to tell the truth."

"That is the truth, sir."

Hampelmann studied his ledger. "How do you explain Herr Kaiser's becoming ill just after he registered a complaint against you with the Lower City Council?"

"I don't even know Herr Kaiser."

"But you knew of the complaint," said Hampelmann.

"I was informed."

"He nearly died, Frau Rosen," said the physician. His prominent red nose reminded Eva of a pig's snout.

"I know nothing about that," she said.

"And your husband did die," said Hampelmann. "Suddenly, and quite mysteriously. How do you explain that?"

"I do not know why Jacob died. No one, not even the

physician, could explain it. He was old. Nearly sixty." Eva lifted her bound hands. "And never did I wish it so. That is the truth. I swear it."

"When a patient's illness is very hard to diagnose," said the physician, "so that the physician himself is in doubt, then witchcraft can be presumed."

"Just because people become ill or die mysteriously, even if it is due to witchcraft, that hardly proves that Frau Rosen is responsible," said Lutz. "All of it could be the work of someone else…one of the witches who was just executed, for example."

Father Streng pointed his quill at Lutz. "Motive, Herr Lutz, motive. Who else would have wanted Herr Kaiser or Herr Rosen dead?"

"I never wished my husband dead!"

Freude poked Eva with the birch rod. "You are not to speak except to answer questions."

"How long were you married, Frau Rosen?" said Father Streng.

"Nine years."

"Nine years and only one child? Were you a good and obedient wife to your husband?"

"*Ja.*"

"Did you make charms and wear them to prevent conceiving?" said the physician, his pig's snout snuffling. "Or to make your husband unable to perform his husbandly duties."

"*Nein!*"

"Did you take herbs or go to a midwife to do away with a child already conceived?" said Hampelmann.

"*Nein.* It was God's will that I should bear no more children." Eva tried to meet Wilhelm's eyes, but he stared at his ledger. Why was he asking these questions, as if he thought she might actually be guilty of such crimes?

"Why have you not remarried?" said Hampelmann. He

looked at her then, his face hard. "There must be some man who wants you."

"There is no man I have wanted."

"No man you have wanted?" Hampelmann tilted his head back and looked down his nose at her. "Why have you not followed the orders of the Lower City Council and chosen a guardian to manage the Rosen Bakery?"

"The nuns taught me my numbers. I can manage my own financial affairs."

"But that means you, a woman, are telling your journeymen what to do," said Father Streng. "A violation of God's ordained order."

"What about the other evidence, Frau Rosen?" said Chancellor Brandt. "The strange rocks and white feathers."

"Those are my daughter's, a few things she's collected."

"These items belong to your daughter?" said the chancellor.

"A child's play things," said Lutz. "They're harmless."

"Don't be so sure," said Father Streng. "The daughter herself is suspicious." He squinted at Eva from behind his spectacles. "Doesn't the girl have a defect?"

"Her left foot is misshapen."

"That's either a *stigma diaboli*. Or a sign of the sinfulness of the mother. Which is it, Frau Rosen?"

Eva had to look away from the priest's pale eyes, which appeared huge, and floating, behind the circles of glass. "Katharina is innocent. Her foot is not a Devil's mark. My daughter bears the mark of my sin. I allowed myself to be seduced before I was married."

"To be seduced?" said Hampelmann. "Or did the seducing yourself?"

"I was seduced," Eva said firmly. "But I confessed that sin and was granted absolution. I have lived chastely since. Katharina's foot has nothing to do with witchcraft."

"Frau Rosen," said the physician, "did you have intercourse during your menses? That can cause deformities."

"I did not choose to."

Chancellor Brandt glanced at Freude. "Search her."

Freude loosened the laces at Eva's neck, then untied her wrists and tugged at the shift. Eva pulled her arms into her chest, her hands gripping the linen. He grabbed the neck of the shift in both hands, ripped the thin cloth, and tore it from her body. Stunned, Eva tried to cover herself with her arms and hands. Her face burned. She could not breathe. Not even her husband had seen her completely naked. And Wilhelm was there, watching her humiliation, doing nothing to protect her.

Her knees buckled, and she collapsed onto the cold floor. Freude pulled a chair to the centre of the chamber, lifted her to her feet, and placed her hands on the back of the chair. Then he started touching her, his gloved hands moving over her skin, poking and prodding. She clenched her teeth to stop the screams in her throat. Unable to look into the men's faces, she watched the torchlight dance across the stone floor.

After what seemed an eternity, Freude said, "Herr Doktor Lindner, would you assist in the examination?"

The physician came toward her. "Where did you get this," he said, peering at her thigh.

"An accident with the razor," said Freude. "She fought me while I was shaving her."

To Eva's horror, Freude forced her to bend over, then touched her where he'd shaved her, in the most private of places, the rod probing. She could hear her heart thudding, her own blood rushing in her ears. The light dimmed, then brightened, then dimmed again. The contents of her stomach rose, too quickly. The vile broth splashed onto the stone floor.

With a disgusted frown at the putrid pool, Freude jerked her upright and handed her the torn shift, which she hastily wrapped around herself. Lindner walked back to his chair. "I can find no blemish, no mark," said the physician.

Freude flashed a knife blade in Eva's face, then cut a length of hemp from a long coil and tied it around her to keep the torn shift closed. Eva tried not to inhale his hateful greasy stink. "I do not think," he said, pulling the rope so tight it cut into her waist, "that means the woman is innocent." He bound her wrists.

"I agree," said Father Streng. "We all know what Jean Bodin has written about the absence of the *stigma diaboli*. The Devil needs to mark only those accomplices whose loyalty he cannot trust. Frau Rosen may enjoy a special trust, such that she needs no mark."

Lutz jumped up. "But didn't we just recommend release for Herr Silberhans because he had no mark?"

"True, Herr Silberhans had no mark," said Hampelmann, "but there was no other evidence against him."

"Frau Rosen, do you still deny the charges against you?" said Chancellor Brandt.

"I am innocent."

"Show her the first instrument of torture."

Freude lifted the thumbscrews from a shelf. He held them close to her face. Her vision blurred. Her bowels churned. The stink of her own vomit made her gag. From a great distance, she heard the chancellor say, "Repeat the questions."

Hampelmann stepped toward her. "How did you know Frau Imhof, Frau Basser, and Fraulein Stolzberger?"

He regarded her coldly, as if she were a stranger, or even worse, a contemptible beggar. Was he still angry, after nearly twelve years?

"I did not know them."

"Where and when did you attend the sabbath?"

"I have never been to a sabbath."

"How did you make Herr Kaiser ill?"

"I had nothing to do with his illness."

"How did you kill your husband?" Hampelmann gave a slight nod toward Freude, who lifted Eva's bound hands and laid them on the cold polished metal.

She gulped back a whimper. "I did not kill Jacob."

"How do you use white feathers and coloured rocks in your rituals?" said Hampelmann.

"I have no rituals. I am not a witch. You know that."

His eyes held the hard glint and impenetrable depth of blue ice, and Eva understood now that he would not help her, not now, not ever. Wilhelm hated her.

"Then why is your daughter crippled?" he said.

"My sin," she whispered. "She suffers for my sin."

"Record her as taciturn," he said brusquely.

Chancellor Brandt brought his gold pomander to his nose. "Take her back to her cell, Herr Freude. If she's not more forthcoming when we question her again, we will be forced to bring in the child."

19

꒰

22 April 1626

Hampelmann stepped out from the darkness just as the Angelus bells started to ring. He blinked in the bright sunlight, then turned toward Saint Kilian's Cathedral and made the sign of the cross, grateful to be free, finally, of the dank chamber's chill and the sour stink of the executioner and the prisoners. His gratitude was tempered, however, by the fact that no carriage awaited him. A fortnight earlier his physician had held a cup of his urine to the light, swirled it, and pronounced that Hampelmann still had an excess of black bile. He'd then prescribed at least two miles of walking daily, in addition to hellebore in his pomander, and teas brewed from feverfew and St. John's wort gathered on a Friday in the hour of Jupiter, the herbs to be obtained only from a licensed apothecary, never a midwife. So now Hampelmann, weary though he was, would have to walk from the Prisoners' Tower to the marketplace before retiring to his home. Such a bother.

Placing his broad-brimmed hat firmly on his head and tucking his ledger under his arm, he began his trek, crossing *Neubaustrasse* to *Dommerschulstrasse*. He made a wide arc around the ragged beggars clustered near the arched gate of the university. Not wide enough. A hump-backed old woman limped toward him, her toothless gums mouthing pathetic entreaties. He tossed a *pfennig* at her so she wouldn't come close enough to touch him with her filthy clawing hand.

Beauty. His whole being craved beauty. He recalled a small, but charming courtyard along the route to the marketplace. He hurried toward it, striding quickly and resolutely past throngs of beggars and stray dogs. Two of the curs were locked in flagrant coitus. A circle of grubby children had formed around them, pointing and laughing. Disgusted, Hampelmann averted his eyes.

When he finally arrived at the courtyard, he sighed with relief. He leaned against the stone fence and embraced the garden's beauty: the shiny yellow flowers, the fragrant white ones, and the bell-like blooms dangling from a gracefully arched stem. The unopened buds were pinkish, the open ones blue. Borage, that's what it was called. Maybe. He wasn't sure. Helena would know, just as she would know the names of the yellow flowers and the white ones, and the buds that had not yet opened. His wife would know the name of the handsome bird, with the rusty face and breast, that warbled from the cherry tree. Helena had time and leisure to learn the names of flowers and birds, to walk among them, to meditate on beauty. She could read poetry: Martin Opitz, and the lyrical couplets of Würzburg's own poet, Walter von der Vogelweide. Burdened by duty, Hampelmann had time only to visit the poet's grave in the Lusam Garden, and there, to meditate on his personal defects and to struggle to write his own mediocre couplets. Every hour of his day was devoted to his responsibilities to Würzburg and the Prince-Bishop, his responsibilities to God. He could not afford the time to contemplate what was serene and beautiful and good, but only what was sordid and despicable and ugly.

That hadn't always been so. He touched his fingertips to his mouth and recalled the sweetness of Eva's lips. She'd been beautiful. She was still beautiful. Thinner than he remembered, but then he'd never seen her naked. And she still had those alluring eyes that were brown one moment, green the next, with gold flecks that caught the light. There'd been a time when he could spend hours meditating on the beauty of those eyes, a time when he could believe that Eva was good as well as beautiful.

The nameless bird stopped singing. Hopping closer, it flicked its tail. Excrement fell onto a yellow blossom. Hampelmann turned away and walked slowly toward the marketplace. Eva was like that bird, or one of the Prince-Bishop's canaries, beautiful and blameless on the outside, her voice sweet, but all the while dropping bits of filth all around her. She used her beauty to seduce men, to tempt them, then polluted them with her vile filth. All the men who came to his father's house had wanted her. Hampelmann had seen the yearning in the hungry eyes that followed her when she served the men wine. Throats cleared and words stuttered as their tongues flicked over bloodless lips.

Hampelmann continued on, passing peddlers and merchants closing up their stands for the day. The air was redolent with the stink of rancid pork and spoiled fish, last fall's rotting cabbage. He picked his way carefully around the piles of refuse.

In the middle of the marketplace, locked in the pillory, stood a plump woman in tattered clothes, her age indeterminate because she wore a brightly painted shame mask, so heavy it pulled her head forward. Blasphemy. That's what the sign posted above her said, which Hampelmann had already surmised from the mask's long red tongue.

He turned away from the woman and her monstrous mask, and her equally revolting crime, and gazed upon what he'd come so far to see: the magnificent Mary's Chapel with its tall arched windows and the stone figures of Christ's apostles adorning its outer walls. It had been built upon the site of a former Jewish synagogue. Hampelmann crossed himself. A triumph of the true faith. The chapel's beauty and grace delighted his weary eyes. He studied the intricately carved sandstone figures of Adam and Eve flanking the chapel's south portal. Eve, naked and alluring, yet seemingly innocent, even as she held the apple at her waist, just below her girlishly rounded breast, and the serpent twined up her leg. Just like Eva, thought Hampelmann. Eva, who was still seductive, even when shaved of her chestnut hair and dressed in a shapeless linen shift. Even her name suggested witchcraft: Eva, Eve. The Devil's accomplice, the primordial temptress leading men into sin. The words of *Der Hexenhammer* sprang to his mind. *For though the Devil tempted Eve to sin, yet Eve seduced Adam. And as the sin of Eve would not have brought death to our soul and body unless the sin had afterwards passed onto Adam, to which he was tempted by Eve, not by the Devil; therefore she is more bitter than death...More bitter than death, again, because bodily death is an open and terrible enemy, but woman is a wheedling and secret enemy.*

A secret enemy. Years ago Eva had seduced him into promising her marriage. She allowed his kisses, but rebuffed anything more. So he offered to marry her, and in the daze of lust, almost believed the promise himself. Eva, so accomplished at deception, was not fooled. Hampelmann ground his teeth as he recalled her stance – imperious, hands on hips, as if she were a lady of noble birth – when she reminded him that he was still subject to his father's will and that Herr Doktor Hampelmann would never allow his son to marry a woman of such low birth, a maidservant with no dowry. She did not believe, she said, that he could summon the courage to defy his father and risk his inheritance.

Infuriated by her impertinence and inflamed with desire, he'd pressed himself against her, forcing his mouth on hers, his hands groping. The memory of his own base lust made him wince, but his shame dissipated when he recalled Eva's coy affectation of horror, as if she'd not invited his advances in the first place, as if she were innocent.

Hampelmann spat into the street. Innocence. Feigned innocence. All women were guilty, even the purest, of leading men into sin and ruin. It was as Saint Jerome had written: *woman is the gate of the Devil, the path of wickedness, the sting of the serpent.* And Ecclesiasticus: *For many have perished by the beauty of a woman, and hereby lust is enkindled as a fire.*

The evening breeze off the Main lifted the brim of

Hampelmann's hat and brought to his nose the river's fulsome odour. It was a fine spring evening, yet everything smelled foul: the river, the piles of garbage in the marketplace, the refuse outside the butcher shops, the unwashed bodies passing by. The stench nearly made him gag. He brought his pomander to his nose.

He really should warn Lutz about Eva's seductiveness, let him know just how skilled she was at pretending innocence. Hampelmann turned away from Mary's Chapel and began walking toward his home on *Hofstrasse*. But then he'd have to admit that he'd known Eva, known her quite well, in fact.

Eva's real nature, the lustful eagerness he'd discerned, showed itself soon after his father announced his betrothal to Helena. Within days, Eva went out and seduced a master baker, a vulgar old widower eager to marry. Sinned with him – before they were hastily wed. She'd even admitted as much today, conceding that her daughter's crippled foot was the result of her sin.

A few paces ahead, Hampelmann saw a skinny dog sniffing around the doorway of a closed butcher shop. He was tempted to kick the mangy cur out of his way, a bitch nursing pups by the look of her drooping teats, but he knew she might whirl around and bite him. He gave her a wide berth.

The sun was low in the sky, gilding splendour and squalor alike with its golden glow. He quickened his pace. Helena would have ordered supper to be ready soon, and she pouted when he didn't return home on time. It was a pretty pout, but annoying all the same. She simply didn't understand the importance of his work. She'd ask a question or two, but when he tried to answer, her lovely ivory face would crumple in bewilderment, law being far too complex for even the intelligent female mind.

Yet her questions lingered, dark wrinkles in the smooth white sheets of his logic, and he'd wake in the middle of the night, plagued with doubts, his skin cold and clammy. Was it possible that he and the other commissioners were condemning innocent women? Or was the Devil using Helena to plant these very doubts in his heart? To bolster his resolve, Hampelmann would go to his library to re-read *Der Hexenhammer* and books by Jean Bodin, Peter Binsfeld, Henri Boguet, and Martin Delrio. Sitting within the warm glow of candlelight, he'd remind himself that the popes had blessed and encouraged these very writings. And then there was Father Streng, a Jesuit of formidable intelligence – and absolute certainty about what he knew to be true. His habit of quoting authorities grated, but it also reassured. How could such a brilliant man, quoting other brilliant men, be wrong? Calmed, Hampelmann would return to his bed to sleep a few more hours.

Arriving at the gates of his house, Hampelmann paused a moment to consider the solidity of the stone, a bulwark against the world, a refuge protecting his wife and daughter, who had little comprehension of just how evil the world could be. A docile shepherd trotted close and sat just beyond the gates. The dog neither moved nor made a sound until Hampelmann stepped through and stroked her head. "Good girl, Wache." Such a pleasing and obedient temperament, he thought. So unlike the mongrels that roamed the streets. Perhaps at the next Lower City Council meeting he'd propose that stray dogs be rounded up and killed rather than allowed to roam free to breed more starving curs to harass the citizens of Würzburg and to entertain the beggars with their lascivious behaviour.

He went into the house, the shepherd following close behind. He handed his hat to a doughy-faced maidservant. "Wine, the Stein Silvaner, in the library," he said, trying to hide his disdain for her ugliness. He'd deliberately asked Helena to hire homely maidservants. He wanted no man who entered his household, including himself, ever to be tempted.

Hampelmann walked toward the back of the house, toward the library, Wache at his heels, and pushed open the heavy wooden door. Anna lifted her sweet face from the book in her lap. Now there was beauty: a heart-shaped face, creamy alabaster skin, a delicate, but noble profile.

"Hello, Papa."

He laid the ledger on his desk, then stepped close to her chair. "What are you reading, *Leibchen*?" He stroked her silky hair, which was so pale it was nearly white, the same colour as his own. It was tied back by a blue satin ribbon. A blue satin flower bloomed over one ear. A strand of hair caught between his fingers and came away in his hand. He tucked it into a pocket in the lining of his breeches.

"A book of poetry Mama picked out. Martin Opitz. I don't like it very much." She thrust out her lip petulantly, then quickly pulled it back and looked down into her lap.

"Where is your mother?"

"Out in the garden, trimming dead blooms. I was helping her, but she sent me in here to be out of the sun."

If Helena was still in the garden, thought Hampelmann, supper was not yet ready. There was time for some reading. The maidservant slipped quietly into the room and set a goblet on the desk.

"What did you do today, Papa?"

"Legal business, *Leibchen*. It's complicated, and not for the ears of little girls. Read a bit longer, then we'll have supper."

Pouting prettily, just like her mother, Anna bent her head over the book.

Hampelmann slid a thick leather-bound volume from the shelves and sat down at his desk. Wache lay on the floor beside him. Opening the tabs on *Discours des sorciers* by Henri Boguet, a French lawyer and judge, Hampelmann turned to the worn pages he'd read again and again: *I would yet have it plainly known that I am a sworn enemy to witches, and that I shall never spare them for their execrable abominations and for the countless numbers of them which are seen to increase every day so that it seems that we are now in the time of the Antichrist, since among the signs that are given of his arrival, this is one of the chief, namely, that witchcraft shall be rife throughout the world.*

Hampelmann nodded. Yes, he should not let his concern for protecting the innocent get in the way of extirpating witches. The world was nearing the end-time, and the righteous were at war with evil. This was not the time to be cautious.

He flipped to another well-worn page. It had always puzzled him that witches craved fornication with the Devil, though they invariably described coitus as painful and without pleasure. As his finger trailed down the page, he recalled the lecherous mongrels. *The Devil uses them so because he knows that women love carnal pleasures, and he means to bind them to his allegiance by such agreeable provocations; moreover, there is nothing which makes a woman more subject and loyal to a man than that he should abuse her body.*

Hampelmann turned then to the real reason he'd selected that book from his collection: Boguet's arguments justifying the calling of children as witnesses against their parents. Hampelmann was uneasy that Chancellor Brandt intended to call Eva's daughter to testify against her. Calling children as witnesses, especially when they were required to testify against their own parents, was not permitted in any other kind of legal proceeding. But then again, Boguet argued, the crime of witchcraft was so secret that sometimes the only witnesses were the woman's own children. Boguet even went so far as to recommend the execution of children who confessed to joining their mothers in witchcraft, reasoning that once they were in Satan's clutches they seldom reformed. Hampelmann wasn't so sure. On the one hand, he preferred giving children the benefit of the doubt. If they failed to reform, they could always be executed later, before they'd done too much harm. On the other hand, if Boguet was correct in his estimate that there were nearly two million witches in Europe, *multiplying upon the earth even as worms in a garden*, perhaps the commission should grasp the opportunity to execute them whenever it could, as early as possible.

It would be a mercy really, saving the children from eternal damnation.

Hampelmann studied Anna's profile, her lips moving as she read poetry to herself. So innocent. Could one so young, just ten years old, really be capable of witchcraft? Boguet thought so. And Hampelmann knew that children were conceived and born in sin; it was only the rite of baptism that exorcised the Devil from them. For some, that exorcism was incomplete. Their natures were flawed. Just as women's natures were flawed – even if they weren't witches. It was only after reading *Der Hexenhammer* that Hampelmann fully understood the true nature of women.

He went to the shelf and exchanged *Discours des sorciers* for the Dominicans' manual. He snapped open the tabs and flipped through the pages. Yes, there it was. He squinted to bring the print into focus. *And it should be noted that there was a defect in the formation of the first woman, since she was formed from a bent rib, that is, a rib of the breast, which is bent as it were in a contrary direction to a man. And since through this defect she is an imperfect animal, she always deceives. And it is clear in the case of the first woman that she had little faith...And all this is indicated by the etymology of the word; for* Femina *comes from* Fe *and* Minus, *since she is ever weaker to hold and preserve the faith...Therefore a wicked woman is by her nature quicker to waver in her faith, and consequently quicker to abjure the faith, which is the root of witchcraft...And, indeed, just as through the first defect in their intelligence they are more prone to abjure the faith; so through their second defect of inordinate affections and passions they search for, brood over, and inflict various vengeances, either by witchcraft, or by some other means. Wherefore it is no wonder that so great a number of witches exist in this sex.*

dancing in the palm of his hand

Lifting the goblet, Hampelmann looked again at Anna. How could he keep her from growing up to be deceptive and lustful? He'd already noticed hints of a coy seductiveness and a bold outspokenness – and had moved at once to quash these tendencies. He disciplined his daughter severely whenever she spoke a sharp or defiant word, smiled flirtatiously, or flashed her pale blue eyes. He'd have no sharp-tongued harpy or seductress in his household. He held before his daughter the image of the Holy Mother, a genuinely pious woman, a silent woman. And his efforts seemed to be bearing fruit. Anna was learning to keep her eyes modestly down-turned, her smile demure, her voice soft, and to speak only when addressed.

Hampelmann was also reassured by the fact that there'd been no sin to taint Anna's birth. True, he was chagrined that she was born almost nine months to the day after he and Helena were married. Their lust made public. But there'd been no sin. He and Helena had waited. And now he struggled to keep his lust strictly in check, as did Helena. They loved chastely, in the way God intended, a model for Anna to follow.

Reaching down to stroke Wache's head, Hampelmann caught a thumbnail on his breeches. He took a small knife from the drawer and pared the ragged nail. There was no fire in the hearth, so he tucked the paring into the pocket that held Anna's strand of hair. With so many witches around, he was scrupulous about disposing of nail parings as well as hair and clippings from his beard. Anything that could possibly be used in a charm against him or his family went into the flames.

He rested his elbows on the desk and felt himself slipping into a familiar despondency. It was occurring more and more often lately. No matter how many miles he walked, no matter what teas the maidservant prepared, his melancholy hovered nearby, always at the ready to enclose him like a dark shroud. It made him feel fatigued and listless, unable to carry out his duties with his former zeal.

Hoping to find a cure, he'd read widely about the condition, finding comfort in Aristotle's observation that a certain amount of cold black bile was necessary for genius. It had pained him, though, to read that Saint Thomas Aquinas considered melancholia a sickness of the soul and believed that a melancholic's despair suggested that he was not sufficiently suffused with joy at the certain knowledge of God's divine love and mercy. Now, during his morning prayers and meditations, Hampelmann prayed for a stronger faith, prayed to know joy. But his melancholy clung tenaciously, black bile flowing through his body.

He'd also read Robert Burton's *Anatomy of Melancholy*. Despite his being an Anglican clergyman and, therefore, in some ways heretical, Burton's contention that miseries encompass life and that it is folly to look for perpetual happiness made sense to Hampelmann. He also found agreeable Burton's observation that the disposition of melancholy men brought about a kind of *enthusiasmus* that caused them to be excellent philosophers, poets, and prophets. But Burton's recommendations to "open up" to friends and to seek out mirth, music, and merry company were beyond ludicrous. Hampelmann couldn't imagine talking to anyone but his physician about his dark moods. And how, when the world was nearing the end-time and evil abounded on all sides, was one to find mirth, music, and merry company?

Recently, Hampelmann had acquired a far more reasonable book by Marsilio Ficino. He fastened the tabs on *Der Hexenhammer*, stood, and slid it back onto the shelf. He reached for Ficino's book and turned to chapter six: "How Black Bile Makes People Intelligent."

20

23 April 1626

Lutz walked swiftly along *Dommerschulstrasse,* eager to reach the university, both to get out of the rain and to meet with Father Herzeim. His most pressing concern was that the commissioners wanted to examine the accused under torture at the next day's hearing. The Carolina Code strictly forbade torture unless there was sufficient evidence that a crime had been committed. Except in the case of the midwife, the evidence was exceedingly sparse. Yet, if he wasn't allowed to challenge the accusers or the evidence or to interrupt the proceedings with questions, how could he protect the old beggar, Fraulein Spatz, and Frau Rosen? Should he protect them? The other commissioners seemed to have little doubt the women were guilty, and those men all had far more experience with witches than he did. The dilemma had vexed Lutz all night long, roiling his thoughts and dreams.

And then there was the question of calling an eleven-year old girl as a witness against her own mother. Lutz had never heard of such a thing.

He yawned broadly, so tired he could hardly think. Not only had he slept poorly, he'd also spent the entire morning sitting through a dreary city council meeting, during which Hampelmann had proposed some nonsense about rounding up mongrels. Shaking his head, Lutz pulled his flapping cape back over his shoulders. In the midst of all the city's turmoil – witches, threats of war from the north, reports of plague from Offenbach, hardly more than fifty miles to the west, grain shortages and the ever increasing number of beggars – Hampelmann expected the councilmen to worry about stray dogs?

Lutz had come home to dinner exhausted, and while Maria changed his soiled cuffs, she lectured him about his health and his need for rest. He nearly fell asleep over his soup. Even so, after dinner, he kept an appointment with a goldsmith who wanted clarifications in a contract Lutz had overseen several months earlier. It had been a relief to think about something as simple and straightforward as a contract. Soon after the goldsmith left, however, Lutz found himself fretting again about the hearings. It was then that he decided to visit Father Herzeim, both to seek advice and to warn him about Hampelmann's suspicions, even if they were unfounded.

Lutz huffed as he climbed the stone steps. He passed by several students in the corridor, paused outside the priest's office to wipe his sweating brow, then rapped on the door. At the muffled *ja*, he cracked it open. Father Herzeim sat at the desk. Across from him sat a sallow young man with a patchy beard, whose thin arms enclosed a tall stack of ledgers and books.

"Come in, Herr Lutz, come in." Father Herzeim turned back to the student. "We can continue this discussion tomorrow morning, Herr Schelhar. I recommend that you re-read what the Carolina Code has to say about theft of Church property, specifically articles 157 and 171, and then re-consider your interpretation of the recent opinion published by the theologians at the University of Cologne."

The young man gathered up his books and nodded deferentially toward Father Herzeim. Clearly annoyed at the interruption, he walked past Lutz without so much as a glance.

Lutz closed the door, shook off his dripping hat and cape, and laid them aside. "Good news, Father. The commission is recommending that Herr Silberhans be released."

Father Herzeim put his hands together as if to pray and looked upward. "Good. They've made the right decision. And the others?"

Lutz sat down in the chair recently vacated by the student. The seat was still warm. "They're to be questioned again tomorrow."

"Tortured?"

Lutz combed his fingers through his beard. "Perhaps, though the evidence warrants it only in the case of Frau Lamm."

"Remind the commissioners of Article 109 of the Carolina Code. It directs jurists to consult with the law faculty of the nearest university before proceeding with torture." Father Herzeim closed the ledger in front of him. "But since they've ignored that article before, your strongest argument is to remind them again that there must be evidence – more than just hearsay. Though the executioner and Father Streng will be deaf, Herr Hampelmann and Chancellor Brandt may yield to reason. If you can convince –"

"But do you think they're guilty? If they are, they *should* be examined under torture."

"Do you?"

"I don't know. The evidence is entirely circumstantial, but I've had so little experience with witches. And if all the other commissioners believe they're guilty…" Lutz raised his hands, palms up. "I've never known a witch, or at least I don't think I have. I don't know what to look for. You've known dozens. What do you think?"

The priest rubbed at a blemish on the ledger's leather binding. "The old woman suffers from ill health and dementia, but is harmless, I think. As to the midwife, it could be that she gives desperate young *frauleins* herbs, and it could be that Fraulein Spatz took such herbs. But is that a crime worthy of death?"

"The Church says it is."

"True, but you know better than I that there's no real proof that either of them did so. There is only a secret birth and a baby nobody wanted, who apparently died in the womb. But no evidence that anyone killed it deliberately."

"If the women are tortured, won't they tell us that?"

Father Herzeim's face looked pained, as if he had an agonizing griping in his bowels. "If they're tortured, they'll tell you anything."

"But isn't torture supposed to free the defendant from the Devil's grasp and elicit truth?"

"That's the theory, but I have my doubts."

"Doubts?" Lutz slid forward on the chair. "Damn, if Jesuits have doubts, what are the rest of us supposed to think?"

"Precisely that. Think."

"I'm not sure anymore what to think." Lutz slid back on the chair, which wobbled beneath his weight. "Based on your experience, Father, do you believe these women are witches? If they are, I should not help the Devil by defending them."

Father Herzeim picked up a white quill and twirled it between his thumb and forefinger. He watched it spin. "By reputation, Frau Lamm is known to help, not harm. And to be honest, but perhaps unkind, Fraulein Spatz seems too simple to be a witch. Why would the Devil enlist women who are stupid? How could they possibly help him? *Nein*, I think their real crime is being poor. And being sinners." He gave Lutz a sidelong glance. "Just like the rest of us."

"I don't know, the midwife seems wicked to me. I think that one is guilty. And what about Frau Rosen? She's not poor, and she's certainly not stupid."

"I can't figure out why Frau Rosen was arrested. I suspect Herr Hampelmann had Herr Silberhans arrested in order to get at me. But Frau Rosen?" The priest hunched his shoulders.

"So you know then that Hampelmann has suspicions about you?"

"I know."

"Yesterday he even warned me not to seek advice from you."

"I warned you not to seek advice from me."

"*Ja*, you did." Lutz smiled uneasily. "But Herr Hampelmann can't really believe you're a sceptic or a defender of witches. He's just irritated with the questions you raise and your complaints to the Prince-Bishop."

"I think he's more serious than that. Be careful, Lutz."

"Ach, he'd never accuse me of being a defender of witches. He knows I'm just trying to carry out the responsibilities assigned to me."

Lutz rubbed his hands on the damp scratchy wool covering his thighs. "And in carrying out those responsibilities, the question I keep coming back to is the question of their innocence. Couldn't it be that Frau Rosen was arrested precisely because she is a witch?"

"By all accounts, she's devoted to the Church."

"But it's common knowledge that witches are skilled at appearing pious and innocent." Lutz pulled on his ear. "I have to admit, though, the evidence against her is hardly compelling." He whistled through his teeth. "And what a beauty…even with her hair shaved off."

"I suppose."

Suppose? Lutz examined his friend's stern countenance. Father Herzeim was a priest, but he was still a man, wasn't he? Or were Jesuits dead from the neck down? "I do wish I could get the names of the people who reported Frau Rosen to the *Malefizamt*," said Lutz. "Then I could determine if their claims have any merit."

"But you can't, can you?"

"*Nein*, the *Malefizamt* won't release any names. Too dangerous for the accusers."

"So they say. And that means there's no way to determine whether the accusations made against Frau Rosen were made in good faith…or out of jealousy or maliciousness."

Lutz had to look away from the priest's accusing eyes. He bent down to pull up his sagging hose and tucked them under the cuffs of his breeches. Father Herzeim's criticisms went straight to the heart of his own doubts.

"I can't say I like the way these hearings are conducted," said Lutz. "Nor do I like the secrecy." He ran a hand through his tangled hair. "I'm disobeying Chancellor Brandt's admonition about secrecy just by discussing these matters with you."

"*Nein*, you're complying with Article 109: consulting with law faculty at the nearest university."

"Even so, could we call this visit a confession?"

"Never would I break your confidence."

Lutz pulled at the lace on his starched white cuffs, already smudged. He'd come here for Father Herzeim's advice, so he might as well share with the priest all of his doubts and concerns.

"Relaxing the rules of evidence and accepting testimony from disreputable witnesses makes me uneasy," he said. "It seems ridiculous to accept malicious gossip as evidence. And grossly unfair that the accused cannot confront their accusers. Yet, when I question the evidence or the commission's procedures, Chancellor Brandt orders me, the defence lawyer, to be silent." Lutz could feel his frustration mounting, but there was also relief in finally releasing it, like steam escaping from a closed pot.

He stood and began to pace. "Now they're even considering calling Frau Rosen's daughter to testify against her. I can hardly believe it: a child testifying against her own mother. It's a violation of the Carolina Code. But I know already what Father Streng will say if I raise an objection: witchcraft is an exceptional crime."

"*Crimen exceptum*." Father Herzeim spat the words. "Eliminates all legal restrictions. Listen, Lutz, you must talk with Katharina. She must understand that the commissioners will try to trick her into implicating her mother. And herself. She must be very, very careful in how she answers."

Lutz leaned forward. "Are you telling me to advise her to lie?"

"*Nein*. Only to be careful."

"And what if Frau Rosen is guilty? What if she has pulled her daughter into her foul rites and rituals? What is Katharina to say then?"

"They are innocent."

"Do you believe any of the accused is guilty?"

Father Herzeim smoothed the quill, intently, as if it were a task of major importance. "I do not doubt there are witches," he said at last, "but I do not believe the newly accused are among them. What I do believe is that the way the trials are conducted – with relaxed rules of evidence, confessions made under torture, and the requirement that accused witches name accomplices – always creates more witches, most of whom are innocent."

"Most of them innocent? That cannot be so." Lutz sank into the chair. "In a crime as secret as witchcraft, the naming of accomplices seems a perfectly reasonable way to identify other witches. How else could we know about them?" He chewed his lip. "I have to admit, though, I'm confused about it all, especially when Herr Freude contends that condemned witches conspired together to accuse Herr Silberhans, an innocent. Couldn't that be true for any of the others as well? And yet the fact that all three condemned witches named the same five accomplices suggests guilt...until I consider Frau Basser's claim that names were suggested to her. I once thought her claim preposterous. Now I'm not sure...of anything. What do you think?"

"Why would she lie?"

"Because she's a witch."

Father Herzeim flicked the quill into the air. The white feather floated lightly to the floor. "That's always the answer, isn't it? Maybe that's why there are so many witches in Würzburg."

"You don't think there are?"

"I don't think there are nearly so many as the commissioners manage to find."

❦

Father Herzeim stood and walked to the window. Raindrops trailed down the panes in crooked paths. He turned to Lutz and looked long into his face, as if trying to read his thoughts, or his heart. Finally he said, "I want you to read something." He locked the office door, then went to a corner and moved a small table to one side. He lifted up a floorboard, pulled out a tattered book, and brought it to Lutz. It was Johann Weyer's *De Praestigiis Daemonum*.

Lutz recoiled as if the book were a serpent. "My God, Father, you could be excommunicated."

"Not just excommunicated. Executed. But just read it. There's merit in what Weyer has to say. At the very least, it's worth considering. And debating." Father Herzeim opened the book. "Weyer claims that the Devil has far greater powers than we acknowledge and has no need for human accomplices. He also claims that women who believe they have satanic powers are deluded and that most women confess to witchcraft only to end the torture."

Father Herzeim pointed to a page of bold type. "Here, just look at what he's written."

"*Nein*, I'll not look." Lutz could hear the tremor in his own voice.

The priest exhaled through clenched teeth. "I've had this book for nearly five years, and I haven't been struck dead yet." He held the open pages directly in front of Lutz's face.

Lutz tried to keep his eyes averted, but his curiosity was too great. Almost against his will, his gaze went directly to where the priest pointed. *Through malicious accusations or the mistaken suspicion of illiterate and ignorant peasants, old women deceived or possessed by the Devil are put by judges into the horrible dens of thieves and caves of wicked demons, and then turned over to be slaughtered with the most refined tortures that tyrants could invent, beyond human endurance. And this cruelty is continued until the most innocent are forced to confess themselves guilty. So it happens that the time comes when these bloodthirsty men force them to give their guiltless souls to God in the flames of the pyre rather than to suffer any longer the tortures inflicted on them by these tyrants.*

"We are not bloodthirsty tyrants," Lutz said in a hushed shout, "and these women are not *guiltless souls*. If they are truly innocent, they go free."

"Read more." Father Herzeim ran a finger down the page. Lutz's eyes followed slavishly. *But when the great searcher of hearts, from whom nothing is hidden, shall appear, your wicked deeds shall be revealed, you tyrants, sanguinary judges, butchers, torturers, and ferocious robbers, who have thrown out humanity and do not know mercy. So I summon you before the tribunal of the Great Judge, who shall decide between us, where the truth you have trampled under foot and buried shall arise and condemn you, demanding vengeance for your inhumanities.*

Lutz jumped up and strode away from Father Herzeim – and the book. He spun to face the priest. "That's precisely why that book is forbidden by the Church. It's wicked heresy to claim that it's the commissioners and not the witches who are evil. Do you really believe that all the popes of the past one hundred and fifty years have been wrong? God would never allow that to happen."

"What I believe is that this *heresy*, as you choose to call it, is important enough to warrant debate in all the law schools in the Holy Roman Empire. This book, and writings like it, should not be forbidden. What harm can there be in debate, in searching for what is true?"

Lutz jabbed a forefinger into the air. "If it's decided that the Church and the popes have been wrong about witchcraft, we will have to doubt everything else as well."

"And what if Weyer is right? How then will you and I stand before the Great Judge?"

"Weyer can't be right. He's been condemned by the Church."

Wearily, his shoulders slumped, Father Herzeim walked to the corner, placed the blasphemous book in its chamber, then carefully replaced the floorboard and table. He sat down at the desk. "I am writing my own book, using the arguments of Weyer, and Adam Tanner. I am also including a thorough legal critique of the way the hearings are conducted."

"*Nein*, this cannot be true."

"If the commission's hearings were conducted like any other legal proceeding," continued the priest, "almost none of the accused would be executed. Even Herr Hampelmann's great favourite, Jean Bodin, admits to that: *The proof of such crimes is so obscure and so difficult that not one witch in a million would be accused or punished if the procedure were governed by ordinary rules.* But instead of seeing the problem of evidence as a reason to proceed cautiously, Bodin uses it to justify relaxing strict legal requirements."

Lutz felt light-headed, as if he were floating near the ceiling. "Hampelmann is right to be suspicious," he whispered.

"*Nein*, I do not doubt the existence of witches. Nor do I defend them. I simply believe the hearings should be conducted in the same way as any other legal proceeding. I defend the innocent, Lutz, not witches." He closed his eyes; his head bent forward. "I feel the weight of every innocent soul who's gone to the stake."

Father Herzeim flipped through his breviary, as if searching for something. He pressed the book open, so that it lay flat before him. "Today is Saint Georg's feast day. Would that I had the courage to slay a dragon." He snapped the breviary closed. "I am a coward, Lutz. I will write my manuscript secretly, publish it anonymously…rather than speak out publicly."

"You would be tried for heresy, Father. And executed." Lutz choked on his own words. "Perhaps rightfully so."

"But then I could stand before the Great Judge, unashamed, a man of courage who worked to protect the innocent." Father Herzeim's restless hands picked up another quill. He ran a fingertip over the nib. "I sometimes wonder why Saint Thomas Aquinas didn't list cowardice among the seven deadly sins. It seems far worse than sloth or gluttony."

He stroked the quill against his dark beard, making a soft rustling like satin skirts, or ghosts. "Will you visit the women yet today?"

"As their lawyer, I must, whether I want to or not."

"I would like to come with you. They will be in need of comfort. I can yet find the courage for that at least."

21

23 April 1626

"He was here, Mama. Right over there." Katharina pointed at the opposite wall. "He sat in a fancy chair. The arms were carved like the heads of serpents with their mouths wide open."

Eva tried to pull her daughter closer. "Shush. It was only a bad dream."

Katharina leaped away, just out of Eva's reach. "*Nein*, Mama. Let me tell you about it. An angel came to rescue me." The girl's bright green eyes flickered with copper lights, though there were no candles, no torches, only the narrow shaft of grey dawn admitted by the small window.

"The Devil smiled and crooked his finger at me." Katharina crooked her own finger, beckoning. "There was a long table set with goblets and plates of silver and gold. The table was piled high with food: dark loaves and jam, honeycakes, tarts, and sweet spiced apples." She spread her arms to show how big the table was, how high the food was piled. She licked her lips.

A child's fancy, thought Eva. A dream. Even so, her heart quickened. Katharina's dreams had become more and more eerie, and frightening. Eva made the girl recite Bible verses every day, as well as the *Pater Noster* and *Ave Maria*. And still, nearly every night Katharina saw the Devil and his red glowing eyes. Eva had begun to blame herself for the girl's malevolent dreams. She'd not thought long enough or hard enough when she'd chosen her name: Katharina. Eva had only thought the name beautiful and had not considered that she was naming her daughter after Saint Katharina of Siena, a mystic who'd begun having visions at the age of six. The saint had also had diabolical dreams.

"I was scared, but I crept closer anyway." Katharina bowed her head, her eyes shifting from side to side. "I'm sorry, Mama. I was just so hungry." She looked up, her face bright now. "But an angel came. He was wearing a white gown with a red cross on the front." She waved her arms in a wide arc, as if to show how big the wings had been. "He carried a long shiny sword. Just like Saint Georg. And there was a white dog at his feet. The dog rushed at me, her teeth like this." The girl bared her teeth and growled. "She kept me away from the Devil."

Eva put her hands to her ears. "Stop." She could not listen any longer. Was it more than a nightmare? Had the Devil really been there, right in their cell, tempting Katharina with food?

"And then, suddenly, the Devil turned into a huge serpent blowing fire from his mouth." Katharina opened her mouth wide and blew. "The angel raised his sword, and the Devil disappeared in a cloud of black smoke. And then the angel was gone, too." She grinned. "But the dog stayed. She lay near me and kept me warm. And even though the food was gone, I wasn't so hungry anymore."

Katharina sat down against the wall, relaxed and smiling. She stretched out a hand, as if to stroke a dog's head.

Unable to watch, Eva looked away. Her fear for her daughter was a stone in her chest. Katharina had dreams – or visions – of the Devil, and now no longer feared him. Had he twined himself into her soul? And yet the girl also saw visions of angels and saints. Was Katharina possessed? Or a mystic?

Like skulking crows, they hovered over her, both of them wearing dark broad-brimmed hats that dripped water onto the floor. Their faces glowed yellow in the candlelight from the lantern.

What would she give, Eva wondered, to be far away from here, outside in the soft spring rain, smelling the damp earth and linden and cherry blossoms, the cold rain cooling her face, which burned with shame? She could not put from her mind that this lawyer looming over her had seen her naked, had watched while the horrid Herr Freude searched her body in the most private of places. She brought her hands together so that her arms covered her breasts.

The priest clutched the wooden cross hanging from his neck. His dark gaze was far away, as if he were deep in thought, or prayer. The stout lawyer swayed from one foot to the other, flicking the copper buttons on his doublet.

"Will they torture me tomorrow?" Eva repeated.

"The Carolina Code specifically forbids examination under torture unless there is evidence that a crime has been committed," said Lutz. "And while your husband's death cannot be adequately explained and the timing of Herr Kaiser's illness is unfortunate, there is no real evidence you've committed a crime."

"But will they torture me?"

Lutz looked away. Father Herzeim closed his eyes. That was her answer.

Why was God testing her so? "Bring me a Bible," she said to Lutz. "I need to read the story of Job."

"He cannot do that," said Father Herzeim, kneeling down beside her, his face too eager. "But I can tell you that story if you want."

Eva ran her fingers over the stubble on her shaved head. The chains on her shackles clanked. Tears gathered. "What I want is to go home." She glanced at Katharina, huddled against the wall. "And to take my daughter with me. We are *not* witches."

Father Herzeim put a hand under her chin and lifted her face. He wiped a tear with his thumb, but there was no comfort in his touch. Eva caught the hateful scent of lye soap.

"Whatever happens tomorrow," he said, "you must insist on your innocence. If you admit to anything, they'll claim you confessed, and use that as evidence to justify torturing you again. You must be strong. You are innocent. God will help you."

He spoke so fiercely that Eva shrank away from him. For a long moment, he looked at his extended hand, no longer cupping her chin, then, finally, dropped his arm to his side and stood.

Lutz cleared his throat. "*Ja*, well…what we can't figure out, Frau Rosen, is why, if you are truly innocent, three condemned witches named you as an accomplice. I know we've been through this before, but I must ask again. Do you know of anyone, besides Herr Kaiser of course, who might have reported you to the *Malefizamt*? Anyone who might have made a false accusation out of spite or jealousy, or sheer malice?"

Eva shook her head. Should she tell them about Wilhelm? It was clear that he hated her, but still, he would never accuse her of witchcraft. Besides, she didn't want to tell that story. It shamed her to remember all that had happened in the Hampelmann household. "I can think of no one," she said.

"Truth," said Father Herzeim. "We can help you only if you speak the truth."

Could this sombre priest see directly into her heart?

"Wilhelm Hampelmann was angry with me once," she said quickly. "A very long time ago."

The lawyer and priest gaped, at her, and then at each other. Lutz leaned closer. "You know Herr Doktor Hampelmann?"

"Years ago, before I was married, I was a maidservant in his father's house. But Wilhelm would never accuse me. He knows me. He knows I am not a witch."

"But you said he was angry with you," said Father Herzeim. "Why?"

"It was nothing."

"But you remember it."

"He made advances…I refused him."

Lutz coughed into his hand. "Did he…did he force–"

"*Nein*!"

"He was just angry about being refused?"

Eva nodded.

Lutz lifted his hat, ran a hand through his white hair, then pulled the hat back onto his head. "And this was what? Ten, twelve years ago?" He shrugged. "Men make advances; virtuous women refuse them. Herr Doktor Hampelmann's an honourable man. He'd not make an accusation of witchcraft and have you arrested for some long ago…embarrassment."

"I believe it's not possible to know what Herr Hampelmann would do," Father Herzeim said sharply.

"Nonsense. It has to be something – or someone – else." The lawyer glanced at Katharina, who was so quiet Eva hoped they'd forgotten her. "What about her?" said Lutz. "She's a bit…odd. Could someone have reported your daughter to the *Malefizamt*?"

"But then it would be Katharina who was accused," said the priest. "Not Frau Rosen."

"Perhaps someone considered the daughter's strangeness evidence of her mother's crimes."

Eva cringed to hear the lawyer speak her own suspicions aloud. It felt like the worst betrayal she could imagine, to believe, even for a moment, that it might be her own daughter who was to blame for their plight.

"People have been kind to Katharina," she said. "Children have teased her now and again, but no one would think her a witch. Or the daughter of a witch."

The priest and the lawyer stood side by side now, arguing quietly with each other, their backs to Eva.

Eva looked down at her torn and ragged fingernails. Katharina's dreams. She couldn't speak of those to the lawyer or the priest. It was all nonsense anyway. A child's fantasies. How could she have considered, even for a moment, that the Devil had been right there in their cell, that her own daughter was possessed?

Father Herzeim stooped down in front of Eva. "You must prepare her," he whispered, nodding toward Katharina. "They may call her to testify against you."

"Not my daughter," Eva gasped. "How can they?"

"By law, they cannot torture her. She has not been accused. But they'll use tricks of language to get her to implicate you. You must instruct her to listen very closely to the questions they ask and to think carefully before she answers. Katharina must deny — over and over again, if necessary — that either of you has ever had anything to do with the Devil or with witchcraft."

"Then she need only speak the truth," said Eva, her throat so tight the words came out in a hoarse whisper.

Father Herzeim turned to Katharina. The girl reached out a hand and smiled at the floor. He turned back to Eva, his dark eyes questioning.

Mother of God, Eva prayed, please protect her, protect us. She must not speak of her strange dreams.

"Pray with me, Father."

22

~

24 April 1626

Stifling a yawn, Lutz took his place at the end of the table beside Hampelmann, who barely glanced up from his ledger even when Lutz's knee bumped his. Lutz felt as if his head were stuffed with wool. He'd lain awake all night, fretting, unable to put Johann Weyer's words, or Father Herzeim's, from his mind. Now and again, he'd been able to convince himself of the lack of merit in Weyer's ideas. The man had been a Calvinist after all, an apostate. Father Herzeim, however, was a man of God, a man of the true faith. Yet, as hard as Lutz tried, he could not find a way to square the priest's words with what he'd read in *Der Hexenhammer*, which Pope Innocent VIII had declared to be true. Even so, Lutz could not bring himself to believe that his friend was a sceptic and a defender of witches. Surely Father Herzeim's concern was only for the protection of the innocent.

When Father Streng had finished recording their names, Judge Steinbach tapped the gavel. "The Commission of Inquisition for the Würzburg Court will now come to order," said the judge. The priest laid the speckled quill beside his breviary and a vial of holy water and stood. As the others rose, their wooden chairs scraped loudly against the stone floor. The men made the sign of the cross and bowed their heads.

"Dearest Father in heaven." Father Streng's boyish voice rang off the walls, creating a buzz in Lutz's wool-filled ears so that he hardly heard the words. At the "Amen," the men crossed themselves again, then sat.

Judge Steinbach picked up a document bearing the

Prince-Bishop's wax seal. It shook so much in his palsied hands the parchment rattled. "Prince-Bishop Philipp Adolf has approved our recommendation to release Herr Christoph Silberhans and to expel him from Würzburg." He glanced nervously at the chancellor.

Chancellor Brandt tugged at the bottom of his silk doublet, pulling it smooth. The flickering candlelight from the lantern danced on the polished silver buttons. He inserted two fingers into the white ruff at his neck and pulled as if to loosen it. "The jailer sent a guard early this morning to inform His Grace that Frau Bettler is dead," he said. "Apparently she died during the night."

"Of what?" said Lutz.

"The Devil killed her," said Freude. "I saw the body. Her neck was twisted. Otherwise, not a mark."

"But why would the Devil do that?" said Lutz.

"To keep her from telling his secrets and from revealing the names of accomplices," said Father Streng. He raised his eyes from his ledger. "Her death proves her guilt."

"I don't understand." Lutz shook his head, trying to clear the wool. "If that's true, why doesn't the Devil kill all witches as soon as they're arrested?"

Father Streng stared at Lutz as if he were a *dummkopf.* "Because, Herr Lutz, God does not permit him to do so."

"Why then did God allow it in this case?"

There was a sudden scrabbling and squealing from the shadows, rats tussling over a scrap left by the guards. Judge Steinbach's chin trembled as he smoothed his little tuft of white beard.

"I doubt we'd have gotten much from the old beggar anyway," said Lindner, ignoring Lutz's question. "And it's one less witch we have to deal with."

"One less I'll be paid for," muttered Freude.

Beside him, Lutz could feel Hampelmann stiffen. Hampelmann placed his hand on the table, fingers flexing, then straightening. "These proceedings are not about money, Herr Freude. They are about waging war against evil."

"I know that, Herr Hampelmann. But there's nothing wrong with getting paid for my work. Soldiers at war get paid."

Chancellor Brandt nudged Judge Steinbach, who tipped the gavel toward the chancellor. "The first order of business," said Chancellor Brandt, "is to determine how to proceed this morning. We still have the charges against Fraulein Spatz, Frau Lamm, and Frau Rosen to investigate. What do you make of the first questioning, gentlemen?"

"I've gone through my report thoroughly," said Father Streng. "Given their evasive answers and the preponderance of evidence, I am nearly certain that Fraulein Spatz and Frau Lamm are guilty. Frau Rosen's case is less clear."

Lutz looked down at his own smudged pages. *Preponderance of evidence?* There was almost no evidence.

"I agree with Father Streng's assessment," Hampelmann said thoughtfully. "And with the old beggar dead, it's clear that the maidservant is the weakest of the three who are left. We should begin with her."

"I agree," said Chancellor Brandt. "Bring in Fraulein Spatz. A few more nights in jail may have prompted that one to discover the truth."

"And if she persists in being taciturn," said Father Streng, "we have all the evidence we need to proceed with light torture."

"Wait." Lutz raised both hands. "I agree that we should question Fraulein Spatz first, but I do not agree that we have the evidence to justify torture. There's a dead baby, but no evidence that anyone killed it." He glanced toward the physician, who sat at the far end of the table near Freude. "Herr Doktor Lindner, didn't you report that there was no sign the infant had been strangled or bludgeoned or harmed in any way?"

"Babies don't die without cause," said Lindner. "Moreover, the girl and the midwife tried to hide the birth…and the death. Why would they do that, Herr Lutz?"

"Under the circumstances, any *fraulein* would."

"That's why we're here," Chancellor Brandt said coolly. "To discover just what those circumstances were."

"And don't forget the mark," said Freude.

"But we've not yet consulted with the law faculty at the university," said Lutz, "as Article 109 of the Carolina Code directs."

"Article 109 was written for inexperienced jurists," said Chancellor Brandt, "not for those of us who have served on the commission time and time again." He turned to the executioner. "Bring her in, Herr Freude."

Lutz shifted on the hard chair. How could Father Streng be so certain the girl was guilty when there was so little evidence? Only a secret death and a questionable Devil's mark. Father Streng's assessment of the evidence seemed far less convincing than Father Herzeim's: the young maidservant was guilty only of being poor and desperate. Lutz rubbed his temples. The young woman must have been frantic at the prospect of having a baby – no husband, no money, only the shame of bearing a bastard that would ruin any chance of marriage she might have had. Perhaps she had gone to the midwife for herbs, but that would make her a murderer, not a witch. And there was no solid evidence that she'd even done that. If one could believe what the midwife had said, that Fraulein Spatz intended to leave the child at the Julius Hospital, the girl was planning for a live baby not a dead one. If she'd only known, Lutz thought wistfully, she could have left the child on his own doorstep. Maria would take in an infant, no matter what the circumstances of its birth. He shook himself to attention. He could not allow himself to drift. He must find a way to defend the poor girl.

The door creaked open. Fraulein Spatz entered, again shuffling backwards. Her scalp was covered with dark stubble. Freude prodded her to turn around. She looked at Lutz, her eyes pleading.

Father Streng stepped forward with the crucifix. "By the belief that you have in God and in the expectation of paradise, and being aware of the peril of your soul's eternal damnation, do you swear that the testimony you are about to give is true, such that you are willing to exchange heaven for hell should you tell a lie?"

Sniffling, she nodded. Her lips formed a silent *ja*.

Freude prodded her toward a chair set beside a small table in the middle of the chamber. The executioner took the gleaming thumbscrews from the shelf and set them before her.

"Fraulein Spatz," said Chancellor Brandt, "during the previous questioning, your answers were duplicitous and disingenuous."

The girl bit her lip. The chancellor might as well have been speaking Portuguese, thought Lutz.

Chancellor Brandt pointed at the priest's ledger. "You claimed –"

Lutz broke in. "Chancellor Brandt means that your answers changed from time to time, leaving us unsure of the truth."

"*Danke* for that clarification, Herr Lutz," the chancellor said through clenched teeth. He turned back to the girl. "You claimed, Fraulein Spatz, that your baby was born dead, then later stated that he *might* have been born alive. You also said that the midwife could not have murdered the child, then later indicated that she *might* have had that opportunity. The child was born – and died – in secret. You deny the charges against you, yet there is the evidence of the Devil's mark – in the most private of places. Tell us, Fraulein Spatz, has the misery of your imprisonment prompted you to find the truth?"

The girl sat up in the chair, a look of resolve on her pasty face.

❧

"I'm telling the truth. I'm not a witch. I've never gone to a sabbath. My son was born dead. Frau Lamm and I kept the birth and the death secret because I didn't want anyone to know."

"So you killed the product of your sin to be sure that no one would know," Father Streng said coldly.

"I did not kill my baby!"

Chancellor Brandt leaned across the judge to consult with Father Streng. Hampelmann leaned in as well. The four men whispered to each other, the priest stabbing a finger at his ledger. Finally, the chancellor nodded at Judge Steinbach, who tapped the gavel.

"We, the members of the Commission of Inquisition for the Würzburg Court," said Judge Steinbach, reading from Father Streng's ledger, "having considered the details of the inquiry enacted by us against you, Fraulein Spatz, and having diligently examined the whole matter, find that you have been equivocal in your admissions. Nevertheless, there are various proofs that warrant exposing you to questioning under torture."

"*Nein*," she shrieked. "*Nein*."

"Please," Lutz said quickly, "because I am new to the commission, would you please review for me the evidence? On the face of it, there seems not enough to satisfy the requirements of Article 58 of the Carolina Code regarding examination under torture."

Fraulein Spatz stared at Lutz, her desperate face hopeful.

Chancellor Brandt's hands curled into fists. "We've already been through this, Herr Lutz. There is the dead baby." He opened his fists to count on his fingers. "A secret birth and a secret death. There are three accusations made by condemned witches, and there is the Devil's mark." He held up seven fingers. "There is more than enough evidence to warrant torture." He turned back to the girl. "Fraulein Spatz, do you wish to reconsider any of your answers before we proceed?"

She shook her head, her cheeks blanching.

"Proceed, Herr Freude."

The executioner puffed out his chest. "You see before you the thumbscrews," he said. "These are considered but light torture. Take your time, Fraulein Spatz, and look around you carefully, at the leg vises that can crush your bones, and at the pulley there." With a wave of his gloved hand, he directed her eyes first to the large wooden wheel, and then to the ceiling. "And the stone weights that can be added to your ankles while you hang suspended. And see the pincers. Imagine them red-hot and pulling at your breasts. I have a razor – you know that I do." He ran two fingers over the stubble on her head. When she flinched away from his touch, his dark teeth showed in a sneer. "It can remove the mark of the Devil from your body – even in the most secret of places. We will have the truth from you, Fraulein Spatz, one way or another. Think carefully how you answer. You can spare yourself – and us – this entire ordeal by telling us the truth now."

Tears spilled from her eyes. "I-I am telling the truth."

"You leave us no choice," Chancellor Brandt said wearily. "Wherefore, that the truth may be known from your own mouth and that henceforth, you may not offend the ears of the commissioners, we declare that on Friday, April 24, 1626–" he glanced at the judge's gold watch "–at 9:10 in the morning, you be placed under torture for questioning. Proceed, Father Streng, Herr Freude."

The priest picked up the vial and stepped forward. He made the sign of the cross over Fraulein Spatz and then over the thumbscrews. Dipping his fingertips into the holy water, he sprinkled both the girl and the instrument. "Dear Father in heaven," he prayed, "may these procedures free this girl from the Devil's grasp and bring forth truth from her lips. *In nomine patris, et filii, et spiritus sancti.* Amen."

dancing in the palm of his hand

Freude grabbed Fraulein Spatz's bound wrists and forced her thumbs under the metal bar. She screamed and tried to pull away, but the executioner held her hands in place and tightened the large centre screw, just enough to secure her thumbs under the bar.

"You have one more opportunity before we begin, Fraulein Spatz," said Chancellor Brandt. "Will you speak the truth?"

"I have," she whimpered. "I have."

"Proceed, Herr Freude."

The executioner tightened the screw. Wailing, the girl rocked back and forth in the chair. Lutz felt his stomach rise into his chest. His fingers curled around his own thumbs.

Lindner leaned forward. "How did you get your mark?"

"No mark," she sobbed. "There is no mark."

"When and where did you first meet with the Devil?" said Judge Steinbach.

"Never," she whispered.

"Who killed the baby?" said Hampelmann.

"No one," she screamed.

"Then how did it die?"

"Born dead. I swear."

At Chancellor Brandt's nod, Herr Freude gave the screw another turn. Blood trickled onto the instrument. The girl vomited, then fainted, her head falling forward onto her outstretched arms.

"So weak," said the executioner, disgusted. He went to a wooden box on the shelf and pulled out a small bottle. He uncorked it and waved it under her nose. The astringent scent of hartshorn mingled with the stink of sour vomit and blood. Lutz gagged.

Herr Freude slapped the girl. Her head bobbed up.

"Who killed the baby?" said Father Streng.

Her eyes fluttered open. "Midwife."

The priest smiled thinly. "How?"

"Potion."

Lutz put a hand to his forehead. So Fraulein Spatz had taken herbs to kill the child. Or had she? What would he say if those were his thumbs being crushed?

"Did you see the midwife eat any part of the infant or drink its blood?" said Father Streng.

"Wait!" shouted Lutz. "Herr Doktor Lindner has already reported that the infant was unblemished."

Father Streng turned slowly, the torchlight reflecting off his spectacles so that Lutz could not see his eyes, only two golden disks. "Herr Lutz," said the priest, "the Devil is the master of illusion. He can make anything appear to be there, and he can make what's there appear not to be there." He adjusted the spectacles. "Fraulein Spatz, did you see the midwife eat any part of the infant or drink its blood?"

She shook her head weakly.

"Were you planning to take the infant to the sabbath to share its flesh with other witches?"

"Bury. Tried to bury…"

"To be dug up later to be used in your foul rituals?" said Judge Steinbach.

"When and where did you first meet with the Devil?" said Chancellor Brandt.

Herr Freude placed his hand on the screw. The girl's plump face contorted with anguish. "Frau Lamm's," she screeched.

"What did he ask you to do?" said Hampelmann.

Her lips moved, but she did not answer.

"Did he ask you to sign a contract granting him your eternal soul in exchange for ridding you of the child?"

She shook her head. Herr Freude gave the screw another turn. "*Ja*," she howled. "A contract."

"In your own blood?"

She nodded.

"How could she sign a contract?" Lutz protested. "She can't even read or write."

Father Streng stopped writing. "Simple, Herr Lutz. The Devil explains the contract to the illiterate, then guides her hand to sign it."

"What was his name?" said Hampelmann

"Name?" she mouthed silently.

Father Streng waved the quill. "Beelzebub? Satan? Lucifer?"

"Lucifer." She blinked rapidly, as if trying to focus her eyes. Her head lolled.

"Was that when you received your mark, Fraulein Spatz, after you'd signed the contract?" said Father Streng.

The girl's face wrinkled in confusion.

"What was it like, fornicating with the Devil?" Hampelmann breathed heavily, as if he'd been running. "Many women have told us that his member is huge and cold, that the act is painful rather than pleasurable. Is that true, Fraulein Spatz?"

Lutz couldn't tell if the girl actually nodded or if she'd simply tried to lift her head and couldn't. He watched Father Streng record her answer, the speckled quill bobbing along hurriedly. How could they believe she was speaking the truth? This was exactly what Father Herzeim had meant. *If they're tortured, they'll tell you anything.* And Weyer, what about Weyer? Lutz had read the passage only once, but it was as if the words had been burned into his head, right behind his eyes. *Tyrants, sanguinary judges, butchers, torturers who do not know mercy. This cruelty is continued until the most innocent are forced to confess themselves guilty.*

"Tell us what you remember of the act," said Hampelmann. "Was the Devil's touch cold?"

"Stop!" Lutz shouted. "In the name of God, stop. The girl is delirious. She doesn't even understand the questions. And you're suggesting to her exactly how she should answer. How can we possibly consider her answers to be true?"

"That is why we use torture," Father Streng said impatiently. "To reveal truth."

"Truth? She'd say anything, anything at all, to stop the torture."

The priest pointed the quill at Lutz. "Are you questioning the sacred teachings of the Church?"

"I'm not questioning anything. It's just...just..." Lutz gestured toward Fraulein Spatz. "Look at her."

Hampelmann patted Lutz on the shoulder. "You're new to this. It's always difficult the first time. We should have prepared you. The girl appears to be in torment, but she's feigning. She's not like us, Herr Lutz. She doesn't even feel the pain."

The buzzing in Lutz's ears had grown louder. He wanted to lay his head on the table.

"The Devil makes them insensible to pain," continued Hampelmann. "That's why we have to use torture. To free them from the Devil's grasp. You'll see."

"When and where did you go to the sabbath?" said Father Streng. "And with whom?"

"No sabbath."

Herr Freude reached toward the screw.

"Easter," she murmured. "With the midwife."

"Did you recognize any of the others there?" said Hampelmann. "Was that where you met Frau Imhof, Fraulein Stolzberger, and Frau Basser?"

"*Ja.*"

"Any others?" Hampelmann leafed through his ledger. "Did you see a young woman named Fraulein Wagner, or a beggar woman who goes by the name of Old Frau Holtzman... or Frau Rosen?"

"Or the Rosen girl?" said Freude.

Lutz stood, nearly losing his balance. He leaned against the table and waited for his vision to clear. He now understood why condemned witches all named the same accomplices. Frau Basser had spoken the truth to Father Herzeim: names had been suggested to her. Dear God, had the woman really been innocent?

"This is not right," said Lutz. "You're suggesting names to her."

"Torture is God's instrument to reveal truth," said Hampelmann. "If these accusations are not true, God will not allow Fraulein Spatz to confirm them."

The girl remained silent, her eyes glazed, chin on her chest.

"See," said Hampelmann. Lutz slumped to his chair.

Lindner approached the girl. "Lift her head," he said to Freude. The physician peered into her eyes. "That's enough for today. No good to overdo on the first day."

"Release her from the instrument," ordered Judge Steinbach.

"*Nein*, not yet," said Father Streng. "We're just beginning to make progress. Have you considered the dangers of the Devil coming to her and strengthening her resolve? Or killing her the way he did the old beggar?"

"Enough is enough," said Chancellor Brandt. "We don't wish to be cruel."

Herr Freude loosened the centre screw and lifted the iron bar. Fraulein Spatz stared blankly at her smashed thumbs. Blood dripped down her arms and spotted her shift. Lutz could not imagine the pain. If she was feigning, she was doing a damn good job. *Tyrants, sanguinary judges, butchers, torturers who do not know mercy.*

Father Streng dipped the quill into the pot of black ink. "Now then, Fraulein Spatz, do you freely confirm the testimony – the answers, that is – that you gave while under torture?"

She shook her head slowly. "Nothing…true. Midwife didn't…kill baby." She paused to breathe. "No Devil…no sabbath."

"Put her back in the screws," hissed Chancellor Brandt.

"*Nein*," she screamed. "*Nein*. What I said before…true…all true."

"Should I put her back in?" asked the executioner.

"*Nein*," said Chancellor Brandt. "She has confirmed her confession freely, without torture. And we have enough new evidence to warrant additional torture if needed."

Confirmed her confession freely? Lutz examined his own thumbnails, smooth and undamaged. This was what they meant by confirming a confession freely? He felt his throat closing. He'd failed the girl, failed her completely. What, in God's name, could he do?

"Take her back to her cell, Herr Freude," said Judge Steinbach. "And instruct the jailer's wife to tend to her."

For a brief moment, Chancellor Brandt regarded Fraulein Spatz almost tenderly, then his face hardened. "Bring us the midwife then. That one is doubly damned, for she is the one who led this young girl to the Devil."

23

~

Lucifer, Behemoth, Leviathan, Belial. They have given me many names. Satan, the fallen angel. Asmodeus, the evil spirit. Apollyon, angel of the bottomless pit. My favourite is Beelzebub. It rolls off the tongue with a clicking of teeth and a popping of lips.

The little Jesuit writes that I, as Lucifer, the rebel who fell from grace, fucked (he purses his lips when he writes "fornicated with") the girl with my huge cold cock. Why would I choose such a simple-minded and doughy-faced fool when I prefer cleverness and beauty?

The priest is not beautiful, but he is clever. His eyes are bright, like polished silver coins, behind the glass disks that help him see the evils of the world more clearly. His logic, though ingenious, confounds me, so much so that I had to chuckle aloud when he claimed that I killed the old woman. Even if I could, why would I kill an old beggar who's already lost her wits? What secrets of mine could she possess? The Jesuit, for all his cleverness, does not understand that I have no secrets not already known to the hearts of men. Already known to his own heart.

They give me their secret desires and call them mine.

I peer over his shoulder as he writes. He feels my cold breath on the back of his neck and pulls his black robe closer. He's recording the midwife's answers now, a monotonous nein, nein, nein. His eyelid twitches. She's not easy, not weak like the girl. Already her thumbs have been smashed to a useless pulp, splattering blood all over the floor. It seeps into the stone, a memory, never to be washed away. Now her arms are bound behind her back. She dangles from the pulley,

❧

kicking in air that reeks of blood, sweat, and shit. She screams, hisses, spits, and pisses herself. The men sweat. Their shirts are damp, but their throats are as dry as Ezekiel's bones. They have not yet found the way to make her tell them what they desire to hear. They cannot even make her weep.

If I could choose my followers, she's the one I'd select.

The executioner lets go of the wooden wheel, then jerks it to a halt. The midwife's shoulders snap. Her legs dance a grisly jig.

The fat one leans to the side and vomits.

24

24 April 1626

Now there was the stink of vomit, right at their feet, to add to all the other abominable odours. Hampelmann felt his own stomach begin to rise. He brought his pomander to his nose and inhaled lavender and hellebore.

Freude lowered Frau Lamm to the floor. Father Streng stood over her. "When did you first meet with the Devil?" he said.

"*Nein.*" A barely audible whisper.

The priest knelt down beside her. He spoke softly, almost wheedling in his young boy's voice. "Surely, Frau Lamm, you know that if you were to confess, and to show contrition, your life could be spared."

Hampelmann twisted his gold ring. He knew that Father Streng was only following procedures recommended in *Der Hexenhammer*, but misleading the accused made him uneasy. Hampelmann had studied the Dominicans' recommendations, and they seemed to him duplicitous at times. *Some hold that if the accused is of a notoriously bad reputation and gravely suspected on unequivocal evidence of the crime, and if she is herself a great source of danger, as being the mistress of other witches, then she may be promised her life on the following conditions: that she be sentenced to imprisonment for life on bread and water, provided that she supply evidence which will lead to the conviction of other witches. And she is not to be told, when she is promised her life, that she is to be imprisoned in this way, but should be led to suppose that some other penance, such as exile, will be imposed on her as punishment... Others think that, after she has been consigned to prison in this way, the promise to spare her life should be kept for a time, but that after a certain period she should be burned. A third opinion is that the judge may safely promise the accused her life, but in such a way that he should afterwards disclaim the duty of passing sentence on her, deputing another judge in his place.*

The midwife's body convulsed. She was weeping. Or laughing. "Bastard," she spat. Father Streng recoiled, and in that moment, Hampelmann glimpsed a dark shadow flit across the wall behind Frau Lamm. He caught his breath. The Devil was here, helping her. Hampelmann crossed himself, then touched the ball of wax at his throat.

"Pull her up again," said Chancellor Brandt. "And this time, add the weights."

"Just a moment," said Lindner. The physician walked around the table to examine Frau Lamm. He directed Freude to hold up her head.

"I recommend that we end the torture for today," said Lindner. "We're getting nothing from her, and if Herr Freude does much more, she may be damaged so badly we'll never get anything."

"I agree," said Freude. "Don't want to lose another one to the Devil."

Hampelmann turned to the chancellor and nodded. The Devil was keeping the woman's resolve far too strong and protecting her from pain. After a few days of sitting and contemplating the torture yet to come, she would weaken, especially after the Devil abandoned her. He had no loyalty to his followers. Hampelmann wondered if he should suggest to Chancellor Brandt that he bring in the Prince-Bishop's reliquary. Surely a thorn from the crown would force the Devil to flee.

"All right," said Chancellor Brandt. "We can continue the torture on Monday."

Lutz raised a hand, pulled it back, then raised it again.

೪

"According to the Carolina Code," he said tentatively, "torture cannot be repeated unless there is new evidence. Frau Lamm has confessed to nothing. There is no new evidence."

"Apparently, Herr Lutz, you did not hear me correctly," said Chancellor Brandt. "I did not say we would *repeat* the torture on Monday. I said we would *continue* it. Continuation of torture is permitted under the Carolina Code." He brought his gold pomander to his nose and breathed deeply of the costly spices it contained: clove and cinnamon. "Herr Freude, take Frau Lamm back to her cell and instruct the jailer's wife to tend to her. But tell her to clean up the mess in this chamber first. The stench is unbearable." He turned to Judge Steinbach. "I suggest we take an early dinner, then return to question Frau Rosen."

"Dinner?" said Lutz, as if he'd never heard the word before. Hampelmann looked at him closely. As always, his collar was rumpled and his starched cuffs smudged, but his doublet no longer strained to cover his belly. His plump face had thinned, and his skin was sallow. His white hair and beard were shaggier than ever. Had he even combed them this morning?

"Two hours, gentlemen," said Judge Steinbach. "Then return here promptly."

As the men pulled on their hats and filed out of the chamber, Hampelmann considered foregoing dinner and returning to the Lusam Garden. He'd been there early that morning, praying for forgiveness for the sin of Onan. He hadn't intended to sin, but when he awakened that morning, the mess was already there. He'd spilled his seed uselessly. While he was praying, he heard a loud flapping of wings. He looked up, expecting to see a wood-pigeon, but saw instead a dark shadow on the stone wall, a shadow as tall as a man. The jagged outline of wings showed over both shoulders. Trembling, Hampelmann bowed his head and waited for the angel to speak, but he heard only the warbling of blackbirds. When he looked up again, the shadow was gone. Hampelmann had waited for as long as he could, praying for the angel to return, but it did not, and by the time he'd left the garden, he was apprehensive, unsure what he'd seen.

Why would God send an angel who would not speak and deliver his message? Or had he been visited by a demon, come to tempt him in the guise of an angel? Tempt him to what?

Stepping out of the Prisoners' Tower and into the warm sunlight, Hampelmann made his decision. He would go to the garden to meditate and to wait. He would be patient and give God's messenger every opportunity to visit him again and to speak. He had nothing to fear from the Devil and his demons. He knew their tricks far too well.

Hampelmann could see the curve of breast through the thin linen shift. He forced himself to look away. Filthy and disgusting as she was, Eva was still seductive. Even her shaved skull was somehow attractive. Only a witch could manage that.

Father Streng stood before her with the crucifix. "By the belief that you have in God and in the expectation of paradise, and being aware of the peril of your soul's eternal damnation, do you swear that the testimony you are about to give is true, such that you are willing to exchange heaven for hell should you tell a lie?"

"I swear, by all that is holy, to tell the truth."

"Frau Rosen," said Judge Steinbach, reading from Father Streng's ledger, "during the previous questioning, you denied having any knowledge of Fraulein Stolzberger, Frau Imhof, and Frau Basser, even though all three confirmed they'd seen you at the sabbath." He paused until the priest had sat down and picked up his quill.

"You denied making Herr Kaiser ill," the judge continued in his thin reedy voice, "denied responsibility for Herr Rosen's inexplicable and untimely death. You also denied collecting suspicious objects like rocks and feathers to use in rituals." He looked up, the white plume on his hat bobbing. "Do you wish to reconsider any of these denials?"

"*Nein.*"

"Are you quite certain?" said Chancellor Brandt.

Eva nodded.

His mouth twisted to one side, Chancellor Brandt drummed his fingers on the table. Father Streng held the open ledger in front of the judge and the chancellor. "There's that. And that. As well as that," said the priest, pointing at the pages and jabbing at one section, then another.

Chancellor Brandt conferred with Judge Steinbach, who then picked up the gavel, tapped it once, and read from Father Streng's ledger. "We, the members of the Commission of Inquisition for the Würzburg Court, having considered the details of the inquiry enacted by us against you, Frau Rosen, find that you have been taciturn in withholding information from us. Nevertheless, there is enough evidence to warrant examining you under torture to get that information."

Lutz leapt up, colour rising into his sallow cheeks. "I object. Frau Rosen cannot be tortured. We have established no grounds." He walked around the table to stand in front of the other commissioners. "The Carolina Code states that no person may be examined under torture unless sufficient evidence has first been found of the criminal act being investigated. I ask you, what evidence do we have that Frau Rosen has committed a criminal act?"

"Herr Kaiser's illness and her husband's death," said the judge. "That's evidence."

"But no one has established that Frau Rosen is responsible," said Lutz, pounding a fist into his palm.

"We have certainly established a reasonable suspicion," said Father Streng.

"Suspicion is not the same as evidence," Lutz insisted. "And the evidence can be explained a dozen other ways than by concluding that Frau Rosen is a witch. It is a travesty of the law to engage in torture on the basis of circumstantial evidence."

Chancellor Brandt ran his tongue over his teeth. "You are new to the commission, Herr Lutz. Does it not strike you as…premature to instruct us in what is and is not a travesty of the law?"

Lutz threw up his hands. "But Frau Rosen doesn't even have a Devil's mark."

"Precisely," said Freude. "The Devil had no need to mark her. She's belonged to him since birth."

"I concur," said Hampelmann, trying not to look at Eva's desperate face. "Her own parents named this woman Eva, Eve. That alone should tell us something about her true nature."

"The nuns at Unterzell chose Frau Rosen to work in their convent," said Lutz. "They kept her, educated her. *That* should tell us about her true nature. Quite obviously they did not believe she was a witch."

Hampelmann picked up one of Father Streng's quills, dipped it into the ink, and made a note in his ledger. That was something to watch, he thought. Some of the nuns at Unterzell might be complicit in the Devil's work.

"And, no doubt, the nuns loved her like a daughter," Lutz added.

Lindner ran a hand over his bald pate. "I have to agree with Herr Lutz in this particular case. The evidence is circumstantial."

Hampelmann held out his ledger. "The reports to the *Malefizamt* are alarming. There is Herr Kaiser's illness as well as men who claim to have become ill after eating bread from the Rosen bakery."

"Probably other bakers," muttered Lutz, "who want to put the Rosen Bakery out of business."

"And there are the accusations made by Fraulein Stolzberger, Frau Imhof, and Frau Basser?" Hampelmann said pointedly. "All three saw Frau Rosen at the sabbath."

"But we've dismissed denunciations before," said Lindner, "when it's obvious they were made with malicious intent."

Lutz squared his shoulders. "And I think we all know how those accusations were secured."

"Are you implying," said Hampelmann, "that there is a problem in the commission's procedures?"

Lutz stood silent.

Eva's lips moved, *in nomine patris, et filii, et spiritus sancti.*

Chancellor Brandt folded his hands and placed them on the table. "It seems we have a dilemma, gentlemen. There is serious disagreement about the veracity of the evidence in this case. We will have to question the girl."

"Not my daughter," Eva wailed.

"But the accusations," said Hampelmann. "They're solid evidence."

The chancellor shook his head. "Accusations alone do not justify torture."

"But calling children as witnesses is not permitted," said Lutz, "particularly when they must testify against their own parents."

Father Streng put a finger to his twitching eyelid. "As you've already been reminded, Herr Lutz, a number of times already, witchcraft is a *crimen exceptum.* We need not adhere to strict legal procedures. And in a crime so secret as witchcraft, sometimes the only witnesses are a woman's own children. We have no choice."

Chancellor Brandt placed an open palm over the gold medallion on his chest. "I understand your concern for the child, Herr Lutz, but these rules are not of our own making, but the rules of civil and ecclesiastical law. Father Streng is right. Frau Rosen has left us no choice. We must question the child."

"*Nein,*" Eva moaned.

Wet, her green eyes were even more alluring. Hampelmann averted his gaze to the floor. If Eva were any kind of mother, she would speak the truth now to protect her daughter. If she chose not to, it was just more evidence against her. "Do you wish now to tell us the truth?" he said.

"I have told the truth."

"Take her away," said Judge Steinbach, "and bring us the girl."

Freude grabbed Eva's bound hands and yanked her toward the door. "But I must be here," she protested, "with my daughter. She'll be terrified."

"Not permitted," said Father Streng. "Your mere presence will keep her from revealing anything."

Freude pulled Eva from the chamber. Lutz returned to his place at the table and bent over his ledger, thumbing through the pages. Chancellor Brandt leaned toward him. "For your own good, Herr Lutz, I urge you to temper your zealous defence. Do not forget the words of Martin Delrio: *It is an* indicium *of witchcraft to defend witches.*"

Lutz closed the ledger with a loud snap, making Judge Steinbach jump. "I am not defending witches, sir. I believe Frau Rosen to be innocent."

"If she is truly innocent," said Father Streng, "she needs no defence from you. God himself will give us a sign."

"Be careful," Hampelmann said to Lutz. "Don't let the woman bewitch you with her beauty, nor allow yourself to be seduced into risking your own life to defend hers."

"But all of you know that I am only carrying out the responsibilities assigned to me."

Chancellor Brandt sniffed. "Carrying them out a bit too zealously, I would say."

Freude returned with the girl. She crept backwards into the chamber, her whole body shaking.

"Unbind her wrists and turn her around," Hampelmann

snapped. "She is *not* one of the accused. And why has she been shaved, Herr Freude?"

"Thought I'd save myself the trouble of doing it later."

Chancellor Brandt's hooded eyes narrowed. "You were hired to follow Würzburg procedures, Herr Freude, not your own."

Freude untied the girl's wrists, then, as if to justify what he'd done, he prodded her to walk across the chamber and display her pronounced limp. She nearly tripped on the baggy shift, which dragged on the floor. The girl looked fragile, as if her neck were too thin to hold up her head. Though Hampelmann had never seen her before, the line of her jaw and her slightly upturned nose were oddly familiar. When Freude stood her in front of the commissioners, Hampelmann saw that her eyebrows and eyelashes were nearly white and the stubble on her shaved head was barely visible. Her hair was as pale as his own. Such a contrast to Eva's dark chestnut hair. The girl had her mother's wicked eyes, though, green-brown flecked with gold, enormous in her small white face.

Her glance darted all around the chamber, taking in the bloody thumbscrews, which were still on the table, the ropes and pulley, and finally the commissioners themselves. She made the sign of the cross. "*In nomine patris, et filii, et spiritus sancti.*"

Father Streng approached her with the crucifix. She shrank away from him. Lutz slid off his chair and went to stand beside her.

"By the belief that you have in God and in the expectation of paradise," said the priest, "and being aware of the peril of your soul's eternal damnation, do you swear that the testimony you are about to give is true, such that you are willing to exchange heaven for hell should you tell a lie?"

Urine pooled on the stones between the girl's feet.

"Do you swear to tell the truth?" Lutz said gently.

She nodded. Freude prodded the girl toward the chair. She sat down, her bare feet dangling above the floor.

The priest resumed his seat and took up a quill. "State your name and age."

The girl remained silent, her gaze fixed on the floor. Lutz placed a hand on her shoulder, but she pushed it off. Freude poked her with a birch rod.

Chancellor Brandt's lips curled as if he were trying to smile. "My dear child, you need not be frightened. You are here only to answer a few questions."

"But you believe my mother's a witch. She's not."

Freude drew back his arm. "You are not to speak–"

Lutz moved quickly to block the executioner's blow. "She is not one of the accused, Herr Freude. She's a witness."

"That's quite correct," the chancellor said kindly. "You have not been accused of anything, child. We're simply gathering information...information that could free you and your mother."

"State your name and age," repeated Father Streng.

Her head still bowed, the girl suddenly grinned. She swept a hand in front of her, then held out her arms as if to cradle a baby. "Fraulein Katharina Rosen, named for Saint Katharina of Siena," she said formally. "I am eleven."

Hampelmann squinted to see the girl more clearly. Katharina, the mystic saint. Eva had chosen a beautiful name for such a damaged child, though she did have a delicate, almost noble, profile. And the girl had spoken with an unusual dignity and composure for the child of a common baker and his low-born wife, for a child who'd just pissed herself.

"Your date of birth?"

"Sixteenth of March, 1615. And I know my numbers and my letters," she said proudly.

"And how have you come by those skills?" said Hampelmann.

"Mama taught me."

Hampelmann smiled. "Very good, Katharina. That's precisely

what we're here to discover…what your mother has taught you."

Judge Steinbach read from Father Streng's ledger. "Did you ever see your mother with Frau Imhof, Fraulein Stolzberger, or Frau Basser?"

"I do not know them, sir."

"You're sure?" said Father Streng.

"*Ja.*" Again, she swept her hand in front of her.

Hampelmann placed his elbows on the table and rested his chin on his laced fingers. "Did you ever see your mother meet with Frau Lamm or Fraulein Spatz?"

"I do not know them either."

"Did you ever see your mother talk with anyone who looked wicked?" asked Father Streng.

Katharina pointed at Freude. "Only him."

The executioner's glare took in both the girl and Lutz.

"Have you seen your mother with anyone of ill repute…or strangers?" said Hampelmann.

"Lots of strangers come into the bakery, but Mama would never let a witch in…if that's what you mean."

Clever girl, thought Hampelmann, to know what he was really asking. Or had Eva prepared her? "And why would your mother not associate with witches?" he said.

"She's deathly afraid of them. She won't even let me watch when they're carted through the marketplace. And she never goes to the burnings. Won't let me go either."

Father Streng dipped the quill. "Is your mother gone a lot?"

"*Nein*, she never leaves the bakery…except to go to mass."

"Why is that?"

"Who would tell Rudolf and Hans what to do?"

"Rudolf and Hans?" said Hampelmann.

"The journeymen."

"And what, exactly, does your mother do with Rudolf and Hans?" said Hampelmann.

"She tells them what bread to make, and when."

"Your mother gives orders to men?" said Father Streng. The mole above his eyebrow jumped.

The girl looked down at her hands.

"Does she sometimes go to the journeymen at night?" asked Hampelmann.

"Mama sleeps with me. She never leaves me. I'd be scared if she left."

"Did you ever hear your mother say that she wished your father would die?" said Judge Steinbach.

"*Nein*. Mama was sad when he died. She cried a lot. That's when I got to sleep in her bed. She cried at night, too."

"Didn't he discipline you and your mother by beating you?" said Hampelmann.

"*Ja*."

"Didn't you – and she – hate him for that?"

She hunched her shoulders, shrinking into herself. "*Ja*," she said softly. "But we didn't want him to die."

Father Streng pointed his quill at her. "How did your mother use the rocks and white feathers?"

The girl swallowed.

"Truth," said Lutz.

"The rocks and feathers are mine, not Mama's. I collect them."

"Why?"

"They're pretty."

Chancellor Brandt leaned toward the priest. "*Bitte*, a clarification, Father Streng." His dark eyebrows came together. "Does the Church forbid collecting feathers?"

"That would depend. If they're used as a sort of charm, that would be forbidden. But if they're merely collected and used in a practical manner, as in a mattress or a pen, that, of course, would be permissible." He stroked the quill against his chin. "To collect them because one finds them pretty would not appear to be expressly forbidden, though it's certainly not advisable as there would always be the temptation to use them in a diabolical manner."

Hampelmann's stomach growled. They were getting nowhere, and he was tired and hungry. He'd gone to the Lusam Garden and waited nearly two hours. Nothing. Nonetheless, he would be patient. God had a message for him.

"Have you ever seen your mother with the Devil?" said Hampelmann.

The girl pulled her feet up onto the bottom rung and gripped her knees.

"Truth," said Lutz.

She began to rock back and forth. "*Ja,*" she said quietly.

Lutz's mouth dropped open. He grabbed the back of the chair.

"When and where?" Hampelmann said eagerly.

"In the cell." The girl looked up at Freude. "When he comes in."

"Fraulein Rosen," said Father Streng, "explain what you mean."

She pointed. "He's the Devil." The girl peered into Freude's face. "Why aren't your eyes red now?"

Freude laughed uneasily. "She's a lunatic...or possessed."

"What did your mother do with the Devil?" asked Hampelmann.

"Do?"

"Have you ever seen the Devil and your mother engage in fornication?"

She stared blankly.

Lutz leaned toward her. "Have you ever seen your mother and the Devil...naked together?"

Katharina brought her small hand to her face and whispered to Lutz.

"What's she saying?" said Chancellor Brandt.

Lutz straightened and took a deep breath. "Fraulein Rosen

claims that when this man – she means Herr Freude, whom she believes to be the Devil – shaved them, her mother was naked. She also says that he touched her mother…in private places, and that he started to take off his breeches, but the jailer's wife came in."

Freude moved to strike the girl. Lutz stepped between him and Katharina. The executioner turned to the other commissioners. "We need to search her," he said. "She has a charm hidden on her somewhere. The Devil's using it to speak through her. She's possessed."

"Herr Freude," Hampelmann said coolly. "Have there been improprieties between you and the accused?"

"Of course not," Freude snapped. "When I shaved Frau Rosen, she was naked – as they all are. She tried her best to seduce me. That's what the girl saw. But I did not succumb to her witch's wiles. And quite obviously, I am not the Devil." He scowled at the girl. "We need to prepare for an exorcism."

"I don't think so," said Father Streng. "Fraulein Rosen's terribly confused. Her mind, as well as her foot, has been damaged. And though she moves her arms a bit oddly now and again, she shows no other signs of possession: no strange voices, no vomiting of foreign objects, no bodily contortions. Am I correct, Herr Hampelmann, in believing that there have been no reports to the *Malefizamt* about the girl herself?"

"Only that her crippled foot may be a sign that her mother's a witch. And, as we all know, witchcraft does run from mother to daughter."

"But we've not yet established that the mother is a witch," protested Lutz. "Fraulein Rosen says that she's seen her mother with the Devil, but if she believes that Herr Freude is the Devil, we cannot possibly conclude that her mother's actually met with the real Devil."

Hampelmann's head was beginning to throb. He breathed lavender through his pomander. They'd been sitting in that cold stinking chamber for hours, and the girl's testimony had only muddled the evidence even more. She'd admitted seeing her mother with the Devil, but since she'd identified Freude as the Devil, Lutz was right to raise the question. What, exactly, could they make of the girl's admission?

Judge Steinbach conferred briefly with Father Streng and Chancellor Brandt, then tapped the gavel. "The child has testified that she's seen her mother with the Devil," said the judge. "Even if she's confused about who the Devil is, the admission certainly provides enough evidence to justify light torture. That, gentlemen, will force Frau Rosen to reveal the truth."

Katharina pulled on Lutz's arm. "Does that mean they're going to hurt Mama?"

Lutz looked as if the executioner had put his thumbs under the screws.

The girl turned to the commissioners, her green eyes glinting. "You're all very wicked men."

25

24 April 1626

Katharina limped toward Eva, who searched her daughter's face for a sign of what had happened. Her heart clenched tight when she saw only fear and distress in Katharina's wild eyes.

Freude reached out to poke the girl with a birch rod, but Lutz wrenched it from his hand and threw it down. The rod clattered across the wood floor, coming to rest at Frau Brugler's feet.

"For God's sake," muttered Lutz, "leave the child alone."

"This is my profession, Herr Lutz. I know what I'm doing."

"Do you? Does it ever cross your mind that an innocent person may have died because of your certainty that you know what you're doing?"

"God would never allow it." Freude pointed a gloved finger at the lawyer. "I'll tell you what does cross my mind: that you might be one of them. You'd do well to heed the chancellor – and keep your mouth shut. You're risking everything…for nothing. It's as plain as the nose on your face that this damned stupid girl is possessed and her mother is the one responsible. Frau Rosen is a witch."

"She is not a witch! And the girl is not possessed!"

Eva rattled the chains of her shackles to attract Lutz's attention. "Please," she said softly, "do not leave us alone with him."

Lutz eyed Freude suspiciously. "I won't," he said.

"They're all guilty…of something," said Freude, sneering at Eva, then at Frau Brugler, and finally at Katharina, who'd pressed herself against the wall. "You know what the Bible says: *From the woman came the beginning of sin, and by her we all die*. Damn them all."

"And what book would that be in?" said Lutz sarcastically.

Freude spat on the floor. "Watch yourself, Lutz." He spun away from the lawyer and strode out the door. Frau Brugler closed it behind him.

"Ecclesiasticus," said Eva.

"What?"

"It's from Ecclesiasticus." She turned to Katharina. "Did they hurt you? Are you all right?"

Katharina moved into her mother's lap, cupped her hands around Eva's ear, and whispered. "The white dog came. She jumped into my lap and growled at them. I was scared, but she kept them from hurting me. And I didn't say anything about her, or about angels or angel wings either."

Eva nodded as if she'd heard nothing unusual, but she felt worms gnawing in the pit of her stomach.

Katharina dropped her hands. "I told them the truth. I told them you're not a witch and you don't know any of the people they asked about."

"You did well." Eva stroked her daughter's face. "What else did you tell them?"

Katharina averted her eyes. "Only the truth."

Gripping his ledger in both hands, Lutz leaned forward. "What is this…about your meeting with the Devil?"

"Mother of God, Katharina, you didn't?"

The jailer's wife wrapped her arms around her waist as if to protect herself, her eyes huge dark circles in a blanched face.

"I only told them the truth, Mama. That he came in and hurt you."

"Hurt me?" said Eva. What are you talking about? I've never even seen the Devil."

"He shaved you. And he hurt you. I saw him."

"Oh dear God," Eva wailed, shaking Katharina by the shoulders. "That's Herr Freude, not the Devil!"

"*Nein*, Mama, he is the Devil. He's the same man who–"

Eva slapped Katharina's mouth to silence her. The girl put a hand to her face and crept away, tears spilling down her cheeks.

"The same man who what?" asked Lutz, watching Katharina.

Hugging the wall, her back to her mother and the lawyer, Katharina rubbed her misshapen foot against her ankle. "The same man who comes to fetch us to answer questions for the other men," she said, sniffing.

"So it's true then?" said Lutz, turning to Eva. "The girl is simply confused about who the Devil is? She's never actually seen you with the real Devil?"

Frau Brugler stepped forward. The keys at her waist jangled. "Well, it's easy to see why the poor girl would think Herr Freude was the Devil himself."

Ignoring Frau Brugler's intrusion, Lutz spoke insistently to Eva. "Have you ever had any dealings with the Devil?"

Eva shook her head. The worms in her stomach still gnawed, twisting her bowels into knots. She desperately needed to purge, but could not shame herself that way in front of the lawyer.

"Would you swear, in the presence of Father Herzeim," said Lutz, "that you have never met with the Devil?"

Eva made the sign of the cross. "I swear it, Herr Lutz. I've never even seen the Devil. You must believe me."

"I do…I think."

Eva studied his face. "What do the other commissioners believe?"

He was silent, unable to meet her eyes.

"They have evidence then?"

"They have evidence."

"When will I be questioned again?"

"Monday morning." Lutz took a deep breath. "Frau Brugler, could you leave us now?"

"*Nein*, not allowed, unless the priest is with you."

Lutz stooped down close to Eva and whispered, so that Frau Brugler couldn't hear. "Listen, Frau Rosen, you could claim to be with child. Legally, they cannot torture a woman who's with child."

"But that would not be true, Herr Lutz. And it would mean that I had not been chaste, as I have claimed." She spoke loudly now. "God will protect me only if I speak the truth." She saw Frau Brugler nod.

Lutz stood and tucked his ledger under his arm. "God and I, we will do what we can." He walked slowly to the door, then turned. "Is there anything I can do for you?"

"*Bitte*, tell Father Herzeim I would like to see him. I need to hear the story of Job." Eva knew the story, nearly word for word, but she needed to hear it from the priest, to be reassured in her faith. God felt so far away.

As soon as Lutz had closed the door, Eva shouted, "Quick, the bucket!"

The jailer's wife rushed to fetch the bucket, which was already half full. Pain ripped through her belly as Eva, hampered by the shackles, struggled to pull the shift out of the way before the foul-smelling liquid splattered into the other wastes. She felt as if she were shitting her own bowels. When the worst of the pain had passed, she wiped herself with straw and tossed it into the bucket.

Frau Brugler made a face at the stench, but then looked upon Eva almost kindly. "I had to dress the others' wounds – a misery. Did they hurt your daughter?"

Eva didn't know how to answer. Katharina bore no visible wounds, but yes, they had hurt her.

Frau Brugler moved closer to the girl, who shrank away from her. "It's all right, child. I won't hurt you. I'm not like Herr Freude." She looked into Katharina's pale face, studied her eyes, then held up her arms, one at a time, and examined her small hands and fingers. "She seems all right. Her eyes are clear." She blew a puff of air through her snaggled teeth. "Pfpft! This girl is not possessed. I've seen women possessed by demons, and there's nothing scarier."

She put her hands on her hips. "Those commissioners make me mad, they do. I bring the prisoners food twice a day, clean up the messes, and tend to the wounds. You'd think they'd want to know what I think about who's guilty and who's not. But they never ask. Not me." She started pacing. "Oh sure, most of those accused of witchcraft are guilty. That's clear enough. But I'm not so certain about some…like you and your daughter…or that poor Fraulein Spatz."

Frau Brugler wagged a finger. "What I'd like to ask those fancy commissioners in all their fancy silk and satin is why there's never any of their wives or daughters in here. Always beggars and whores. Or spinsters. Or widows like yourself. How come there's never a Frau Lutz, a Frau Hampelmann, or a Frau Brandt? That's what I'd like to know."

Eva was hardly listening. Her gut – and her heart – still ached.

"I'm willing to bet there's some witches among the high and mighty, but their husbands and fathers protect them." The jailer's wife leaned closer to Eva. "Makes sense, doesn't it? Why wouldn't the Devil choose followers from among the rich and powerful instead of carousing with ugly old spinsters and widows?" She laid a finger on her chin. "Well, you're not old and ugly, and I don't mean to offend, but, honestly, why would the Devil waste his time with you or Fraulein Spatz when he could be seducing somebody who has some real power in this world?" She shrugged. "But they never ask what I think."

Frau Brugler picked up the bucket and left, locking the door behind her.

Still holding a hand over her mouth, Katharina came to her mother and sat in her lap. Eva wrapped her arms around her. Dear

God, she wondered, what would the commissioners do to them now? Why had Katharina told them she'd seen her mother with the Devil?

"Why, oh why, child, do you see the world the way you do? Herr Freude is evil, but he is not the Devil."

"Oh, but he is." Katharina was silent for a long time. "When I was over there by the wall and that old woman was talking, I was wishing I'd never been born."

Eva put her fingers over Katharina's lips, but the girl pulled her hand away. "You were right to hit me, Mama. Because of me, they're going to hurt you. I'm a curse to you."

"*Nein, Liebchen!*" Eva said the words, but felt the terrible truth of what Katharina had said. She had thought it herself.

Tears stung her eyes. Had her heart and soul died? How could she wish that Katharina, the only good thing in her life, had never been born? She hugged her daughter to her chest. "You are not a curse, *Liebchen*. You are a blessing. A wonderful blessing."

Eva was startled awake by the rasp of the key. Yellow light shone at the small barred window. The door creaked open, and a wedge of light sliced through the dark. A rat scurried along the wall until it found the shadows. Carrying a lantern before her, Frau Brugler came in. Wilhelm stepped in behind her, a lantern in his own hand.

Eva gasped. What could he want?

"Such an hour," Frau Brugler said nervously. "Decent folk are asleep in their beds."

"Leave us," Wilhelm said quietly, but firmly, breathing through his pomander. "And give me the key, then you can leave and go to your bed. I'll leave the key with the guard downstairs."

"That's not allowed," said Frau Brugler.

"Leave us," he shouted, the black plumes on his hat fluttering. "Or do you forget, old woman, that I am head of the *Malefizamt*?" He held out a gloved hand.

Katharina crept from Eva's arms to crouch in the shadows against the wall. Eva held her breath. Would he try to force her the way Herr Freude had? The way he'd once tried? Would he force Katharina?

Frau Brugler set down the lantern, unscrewed a key from the ring at her waist, and placed it into Wilhelm's palm. "This is not right, sir," she mumbled. She picked up the lantern and scurried out the door.

Wilhelm slipped the key into his breeches and walked slowly toward Katharina. Flipping his cape over one shoulder, he stooped down beside her and held the lantern close to her face. She edged away from him, but he reached out and cupped her chin in his gloved hand, turning her terrified face from one side to the other. With a forefinger, he traced her nose, chin, and jaw. He touched the stubble on her scalp. Finally he stood and came toward Eva. The gold thread in his brocade doublet gleamed in the candlelight.

"Who is that child's father?" he said bluntly.

"Jacob Rosen."

"Doubtful. The line of her nose and jaw bears a certain... nobility. Jacob Rosen was no noble."

"Her father was Jacob Rosen." Eva's voice shook.

"And you would swear that to be true...just as you have sworn to all your other lies before the commission?"

"Everything I've told the commissioners is true. I am not a witch, Wilhelm. You know that. How can you possibly believe that I am?"

"Would you swear before the commission that Jacob Rosen is the father of your daughter?"

Eva pressed her lips together.

"So I am right." Wilhelm bared his teeth in a grimace. "How did you seduce my father?"

"I didn't. I swear I didn't."

"It hardly matters what you swear – daughter of Eve." His eyes were an icy blue. "You rejected me…then seduced him."

"I was forced."

"Forced!" Wilhelm barked a harsh laugh. "Never would my father do such a thing. Never." He pointed at Katharina. "And there's the evidence, Eva. You conceived a child."

"He forced me."

"But conception requires pleasure."

Eva ran a hand over the prickly stubble on her scalp. "There was no pleasure, Wilhelm. Only shame. Only shame."

"My father was an honourable and righteous man. How could you do such a thing?" Wilhelm held the lantern close to her face. "You are truly a witch. You will pay for this with your life." He started toward the door, then turned back. Towering over her, he raised an arm. Eva readied herself for the blow.

His arm dropped to his side. "Damn you, Eva. Damn you."

26

25 April 1626

Eva watched a black rat creep along the wall, sniffing, perhaps drawn to the scent of her blood. There was nothing but dirty straw to soak up the darkness of her womb. She closed her eyes. She would not think of rats licking at bloody straw.

The morning bells rang out, prompting memories of the bakery and the warm fragrance of yeast and bread. Were the journeymen even baking bread anymore? Was anyone buying it, or did everyone believe the accusations against her?

Eva had been awake all night, her mind and heart roiling with contrition, sorrow, and deep foreboding. *Daughter of Eve*, Wilhelm had called her. A wicked temptress who'd seduced his father. She leaned against the wall, her whole body weighted down with shame. Wilhelm was right: she was a seductress. But it was not his father she'd seduced, but Jacob, as soon as she'd realized she was carrying a child. She couldn't bear the thought of being publicly dismissed from the Hampelmann household and having all of Würzburg know her shame, so she'd had to choose, quickly, a man who would marry her, a man who would believe her when she claimed the child was born early. Eva chose Jacob, an old childless widower, who was astounded and delighted by her attentions.

She had seduced a man, and she had lied to him. And for her sins, God had crippled her daughter. Jacob had been right to beat her.

Katharina dozed in Eva's lap, her arms held out to embrace the white dog. In the darkness before dawn, she'd stirred from her sleep to tell her mother that the white dog had kept the Devil away. She'd seen no visions in the night.

The white dog. Why did her daughter see it? What in the world was it? Mother of God, Eva prayed, please don't let her speak of the dog to anyone, especially the commissioners.

The commissioners. Her bowels twisted in her gut. All through the night Eva had wondered, again and again, what Wilhelm would do. Now that he knew Katharina was his sister, would he find a way to protect her, or, in his wrath, would he be determined to see her die, as if she had never been?

Eva had little doubt what he'd do to her. She'd seen the fury in his icy eyes. And Herr Lutz had no power to protect her. She'd seen that, too. But God had the power to save her. And surely he would. She might be guilty of other sins, but she was innocent of witchcraft. God protected the innocent.

She put her hands to her face and felt the wetness of tears. She knew the story of Job all too well. God had permitted Satan to test Job, a man who was righteous and upright in all ways. God had allowed Satan to destroy all that Job owned, to kill all of his sons and daughters, to make him ill and despised. Yet Job never lost faith.

Was God allowing Satan to test her, a woman who'd grievously sinned? Eva tried to wipe the back of her hand across her cheek, but the shackle scratched her skin. Was her faith strong enough to withstand the test? To withstand losing everything, even her only child?

The rat scuttled into a crevice. Eva turned toward the sound of the key and saw Father Herzeim's face in the window. Stepping quietly into the cell, the priest made the sign of the cross. "Herr Lutz said you wanted to see me."

"You must tell me the story of Job, Father. I must be strong in my faith. Like Job. I am to be tortured on Monday."

His haggard face paled.

"*My soul is weary of my life,*" she recited, recalling a lament from the Book of Job. She could not stop the flow of tears. "*I should have been as if I had not been, carried from the womb to the grave.*"

Father Herzeim knelt down in front of her. He placed his breviary by his knee and laid a hand on Katharina's forehead. A blessing. "Job was a righteous and faithful man," he said. "Yet he suffered – suffered horribly. He was not the author of his own suffering, Frau Rosen. Just as you are not the author of your suffering. Remember Job also said: *If we have received good things at the hand of God, why should we not receive evil?* Suffering is a mystery only God understands. But you must continue to have faith. And to insist on your innocence…no matter what they do."

"I am innocent." Eva looked away. "At least of witchcraft."

Father Herzeim put a hand to her cheek and wiped away a tear with his thumb. His touch was warm, and she tried not to flinch away from the fragrance of soap. His dark eyes held hers, and Eva saw not only kindness and grief, but also despair at her despair. She realized, in that moment, that she could love this man, his gentleness and his strength. But it would be a sin. He was a priest, a man of God, not an ordinary man. Were there no bounds to her sinfulness?

"If I tell the truth, will God protect me?" she asked.

His hand dropped. "God protects the innocent – in his own way. But you must help. No matter what the commissioners do, you must give them no grounds to continue the torture."

Katharina lifted her head. "Will God stop those awful men from hurting Mama?"

"The truth will stop them. And innocence." The priest's words lacked conviction, as if he did not believe them himself.

Eva touched his black sleeve. "*Bitte*, confess me, Father."

He scanned the cell. "What sins could you have committed while confined in this place?"

⇛

"Wicked thoughts."

Father Herzeim placed one hand on his breviary and the other on her bowed head.

"Forgive me, Father, for I have sinned. I have been weak. I have been guilty of losing faith, and I have doubted God's love and protection." Eva paused.

"Is there anything else you wish to confess?"

"I have thought wicked things about the commissioners…and about my daughter." Eva took a hiccupping breath. "I have blamed her when the fault is not hers." She began again to cry. Had she not wept every tear within her?

"*Let the day perish wherein I was born,*" she whispered, feeling Job's curse in the marrow of her bones. "*Let darkness, and the shadow of death cover it, let a mist overspread it, and let it be wrapped up in bitterness.*"

She felt his hand cup her chin. "*Nein,* Eva, *nein.* Do not lose faith. There are those who will be punished, severely, in the eternal life to come, but you are not among them."

"But what of this life, Father?" She looked up and saw a tear threatening to spill onto his own cheek.

"You are forgiven," he said. "Everything. *Ego te absolvo, in nomine patris, et filii, et spiritus sancti.*"

21

25 April 1626

Fraulein Spatz stared at her damaged hands. The mutilated thumbs made Lutz cringe. Herr Hampelmann was wrong about them feeling no pain. Lutz and Father Herzeim had visited the midwife earlier that day, and she'd been nearly out of her mind with pain, both arms useless, pulled from their sockets. The visit had been brief, very brief. Frau Lamm had spat at them only one word: *schwein*.

Fraulein Spatz talked to herself as she rocked back and forth. "I'm dead…dead. They'll burn me. Lies. All of it. I never did those things. The midwife never did those things. Why didn't God protect me? I must be wicked. I must be guilty." She turned to Father Herzeim. "What can I do?"

Lutz stepped toward her. "When you are questioned again, you must retract your lies. You must insist on your innocence."

Father Herzeim grabbed Lutz's arm and spun him away from Fraulein Spatz. "Don't do this," he whispered. "If she has truly confessed, it is done. If she withdraws her confession, they'll torture her until she confesses again. Doing what you ask will only prolong her agony."

"But if she's put to the test and maintains her innocence, they'll have to believe her."

The priest grimaced. "You saw Frau Lamm. Do you think this girl can withstand that? And there is more Herr Freude can do, much more. He has only begun with Frau Lamm. Because of Fraulein Spatz's confession, the commissioners have all the evidence they need to proceed to the third degree. The girl would never survive it."

"But if she's innocent, God will help her. He protects the innocent. Doesn't he?" Lutz could hear the pleading in his own voice.

Father Herzeim put a hand on his cedar cross. "Do not encourage her to retract her confession. That will only make it worse for her...and more dangerous for you."

"But what can I do?"

"Nothing. She is my responsibility now."

Stunned, Lutz stepped back. Nothing? He could do nothing? He brought his pomander to his nose. The scent of hartshorn was unpleasantly sharp, but it kept him from fainting.

"What can I do?" said Fraulein Spatz, echoing Lutz's question.

Looking older and more haggard than Lutz had ever seen him, Father Herzeim knelt down beside the girl. "Unless you truly believe you can withstand more torture, do not retract your confession to the commissioners."

"No more," she mouthed. Tears made dirty trails down her cheeks and dripped from her chin.

Lutz felt hollow, impotent, useless. He had failed, utterly, to protect this girl. Why hadn't God protected her?

"You must confess your sins," said Father Herzeim.

Fraulein Spatz bowed her head, tried to make the sign of the cross, then cried out in pain. "Forgive me, Father, for I have sinned. I lied to the commissioners. All of it lies. Frau Lamm will die because of me," she wailed. "They're right. I am wicked. And evil. I am a murderer."

"*Nein*, child, you are not evil. And if you are a murderer, it is only because they have made you so. It is their sin, not yours." Father Herzeim's words were hard and bitter. He made the sign of the cross over her. "*Ego te absolvo, in nomine patris, et filii, et spiritus sancti.* All of your sins are forgiven, Fraulein Spatz."

"Forgiven?" She did not lift her head. "Even Frau Lamm's death?"

"Forgiven."

"Will I burn in hell?"

"If you have confessed the truth now, you will not burn in hell. *Ego te absolvo, in nomine patris, et filii, et spiritus sancti.*"

"Will I burn here?"

Father Herzeim laid a hand on her shoulder. "If you do not retract your confession to the commission, you will be beheaded or strangled first." His voice cracked.

She slumped against the wall. "Thanks be to God."

28

26 April 1626

Shifting on the hard wooden bench, Lutz glanced around the crowded cathedral. His own thoughts buzzed so loudly he could hardly hear the priest's droning voice. He could not remove Fraulein Spatz from his mind. He had little doubt now that she'd confessed the truth to Father Herzeim. She'd been terrified for the fate of her soul.

Lutz rubbed his temples, trying to ease the throbbing. Would he ever know such torment that beheading or strangling would seem a mercy? That he'd be grateful to God for such a mercy?

How could Father Streng be so certain the young woman was guilty? Lutz craned his neck, looking for the young priest, who sat near the front of Saint Kilian's with the other members of the Cathedral Chapter. Father Streng also claimed it was the Devil who helped Frau Lamm, not God. How could he be so sure? As a Jesuit, did he have some secret knowledge that Lutz wasn't privy to? But Father Herzeim was a Jesuit, and he and Father Streng couldn't be further apart on the question of who was helping the midwife. Father Herzeim had even made Lutz doubt his own certainty about Frau Lamm's guilt.

He felt a shiver of fear go through him. Was it possible that he – and Father Herzeim – were being deluded by the Devil into believing the accused were innocent? Perhaps that's why God hadn't helped them. They were guilty. Or was the Devil, with all his powers, deluding the other commissioners into believing that innocent women were guilty? Either way, the Devil won.

Lutz had thought himself into a tangle, a maze with no escape. He felt as if his head would explode, as if he were living a nightmare. One huge unending nightmare that had encompassed them all. Where was truth?

He looked up. It seemed wrong that the sun should stream through the stained-glass windows and warm the cathedral with cheery rainbows of light. Everything should be in black and shades of grey.

Maria elbowed him in the belly. Lutz moved to his knees, folded his hands for prayer, and tried to listen to the priest, but his thoughts – and his gut – churned, bringing a burning pain to his chest and throat. He stared at the crucifix. Where was God in all of this? Lutz had seen the doubt in Father Herzeim's eyes, heard it in his voice. The priest didn't believe that God protected the innocent. At least not in this earthly life. Why were the commissioners so certain he did? Lutz studied the suffering figure of Christ. His own son had been innocent, and God hadn't even protected him.

Lutz bowed his head. Dear Father, he prayed, forgive my doubts. Forgive my weakness. But please give me a sign. Show me your will. Grant me the strength and courage to do whatever it is I must do. If they are truly innocent, help me to protect Frau Lamm and Frau Rosen. If they are not, help me to know that.

Maria touched him lightly on the shoulder, her concerned face close to his. He looked around. No one else was kneeling. He slid back onto the bench and scrubbed his face with his hands. He hadn't slept at all the night before, tossing and turning, tangling the bed linens, soaking them with sweat. Maria had wondered aloud if he were ill. Perhaps he was. For the first time in his life, even the thought of food was revolting.

Maria slipped her hand into his. He forced a smile. He wanted desperately to talk with her about the hearings and about his doubts. And his fears. He wanted her reassurance that he was not a monster. But Maria was already afraid. Twenty times a day, her hand fluttered like a bird across her chest, making the sign of the cross. Every morning, she came to Saint Kilian's to light candles and pray. Telling her anything more would only add to her terror.

"St. Augustine himself has written," shouted the priest from the raised pulpit, "that he *most firmly holds and in no way doubts that not only every pagan, but every Jew, heretic, and schismatic will go to the eternal fire, which is prepared for the Devil and his angels, unless, before the end of his life, he be reconciled with and restored to the Catholic Church.*"

Eternal fire. Lutz had never given it much thought before, but now he wondered. Would all those people, whose only sin was to believe the wrong thing about God, really be condemned to burn? It would be heresy to voice that question aloud. Lutz searched the cathedral for Father Herzeim. The Jesuit's face was unreadable even as he listened attentively to the priest. Damn, if in nothing else, his friend was right in one thing: people ought to be allowed to debate and discuss, to give voice to their doubts without fearing for their very lives.

"Indeed," the priest intoned, "one has only to look at the evidence to see that the poor harvests and pestilence now plaguing Würzburg are the wages of sin. And sloth." He dipped his head toward Prince-Bishop Philipp Adolf, who sat at the very front of Saint Kilian's in an ornately adorned cubicle. Lutz imagined the deep scowl the priest's words had brought to His Grace's face. *Wages of sin and sloth.* The Prince-Bishop must be seething.

"In his forty years as Prince-Bishop," continued the priest, "the great Julius Echter approved the execution orders for hundreds of witches. In the year before he died, 300 were beheaded and burned. And Würzburg knew peace and prosperity."

The priest lowered his voice, almost to a whisper, yet his

words resonated through the cathedral. "But then came Prince-Bishop Johann Gottfried. In seven years, less than a dozen killed." His lip curled. "Apparently he had no interest in witches."

His voice grew louder, its pitch higher. "And that is why Würzburg suffers today. The wrath of God is not diminishing in this age of wars, privations, and pestilence, as the world goes through its agonizing death throes approaching the end-time. Instead, God's wrath grows fiercer everywhere, because all manner of sins and vices are gaining the upper hand in this Godless world."

The priest raised his arms in a sweeping gesture toward the Prince-Bishop. "But now His Grace is putting things to right. Despite the grave dangers to his own person, he is pursuing the Devil's agents with utmost zeal. Würzburg shall once again be a city of the righteous, a city of God."

Lutz imagined the Prince-Bishop's scowl relaxing into a broad smile.

How many of those hundreds put to death had been innocent? And who was responsible? The Prince-Bishop or the commissioners? Or God himself, for allowing the deaths to happen, for not protecting the innocent? Lutz thought of Father Herzeim's book, the one he kept hidden. *But when the great searcher of hearts shall appear, your wicked deeds shall be revealed, you tyrants, sanguinary judges, butchers, torturers...the truth you have trampled under foot and buried shall arise and condemn you.*

Where was truth?

Lutz felt as powerless and inconsequential as one of the motes floating in the rainbows of light, moved hither and thither by unseen forces.

God or Satan? What force was moving him?

29

21 April 1626

Judge Steinbach tapped the gavel, startling Hampelmann, who'd been paging through his ledger, but thinking about his father. And Eva. Together. It made his stomach turn.

"We've lost another one," said the judge. "Fraulein Spatz is dead. Her throat slit."

"Oh my God," said Lutz. "That poor girl."

"Poor girl?" Father Streng threw down his quill. "This is exactly what I feared. We stopped the questioning too soon. Now the Devil has killed our most valuable informant."

"How can you be so sure it was the Devil?" said Lutz.

"It's just like Frau Bettler," said the priest. "The Devil kills them before they can reveal anything more."

Lutz's face took on its customary look of befuddlement. "But if the Devil can come into the jail with a knife," he said, "why doesn't he just slit the throats of the guards and free the accused?"

Behind his spectacles, Father Streng rolled his eyes. "Herr Lutz, surely you must realize that God himself assists us in our work. He does not allow the Devil to liberate witches who've been arrested. Nor does the Devil want to free them. They're of no use to him once they've been revealed as witches. He wants them to die before they can escape from him by obtaining pardon from God through sacramental confession."

Hampelmann had heard these arguments before, but he wasn't entirely convinced that the deaths of witches in jail were always the work of the Devil. There were times when he suspected Frau Brugler of having altogether too much pity for the accused and of smuggling to them the means to take their own lives. It always amazed him that, even with all their contact with witches, so many jailers and guards failed to comprehend just how dangerous they were. Only a few months ago, the Prince-Bishop had had to order the execution of a guard who'd helped an accused witch to escape. That was part of their menace: witches could so easily seduce or deceive unwary or stupid people into helping them.

"But Fraulein Spatz had already confessed," said Lutz. "I was there when she made her confession to Father Herzeim."

Father Streng held up a hand, palm toward Lutz. "She should not have confessed while you were there, and you cannot reveal what she said. But if Fraulein Spatz has confessed and been reconciled with God, then the commission has done its work well. We have saved her eternal soul."

"But then why would the Devil kill her?" said Lutz, his jaw clenched.

"So she couldn't reveal anything more to us," said Chancellor Brandt. "A pity. It really is. Now we have only Frau Lamm, who is entirely uncooperative, and Frau Rosen, whose case is weak."

"And the Rosen girl," added Freude.

"She has *not* been accused," said Lutz.

Father Streng polished his spectacles on the sleeve of his cassock. "What do we do about the Rosen girl?"

The Rosen girl. Hampelmann had been obsessed with her since the questioning three days ago when he first noticed her striking resemblance to his own daughter. He'd noted Katharina's date of birth, quickly calculated backwards, and realized that, unless one took as truth Eva's dubious claim that Katharina was born early, Eva had been working in the Hampelmann household when she conceived, at least two months shy of her betrothal to Jacob Rosen. Hampelmann thought he was prepared when he went to her cell; even so, he was shocked by what he heard from Eva's own lips. He fell into a blackness then that no amount of St. John's wort or hellebore could relieve. For two days and three long nights, he couldn't eat, couldn't sleep, couldn't even clear his mind for meditation and prayer in the Lusam Garden. He was hardly surprised the angel didn't return, not when he could think of nothing but Eva. And his father. And the product of their sin. The girl was of his own blood. Noble blood corrupted by witch's blood. A cripple. He bore no responsibility, but still, he felt ashamed, as if the sin were his own.

A hand closed on his arm. He looked from the pale hand to Father Streng's perplexed face, then down to the pile of paper fragments before him, the remains of a page from his ledger Hampelmann's fingers had just shredded.

"The girl is possessed," said Freude. "And her mother is responsible."

Lindner sat, clicking his thumbnail against his front teeth. "Possession is nearly always evident from its outward signs: voices, flailing, contortions," the physician said thoughtfully. "The Rosen girl seems more dim-witted and confused than possessed. I recommend that we proceed to the questioning of Frau Rosen under torture. The girl's testimony has provided enough evidence for that at least."

"*Nein!*" shouted Lutz. "There is no evidence. If the girl is dim-witted, her testimony should be discarded."

"Not in cases of witchcraft," said Father Streng.

"I concur," said Chancellor Brandt. "What do you think, Herr Hampelmann?"

Hampelmann rubbed his gritty eyes and tried to recall what had just been said. "I-I'm not sure. Are you asking about the girl's possession or discarding her testimony? Or the questioning of Frau Rosen?"

"Not sure?" The chancellor gave Hampelmann a withering scowl, then pointed at the judge's gavel.

"Herr Freude," said Judge Steinbach, "bring in Frau Rosen."

Lutz released a long exhalation that whistled through his teeth.

Father Streng turned to Hampelmann. "What is wrong with you? Are you ill?"

"It's nothing. A mild griping of the bowels. I slept poorly." Hampelmann cupped his pomander in his palm, examined the gold filigree, then brought it to his nose. Lavender and hellebore, always lavender and hellebore. He should have put in hartshorn, something to clear his head of the fog. He needed to prepare himself for Eva's questioning. He ground his teeth. How could she have chosen his father over him? How could she have led such a good and pious man into sin? Claiming he'd forced her was ludicrous. His father, the righteous and upstanding Herr Doktor Hampelmann, forcing a maidservant? Impossible. Hampelmann stared at his gold ring, the family crest. He polished it on the sleeve of his silk doublet. But at the very least his father had allowed himself to be seduced. By a witch! Had his father confessed to his lust before he died? Or was he writhing in hell at this very moment?

Freude returned with Eva, who stepped backwards into the chamber, a rusty-brown stain on the back of her shift. The executioner prodded her, and she turned to face the commissioners. Looking directly at Hampelmann, her green eyes held a desperate plea. He seethed. How dare she appear before them as if she were weak and helpless?

Father Streng came forward with the crucifix. "By the belief that you have in God and in the expectation of paradise, and being aware of the peril of your soul's eternal damnation, do you swear that the testimony you are about to give is true, such that you are willing to exchange heaven for hell should you tell a lie?"

"I swear, by all that is holy."

The priest noticed the drops of dark blood between Eva's bare feet and scrambled backwards. "The filth of women," he muttered, taking his seat at the table.

"Frau Rosen," said Judge Steinbach. His voice quavered. "In your previous questioning, you persisted in denying all the charges against you – killing your husband, making Herr Kaiser ill, attending the sabbath. Do you wish to reconsider those denials?"

"*Nein*, I do not."

"Are you quite sure?" said Chancellor Brandt. "Because your own daughter claims that you have, indeed, met with the Devil."

"But Katharina believes that Herr Freude is the Devil," said Lutz, "so it is not accurate to say that Fraulein Rosen testified that her mother met with the real Devil."

Chancellor Brandt ignored Lutz's protest. "Look around you, Frau Rosen, at the tools we can use to extract the truth. I ask again, are you quite certain that you wish to deny all the accusations against you? Or do you wish to confess now – and spare yourself?"

Hampelmann twisted his ring. His palms were damp.

Eva looked at the thumbscrews, which had been cleaned and polished since they'd been used on Fraulein Spatz and Frau Lamm. "I am innocent, and by the grace of God, my innocence will be proved."

"Very well then." Judge Steinbach banged the gavel, its ring reverberating through Hampelmann's aching head. "We, the members of the Commission of Inquisition for the Würzburg Court, having considered the details of the inquiry enacted by us against you, Frau Rosen, find that you have been taciturn in withholding information from us. After questioning Fraulein Katharina Rosen, there is now enough evidence to warrant examining you under torture. You may proceed, Father Streng, Herr Freude."

Lutz laid his head on the table and groaned.

Herr Freude prodded Eva toward the chair. Careful to avoid defilement by the blood on the floor, Father Streng stepped forward and made the sign of the cross over Eva and the thumbscrews, then sprinkled holy water over both. "*In nomine patris, et filii, et spiritus sancti.*" He returned to the table and picked up his quill.

Freude grabbed Eva's bound hands and placed her thumbs under the metal plate. He tightened the centre screw just enough to hold them in place. Her lips trembled, but Eva did not pull away or try to resist.

"Do you wish to confess now, before I begin?" Freude growled.

"I have nothing to confess."

The executioner turned the centre screw. Eva cried out, and Hampelmann nearly screamed with her, so great was the shooting pain in his own thumbs. His fingers curled tightly around them. He forced himself to straighten his fingers and look at his thumbs. They were undamaged.

"When and where did you first meet with the Devil?" said Father Streng.

"Never," she wailed.

Herr Freude gave the screw another turn. Hampelmann heard the sickening crunch. Blood trickled onto the instrument. Pain shot from Hampelmann's thumbs to his forearms. Dear God, what was happening?

"When and where did you meet with the Devil?" repeated Father Streng.

"*Nein,*" she whispered.

Herr Freude gave the screw yet another turn, and Eva's head fell backward. Though she held her lips tightly together, an animal cry escaped.

Hampelmann couldn't draw breath. The pain was unbearable. He'd watched this procedure dozens of times and never felt this.

He saw blood gathering under his thumbnails. Horrified, he put his hands under the table.

"When and where have you met with the Devil?" repeated Father Streng, his voice rising.

Eva lifted her head. "*The Lord gave, and the Lord hath taken away. As it hath pleased the Lord so is it done. Blessed be the name of the Lord.*"

The priest leaped up. "She dares quote to us from Job!" Behind his spectacles, his grey eyes were enormous. Freude forced Eva's jaws open, and Father Streng poured holy water into her mouth. Eva sputtered and choked.

"Surely that will free her from the Devil's grasp," said Father Streng. "Proceed, Herr Freude."

"*I will say to God, Do not condemn me. Tell me why thou judgest me so.*" Eva's voice was barely audible. "*And shouldst know that I have done no wicked thing.*"

Hampelmann blinked, then blinked again at the strands of thin white mist her words had woven around her. Job's lament. Without thinking, he completed the lament, murmuring to himself, "*Thy hands have made me, and fashioned me wholly round about, and dost thou thus cast me down headlong?*"

Lutz opened and closed his fists. Hampelmann saw blood oozing from his thumbnails as well. He glanced at Judge Steinbach's hands, which lay folded upon the gavel. Blood pooled beneath them.

Eva looked at Hampelmann, her eyes wide and distant. "*Thou hatest all the workers of iniquity. Thou wilt destroy all that speak a lie.*" Her head sank to her chest. "*Deliver me from my enemies.*"

Agitated, Father Streng danced around the chamber, pointing at Eva. "The witch now dares to quote from Psalms?"

A loud chuckling erupted from the shadows. Hampelmann saw a tall dark man with glowing red eyes and a broad grin. His exposed member was huge and erect, and he shoved his hips forward obscenely. Staring at Hampelmann, he raised his arm and crooked his long bony finger, beckoning.

Hexen gestank. Hampelmann nearly choked on the stench. Though the pain in his thumbs was excruciating, he laid one shaking hand on Father Streng's breviary and, with the other, touched the ball of wax at his throat. "*In nomine patris, et filii, et spiritus sancti,*" he whispered.

Eva raised her head and fixed her gaze upon the man. His arm dropped, his grin became a grimace, and his member withered. He began to fade, until all that was left was a wisp of black smoke smelling faintly of witches' stench.

Hampelmann gasped and turned to Chancellor Brandt, but his face was impassive. Did he not see that? Hampelmann spread his hands. The pain had subsided. There was no blood under his nails, no blood on the table. Was this the message the angel in the Lusam Garden had come to deliver? A sign from God that Eva was innocent? But the other men were so calm. Had no one else seen Eva save them?

"When did you meet with the Devil?" said Father Streng.

"*Nein,*" Eva sobbed. Her head rested on one shoulder. "It would be a sin…to confess…to something I did not do. I would rather die here…than die to eternal life."

"Proceed!" The priest's voice was shrill.

Freude shook his head. "I cannot tighten the screw any more."

Lutz stood. "It is done then! She has withstood the test. She has shown herself to be innocent."

"We must proceed further," insisted Father Streng.

"*Nein!*" shouted Lutz.

"But the Devil is helping her. We must continue."

Judge Steinbach feebly tapped the gavel. "Order! Order!"

Hampelmann stood, swaying. He leaned against the table. "It is not the Devil who is helping her. It is God. Frau Eva Rosen is innocent."

30

He cannot admit, even to himself, that he desires the woman, has always desired her. So the man with the pale hair conjures me to give him a sign. I chuckle out loud. Me? Bring a sign from God?

He has been taught that I am a dark man, so he sees darkness and black smoke. It is the little girl who told him that my eyes are red and glowing.

His lust has almost destroyed the woman. Now it may save her. Lucky woman.

The midwife is not so lucky. No one will conjure a sign for her. She stands, shoulders slumped, arms hanging limp, wrists bound.

The little priest prays and sprinkles holy water. He is red-faced, and stinks of sweat and fear.

They ask their questions. Always the same: when and where did she meet with the Devil? How and when and in what positions did she fuck me? (Though they are always careful to say 'fornicate' or 'sexual intercourse.') They are sure my cock (they say 'member') is huge and cold, but desirable to spinsters and widows nonetheless.

She curses them. Sons of whores. Sodomites. Fuckers of sheep and goats. And little boys.

The men flinch. Some of them have never heard such words from the mouth of a woman.

The executioner prods the midwife to the floor. He pours water into her mouth, then forces a wet rag down her throat. The rag is attached to a hemp cord. He yanks the cord and pulls the rag from her gullet. There is blood.

The fat lawyer, who is not so fat anymore, covers his face with his hands.

They repeat their questions. She is silent, except for her choking moans.

The executioner grits his teeth, furious with the silence that defies him. He forces the rag down her throat again. More questions. The midwife gags on the cord, but does not answer. The rag comes up. More blood.

He unties her wrists, rolls her over, and yanks her arms behind her back. She screams, then collapses, and for a few moments, feels no pain. He binds her arms to the thick rope hanging from the pulley on the ceiling, turns the wooden wheel to lift her up off the floor.

She dangles. *Nun fuckers*, she screams.

He ties stone weights to her ankles.

They repeat their questions again. So tedious.

The executioner draws her up, then lets her fall, jerking her to a halt before the stones can crack against the floor. The fat lawyer covers his ears to shut out the popping and snapping of bones and joints. Her screams ring off the walls. The fat lawyer screams with her.

The midwife's body goes as limp as the bloody rag.

The physician raises a cautioning hand. They cannot afford to lose another one, he says.

31

21 April 1626

Eva puked, again and again, every jerking movement provoking fiery pain. Her thumbs throbbed with every beat of her heart. Yet her heart was comforted. God had protected her! She had withstood the torture, and Wilhelm believed she was innocent.

When would someone come to release them?

Katharina huddled against her mother. She studied Eva's face, but would not look at the smashed thumbs.

The rasp of the key. At last! The door creaked open and Frau Brugler stepped in, Herr Lutz and Father Herzeim close behind.

"When will they let us go?" said Eva.

Lutz bowed his head. Father Herzeim laid a hand over his wooden cross. The jailer's wife scuttled out the door.

"They know now that I am innocent," said Eva, her terror rising. "They have to release us!"

"They wish to question Katharina again," Lutz said quietly.

Eva threw back her head and howled. She had proved herself innocent. How could they do this to Katharina? To her? She pulled at her shackles, then cried out in pain.

Father Herzeim knelt down beside her. He tenderly took her hands in his, but even the slightest touch caused agony. Eva nearly fainted from pain. He released her hands and grasped her shoulders.

Eva wanted desperately to move into his embrace, to accept the comfort he offered. But not from a priest. Mother of God, not from a priest.

He leaned close, his melancholy face only a hand span from

hers. She could see the web of fine lines around his eyes. "You must continue to be strong, Frau Rosen. You have won a great victory. And God willing, Katharina will win another."

"And what if God is not willing?"

Katharina wiped at the tears on Eva's cheek. "Mama, I will be strong for you. The angels will help me." The girl turned and smiled, then reached out and hugged empty air to her chest. "I knew you'd come back," she whispered.

Lutz tilted his head toward Katharina. "Who'd come back?"

"The white—"

"Father Herzeim," Eva said quickly. "She finds his presence a great comfort."

Though the priest's expression did not change, Eva could see the question in his dark eyes. "Katharina," he said, "you must be strong for your mother."

"When will they question her?" asked Eva.

"Tomorrow morning," said Lutz.

Father Herzeim squeezed Eva's shoulders, then stood. "Is there anything you need, Frau Rosen?"

"God."

Eva clenched her teeth to keep from screaming.

Cooing softly, as if she were bathing a newborn baby, Frau Brugler carefully washed Eva's hands in warm water stained a pale brown by leaves of comfrey and purslane. The woman patted them dry, then dabbed a foul-smelling ointment over the wounds. "There now, I know this hurts, but it'll help them to heal without festering." She wrapped Eva's hands in clean rags, then, with a long sigh, locked her wrists into the shackles. "I wish I didn't have to do this to you. I knew all along you and your little girl weren't witches."

She put a stoneware mug to Eva's lips. "Here, drink this. It's wretched tasting, but it'll ease the pain."

Eva caught the scent of hellebore and valerian. The draught was so bitter she could hardly swallow without choking.

The jailer's wife left and returned with two bowls of soup and fresh bread. She fed Eva spoonfuls of the hot rich broth, which contained chunks of real meat, pork. "It's from my own table," said Frau Brugler.

Eva wept at the woman's kindness.

"The midwife won't give them a thing," said Frau Brugler, lifting the spoon to Eva's mouth. "She's a tough one. Most women would've been long dead by now."

Eva looked at her bandaged hands. They'd smashed her thumbs, and that had been agony. What else had they done to the midwife? What else would they do to her? To Katharina? Dear God, she prayed, please help Katharina to be strong. Give her the words that would free them.

"Proves she's a witch," continued Frau Brugler. "I always knew she was. I could tell by her evil eyes. I can always tell by the eyes. That's how I knew you and your daughter were innocent. But do they ever ask me? Never. Those high and mighty commissioners would never think of asking the opinion of an old crone like me."

She winked at Eva. "But I have my ways. Fraulein Spatz was innocent, too. *Ask, and it shall be given you.* That's what I live by. So I gave the poor girl a bit of help when she asked."

The woman wagged a finger at Katharina, who was eagerly stuffing fresh bread into her mouth. "Girl, you've got to be strong for your mama tomorrow. Don't give the bastards anything. Even if they hurt you."

"They can't hurt me," Katharina mumbled around a mouthful of bread.

"Oh, but they can, girl."

"*Nein,* they can't, because–" She stopped, finally heeding her mother's warning glare. "Because we are innocent," she murmured.

"I hope you're right, child."

When Frau Brugler left, Katharina settled at Eva's side. The girl stroked the air over her own lap. "Mama," she said, "can I tell no one about the white dog?"

"No one," said Eva. "Even a whisper about her could mean death for both of us."

"But why? She's a good thing, like an angel."

"The commissioners would not understand, *Liebchen*."

"But she is true."

Eva stared at the space over Katharina's lap, trying to discern at least the dim outline of what her daughter saw and believed to be true. She saw nothing. "They do not see her," she said finally, "so it is not a falsehood to say nothing of her."

Eva was startled from a feverish aching sleep. A dim glow at the window. She heard rats scrambling as the door swung open. The lantern the guard carried illuminated the dark frown on his face. "There's someone here to see you," he said.

Wilhelm stood behind him. "Leave us," he said gruffly. "And leave your key. I will let myself out."

"*Nein*, I cannot," said the guard.

Eva shivered, with cold and with fear. Had Wilhelm come to test her? Did he no longer believe she was innocent? Had he come to kill Katharina? Eva glanced at her helpless daughter, sleeping in the straw beside her, and desperately hoped the guard would stay.

"Leave us! I am head of the *Malefizamt*. You take your orders from me."

The guard's scowl deepened. He gave Wilhelm a measuring look, then handed over a single key from the iron ring and left, the door scraping closed behind him. Katharina stirred, then turned and lay still, pretending to sleep, but Eva could feel her trembling.

Wilhelm's demeanour changed at once. Placing his own

lantern safely away from the straw, he knelt down in front of Eva and put his hands to her face. His fingers were dry and cool. There was a softness in his blue eyes that Eva had seen only once before: the day twelve years ago when he told her he wanted to marry her.

"I have seen a sign," he said. "When you were tortured, I felt the pain in my own hands."

Anger surged through Eva. She held out her bandaged hands. "How could you *possibly* feel my pain?"

He took her hands into his own and kissed them gently. "I felt it, Eva. I bled with you. And I saw a sign from God confirming your innocence."

"A sign from God?"

"I saw you do it. With a single glance you banished the Devil from the chamber. Eva, you proved what Jean Bodin has written: *It cannot be denied that witches occasionally conspire maliciously to accuse a totally innocent person of complicity in their crimes. But in such cases, Almighty God has invariably revealed the innocence of such persons in a miraculous manner.* I saw a miracle." Wilhelm was almost giddy.

"Forgive me," he said, "for ever desiring you, for even thinking of defiling you." He bowed his head. "And please forgive my father. It was his sin, not yours, that crippled Katharina. Never should you have been forced to know a man. You are like the Holy Mother, pure and good."

He reached out and ran his fingertips over her bare scalp. "Your hair. Your beautiful hair. Your crowning glory." Wilhelm placed his hands on her shoulders then, just as Father Herzeim had, but Eva felt no desire to accept comfort from this man. She wanted to pull away from his embrace. Instead, she held her breath, afraid to move.

"I will forgive you," she said finally, "if you will stop them from questioning Katharina, if you will make them release us."

Wilhelm looked away, his lips pressed tightly together. "I cannot stop them from calling your daughter to testify, but I can protect her. I will not allow that odious Herr Freude to touch her. And I will insist that the commission recommend to the Prince-Bishop that you and your daughter be released."

His blue eyes lost their softness, and his words took on a bitter edge. "I understand now that it was the evil of others that led to your arrest. Witches conspired to name you as an accomplice. And when Herr Kaiser filed his complaint with the Lower City Council and claimed later that you'd made him ill, I should have questioned his motives. I am certain now that he was plotting with other bakers to put the Rosen Bakery out of business. It was another baker, Herr Russ, who filed the report with the *Malefizamt* claiming that the death of your husband was by witchcraft. I promise you, Eva, you shall have justice. I will have these men, and anyone else who has accused you, arrested."

"*Nein*, Wilhelm. Arrest no one on my account."

"But they must be punished."

"Please! No more arrests! I want nothing from you but freedom."

He dropped his hands from her shoulders and rocked back on his heels. "I believe these men should be punished for causing such harm to an innocent. But because I am begging your forgiveness, Eva, I will do as you ask. And because I have allowed myself to be led astray by the malice of others, I will beg God's forgiveness as well. And I will ask his help in freeing you. And Katharina…my sister."

32

~

28 April 1626

Judge Steinbach laid his gold watch on the table. "Bring in the Rosen girl, Herr Freude."

Lutz's feet jiggled nervously. Beside him, Hampelmann sat straight-backed, calm and composed. Had he really seen a sign from God? He'd managed to convince them all – except Freude – that he'd seen Frau Rosen banish the Devil from the chamber. Lutz had seen nothing of the sort, nor had any of the other men, and they'd remained sceptical enough to insist on questioning Katharina at least one more time.

Freude and Katharina appeared in the doorway. The girl looked fragile, her bald head perched on a willowy stalk. She was shaking, either with cold or fear. Lutz wished he could wrap her in a thick wool blanket, take her bare feet into his hands, and rub them until they were warm and pink. He wanted to see the child smile and to hear her laugh. She was so delicate he imagined her laugh would sound like finely tuned chimes.

The executioner nudged her forward. Katharina stepped into the chamber, her arms held oddly before her, as if she were dancing. Lutz went to stand beside her.

Father Streng approached Katharina with the crucifix. "By the belief that you have in God and in the expectation of paradise," said the priest, "and being aware of the peril of your soul's eternal damnation, do you swear that the testimony you are about to give is true, such that you are willing to exchange heaven for hell should you tell a lie?"

"I shall speak only truth." Katharina made the sign of the cross. "*In nomine patris, et filii, et spiritus sancti.*"

Father Streng returned to the table, and Freude prodded the girl toward the chair. Before she sat down, she peeked up at Lutz. He leaned forward and spoke into her ear. "Truth, Katharina. But nothing more."

"State your name and age," said Father Streng.

"You know already that I am Fraulein Katharina Rosen, and I am eleven."

Chancellor Brandt placed an elbow on the table and rested his chin in his hand. "In your previous testimony, Fraulein Rosen, you claimed that your mother had met with the Devil and had even been naked with the Devil."

Katharina pointed at the executioner. "I meant only him. He's evil."

Freude looked as if he wanted to throttle the girl. "Possessed, I tell you. The girl is possessed."

"And is this man the only devil you've ever seen with your mother?" asked Lutz. Freude shifted his venomous glare to Lutz.

"*Ja*," she said, with a little jerk of her chin.

"Have you or your mother ever seen the Devil?" said Father Streng. "The real Devil."

Katharina hugged her arms to her chest.

"Truth," said Lutz. "The truth will protect you."

"*Ja*, I have," she said softly.

Lutz felt his stomach drop to his knees. Mother of God, why had she said that!

Freude smirked. "When and where?"

Katharina straightened her narrow shoulders. "Only here. And in our cell. But Mama does not meet with him," she added quickly. "It is like Herr Hampelmann has seen. She banishes the Devil from her presence with a single glance. My mother is pure and good, like the Holy Mother."

Lutz grabbed the chair to steady himself. How could Katharina know what Hampelmann had seen? No one had told

Frau Rosen. The girl could know only if it were true and her mother had told her. And if Katharina had actually seen her mother banish the Devil at other times, then it had to be true.

Lutz glanced at the other commissioners. They were as stunned as he was. Their mouths hung open. Even Freude looked taken aback.

"Your mother has never spoken with the Devil, or met with him?" asked Father Streng, almost timidly.

"Never. Mama is not a witch, and all of you know it."

Triumphant, Hampelmann stood. "Enough questions. The girl's testimony confirms the sign from God. Eva Rosen is innocent."

Judge Steinbach consulted with Chancellor Brandt, then tapped the gavel. "Take her back to her cell, Herr Freude. And treat the girl gently."

Lutz returned to his place at the table and brought his pomander to his nose to clear his head. Chancellor Brandt drummed his fingers. Left eye twitching, Father Streng thumbed the corner of his ledger, the sound like cards being shuffled. Judge Steinbach blinked his watery eyes, his wrinkled face crumpled in confusion. Lindner sat, thoughtfully clicking his thumbnail on his front teeth. Vindicated, Hampelmann nodded knowingly at each of them.

Lutz gripped the pomander and prayed. Was it possible that Frau Rosen and Katharina would walk free that very day?

Finally, the executioner returned. He threw several logs onto the glowing embers in the wire basket, then took his place at the end of the table.

"This is one of the most baffling cases we've ever had," said Chancellor Brandt. "How should we proceed?"

"Recommend to the Prince-Bishop that Frau Rosen and her daughter be released at once," Hampelmann said adamantly.

"They must be released," agreed Lutz.

"*Nein*," said Freude. "I don't believe the girl. Her mother should be questioned under torture. Then we shall have the truth from her. The Rosen girl is possessed. That's how she knows what she claims to know."

"There is not one bit of evidence to justify torture," said Lutz. "And Katharina is not possessed, Herr Freude."

Lindner pulled at his fringe of sandy hair. "I have to agree with Herr Lutz. That girl shows no real signs of possession. She could know what she knows only if what Herr Hampelmann reported seeing is true."

"Of course it's true," snapped Hampelmann.

Father Streng ran a finger down a page in his ledger. "On the one hand, gentlemen, we have the evidence against Frau Rosen: the accusations from three condemned witches, Herr Kaiser's illness, and the suspicious death of her husband. On the other hand, we have two relevant findings: she has withstood the first degree of torture, and Herr Hampelmann has seen a sign from God that the woman is innocent, a sign that would appear to be confirmed by her daughter's testimony. I recommend that we submit this case to the law professors at the university. All of the relevant facts are here in this report, in detail."

"But the evidence is clear," said Lutz. "Why do we need an external review?"

"Article 109 of the Carolina Code," said Father Streng. "As you, yourself, reminded us, jurists are directed to consult with the law faculty of the nearest university regarding the use of torture."

"I agree with Herr Lutz," said Hampelmann. "The evidence is clear. The accusations made by condemned witches were obviously a malicious conspiracy, just as they were in Herr Silberhans' case. And the reports made to the *Malefizamt* were also malicious and without merit." He slapped the table with an open palm. "And I have seen a sign. A sign confirmed by Katharina herself."

Chancellor Brandt rubbed his gold medallion between a thumb and forefinger. "I think Father Streng is right. Let men who can review this case more dispassionately than we can make the decision. Judge Steinbach can have the report sent by courier yet today." He glanced pointedly at the judge.

Lutz's stomach churned. Damn, Frau Rosen and Katharina would be left sitting in that wretched cell for at least another few days. He rotated his shoulders, trying to make himself relax. God had helped Frau Rosen through the torture, he assured himself, and even sent Hampelmann a sign. Surely God would not allow the professors at the university to decide against her now. And Father Herzeim would be among the men consulted. His arguments would assure her release.

Chancellor Brandt picked up the judge's watch, then laid it back down. "And now, gentlemen, we must deal with Frau Lamm. Her case, though difficult, is at least clear."

"Bring her in, Herr Freude," said Judge Steinbach.

Before he left, the executioner added more wood to the roaring fire. He placed the pincers on the hot coals. Lutz dreaded what was to come. Yesterday, he'd made a fool of himself by screaming when the midwife screamed. Hampelmann was right. Lutz didn't have the stomach for this. He felt a constant churning in his gut, a painful burning in his chest and throat. He almost wished the midwife had died – or the Devil had killed her. He hated it that he couldn't help her. Nor shouldn't. He felt, instinctively, that Father Herzeim was wrong in this case. Frau Lamm was evil. Lutz had re-read what *Der Hexenhammer* said about witch midwives, that they surpassed all other witches in their crimes. He wished, though, that the commission could just dispatch her quickly, mercifully, and be done with it, but he knew that *Der Hexenhammer* also said that a witch should not be condemned to die unless convicted by her own confession. In order to execute her, they had to get a confession, and so far, she'd given them nothing.

"Would that we had the Prince-Bishop's relic," said Hampelmann thoughtfully. "A thorn from the crown would keep the Devil from this chamber and prevent him from helping Frau Lamm."

Chancellor Brandt pulled at his dark beard. "If Frau Rosen's glance can banish the Devil, why not bring her in?"

"That would be highly irregular," said Judge Steinbach, sliding the gavel from one shaking hand to the other.

"But it might work," Father Streng said excitedly.

"I don't think we should," said Lutz. "It's a departure from proper procedure." And the ordeal would be terrifying for Frau Rosen. How could she not see herself in the midwife's place?

"But if she helps us to get a confession from Frau Lamm," said Hampelmann, "it would be more evidence confirming her innocence."

Freude returned, carrying the midwife, who could no longer walk. He set her in the chair and, when she started to slide off, tied her upright with hemp ropes around her waist and chest. Her head drooped. Her bare feet and ankles, bruised a vivid purple and black, were so swollen the discoloured skin looked as if it might burst.

"Herr Freude," said Chancellor Brandt. "Bring in Frau Rosen as well."

The executioner flinched.

"If she can keep the Devil away," explained Hampelmann, "she can assist us in the questioning of Frau Lamm."

"*Nein*, that's a complete departure from proper procedure," said Freude.

Chancellor Brandt glowered. "Get her, Herr Freude."

The executioner left, grumbling under his breath.

Father Streng stepped forward with the crucifix and made the sign of the cross over Frau Lamm. "By the belief that you have in God and in the expectation of paradise, and being aware of the peril of your soul's eternal damnation, do you swear that the testimony you are about to give is true, such that you are willing to exchange heaven for hell should you tell a lie?"

The midwife didn't move. Reluctantly, Lutz pushed himself up from the table and went to stand by her side. "Do you swear to tell the truth, Frau Lamm?"

Her head flopped to one side, and she considered Lutz with the one eye that had not swollen completely shut. She mouthed the word *ja*.

Father Streng made the sign of the cross and sprinkled holy water over her, then walked to the fire and flicked a few drops onto the pincers. The water hissed and sputtered. He took his place at the table.

Freude returned with Frau Rosen, but appeared unsure whether she should be made to step backwards into the chamber or if she could now enter facing the commissioners.

"Just bring her in," Chancellor Brandt said impatiently.

Bewildered and obviously frightened, Frau Rosen looked from Hampelmann to Lutz, and finally, to Chancellor Brandt.

"You are not here for questioning, Frau Rosen," said the chancellor. "You are here to free Frau Lamm from the Devil's grip, to rid the Devil from this chamber."

The executioner led her to a place in front of the table. She sat down on the floor, facing Frau Lamm.

"Frau Lamm is already sworn, Herr Freude," said Judge Steinbach. "You may proceed."

The executioner grabbed the top of the midwife's shift and ripped it open, revealing shoulders as swollen and discoloured as her feet and ankles. The movement made her cry out.

Lutz pulled at his starched collar. Sweat dripped down his back. The heat in the chamber was stifling. He couldn't breathe. The men's flushed faces gleamed.

"Do you wish to make your confession now, Frau Lamm? Or later?" said Freude.

She shook her head weakly.

Freude pulled down the shift to expose her breasts, then stepped to the wire basket. Placing a protective pad over his hand, he picked up the red-hot pincers. He approached the midwife, then quickly pierced her right breast with the pincers and pulled, slicing through it. The midwife released a scream that echoed off the walls.

Bright red blood splattered onto Lutz's white cuffs. He grabbed the back of the chair. The sight, the sound, the smell of blood and burning flesh. His vision spun, then faded to black. When he came to, he was lying on the floor and Freude was waving hartshorn under his nose. The executioner sneered. "You might want to take a seat at the table, Herr Lutz."

Lutz struggled to his feet, then leaned against the wall, his pomander to his nose. He was panting, and sweating. Frau Rosen crouched on the floor, rocking herself, her bound and bandaged hands over her face.

"When and where did you meet with the Devil?" said Hampelmann.

His handsome face was calm and composed, his pale blue eyes impassive. Such a contrast, thought Lutz, to the man's agitation when Frau Rosen was in the thumbscrews. Then, he'd seemed ready to jump out of his skin. Just the way Lutz felt now.

"*Nein,*" the midwife mouthed, watching her own blood soak her shift.

Freude placed the pincers near her left breast.

She began to weep. "Tell me...what you want me...to say...and I'll say it."

The pincers tore through the breast, ripping the nipple.

Lutz retched, green bile splashing onto the stone floor.

"Did you attend the sabbath with Frau Basser, Frau Imhof, and Fraulein Stolzberger?" said Hampelmann.

She nodded weakly.

"Is that where you fornicated with the Devil?" said Lindner.

Silence.

"Answer!" shouted Chancellor Brandt.

"*Ja*," she mouthed.

"Did you trample the host?" said Judge Steinbach. "And spit upon the crucifix?"

Her head lifted, then dropped.

Father Streng was scribbling frantically, the quill scratching across the page. "Did you kill Fraulein Spatz's baby?" he asked.

Silence.

Freude held the hot pincers near her breast.

Again, her head lifted and dropped.

"Did you take the baby to the sabbath to share its flesh and blood with other witches?" Father Streng demanded.

The slightest of nods.

Lutz leaned against the wall and stared at the grey stone. A confession obtained in this way couldn't possibly be valid. But what did that matter? The woman was guilty, and obtaining her confession meant it would soon be over. For everyone.

"Who else was at the sabbath with you?" said Hampelmann, squinting at his ledger. "Did you see a young woman named Fraulein Wagner, or a beggar woman who goes by the name of Old Frau Holtzman?"

The midwife gave a single nod.

"And Father Herzeim, your confessor?" said Hampelmann.

Lutz roused himself. "I object," he said, glaring at Hampelmann. "You cannot suggest names to the accused."

For the first time since she'd been brought in, Frau Lamm raised her head and looked at the commissioners. Her one good eye locked on Hampelmann. "*Nein*, not the priest," she said with obvious effort. "I saw Frau Hampelmann."

Hampelmann leaped up. "Do not record that!" he shouted at Father Streng. "She's lying." He strode toward the midwife, touching Frau Rosen on the shoulder in passing. "Fix your eyes upon her so that Frau Lamm cannot lie again."

Slowly, Frau Rosen lowered her hands. Her eyes were huge and dark in a white and terrified face.

Hampelmann grabbed a birch rod and raised it over Frau Lamm. "Tell us, you witch, who you really saw."

The midwife considered each commissioner in turn, her one-eyed gaze coming to rest on Lutz. He held his breath. Oh, God, no, please don't let her name Maria.

"Frau Hampelmann," she repeated. Then cackled.

The blow was so hard Lutz was sure it had snapped the woman's neck. He and Freude moved to restrain Hampelmann from hitting her again, then the executioner put the pincers to her right breast, which had already been torn nearly in half. Her shift and the stones beneath her were soaked with blood. "Tell us the truth," said Freude.

She gasped, then her head dropped.

Lindner stepped forward. Freude lifted the midwife's head so the physician could examine her face. "That's all she can take for today," said Lindner. "We have obtained a confession and names of accomplices. That's all we need."

"But she's not yet retracted her lies," screamed Hampelmann. "We cannot stop."

"I understand your concern," said Lindner, "but anything more will almost certainly kill her."

Judge Steinbach tapped the gavel. "Take her back to her cell, Herr Freude. Then come back for Frau Rosen."

Father Streng smiled at Frau Rosen. "*Danke*, Frau Rosen. Your presence appears to have freed the midwife from the Devil's grasp. I'll be sure to include that in the report to the university."

33

28 April 1626

Lutz tossed his hat to the side and sank into the rickety chair opposite the desk. "They will recommend release, won't they?"

Candlelight cast Father Herzeim's face in shadow, accentuating its grim and angled aspect. "It is not a foregone conclusion," he said. "But there are only five of us, so I need convince only two to vote with me. The professors are stubborn and arrogant in their certainty, but the evidence in Frau Rosen's case is so weak they may be willing to listen to reason." He glanced toward the corner where his manuscript and heretical books lay hidden. "I promise you, Lutz, I will do everything I can to protect her and Katharina. Everything."

He turned back to Lutz. "If only you – or someone else – had seen the sign Herr Hampelmann saw, the arguments for release would be that much stronger."

Signs. Lutz had never seen a sign in his life. Not one that he recognized anyway. He wished now that he'd seen whatever Hampelmann had, or at least had thought quickly enough to claim he had. He was willing to lie to save Frau Rosen's life. There would be time enough later to beg God's forgiveness. Now, there were larger truths at stake. "Do you really believe Hampelmann saw a sign?"

The priest's mouth twisted on one side. "With God, all things are possible. I would certainly like to believe he intervened on Frau Rosen's behalf. It would give me greater confidence that he will guide the professors to make the right decision. Have you told Frau Rosen about the commission's decision?"

"I just came from her cell," said Lutz. "She is hopeful, especially since I told her that you would be among the professors who will be making the decision. She knows you believe her to be innocent."

"A woman of great faith. Perhaps greater than mine." Father Herzeim's fingers trailed over his cedar cross. "I can only hope her faith in me is not unfounded."

The candle had burned down to a flickering nub. Father Herzeim reached into a desk drawer for another and placed it into the holder. Hot wax dripped onto his thumb and forefinger, but he seemed not to notice. "And what of Frau Lamm?" he said.

Though he tried, desperately, Lutz couldn't stop the flood of images, sounds, and smells provoked by the mention of the midwife: red-hot pincers tearing at breasts, blood spurting, vomit, joints popping, piss, bones grinding, shit. The small bit of dark bread and fish he'd eaten for supper rose into his throat. He swallowed it back. "She finally made a confession today."

"Confession," spat the priest. His face showing fierce disgust, he stared into the candle flame. "How can they continue to do this? I visited her today. The woman is barely alive."

"It's horrible, I know, but she's guilty. She deserves her punishment."

"Does she? Did the commissioners have one shred of solid evidence she'd committed a crime worthy of such torture, worthy of such a death?"

"There may be no evidence, but the woman just...just–"

"Just what?"

"Just seems evil."

"Why?" His dark eyes narrowed to slits. "Because she defied the commissioners and refused to lie? Refused to confirm the foul conjurings of their own minds?" Father Herzeim slammed a fist on the desk, making the small flame waver. "Damn them." He looked toward the ceiling, tears in his eyes. "Would that I had her courage. She may be the bravest one of us all, Lutz."

"I admire her courage, but I still believe she's guilty." Lutz saw again the midwife's evil eye fixed upon him. Guilty. And wicked enough to accuse an innocent: Frau Hampelmann. Thank God she hadn't named Maria.

"You should know," Lutz said, pulling his fingers through his tangled beard, "that when Hampelmann suggests names to the accused, yours is the name he mentions most often."

Father Herzeim gave Lutz his crooked half smile. "I am like a thorn in his soul. In a secret part of him, he knows that what I say is true. The thorn pricks at his own doubts, and the pricking drives him to try and silence me."

"I've heard precious few doubts from Hampelmann."

"Even Father Streng has his doubts."

Lutz snorted. "*Nein*, the Jesuit seems absolutely certain about what he and the other commissioners are doing."

"Why then are they so quick to quote to each other long passages from Jean Bodin, Martin Delrio, and *Der Hexenhammer*, if not to reassure themselves and to quell the doubts that plague them?"

Lutz fingered his starched cuff. The spots of red blood, the midwife's blood, had turned brown. He touched the ball of wax at his throat. *Doubts*. Possible, but not likely. It was only he who seemed plagued with doubts about the commission's work.

Father Herzeim gazed into the darkness beyond the window. A few evening stars had appeared in the clear night sky. "Sooner or later," he said, "Hampelmann will get what he wants: three accused witches who are willing to name me as an accomplice. And then he can send the Prince-Bishop's bailiff to arrest me. I only hope that I can complete my manuscript before he does."

"They cannot arrest you, a Jesuit." Even as he said the words, Lutz knew them to be untrue. Hampelmann could, and he would, if he could find a way. Yet Lutz couldn't bear just to sit there and listen to his friend speak calmly of being arrested for witchcraft. Father Herzeim had to know the commissioners would treat him – a man of God who'd betrayed the true faith and turned to the Devil – even more brutally than they did the midwife.

Could it be that his friend was truly guilty of turning from God, of being in league with the Devil? He was, after all, claiming that even the midwife was innocent. Lutz shook his head, vigorously, to erase these suspicions from his mind. Father Herzeim defended the innocent. He might err now and again in going too far in that zealous defence, but he was not in league with the Devil. He couldn't be.

The priest placed his elbows on the desk and brought the fingertips of both hands together. "If I cannot persuade the other professors to recommend release, we must teach Katharina how to feign possession."

"What?" Lutz started as if he'd just been awakened from a deep sleep.

"Possession is always caused by someone else: the Devil or a witch. So the blame cannot fall on Katharina. She can be exorcised, but not tortured."

"But the blame will almost certainly fall on Frau Rosen."

Father Herzeim pressed his fingers to his lips, as if to stop the flow of his own words. "I know that," he said. "But Katharina will be spared. Frau Rosen is a mother. It is what she herself would wish."

34

29 April 1626

Hampelmann twisted the gold ring around his finger. What to do about the midwife? Her testimony could not be allowed to stand. Though Father Streng had assured him he hadn't recorded Helena's name in his ledger, Hampelmann knew he couldn't rest until Frau Lamm had retracted her false accusation. He rubbed his eyes, which felt raw and burning, and tried to bring his attention back to the hearing.

"The documents relating to Frau Rosen and her daughter were sent by courier to the university late yesterday," said Father Streng. "Has Frau Rosen been informed?"

"She has," said Lutz, "and she's waiting anxiously for a decision." The dark half moons under his eyes stood in stark contrast to his pallid cheeks.

"You can tell her that the professors agreed to act quickly," said the priest. "They will then send the documents – and their recommendations – to the Prince-Bishop. We may have their recommendations, as well His Grace's decision, as early as tomorrow afternoon. Friday morning at the latest."

Chancellor Brandt flicked the chain on the judge's gold watch, then carefully pulled it straight again. "How shall we proceed with Frau Lamm, gentlemen?"

"I examined her more thoroughly yesterday afternoon," said Lindner, crossing his arms over his thick chest. Red blood vessels webbed the physician's eyes and his bulbous nose glowed.

Drinking heavily last night, thought Hampelmann. This wretched business was wearing on all of them. Except Freude and

Father Streng, who looked rosy-cheeked and rested. Everyone else looked sallow and unwell, especially Lutz, who appeared to have aged at least ten years. Hampelmann brought his pomander to his nose and inhaled lavender and hellebore. Headaches, constant headaches. He couldn't remember how it felt not to have a headache.

"I doubt the woman can withstand more torture," continued Lindner. "She's lost a lot of blood, and some of her wounds are beginning to fester. She cannot eat. She can barely swallow water."

"But she must be made to retract her false accusations," Hampelmann insisted.

"Herr Hampelmann," said Father Streng, "I assure you – once again – your wife's name was not recorded. I knew full well that accusation was false. And malicious." He smoothed the quill between a thumb and forefinger. "But we need to proceed carefully. If Frau Rosen is released and Frau Lamm dies, there will be no one left to go to the stake. The commission will have nothing to show for all of its hard work."

"But we must have more names," said Hampelmann, "true names. Surely the midwife can name many more accomplices. We must get those names."

Freude combed his fingers through his greasy beard, trapping a louse. "I agree with Father Streng. At this point, it's more important to have a public execution than to obtain more names. And that one'll give us nothing more unless I put her in the Spanish boots."

Judge Steinbach cringed. Hampelmann, too, found the leg vises revolting. The grinding crunch of bone and the oozing of pink marrow nearly always made his stomach heave. Still, he wanted to force the midwife to retract what she'd said about Helena. He'd even be willing to endure watching the boots for that.

Linder shook his head. "She'll never survive the boots."

❧

"Then just threaten her with them," said Hampelmann.

Freude snorted. "When has Frau Lamm given us anything just by being threatened?"

"Then bring in Frau Rosen again," said Hampelmann. "That loosened the witch's tongue yesterday."

"We cannot delay any longer," said Chancellor Brandt. "I recommend that we bring in Frau Lamm, have her confirm her confession freely, then send the documents to the Prince-Bishop for his review. Soon. Before she can die."

There were nods all along the table, except for Hampelmann, and Lutz, who sat morosely with his head in his hands.

"Father Streng," said the chancellor, "has Frau Lamm's confession been written out? Is it ready for her to sign?"

"Of course."

"Herr Freude, bring in Frau Lamm," said Judge Steinbach.

After the executioner left, Chancellor Brandt continued, "We'll recommend that His Grace set the date for Frau Lamm's public trial and execution for next Monday. Are we all agreed?"

Again, everyone but Hampelmann and Lutz nodded. Hampelmann sat, silently fuming. He would yet force the midwife to retract her lies about Helena.

Freude returned, carrying Frau Lamm, who hung limp in his arms. He tied her upright in the chair facing the commissioners. Were it not for her laboured breathing and occasional groans, Hampelmann would have thought her dead. The jailer's wife had changed the woman's shift, but there were bloodstains on her chest, bright red and dark brown. The cloying stink of blood and putrid stench of infection hung thick in the air.

Chancellor Brandt put his gold pomander to his nose. "Frau Lamm, you have been brought before the Commission of Inquisition for the Würzburg Court to confirm your confession on this day, the twenty-ninth of April, 1626. Father Streng, read Frau Lamm her confession."

The priest stood and began reading his account of the previous day's interrogation. As was customary, he'd numbered the questions – and the answers. Hampelmann listened closely as Father Streng droned on and on. The confession was at least ten pages long and described in grisly detail – much of it added by the young Jesuit – the crimes to which Frau Lamm had finally admitted: turning away from God and signing a pact with the Devil, fornication with the Devil, killing Fraulein Spatz's baby and taking its body to the sabbath to share its flesh and blood with other witches.

Judge Steinbach trembled as if he were witnessing the crimes himself.

Lutz raised a hand, his brow furrowed in puzzlement. "My understanding was that Fraulein Spatz was caught trying to bury the child's body."

"Doesn't matter," said Father Streng, clearly annoyed at being interrupted. "Even if the Devil only deluded Frau Lamm into believing she carried the child's body to the sabbath, her intentions were evil. And merit death."

Lutz sat, scratching his chin, his face still perplexed.

When Father Streng finally sat down and picked up his quill, Hampelmann let out a long sigh. Just as he'd claimed, the priest had not listed Helena among the newly accused.

Chancellor Brandt leaned forward. "You have had a day to think about your confession, Frau Lamm, and you are no longer under torture. Do you confirm your confession freely?"

"But Frau Hamp…" She was too weak to continue.

Hampelmann gripped the edge of the table. He could strangle the woman, right then and there. Father Streng laid a hand on his arm. "Relax, Herr Hampelmann, we know that accusation is false."

Hampelmann stood. "You have nothing to lose, Frau Lamm, and everything to gain from God by retracting the names of those you've falsely accused and giving us the names of true accomplices."

"That is quite enough!" Chancellor Brandt glared at Hampelmann, who sank to his chair. The chancellor turned back to the midwife. "Do you confirm your confession freely?"

"If I do not…" Her words were barely audible.

Freude leaned in close. "If you recant now, or tomorrow, or the day after tomorrow, you will come again into my hands, and then you'll learn that up to now I've been only playing with you. I'll plague and torture you in such a way that even a stone would cry out."

"Are you prepared to sign your confession, Frau Lamm?" said Judge Steinbach.

The midwife sat, her mouth working. Never had Hampelmann wished more fervently for the death of a witch. After a long silence, she spat on the floor, a glob laced with bright red blood.

Chancellor Brandt flushed. "Are you prepared to sign your confession?"

With great effort, the woman raised her head, but it fell back to her chest.

Father Streng brought the written confession and a quill toward her. He looked at her hands, then pursed his lips. "Do you authorize me to sign for you, Frau Lamm?"

Her head bobbed slightly. The priest drew a large black "X" at the bottom of the last page. Beneath it, he wrote her name in bold and elegant script.

"It is done then," said Judge Steinbach. "His Grace willing, Frau Lilie Lamm's public trial will be Monday, the fourth of May, in the year of Our Lord 1626." He tapped the gavel lightly on the table.

"You have five days to make your peace with God, Frau Lamm," said Father Streng.

"A special guard should be posted outside her cell," said Hampelmann, "so that she cannot take her own life or be killed or rescued by the Devil. She is, after all, one of his specially anointed servants, and tomorrow night is *Walpurgisnacht*. She'll want to join the other witches and the Devil in their obscene celebrations on Fraw Rengberg."

Chancellor Brandt nodded gravely. "Agreed. You will instruct the jailer and the selected guard yourself, Herr Hampelmann. They must understand the importance of not allowing Fraw Lamm to escape just punishment for her crimes."

He turned then to the midwife. "Because you have confessed to your crimes, this commission will recommend that you be mercifully beheaded before your body is burned. Your final sacramental confession is between you and God, Frau Lamm, and I would remind you that your eternal soul hangs in the balance. I would also remind you that, if you publicly recant your signed confession to the Commission of Inquisition for the Würzburg Court, you shall be burned alive."

35

30 April 1626

The guard unlocked the tower door for Lutz, then, with a deferential nod, withdrew from the chamber. For the first time since the commission had begun meeting, Lutz had arrived early, leaving his dinner untouched and Maria clucking her tongue, her eyes filling with tears yet again.

Sitting alone at the table, Lutz tried not to inhale the ever-present odours of blood and vomit and piss. He toyed with his pomander, turning it in his palm and examining his distorted reflection in the tarnished silver. He'd been waiting only two days for the professors' recommendations, but it felt like weeks. He'd been unable to sleep. Whenever he closed his eyes, he saw mutilated flesh and blood, heard the midwife's haunting screams.

Dressing that morning, he'd been surprised at the looseness of his doublet. Maria had put her soft hands to his face and wept. He'd wrapped his arms around her, and she buried her face in his neck, sobbing. When he finally released her, there were tears on his own cheeks, but he could not think for whom or what he was weeping. The midwife was guilty. She'd brought her horrible suffering upon herself. And surely Frau Rosen would be released. Were his tears for Fraulein Spatz? The old beggar woman? Or for himself, because he'd failed them so miserably?

In the flickering torchlight, the pomander reflected the dark hollows under his red-rimmed eyes. How relieved he would be when this nightmare was finally finished and he could return to his old clients with their old complaints about contracts, when he could return to a courtroom where the law was the law and there were no *crimena excepta*. A courtroom where no one was tortured.

Lutz rubbed his stinging eyes before they could leak more tears. He'd never be finished with this. He'd never sleep peacefully again. He'd always see the blood, and hear the screams and the grinding crunch of bone. He'd always know that innocent women had suffered and died because he had failed to protect them. Lutz felt a burning pain in his chest and tasted bitterness at the back of his throat.

The door creaked open and Hampelmann came in, looking as drawn and weary as Lutz. He sat down at the table. "If there's a God in heaven," he muttered, "they must recommend release." He stretched out his hands, then clenched them to still their trembling.

Freude, Lindner, Father Streng, and Judge Steinbach filed slowly into the chamber. They nodded to each other, hung up their hats, then all but Freude took their places at the table, once again shoulder to shoulder, knee to knee. Freude lit a few more torches before he sat down, the light and shadow dancing eerily across the stone walls.

Finally, Chancellor Brandt arrived, a sheaf of documents tucked under his arm. The top one carried the Prince-Bishop's seal, but Lutz could not read the words. He studied the chancellor's face for a sign, but his fixed expression revealed nothing.

Judge Steinbach tapped the gavel. The men rose together, crossed themselves, and bowed their heads. Lutz hardly heard Father Streng's words, he was praying so hard himself. Please, God, please, let the decision be for release. Let me believe again that you protect the innocent. *In nomine patris, et filii, et spiritus sancti.* The men crossed themselves and sat down.

Chancellor Brandt folded his hands and placed them on the documents. "I have before me Prince-Bishop Philipp Adolf's decision about the Commission of Inquisition's recommendations regarding the case of Frau Lilie Lamm. He has approved our recommendations, gentlemen. Her public trial and execution will be on Monday, the fourth of May, 1626."

He ran his tongue over his teeth. "I also have before me the recommendations from the professors of ecclesiastical and civil law at the University of Würzburg regarding the case of Frau Eva Rosen, as well as His Grace's approval of those recommendations."

Lutz felt as if his heart would explode from his chest.

Chancellor Brandt looked toward the pulley on the ceiling. "His Grace's decision is that there is enough evidence to warrant the further questioning of Frau Rosen under torture."

"*Nein!*" shouted Lutz. "*Nein!*"

"Moreover," the chancellor continued, ignoring Lutz's outburst, "the professors recommend, and the Prince-Bishop concurs, that Fraulein Rosen should be questioned under torture as well." He turned to Lutz, who sat, stunned into silence. "The recommendation was four to one against release, Herr Lutz. And His Grace has reminded us that witchcraft is high treason against God's majesty, *crimen laesae maiestatis divinae*, and not to be dealt with lightly."

Lutz closed his eyes against Freude's lurid grin. He felt tears pushing against his eyelids. Four to one? How could that be?

"But-but I saw a sign from God," stammered Hampelmann. "Frau Rosen is innocent."

"If she is truly innocent," said Father Streng, "it will be proved so under torture."

"We cannot do this," said Lutz, weeping openly now. "It's wrong." He wiped the back of his hand across his cheek.

Father Streng cleared his throat. "I believe a quote from Ignatius may help us to see how we should proceed in this matter: *Look upon your superior, whoever he may be, as the representative of Christ.* And Prince-Bishop Philipp Adolf is, after all, our superior, gentlemen." He pointed the grey quill at Lutz. "Ignatius also wrote: *Obedience in execution consists of doing what is ordered; obedience in will consists of willing the same thing as he who gives the order; obedience in understanding consists of thinking as the superior thinks and in believing what he ordains is rightly ordained. Otherwise obedience is imperfect.* We have no choice but to obey."

It was not the words of the Jesuit founder that flooded Lutz's brain, but the words of Johann Weyer: *So I summon you before the Great Judge, who shall decide between us, where the truth you have trampled under foot and buried shall arise and condemn you.* "We cannot do this," he gasped. "The woman – and her daughter – are innocent. We will all be condemned to hell."

"In that, you are quite wrong," said Father Streng. "If I might quote the honourable Jesuit Alfonso Rodriguez in that regard: *The superior may commit fault in commanding you to do this or that, but you are certain that you commit no fault so long as you obey, because God will only ask if you have duly performed what orders you have received, and if you can give a clear account in that respect, you are absolved entirely…The moment what you did was done obediently, God wipes it out of your account, and charges it to your superior.* If what we do here is wrong, Herr Lutz, the sin will be charged to the Prince-Bishop, not to us."

Hampelmann's face had gone from stark white to flaming red. "What then, do you make of what Ignatius wrote at the very beginning of the *Spiritual Exercises? Preserve always your liberty of mind; see that you lose it not by anyone's authority.*"

The priest sniffed. "I think Ignatius' thoughts on this matter are made perfectly clear in the thirteenth rule of the *Exercises: To make sure of being right in all things, we ought always to hold by the principle that the white that I see I would believe to be black, if the hierarchical Church were so to rule it.*"

Chancellor Brandt elbowed Judge Steinbach, who quickly tapped the gavel. "Gentlemen, enough debate," said the chancellor. "We have no choice in this matter. His Grace has given us his decision. However, we need not act on that decision today."

He looked up and down the table. "All of us are weary and distressed by our duties. We need a day of rest and contemplation. I suggest that we meet tomorrow morning at eight to continue the questioning of Frau Rosen and her daughter. Herr Lutz, you may inform Frau Rosen of the professors' recommendations and the Prince-Bishop's decision."

The hell he would. Lutz couldn't bear even to think of facing Frau Rosen with this news. What could he do now? Resort to teaching Katharina how to behave as if she were possessed? Causing the possession of her own daughter would be enough to justify torturing Frau Rosen even more viciously than the midwife.

Lutz put his head in his hands. He no longer believed that God protected the innocent. What else had he ceased to believe? He'd become a heretic – a heretic without the courage to say so out loud.

Standing abruptly, he stormed from the chamber. He had to see Father Herzeim. Four to one against release! What in the world had gone wrong? Why had God failed them?

By the time he reached the university, Lutz was panting. The brief walk had done nothing to calm his outrage or his grief. He burst into Father Herzeim's office. "Four to one! How could you allow that to happen?"

The priest stared at the stoneware goblet in his hands. When he finally turned, he looked like a man condemned. "I have failed her, Lutz. Failed her. I used every argument, even Weyer's and Tanner's, and I failed to convince even one of them. I succeeded only in making them more suspicious of me." He raised the goblet to his lips and gulped. "I am quite certain they will report me to the *Malefizamt*."

"The *Malefizamt*!" Lutz placed his hands on the desk and

peered into Father Herzeim's haggard face. The priest reeked of wine. "Dear God, what can we do?" said Lutz.

"Free her." His dark eyes sparked with an odd light.

Lutz backed away. "Her? Father, I was talking about you."

"I have a plan. It's not a good one, but—"

"A plan?"

"If I can just get Frau Rosen and her daughter to Nuremberg, they will be safe. My family will take them in."

"Nuremberg?"

"It's a free city. Ruled by a town council, not a prince-bishop. They stopped killing witches years ago. They'll refuse to send her back to Würzburg."

Free Frau Rosen? Impossible. Lutz brought his pomander to his nose and inhaled deeply to clear his head. "But you'll be arrested."

"I will be arrested no matter what I do...or fail to do." Father Herzeim picked up the empty goblet and rolled it between his hands. "Would that I could free Frau Lamm as well."

"*Nein*," shouted Lutz. "Not the midwife."

"*Nein*, not the midwife," Father Herzeim echoed wearily. "She would never survive the journey."

Lowering himself to the chair opposite the desk, Lutz felt again the painful burning in his chest. "What is this plan?" he asked.

Father Herzeim filled the goblet from a decanter on his desk. "Wine?"

"*Nein*," Lutz said firmly. "I want to hear about this plan."

The priest licked his lips. "Well," he said finally, "I'll go to Frau Rosen late tonight, just before dawn. The guards will always admit the final confessor, no matter what the hour. A few of the commissioners already suspect that Katharina might be possessed, so I'll teach her how to behave as if she really is. I'll show her how to scream and howl, how to contort her body and speak in tongues. Then I'll arrange myself as if she's thrown me against the wall. When the guard comes running, someone will come from behind the door, strike him on the head, and knock him out. With any luck – or by God's grace – the guard will believe that Katharina's demons attacked him."

"Demons?" Lutz said sceptically. "And just who is this *someone* who will come from behind the door?"

Father Herzeim waved a hand as if Lutz's question were of no concern. "God will provide."

"Might I remind you, Father," said Lutz, "that God has failed to provide so far."

The priest took another large gulp of wine, then continued as if he'd not even heard Lutz's objection. "We'll take the keys, unlock the shackles...and be gone." He spoke hurriedly now, as if embarrassed by the foolishness and insufficiency of his plan. "God has already provided a yeoman with a hay cart to wait in the alley near the tower. He can leave the city by the gate at the Sander Tower at dawn without attracting notice."

"A full hay cart? Leaving the city?"

Father Herzeim shrugged one shoulder. "Perhaps no one had *kreuzer* enough to buy the hay."

"How can you trust this man to take them all the way to Nuremberg? That's at least 60 miles away. More than three days of hard travelling, especially in a hay cart."

"He's been paid only half of what he asked. He'll receive full payment only when he delivers my letter – and Frau Rosen and her daughter – to my family."

"What if he gives the letter to the *Malefizamt*?"

"I'll have to take that risk."

Lutz leaned forward. "It's a child's plan, Father...or one inspired by drink...and desperation. You've not thought it through. Someone will see you."

The priest smiled sheepishly. "Tonight is *Walpurgisnacht*.

Everyone will be too frightened to be out in the dark while witches and demons are gathering."

"But the guard will be scared when he hears voices and screaming. He'll bring another guard with him. Frau Rosen's cell is just below Frau Lamm's, and Hampelmann has ordered that a special guard be posted outside the midwife's cell specifically to prevent her escape on *Walpurgisnacht*."

"Faith, Lutz, faith. God will provide. Perhaps only one guard will come. Perhaps the commissioners will believe the Devil freed Eva to attend the great festival of witches and demons on Fraw Rengberg."

Lutz rolled his eyes. "What they'll believe is that you freed Frau Rosen so you both could attend the festival together."

Father Herzeim glanced toward the floorboards that hid Johann Weyer's book and his own manuscript. "I must do this one courageous thing before the Prince-Bishop's bailiff comes for me. I have nothing to lose. And eternal life to gain."

One courageous thing. As if Weyer's heretical pages were once again before him, Lutz could see the bold print. *The great searcher of hearts, from whom nothing is hidden…the tribunal of the Great Judge…the truth you have trampled under foot and buried shall arise and condemn you.*

"God has provided," Lutz whispered. "I will be that someone."

Father Herzeim came around the desk and put his hands on Lutz's shoulders. "I cannot allow you to take that risk. There is no doubt they will come for me, but you are safe yet."

"But I must, Father. Or I am damned for all eternity."

36

30 April 1626

The ring of keys at her waist jangling, Frau Brugler shuffled in, carrying a basin of steaming water and clean bandages draped over her scrawny arm. The throbbing in Eva's thumbs had eased only a little, and she bit down on her lip to keep from screaming as the woman peeled the bloody strips of cloth from her hands.

When Eva could finally speak, she asked the question that had worried her all day. "Why has Herr Lutz not come?"

"I wouldn't know," the woman grumbled. "Nobody tells me anything."

"Has no decision been made?"

Her eyes flicked away from Eva's. "I wouldn't know."

The jailer's wife was unusually quiet as she dressed Eva's hands. When she'd finished, she said, "Be strong, Frau Rosen. For the girl's sake, be strong." She looked down at the floor. "And if you ask," she whispered, "I will bring you a razor."

"Tell me what you know," Eva begged.

Shaking her head sadly, Frau Brugler picked up the basin and dirty cloths and left.

Eva waited into the night. Where was Herr Lutz?

To calm herself, she tried to pray, to be thankful that God had protected her and given her strength to endure the torture, that he'd protected Katharina. Surely he'd not forsake them now. She must be faithful, like Job.

The scrape of the key startled her. She looked anxiously toward the small square of light, but could see no faces. The door opened, the wedge of flickering light slowly widening. Eva's ears caught whispered mutterings as Frau Brugler came into the cell. "Visitors at ungodly hours...*Walpurgisnacht*...witches and demons about."

Wilhelm stepped in behind her.

Eva stopped breathing. Why was he here?

"Leave us," he ordered.

"Improper," snapped the jailer's wife. With a look of disdain for Wilhelm, she drew herself up and stomped out the door.

Eva laid a protective hand on Katharina. The girl still slept quietly beside her, her body curled around the hollow she'd made for the white dog.

Setting his lantern aside, Wilhelm knelt down in front of Eva. "Don't be afraid. I will protect you."

"Protect me?"

There was a long aching silence while he studied her face. "You haven't been told?"

"Told what?" Eva's heart pounded, making the throbbing in her thumbs nearly unbearable.

Wilhelm put his hands together, as if to pray, then brought his forefingers to his lips. His gold ring flashed in the candlelight. "The recommendations from the university, and the Prince-Bishop's decision, came back this morning." He put his hands on her shoulders. "We have been directed to question you and your daughter again. Under torture."

Eva released a strangled wail.

Katharina sat up and rubbed her eyes. Eva looked at her daughter's small fists and tried not to imagine her thumbs in the screws. Why had God abandoned them?

Wilhelm's face came close to hers, a frightening intensity in his eyes. "You must be strong, Eva. I will protect you. God will protect you. He has shown me that you are innocent." He embraced her, bumping her hands and bringing excruciating pain to her thumbs.

"I won't let them hurt you," he said, releasing her. "Even if they accuse me of being a defender of witches, I will protect you." He put a hand to her cheek. "You are good and pure. And innocent."

"Leave me now."

"But I would stay a while. And comfort you."

What comfort could he offer? She'd seen what they'd done to the midwife. How could she possibly withstand that? How could Katharina? God had forsaken them. They were not like Job. They were like Job's children. Their lives meant nothing to God.

She felt numb, as if she were already dying. If this was death – a numbing of all pain – she would welcome it. But she would not suffer the way Frau Lamm had suffered. She would ask Frau Brugler for the razor. But what of Katharina?

"Leave me."

Wilhelm picked up the lantern and slowly backed away, the candlelight illuminating the anguish on his face. He knocked on the door and called out.

Frau Brugler was there at once, as if she'd been waiting, and listening. As the door opened, Eva caught another stream of grumbling invective. "No sleep…running a brothel… *Walpurgisnacht*."

Wilhelm turned. "Be strong, Eva. God is with you." Then he and Frau Brugler were gone, the light with them.

Katharina put her arms around Eva's waist. "Mama?"

"We will be all right, *Liebchen*. Go back to sleep."

"But Mama?"

Eva stroked Katharina's face with the heel of her hand, then brought her palms carefully together. She needed to pray. But to whom? Wilhelm was wrong. God was not with her. God had abandoned her. She would pray to the Holy Mother. Never would the Holy Mother have given Satan permission to slaughter Job's children just to test Job's faith. Eva would pray to her.

She recited the *Ave Maria*, but could not keep her thoughts from the terror to come: the ropes and pulley, red-hot pincers, leg vises, eye gougers. The midwife's screams. Her maimed and broken body.

Why had Herr Lutz not come to tell her about the decision? Would he no longer even try to protect them? Would Wilhelm? No. He might try, but he could not. Eva knew now that no matter what she said, or did, they would find a way to kill her – and Katharina. God would not protect them.

Her shoulders shook with her weeping. And yet, to slit her own throat, and Katharina's, would be sin, grievous sin, for which there could be no forgiveness or redemption.

37

🔊

30 April 1626

Hampelmann waited until Frau Brugler had turned the key in the lock. "Go on to your bed now," he said. "I want to speak to the guard upstairs."

She gave him a quick nod and descended the stairs. Hampelmann watched until the light of her lantern had faded away. An old crone, he thought, suspicious in manner and looks. There'd been no reports about her to the *Malefizamt*, but still, he should investigate. Perhaps it was she, acting as an agent of the Devil, who'd killed Frau Bettler and Fraulein Spatz.

He turned and climbed the winding stairs as quietly as he could. His lantern cast long shadows on the grey stone walls, shadows that appeared to be stalking him. More than once, he turned to look behind him.

He heard the low rumble of snoring even before the glow from his lantern revealed the guard slumped against the cell door. "Herr Klingen," Hampelmann shouted, furious.

The guard started, then jumped to his feet. "H-h-herr Hampelmann," he stammered. "I-I was asleep for only a moment, sir. Only a moment. I wake at the slightest sound, and it's been quiet all evening."

"I came all the way up the stairs without you waking, and the candle in your lantern has burned out, you fool." Hampelmann glowered at the guard, then held up his own lantern and peered in the small barred window.

Frau Lamm lay completely still. Just the sight of her made the bile rise in his throat. He wished she were writhing in pain.

The filthy bitch. "She's not dead?"

"*Nein*, sir. I've heard her moan now and again. Not much, but enough to know she's still alive, sir."

"And you've heard or seen nothing strange tonight?"

"Nothing, sir."

Hampelmann held up the lantern so he could see the young guard's face and eyes. "You are absolutely not to leave this post, Herr Klingen, except to prevent Frau Lamm's murder or escape. And you are not to admit Frau Brugler to this cell. I'll not have her killing another one." He hissed through his teeth. "And you are not to sleep, no matter how quiet it may be. The Devil never fails to take full advantage of our weaknesses. Do you understand?"

The guard gulped and nodded.

"And for God's sake, man, replace that candle. Do you want to be caught in the dark with demons?" Hampelmann took one last look at the midwife, waited until the guard had lit a new candle from his lantern, then descended the stairs.

He stopped outside Eva's door, longing to go back into the cell, to hold and comfort her through this long dark night. He peeked in the window. She appeared to be sleeping, Katharina nestled at her side.

Hampelmann squared his shoulders. Only he could protect them. Herr Lutz was too weak and stupid, and the priest would be arrested in the morning. He felt some regret about that, since the Jesuit had argued so fervently for Eva's release. But it was, after all, the right thing to do. The other professors had reported Father Herzeim as a defender of witches.

That left only him. And with God's help, he would do all that he could to protect Eva. He had to. She was innocent. He had seen God's sign.

How could his father have forced such a good and holy woman? His father's sin grieved Hampelmann, creating an aching hollowness in his chest. Had his father confessed and begged God's forgiveness before he died?

Reluctantly, he continued on, winding his way past the doors of two empty cells before he reached the lowest chamber. He knocked on the thick door, then heard the key turn from the other side. He pushed it open and saw a guard and Frau Brugler, who was just sitting down at the curved table, the commissioners' table. They'd been drinking beer and playing cards. A few shiny *pfennigs* lay between them. A small fire burned in the wire basket, and white rags had been hung on the wooden wheel to dry. The pine torches guttered as Hampelmann strode through the chamber.

Frau Brugler stood up again to unlock the outside door. She gave him a gap-toothed grin. "Business all done, is it?" she said derisively. "Good night, Herr Hampelmann."

With a barely civil nod toward the guard and Frau Brugler, Hampelmann stepped out into the cool night air. He heard the door lock behind him. It was a clear night, but the wind was whistling and howling around the Prisoners' Tower and the scattered buildings nearby. A few wispy clouds raced across a crescent moon, its outline fuzzy to Hampelmann's eyes. He looked up at Marienberg Castle, ghostly white in the pale moonlight, and wondered how he would persuade the Prince-Bishop that he'd erred in his decision about Eva. He'd tried to visit His Grace that afternoon, but been turned away, the Prince-Bishop having been ill with a griping of the bowels. Hampelmann would go to him again tomorrow and quote to him Jean Bodin and his words about God's miraculous signs. If he could somehow silence Father Streng, Hampelmann was sure he could persuade His Grace of Eva's innocence.

He glanced around him then, squinting into the darkness. He could see no other lanterns. No one ventured forth on *Walpurgisnacht*, not even the beggars. He imagined the great orgiastic festival on Fraw Rengberg, and shuddered. The witches and demons would be there now, fornicating lasciviously with each other, engaging in sodomy of all sorts and a myriad of other abominations.

He walked quickly, his lantern swinging in front of him, the candle burning low. As he passed Saint Stephan's, he was startled when the candlelight revealed two beggars huddled on the church steps, a skinny cur at their feet. Witches? Hampelmann's heart raced. The man and woman turned toward him, their faces deeply lined, their ancient eyes shadowed by the hoods of ragged cloaks. The cur snarled. Hampelmann saw the glint of metal in the old man's bony hand. A knife?

Hampelmann reached into the pouch in his breeches and tossed a handful of coins. "God bless you," he yelled. "That's all that I have."

He broke into a run down the dark street, slowing only when he was certain he could hear no footsteps behind him. He put a hand to his throat and gasped for air. His chest burned. The candle in the lantern flickered, then went out. He looked to his right, toward the dark forest beyond the city wall. The tops of the trees swayed in the wind. He heard a strange roaring then, as if it came from within his own ears. Then he saw them, shapes flying across the face of the moon, swirling around the white crescent, hundreds of them, capes straight out behind them: *wutenker*. The flying demons were screeching, hurtling curses, and barking like wild dogs. They were on their way to Fraw Rengberg, but Hampelmann knew they were also looking for him, a prosecutor of witches. Touching the ball of wax at his throat, he withdrew into an alley where he hid behind a huge pile of stinking offal, black rats scattering all around him.

He stayed there, praying, hardly daring to look up at the sky until long after the roaring had died away. He crept out from the alley then, crossed himself, and made his way home as quickly as he could. He stole quietly into the house and went to the bedchamber, where he took off his silk doublet and breeches, and his linen shirt, which stank of offal. Even his skin stank.

He pulled on his nightshirt and slipped into bed beside Helena, beautiful Helena, her shoulder milky white in the sliver of moonlight. Her breathing was peaceful and even, just as it had been when he'd slipped away. He leaned closer to smell the clean scent of her skin, the fragrance of pears. He wanted desperately to press himself against her, wrap his arms around her, and pull her in to fill the hollowness he felt inside. But he dared not. Not now. Not when it meant succumbing to Saint Thomas' third deadly sin: lust. He would not be like his father.

38

⁓

1 May 1626

Eva woke with a start. The door creaked open to grumbling complaint. "Holy Mother of God…decent people." Frau Brugler crossed herself as Father Herzeim stepped in, his arms held stiffly at his sides. Lutz followed behind.

Eva sat up. She'd waited all day for them. Why had they come in the middle of the night?

Father Herzeim gently chided the jailer's wife. "You would stand in the way of sacramental confession?"

"But now, at this hour? On *Walpurgisnacht*?"

"God's forgiveness knows no hour or day. *Bitte*, leave us now. Go to your bed, Frau Brugler. We may be here some time. The guard can let us out."

The jailer's wife nodded deferentially, then left.

When the door had been closed and locked, two dark cloaks and a thick wooden rod dropped from beneath the priest's cassock. Father Herzeim handed the rod to Lutz. "Let's pray she goes to bed soon," said the priest.

Lutz raised his eyebrows. "There is still the guard just one floor above us."

"May God be with us." Father Herzeim stepped closer to Eva and Katharina.

Eva shook herself. Was she still sleeping, still dreaming? She could make no sense of what the men had said, no sense of the cloaks and rod.

Lutz placed the lantern safely away from the straw, then knelt in front of Eva. "We're taking you out of here," he said quietly.

Eva recoiled. "They would torture me now?"

"*Nein.* We're trying to get you to somewhere safe."

"Safe?" The word felt strange in her mouth, like a word from a language she did not know.

"Please, just do as we say. It's your only chance." Lutz laid the rod across his thighs and sighed deeply. "And may God help us."

As Father Herzeim talked to Katharina, who was now sitting up, wide awake, his voice was hushed but urgent. She followed his words and gestures intently.

"The plan," said Lutz, "is that Katharina will pretend to be possessed–"

"*Nein!*"

"Just listen," Lutz pleaded. "Katharina will pretend to be possessed, screeching and shrieking. And when the guard comes running, I'll knock him out. We're hoping he blames the demons."

"Demons?"

"It is *Walpurgisnacht.*" Lutz shrugged sheepishly. "Then we'll take the guard's keys and get you and Katharina out of here. There's a wagon waiting to take you to Nuremberg."

"Nuremberg," Eva breathed. She had never travelled that far. Could she trust these men? Why were they taking this risk for her and Katharina? And yet, what choice did she have? If they caught them now, at least their deaths would be quick.

"It would help if you could scream and shriek as well," Lutz added, "as if you're afraid of your own daughter. We must wait, though, until Frau Brugler has gone to bed. There's just one guard downstairs, and another upstairs, outside Frau Lamm's cell."

Too bewildered to ask any more questions, Eva watched Father Herzeim instruct Katharina. He had positioned her in the middle of the cell and was showing her how to contort her limbs, how to open her eyes wide and stare without blinking, how to hold her head at an odd angle. Katharina smiled, actually laughing once. The musical sound pierced Eva's heart.

The priest sat Katharina down and carefully taught her words of Latin and other languages Eva didn't recognize. He made the girl repeat the words again and again. Katharina mimicked the priest like a parrot, as if it were all an exciting new game.

Father Herzeim looked up at the window and pressed his lips together. The night sky was just beginning to pale. He turned to Lutz. "We can wait no longer." He bowed his head and made the sign of the cross.

Lutz went to stand behind the door. The priest slumped against the wall opposite the door, pulled his cassock into disarray, and cocked his head at a seemingly impossible angle, as if his neck had been broken. "Now, Katharina," he said.

The girl let out a horrifying, unearthly shriek, then wailed, "*Domino niger! Dieu noir! Pere mauvais!*" Eva and Father Herzeim screamed and shrieked with her, the chorus echoing off the walls. Lutz pounded on the door, then raised the rod, clutching it in both hands.

Glowing light, then a pair of eyes appeared in the barred window. "It's the priest!" shouted the guard. "He's been hurt."

The key turned and the door burst open. Katharina tilted her head and bared her teeth. Hissing and growling, her wraith-like arms flung over her head, she gave the guard her most wild-eyed glare.

"Christ Almighty!" the man yelled before the birch rod came down and he fell to the floor. Frau Brugler stood behind him, hands to her mouth. She turned and looked at Lutz just before the rod cracked against her forehead.

Father Herzeim leaped up and unhooked the ring of keys from the leather belt at her waist. Lutz stood still, ready for the other guard.

Fumbling with one key after another, the priest finally found the one that unlocked Eva's shackles. Careful of her hands, he helped her to her feet and draped a black cloak over her shoulders. He wrapped the second cloak around Katharina. It dragged the floor.

"Hurry," said Lutz. "Before the other guard comes." Holding fast to the rod, he picked up Katharina and settled her on one hip. She wrapped her arms around his neck.

Father Herzeim looked out into the stairway, putting his hand to his ear to listen. He picked up the lantern and, with an arm around Eva, guided her swiftly out the door and down the narrow steps, which seemed to go on forever in a winding spiral. The stone was cold and smooth beneath Eva's bare feet. Carrying Katharina, Lutz followed closely behind. They paused only a moment when they reached the door to the lowest chamber. They listened for footsteps coming behind them. Silence.

Father Herzeim blew out the candle in the lantern and crossed himself. "Pray that God has kept the jailer to his bed and that no one else has come." His hand shaking, he slowly pushed on the door, which, in their haste, the guard and Frau Brugler had left unlocked. He scanned the chamber. Eva stood on tiptoe and peeked over his shoulder. The torches flickered. Cards lay scattered across the table, and shards of a goblet lay on the floor in a pool of dark beer. But there was no one in sight. Even so, Eva had to force herself to follow Father Herzeim into the chamber, that horrifying chamber. The smell of it made her gag.

Quickly, they crossed the cold stone floor. Father Herzeim unlocked the heavy door to the street and cracked it open. Tossing the keys to the floor, he peered out into the darkness. He waited for a pack of stray dogs to pass before he led them all out of the tower. They ran across the open space, then rested briefly within the shadows of a neighbouring building. The wind whipped their cloaks around them, but covered the sounds of their passing. Grass, Eva felt real grass under her feet.

They moved from shadow to shadow, Eva's thumbs protesting with every jerking movement. Finally, they turned a corner into a narrow alley where a horse and wagon waited. As if carved from granite, the driver didn't move or acknowledge them in any way. Lutz laid Katharina in the wagon bed and began covering her with armfuls of hay. Awkwardly, Father Herzeim smoothed the cloak over Eva's shoulders, then tied the ribbon under her chin, his fingers brushing her skin.

"*Danke*," she said. "For everything." She put a bandaged hand to his cheek. "What is your name?"

Startled, Father Herzeim blinked. "Friedrich," he said. He reached out and pulled her close. And for one brief moment Eva accepted the comfort he offered.

"Hurry," said Lutz.

Father Herzeim helped Eva onto the wagon, then he and Lutz arranged the cloak to cover her and piled hay on top of her. Katharina snuggled in close. "The white dog wants to come with us, Mama. Is that all right?"

"Of course, *Liebchen*." Ravenously, Eva breathed in the sweet scent of hay. She cleared away the hay covering her eyes. The sky above her was a rich, dark blue dotted with stars. How long since she'd seen stars?

"Go with them, Father," said Lutz. "Stay there, in Nuremberg."

"*Nein*, I have work to do here."

"What work? You'll be arrested soon."

"It's you who should go. Frau Brugler saw you. She knows it wasn't demons."

"And leave Maria? Never. You go. If you stay here, you're a dead man."

"If I go, I'm a dead man. Dead to eternal life. Remember what you said to me? *I must. Or I am damned for all eternity.*"

The sound of a blacksmith's hammer rang out.

"Whoever's going," growled the driver, "we need to leave. Now!" He snapped the reins and the wagon lurched forward.

Eva's heart lurched with it. She wanted them both to come with her. She loved them for what they'd risked for her and Katharina.

She called out through the hay. "May the Holy Mother be with you."

Father Herzeim's voice was soft, but clear. "And with you…Eva."

39

1 May 1626

Lutz watched Maria sleep. Should he wake her and flee before they came to arrest him? He scrubbed his face with his hands. He should have gone with Frau Rosen. And left Maria? They'd come for her then. Why hadn't he thought of that last night, and brought her with him? All of them could be on their way to Nuremberg right now.

He reached out and touched the back of her hand. She pulled it under the coverlet. She'd never have gone, just as she'd not go now. And she'd never understand why he'd helped an accused witch to escape. That was his fault. Thinking to spare her, he'd never shared with her his deepest doubts and fears.

Lutz studied his wife's face, every beloved line and wrinkle, then leaned forward and kissed her lightly on the forehead. He rested his elbows on his knees and laced his fingers, thumbs crossed. If he wasn't going to flee, should he go to the hearing? Or just sit here and wait for the Prince-Bishop's bailiff?

Sitting up in the chair, he thrust out his chin, defiant. He was not ashamed of what he'd done. He would not cower and hide, and wait for them to come for him. He would not force Maria to watch them bind his wrists and drag him away. He would change his rumpled doublet and breeches, don a clean white collar and cuffs, and face them with whatever courage he could muster. He'd conceal a razor in his doublet, though. And no matter how much they tortured him, he'd give them no names. No more names. He'd slit his own throat before he'd give them more names.

He rose and walked from room to room then. In the pale light of dawn, he considered the furniture, the paintings, the dishes, the tapestries – everything he and Maria had collected over twenty-four years. He stepped out into Maria's garden and watched the interplay of colour and shadow in the angled golden light. He inhaled deeply and tried to impress upon his memory the fragrance of earth dampened by dew, of lily-of-the-valley, lilac, and linden. These were the last beautiful scents he would know, the last beautiful colours he would see. He felt tears wetting his cheeks and beard.

How could he explain it all to Maria? She'd never understand why he'd had to do it, never understand his one act of courage, that he did it because he loved her.

Lutz went to his library, sat down at his broad rosewood desk, and picked up a grey quill. He dipped the sharpened nib into a pot of black ink.

> *Dear Maria,*
> *Whatever anyone tells you, whatever they make me say, know that I am guilty only of freeing an innocent woman and her daughter. The Church says there are witches in this world, so there are witches in this world. But know that neither they, nor I, are among them. Nor am I a defender of witches. I am a defender of the innocent. If I am guilty of any sin, it is only that I did not defend the innocent well enough. Not nearly well enough. I do not regret what I have done. I regret only that I did not have the courage to do more to protect them. And I regret that I will be taken from you. Do not grieve. We have lived and loved well, you and I. Perhaps God will protect me in this life. If he does not, surely, with your prayers, he will welcome me into the next. And as surely as there is a God in heaven, I will be waiting for you there. God be with you.*
> *Your loving husband, Franz.*

Lutz blotted the ink, then folded the single page and placed it under a candleholder – a place where Maria would be sure to find it when she cleaned. Would she continue to dust his things after he was gone?

He felt as if the executioner had already placed a crushing weight upon his chest.

Lutz sat quietly while the other commissioners filed in and took their places at the table, exchanging no greetings or pleasantries. Their faces were sombre, all but Hampelmann's. He looked badly in need of sleep, but oddly calm, almost bemused, with the hint of a smile on his lips.

Chancellor Brandt swept in, banging the door behind him. He didn't even pretend to defer to Judge Steinbach. "All of you have heard by now. All of Würzburg has heard!" He gave Lutz a penetrating glare. "The Prince-Bishop's bailiff and his men are searching for them now. I do hope you have an explanation for us, Herr Lutz. Go get the jailer, Herr Freude."

No accusation? No arrest? Lutz put a hand to his forehead to cover his face. What did the chancellor know?

Father Streng started to stand. "Not this morning," Chancellor Brandt said irritably. "I haven't the energy."

Lips pursed, the priest sat back down and crossed himself. "*In nomine patris, et filii, et spiritus sancti.*"

Chancellor Brandt turned to Lutz. "What happened last night?"

Lutz opened his ledger and flipped through the pages, delaying. What should he say? The truth? That would only implicate Father Herzeim. No, he'd claim that he acted alone, that he attacked the priest, the guard, and the jailer's wife, then freed Frau Rosen and Katharina. That would fit with whatever Frau Brugler had reported.

"Father Herzeim and I went to visit Frau Rosen." Lutz could hear his voice quavering. "To inform her of the Prince-Bishop's decision–"

"In the middle of the night?"

"I-I had delayed because I could not think how to explain it to her. So after the meeting yesterday, I went to Father Herzeim. He thought it would be terribly difficult for her and wanted to offer solace and, if she wanted, sacramental confession."

"In the middle of the night? On *Walpurgisnacht*?"

Lutz shrugged gamely, keeping his hands under the table to hide their trembling. "Father Herzeim and I discussed the situation long into the night, and I persuaded him that it would be cruel to leave Frau Rosen waiting–" Lutz was interrupted by the appearance of Freude in the doorway, the jailer at his side.

"What happened last night, Herr Brugler?" demanded Chancellor Brandt.

The scrawny man shuffled into the chamber, clutching his gnarled hands protectively in front of his groin. His milky eye stared off to the side. His other eye fixed on Chancellor Brandt. "Well…um…"

Father Streng stood and picked up the cross.

"What happened!" The chancellor's face was bright red.

The priest raised a hand in protest. "The man has not yet been sworn."

Chancellor Brandt turned his glower upon Father Streng, who quickly sat down and picked up his quill.

Brugler licked his thin lips. "All I know is what the wife told me. The Rosen girl is possessed."

"Just as I've said all along," said Freude, looking vindicated. "Now you know."

"I don't believe it," said Hampelmann. "Katharina is not possessed."

Grabbing the gavel from Judge Steinbach, Chancellor Brandt banged it sharply to silence them. "How did the girl and her mother escape?"

The jailer gulped. "*Walpurgisnacht* it was."

"I know what damn night it was. How did they escape?"

"Well...um...what the wife said was that sometime in the night, towards morning, there was a terrible commotion in the tower. She and a guard went to see about it. And both of them got knocked out. By the girl. When they came to, Frau Rosen and the girl were gone."

Knocked out by the girl? Lutz nervously twisted a tuft of beard. Had Frau Brugler said nothing about Father Herzeim or him?

"What did the guard report?" said Chancellor Brandt.

"He was knocked silly. Doesn't remember much at all."

"What about the guard outside Frau Lamm's cell?"

"Herr Klingen heard the commotion, sir, but he had orders not to leave his post except to prevent Frau Lamm from escaping. And he reported that she never moved at all, sir."

"And where were you?"

Brugler looked down at his feet. "Sleeping, sir. I didn't hear a thing." He hunched one shoulder and pointed to the left side of his head. "I'm deaf in this ear."

The chancellor's face had turned nearly purple. "Herr Freude, go get Frau Brugler. We need to hear an explanation directly from her."

The jailer scrambled to follow Freude from the chamber. "Herr Brugler," said Chancellor Brandt, "you will remain here."

Lutz bowed his head. This was it. Frau Brugler would tell them what had happened, and then he would be arrested.

The jailer's wife soon appeared at the door, as if she'd been waiting on the stairs. There was a large dark bruise on her forehead. She stepped into the chamber, her hand covering the mole on her cheek.

"What happened last night, Frau Brugler?" said Chancellor Brandt.

Her lower lip quivered. "W-well, it was *Walpurgisnacht.*"

"What happened!"

Her whole body shaking, the woman glanced toward Lutz. "H-herr Lutz and F-father Herzeim came to see Frau Rosen. To offer sacramental confession, the priest said."

Lutz closed his eyes. Dear God, don't let her blame Father Herzeim.

"What happened then?"

"Sometime later, I heard screaming and shrieking – in tongues. And thumping, too. It being *Walpurgisnacht* and all, I was scared out of my wits. All kinds of strange things happen on *Walpurgisnacht*. Demons and ghosts about. Witches, too."

"Get on with it!"

"Well, like I was saying, there was this horrible commotion. The guard and I rushed up the stairs to see what was happening. He looked in the cell and saw Father Herzeim knocked against the wall. When the guard opened the door, the poor girl's demons got him right away, then I felt a blow to my head so powerful I knew that only a demon could've done it." She looked directly at Lutz and rubbed the bruise on her forehead.

"And where was Herr Lutz?"

"Oh, he'd been knocked out, too."

Lutz felt faint. God bless her. He didn't know why she'd lied, but God bless her for it.

"Could it be," Hampelmann said thoughtfully, "that it was an angel rather than a demon who assaulted all of you and then freed Frau Rosen and her daughter? God has, after all, given us a sign that the woman is innocent."

Frau Brugler pulled at her apron. "I-I've never seen an angel, sir. It seemed like demons to me, what with the voices and all."

"What happened then?" persisted Chancellor Brandt.

"When I came to, Father Herzeim and Herr Lutz were bending over me, but the guard was still knocked flat. He took such a knock on the head, he doesn't remember a thing." Her eyes flashed back to Lutz.

"And where were Frau Rosen and her daughter?"

Frau Brugler raised her hands, palms up. "Gone! Just gone. The three of us searched everywhere, sir. When we didn't find them, I told Father Herzeim and Herr Lutz to go on home, being that the morning bells had started to ring." She dipped her head toward Brugler. "I told them I'd send the husband to tell the bailiff that Frau Rosen had escaped. Then I went to tend to the poor knocked-out guard."

Chancellor Brandt gripped the gavel. "And what do you know of all this, Herr Lutz?"

"Well...the Rosen girl seemed all right when Father Herzeim and I first got there, but then she began acting strangely. Suddenly, I saw the priest knocked against the wall, then I felt a terrific blow to the back of my head." He rubbed his head. "I don't remember a thing until after I woke up, then it was just as Frau Brugler has said. We searched, but Frau Rosen and her daughter were gone."

The chancellor's dark eyebrows came together in an expression that was clearly sceptical. "Once in a great while, prisoners do escape. But demons and angels aside, never before has a prisoner escaped by herself, without the assistance of a guard – or of someone else who had access to her cell. You and Father Herzeim are the only ones who visited Frau Rosen."

"There was someone else," Frau Brugler said softly.

"Oh?"

She jerked her bony chin toward Hampelmann. "That one there. He visited."

Chancellor Brandt tilted his head toward her. "Go on."

The woman's mouth worked. "Herr Hampelmann came to Frau Rosen at least three times," she said finally. "Late at night. And he always ordered me or the guard to leave them alone. He came again last night."

Lutz saw Hampelmann's hands clench. Could that be true?

Why had Frau Rosen never told him about Hampelmann's visits?

"Herr Hampelmann, why did you visit Frau Rosen last night?" asked Chancellor Brandt.

"To inform her of the Prince-Bishop's decision."

"That's Herr Lutz's responsibility, not yours. Were you alone with her?"

"*Ja*," said Frau Brugler. "Like I'm running a brothel."

"A serious breach of procedure," said Father Streng, his grey eyes wide behind his spectacles.

"And why, Frau Brugler," said Chancellor Brandt, purpling yet again, "against all orders, did you leave Herr Hampelmann alone with Frau Rosen?"

"He ordered me to. I couldn't very well disobey the head of the *Malefizamt*, could I?"

"Why were you there, Herr Hampelmann? The truth this time."

There was a prolonged silence. Hampelmann twisted the gold ring around his finger. "Because–"

"'Cause he lusts after her," blurted Frau Brugler.

"That's not true!" yelled Hampelmann.

As one, the commissioners turned toward him.

Emboldened by the effect of her words, Frau Brugler continued, "And by the looks of the girl, I'd say he's been lusting after Frau Rosen for quite some time."

Father Streng's forehead wrinkled in puzzlement.

She flicked a hand toward Hampelmann. "Any fool can see that the Rosen girl looks just like him."

In the shocked silence, Lutz studied Hampelmann's face. Why had he never seen it before? The same pale skin and colourless lashes, the same white-gold hair, the same chin and nose.

"She's lying," shouted Hampelmann. "Question her under torture and you'll get the truth."

"Torture?" said Lindner. "Frau Brugler hasn't even been accused of anything. Not yet anyway."

"I swear by Almighty God, Katharina Rosen is not my daughter." Hampelmann set his jaw, defiant. "And if I have any love at all for Eva Rosen, it is a chaste love, the same kind of love one has for a saint who is pure and holy."

The jailer's wife snorted. "Chaste love don't make for bastard children."

"I wonder, gentlemen," said Father Streng, "if we have here before us evidence of an unholy – and lascivious – alliance among the Devil, Frau Rosen and her daughter, and Herr Hampelmann and his wife? The midwife did, after all, name Frau Hampelmann as an accomplice."

"That's outrageous!" said Hampelmann.

"Is it?" Father Streng regarded him with contempt. "And it would appear to be an alliance of quite long standing. Isn't it true, Herr Hampelmann, that Eva Rosen worked as a maidservant in your father's household for several years before either she or you were married?"

"*Ja*, but Katharina is not–"

The priest cut him off. "Moreover, Herr Hampelmann has argued adamantly for Frau Rosen's innocence, even claiming to have seen a sign from God – a sign no one else saw. Even now he would argue that it was an angel, not demons, who freed Frau Rosen and her daughter." His mouth twisted into a sneer. "Could it be that Herr Hampelmann freed them so they could all go together to Fraw Rengberg for the *Walpurgisnacht* festival?"

"How can you possibly believe such idiocy? I am head of the *Malefizamt*."

"The perfect place for a protector and defender of witches," said Chancellor Brandt. He brought his pomander to his nose as if he smelled something foul. "Herr Freude, escort Herr Hampelmann to a cell. If he is in league with the Devil, he must not be here to intimidate the other witnesses when we question them."

"But I am innocent."

Freude smirked. "That's what they all say."

Mouth gaping in disbelief, Hampelmann did not resist as Freude bound his wrists. "Freed Eva?" he murmured to himself. "Both of us, we are innocent."

Lutz's throat burned, and his chest ached. He could not remain silent and let another man die for what he had done. "Chancellor Brandt," he gasped.

"Herr Lutz, I haven't the patience for your objections. Not this morning."

"But—"

"Silence!"

"Gentlemen," Lutz persisted. "There is no alliance among Frau Rosen, the Devil, and Herr Hampelmann. She is innocent, and he is innocent."

"What? You've seen a sign from God?" Father Streng's words dripped with sarcasm.

Lutz took a deep breath. "I know he did not help Frau Rosen to escape. It is I who helped her, not him."

"*Nein*," shouted Frau Brugler. "The blow to his head has addled him."

Hampelmann's head jerked up, his icy blue eyes furious. "You freed Eva?"

Lutz shrank from the intensity of his anger. "I cannot let an innocent man die for what I have done."

Chancellor Brandt spread his hands, his face weary and strained. "First, it was demons that freed her. Then it was Herr Hampelmann. Now it's Herr Lutz." His shoulders slumped, as if his duties were too much to bear. "Herr Freude, find a cell for Herr Lutz." He glanced at the judge's watch. "We will adjourn, then return to this chamber in two hours to determine how to proceed. There are the guards yet to be questioned. And Father Herzeim, who is already in custody on other charges. We will find out who is responsible."

40

The tall Jesuit stands before them, his wrists bound, as if he were dangerous. The men ask him questions about the woman and the child. What happened? Who helped them? What does he know?

What he knows, he says, is innocence. The woman and her daughter are innocent. Their escape was the will of God.

Will of God? The men pull at their beards. The old one twitches.

They ask their questions again. The executioner's palms itch. He desires to lay hands upon the Father Confessor, who knows the hearts of witches.

The Jesuit would answer them plainly and admit to what he has done. His own heart is at peace, but he is afraid for his friend, who no longer sits at the table.

The Holy Church says there are witches in the world, he tells the men, so there are witches in the world. But the woman and the child are not among them. Even if they were, their lives should be spared, for witchcraft is merely delusion induced by the Devil.

Or delusion induced by men, I shout. But no one hears me.

If witches truly have diabolical powers, he says, why are they always so poor, their lives so wretched and miserable? Why are they not rich and powerful?

The men cannot hear him. His words offend their ears.

The Jesuit looks from one man to the next. The Devil needs no help from mortal women to work evil in this world, he says.

In that, I know he is right. The men's fervent belief suffices.

Early this morning, before they came for him, the Jesuit completed his manuscript. Remembering well what he wrote only a

~

few hours ago, he repeats it for the men. You force them to name names, he says, names put into their mouths by your own tongues. And so it goes on…and on. Eventually, you who have clamoured most loudly to feed the flames will yourselves be accused, for you have failed to see that your turn will come. His voice resonates within the stone chamber, making the ropes quiver. Thus will heaven justly punish you who have created so many witches, he says, and sent so many innocents to the fires.

He points his bound hands at the small Jesuit sitting at the table, the one who is scribbling feverishly. This, he proclaims, you should record in red ink: no one is safe, no matter what sex, fortune, condition, or dignity. No one.

The men recoil, assaulted by his words. Yet each wonders, remembering that two from among their number have already been taken. Accused.

The small priest jumps up, beads of sweat on his flushed and boyish face. You would be wise, he says, to realize how foolish and noxious it is to prefer the ravings of heretics to the judgement of the Holy Church.

The tall Jesuit looks to heaven and sighs. I would quote to you from a true man of God, he says. Johann Weyer.

The men gasp and touch the balls of wax at their throats.

When the tall priest speaks again, even the stones listen. I summon you before the tribunal of the Great Judge, Weyer has written, who shall decide between us, where the truth you have trampled under foot and buried shall arise and condemn you, demanding vengeance for your inhumanities.

The men murmur among themselves. They are now more worried about the Jesuit's heresy than about the woman and the child. How do they prosecute a man of God who has turned from God? A priest who is now an instrument in the Devil's hands?

Their own hands tremble, their knees shake, and their feet dance. They have erred. They recommended release for a girl possessed and her mother, a witch. *The Prince-Bishop was right. But now the woman and her daughter have escaped, with the help of the very men who were charged by God with prosecuting them. The same men who have sat at this table with them.*

They now have no doubt that they are surrounded on all sides by witches and their defenders. They must let no one escape just punishment. Or they will all be destroyed by the wrath of God.

The men are more afraid than they've ever been. And thus are they dangerous.

Heretic, shouts the boyish priest. He comes from behind the table and steps close to the tall Jesuit. He points his quill. *You will no longer teach,* he says. *You will no longer speak your heresy to anyone. I will write the recantation myself, and then you will sign it. Publicly, in the marketplace, kneeling before the Prince-Bishop.*

Or you will die a heretic's death.

Two Jesuits, face to face. Each believes he works for the greater glory of God, ad majorem Dei gloriam. *One has chosen obedience to the Church, the other, obedience to his own heart.*

Do not waste your precious ink, the tall one answers.

41

1 May 1626

Lutz stared at the patch of blue sky beyond the high narrow window. He wished desperately to believe that God would protect him, that he would live and return home to Maria. Had she found his letter? Was she weeping for him even now, as he was weeping for her?

He'd been foolish to come to Hampelmann's defence. Likely, the man would die anyway. All of them would die. Horribly. Yet he knew he could not have remained silent and let another man be condemned for what he had done.

The rasp of the key. Lutz wiped his cheeks with the back of his hand, rattling the chains on his shackles.

Carrying a wooden bowl, Frau Brugler came in, the bruise on her forehead a dark purple. She gave an exasperated shake of her head. "Just couldn't keep your mouth shut, could you?"

"Why did you lie?"

The woman sucked her teeth, considering. "I'm telling you this just once, Herr Lutz. From then on, it's the demons…or Herr Hampelmann."

"Why did you accuse an innocent man instead of me?"

"Herr Hampelmann? Innocent?" She laughed bitterly. "It's the good Father who's innocent. I was trying to protect him. And if you care about him, you'll stick with my story."

She handed Lutz the bowl and spoon. "The good Father doesn't know I've said anything about Herr Hampelmann. And if it's up to me, he'll never know. Cause I know what he'd do. Same as you, you damn fool."

Frau Brugler rubbed her forehead. "You didn't have to whack me so hard, Herr Lutz. But what you did – it was a good thing. That woman and her little girl aren't witches. Any *dummkopf* can see that. And no matter what you say, I'll stick to my story and say that you've been deranged by *Walpurgisnacht* demons. Even if they torture me, that's the story they're getting."

Lutz gagged at the rancid smell of the greasy broth. He set the bowl aside.

"Listen to me," she said. "The good Father'll not say a word that'll damn you. So don't you be saying anything that'll damn him. Leave it alone, Herr Lutz. You'll only make things worse for him if you claim it was you who helped Frau Rosen."

Lutz pressed the heels of his hands into his eyes. What now? It was one thing to condemn himself, quite another to condemn Father Herzeim. When the commissioners questioned him again, he'd have to find a way to claim that both Father Herzeim and Hampelmann were innocent. Only he was guilty.

"The only evidence the commissioners have," she continued, "is the professors claiming he's a defender of witches. So I'm thinking the good Father – and you – will be like Herr Silberhans. They arrested him for being a defender of witches, then let him go, with just a warning."

Lutz wished he could believe that, but he doubted that either he or Father Herzeim would be as fortunate as the young law student. The Prince-Bishop's bailiff and his men would search the priest's office and find the book by Johann Weyer. And Father Herzeim's own manuscript. That would be more than damning.

His throat tightened. "How is Father Herzeim?"

"He's strong. A true man of God, that one. Believe me, I've seen it. He's done more good for more souls than any of the high and mighty commissioners sitting at that table. You're both innocent of doing anything wrong. They'll have to let you go." Frau Brugler patted the ring of keys at her waist. "And if they don't…well, I still got the keys, don't I? I'm willing to help God help the innocent."

Lutz was sorely tempted to grasp at the hope she offered. He guessed, however, that Frau Brugler would be removed from her position, and perhaps even arrested, before she ever got a chance to help another prisoner.

She wagged a gnarled finger at him. "Eat that broth. You'll be needing your strength. And remember, Herr Lutz, from now on, it was the demons."

42

3 May 1626

Every jolt and bump of the wooden wheels over the rutted road caused pain, but it was an exquisitely welcome pain. She was here, not there. Hay still covered her, but Eva had cleared a small circle around her eyes so she could study the sky, the beautiful blue sky, so wide above her. There were still moments of terror, especially when she heard riders coming behind them. She prayed then to the Holy Mother to shield them from the Prince-Bishop's bailiff and his men, and if she could not, to at least give Eva the means, and the courage, to kill herself and Katharina before they could take them back to Würzburg.

This morning, though, Eva was not afraid. She could hear cathedral bells ringing, calling people to mass. Neustadt, the driver had muttered when she asked. They were passing through Neustadt. She had never been so far from home, and she longed to sit up and gawk at everything. But she dared not.

On this rare morning, Katharina sat up beside the driver. She wore a chemise and gown they'd found tucked in the corner of the wagon. A bright kerchief covered her shaved head. She chattered away excitedly, talking to the horse and describing people, buildings, and other sights, so that her mother could hear. The driver answered the girl's questions with guttural grunts.

A wary man, he rarely spoke. He'd not even told them his name, nor asked theirs. He wasn't old, but deep lines of worry creased the ruddy skin around his mouth and eyes. Eva could see that he was suspicious of her, never laying a hand upon her, even to help her into and out of the wagon.

⁓

When they'd stop on the road to eat and rest, the driver's eyes would dart all around. He was especially watchful when they stopped in the forest, alert for the bailiff and his men, as well as for brigands hiding among the trees. While he watched for danger, Katharina would gather herbs and roots and set them to boil, then bathe Eva's hands in the cooled broth. She would make a poultice of comfrey leaves, all the while telling Eva about comfrey and hellebore, about the bark of willow and elm.

How did Katharina know all that? Who had taught her that wisdom?

When Eva was afraid, Katharina would comfort her, telling her, in her childish certainty, that no one could hurt them. The white dog was with them. Eva wanted to believe Katharina, to believe that the white dog her daughter saw was a good thing.

Eva was no longer sure what she believed. But she still prayed. Not to God, but to the Mother of God.

The bells rang out, lovely and clear, a chiming through the morning sky. Eva lay still and tried to imagine herself at mass. Safe. Her lips could hardly form the word. Had she ever been safe? No one was safe, not any longer. Even now, they might be torturing Herr Lutz and Father Herzeim. Friedrich. A fresh grief stabbed at her heart.

She folded her damaged hands on her chest. Mother of God, she prayed, please protect them. Please reward the goodness of their hearts.

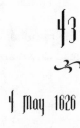

43

4 May 1626

Lutz turned the shackles to ease the rawness on his wrists. He'd been there three days, three long nights, and it was more dreadful than he'd ever imagined: the stink and filth, the black rats, the same dull grey stone, the rancid broth, the loneliness. And the terrible grief for Maria. And fear.

Why hadn't they questioned him again? Why hadn't Freude come to strip and shave him?

He could hear commotion outside the tower: voices calling out, horses snorting, monks chanting that the end of the world was near. He'd heard a dozen swift footsteps pass on the stairs outside the door.

Lutz turned toward the sound of metal scraping on metal. The door opened, and as he expected, it was the new jailer's wife, hefty and gruff, and as silent as Frau Brugler had been talkative. For two days now, she'd brought his food, emptied the slop bucket, changed his straw, and hardly said three words. Lutz had begun to wonder if the woman was deaf.

She carried a broom and a basket in her beefy arms. Setting down the basket, she gestured for him to stand, then, with wide strokes of the broom, began sweeping up the soiled straw.

"Any news of Frau Rosen?" said Lutz.

Silence.

"Have they found her?"

Her coarse face darkened. "Why ask about witches?"

"Please, just tell me. Have they found her?"

"Leave me alone," she muttered, her round chin trembling. "I can't talk to you."

"Just a word," he pleaded.

She kept her head down and continued sweeping. "*Nein*," she whispered.

"*Nein* what?"

"They haven't."

Was it possible they'd made it safely to Nuremberg? Oh God, let it be so. Lutz opened his mouth to thank the woman, then clamped it shut. It wouldn't be good to seem pleased that Frau Rosen had escaped. "That's terrible," he said. "Chancellor Brandt and the other commissioners must be furious."

She bobbed her head, but said nothing more. She quickly swept the straw into the basket and left. Never once had she actually looked at him.

Lutz sat down on the bare wood floor. She was afraid, he thought. Of me. What have they told her?

The clamour outside the window quieted. There was only the murmur of the monks' chanting. Suddenly, loud shrieks broke the silence. The midwife. Where had the woman found the strength? She'd been close to death when Lutz saw her last.

Her screaming denials rang out through the clear morning air.

Where, in God's name, had she found the courage to recant, knowing she'd be burned alive? Could he ever find that kind of courage within himself? Lutz lowered his head into his shackled hands. The woman's screams pierced his heart. Maybe he'd been wrong all along. Maybe Frau Lamm was innocent, too.

He stood and ran his fingers along a crevice between the cold grey stones, a crevice he could reach even when shackled. That's where he'd hidden the razor. It would be there when he needed it.

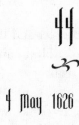

Hampelmann stared at the grey stones. The sins of the father. That's why he was here. That's why he suffered. He closed his eyes to bring the words of Moses clearly to mind: *The Lord is patient and full of mercy, taking away iniquity and wickedness, and leaving no man clear, who visitest the sins of the fathers upon the children unto the third and fourth generation.*

He heard distant screams from outside the city walls and knew, by their pitch, that Freude had kindled the flames. He'd soon be assaulted by the dreadful *hexen gestank*. Why had the witch recanted? More proof that *Der Hexenhammer* was right. Witch midwives surpassed all other witches in their wickedness. She'd not only burn here, but for all of eternity.

He put his shackled hands over his ears to shut out the screams. He would not think about the midwife. He would meditate on his own innocence. He was suffering for the sins of his father, but he, himself, was innocent. Therefore, God would send them a sign, just as he'd sent a sign to show him that Eva was innocent.

He tried to recall the details of that night, concentrating on remembering exactly how he'd done it, but everything was fragmented and hazy, as if he'd acted in a dream. When he first went to Eva, he'd felt the presence of something strange and ethereal in the cell, but it was not demons. Katharina was not possessed. Hampelmann knew that. It was God's hand that had guided him, not the Devil's.

He had a vague recollection of whisking them out of the

tower, past Frau Brugler and the guard, who were distracted with their beer and cards. He'd handed them over to an old man and woman disguised as beggars. How much had he paid the couple to hide them? He wasn't sure, but he did recall, with pleasure, the wistful longing on Eva's face when he'd had to leave her.

On his way home, he'd encountered the *wutenker*, who were searching for him, furious that he'd freed an innocent. He'd been terrified, but God had protected him.

Hampelmann's plan was for Eva and Katharina to remain hidden until he could convince the commissioners to declare them innocent. All of them knew Eva was innocent. He'd only done what every man among them had wanted to do. But no one else had had the courage.

Why had Lutz spoken up?

It could only be envy, Saint Thomas' fourth deadly sin. Lutz had always been jealous of his noble lineage, his membership in the Upper City Council, his position of power and authority in the *Malefizamt*. And now, the weak-willed lawyer envied him in being God's faithful servant in the rescue of Eva and Katharina. Lutz wanted to claim that honour for himself.

Hampelmann dropped his hands. He'd never allow Lutz to lay claim to what was rightfully his.

He'd acted with courage in saving Eva and Katharina, and God would reward him. God would protect him the way he'd protected Eva. He would walk free, and then he would find her. And she would love him.

They would love chastely, in the way God intended.

Hampelmann looked at the shackles, and smiled. These were the very same shackles that had embraced her wrists, the very same walls that had witnessed her holy gaze. That, in itself, was a sign from God. A sign that, in this place where Eva had dwelt, he had nothing to fear from the Devil.

Nothing to fear from the Devil. But everything to fear from the men who sit at the table.

His fear will conjure me. He will see me in the cell. He will see me in the chamber. He will see me in the night, a dark man with glowing red eyes and a huge cock. His fear will torment him, for he does not know I dwell within, not without. I am with him always.

Like the tall Jesuit and the fat lawyer, he will talk and talk and talk. He and the priest and the lawyer will use different words, but the men at the table will hear none of them. Their fear stops their ears.

In a strange and wondrous alchemy, their fear hardens their certainty.

46

∾

4 May 1646

He sits in Maria's garden, a wool coverlet over his bony knees. He's a thin man now, with the look of an ascetic. His hair and beard have long since grown back, as white as before, but his bright blue eyes have faded to the colour of clouded ice. When he closes them, he sees it all again. So he keeps them open and takes in the colours all around him: blue forget-me-nots, pink cherry blossoms, shiny yellow buttercups, purple violets, deep red blooms of bleeding heart. He wills himself to forget, but his heart remembers, and bleeds, and at odd moments, he weeps uncontrollably. He no longer tries to contain his grief. The effort is beyond him.

He rarely goes out. Even more rarely does anyone come to the house. No man trusts a lawyer who is still, twenty years later, rumoured to be a defender of witches. No matter. He cannot write contracts anyway. His writing is hardly legible, and his thumbs ache with the effort. His circumstances are much diminished. But there is still the garden with its lovely colours and scents. He would bury his nose in green grass, in earth dampened by dew.

Maria still fusses. She takes him to Saint Kilian's every Sunday. He keeps his eyes open there as well. He studies the crucifix, the Son's suffering. And wonders about God the Father.

He did not go to see Hampelmann burn. He'd tried to defend him. But failed. Yet again.

True to her word, Frau Brugler kept to her story, even when tortured. But neither she nor Lutz could save Father Herzeim, who refused to recant his heresy. Addled by demons, Lutz was no threat. They were willing to release him. But they knew the Jesuit was dangerous.

Lutz went to the execution. He would give his friend one kind face to look upon. It hadn't been hard for Father Herzeim to spot him. Lutz had stood at the front of the jeering crowd, empty space all around him. No one would stand near to a man who'd been shaved of his hair and beard, a man whose thumbs had been mutilated and smashed.

He didn't turn his eyes to the ground this time. He watched. He still sees the terrible look of resolve, even of exultation, on his friend's face as the flames caressed his bare feet. Then there was the exquisite look of agony.

A month later, when he thought he could bear it, Lutz went to the priest's office to claim his breviary. And found the manuscript. At his own expense, he arranged to have it smuggled to Nuremberg and published. It was the least he could do.

It has ended. Finally. But not before nine hundred women, men, and children burned. Lutz went to every execution so there would be one kind face for innocents to look upon.

It has ended. It ended when Prince-Bishop Philipp Adolf von Ehrenberg and Chancellor Johann Brandt were themselves accused. Just a year later, King Gustavus Adolphus and his Swedish troops marched into Würzburg, and His Grace fled.

It has ended. But Lutz still smells the stink of burning flesh clinging to the city like an invisible foulness that cannot be washed away. He keeps the razor tucked away in his doublet.

There is but one memory that can make him smile: Eva Rosen. The Prince-Bishop's bailiff never found her. Lutz did not fail them all.

47

> *It has not ended. Their fear conjures me yet. Their fear keeps them dancing in the palm of my hand.*

acknowledgements

I am deeply grateful to members of Northern Writers – Tom Joseph, Michele Bergstrom, and Phil Paterson – and to Pat Byrne of Memorial University of Newfoundland for careful readings of and insightful comments on all versions of the manuscript, from rough draft to final copy. I appreciate their unstinting support and enthusiasm for this project.

I also thank my editor at Breakwater, Tamara Reynish, for her careful and sensitive editing of the manuscript. She was a joy to work with. Thanks go to Rhonda Molloy as well for designing the cover and manuscript so beautifully and appropriately.

Thomas Mallon, Carolyn Cooke, and Mira Bartok at the 2001 Bread Loaf Writers' Conference, as well as Elizabeth McCracken and Eric May at the 2002 Stone Coast Writers' Conference, offered perceptive comments and advice on the novel. Laurel Yourke at the University of Wisconsin-Madison provided thought-provoking discussions about point-of-view.

I cannot thank enough the wonderful librarians at the Minocqua Public Library who obtained for me, through interlibrary loan, all the arcane research materials I needed to complete this novel.

I also thank Katra Byram for her invaluable translation of Christel Beyer's *Hexen-leut so zu Würzburg Gerichtet*, and Hans-Peter Baum of the Stadtarchiv in Würzburg for so generously providing information on seventeenth century Würzburg. All errors, however, are mine.

bibliography

~

Primary sources

The Holy Bible, Douay Rheims Version. 1609. Translated from the Latin Vulgate. Rockford, Illinois: Tan Books and Publishers, Inc., 1899.

Binsfeld, Peter. *Tractatus de Confessionibus Maleficorum et Sagarum.* Treves, 1589.

Bodin, Jean. *De la Demonomanie des sorciers.* Paris, 1580.

Boquet, Henri. *Discours des sorciers.* Lyons, 1602.

Delrio, Martin. *Disquisitionum Magicarum.* Louvain, 1599.

Institoris (Kramer), Heinrich and Jakob Sprenger. *Malleus Maleficarum.* Cologne, 1486.

Remy, Nicolas. *Demonolatreiae.* Lyons, 1595.

Weyer, Johann. *De Praestigiis Daemonum.* Basel, 1563.

Secondary sources

Asch, Ronald G. *The Thirty Years War: The Holy Roman Empire and Europe, 1618-48.* New York: St. Martin's Press, Inc., 1997.

Barstow, Anne L. *Witchcraze: A New History of the European Witch Hunts.* London: Pandora (HarperCollins Publishers), 1994.

Behringer, Wolfgang. "Witchcraft Studies in Austria, Germany and Switzerland." *Witchcraft in Early Modern Europe: Studies in Culture and Belief.* Eds. Jonathan Barry, Marianne Hester, and Gareth Roberts. Cambridge: Cambridge University Press, 1996.

Behringer, Wolfgang. *Witchcraft Persecutions In Bavaria: Popular Magic, Religious Zealotry, and Reason of State In Early Modern Europe.* Trans. J. C. Grayson and David Lederer. Cambridge: Cambridge University Press, 1997.

Beyer, Christel. *Hexen-leut so zu Würzburg Gerichtet.* Frankfurt: Peter Lang, 1986.

Brauner, Sigrid. *Fearless Wives and Frightened Shrews: the Construction of the Witch In Early Modern Germany*. Amherst: University of Massachusetts Press, 1995.

Briggs, Robin. *Witches & Neighbors: The Social and Cultural Context of European Witchcraft*. New York: Penguin Books, 1998.

Bunn, Ivan and Gil Geis. *A Trial of Witches*. London: Routledge Press, 1997.

Clark, Stuart. *Thinking with Demons: The Idea of Witchcraft in Early Modern Europe*. Oxford: Oxford University Press, 1997.

Hester, Marianne. "Patriarchal Reconstruction and Witch Hunting." *Witchcraft in Early Modern Europe: Studies in Culture and Belief*. Eds. Jonathan Barry, Marianne Hester, and Gareth Roberts. Cambridge: Cambridge University Press, 1996.

Hinckeldey, Christoph. *Criminal Justice Through the Ages*. Trans. John Fosberry. Rothenburg: *Mittelalterliches Kriminalmuseum*, 1993.

Hollis, Christopher. *The Jesuits: A History*. New York: The Macmillan Company, 1968.

Hufton, Olwen. *The Prospect Before Her: A History of Women in Western Europe, 1500-1800*. New York: Alfred A. Knopf, 1995.

Klaits, Joseph. *Servants of Satan: The Age of Witch Hunts*. Bloomington: Indiana University Press, 1987.

Kors, Alan C. and Edward Peters. Eds. *Witchcraft in Europe 1100-1700: A Documentary History*. Philadelphia: University of Pennsylvania Press, 1972.

Kunze, Michael. *Highroad to the Stake: A Tale of Witchcraft*. Trans. William E. Yuile. Chicago: University of Chicago Press, 1987.

Levack, Brian P. *The Witch-Hunt in Early Modern Europe*. London: Addison Wesley Longman, Ltd., 1995.

Levack, Brian. "State-building and Witch Hunting in Early Modern Europe." *Witchcraft in Early Modern Europe: Studies in Culture and Belief*. Eds. Jonathan Barry, Marianne Hester, and Gareth Roberts. Cambridge: Cambridge University Press, 1996.

Midelfort, H. C. Erik. *Witch Hunting in Southwestern Germany 1562-1684: The Social and Intellectual Foundations*. Stanford: Stanford University Press, 1972.

O'Malley, John. *The First Jesuits*. Cambridge: Harvard University Press, 1993.

Ozment, Steven. *Flesh and Spirit: Private Life In Early Modern Germany*. New York: Viking, 1999.

Parker, Geoffrey. *The Thirty Years' War*. London: Routledge & Kegan Paul, 1987.

Robbins, Rossell Hope. *Encyclopedia of Witchcraft and Demonology*. New York: Crown Publishers, 1959.

Roper, Lyndal. *The Holy Household: Women and Morals in Reformation Augsburg*. Oxford: Clarendon Press, 1989.

Roper, Lyndal. "Witchcraft and Fantasy in Early Modern Germany." *Witchcraft in Early Modern Europe: Studies in Culture and Belief*. Eds. Jonathan Barry, Marianne Hester, and Gareth Roberts. Cambridge: Cambridge University Press, 1996.

Sebald, Hans. *Witchcraft: The Heritage of a Heresy*. New York: Elsevier North Holland, Inc., 1978.

Summers, Montague. Trans. *The Malleus Maleficarum of Heinrich Kramer and Jakob Sprenger*. New York: Dover Publications, 1928.

Wiesner, Merry. "Women's Defense of Their Public Role." *Women in the Middle Ages and Renaissance: Literary and Historical Perspectives*. Ed. Mary Beth Rose. Syracuse: Syracuse University Press, 1986.

Wiesner, Merry. *Working Women in Renaissance Germany*. New Brunswick, New Jersey: Rutgers University Press, 1986.

Wiesner, Merry E. "Nuns, Wives, and Mothers: Women and the Reformation in Germany." *Women in Reformation and Counter-Reformation Europe: Public and Private Worlds*. Ed. Sherrin Marshall. Bloomington: Indiana University Press, 1989.

Also by Annamarie Beckel

৵৴

ALL GONE WIDDUN

A novel of William Cormack's quest to save the Beothuk from
extinction, his love for Shanawdithit, a young Beothuk woman,
and the tragedy of her life and the lives of her people. Based on
historical and ethnographic accounts of the Beothuk, it is a fresh
glimpse into a pivotal period of Newfoundland's heritage.
Winner of the *1999 Book Achievement Award* from Midwest
Independent Publishers Association.

ISBN 1-55081-147-9 / $ 19.95 PB / 5 X 8 / 392 PP

Praise for All Gone Widdun

ॐ

All Gone Widdun is a very powerful, well-written novel
which truly brings alive the character of Shanawdithit...
This novel will provide many hours of reading enjoyment and at
the same time highlight one of the saddest chapters in our history.
Mike McCarthy, *Evening Telegram*

All Gone Widdun's portrait of sanctioned inhumanity
is near brilliant... a captivating story, very well told.
Jim Bartley, *Globe & Mail*

Beckel offers us a new world and new insights into
the human heart. It's a beautiful story, beautifully rendered.
Marshall Cook, *Creativity Connection*